DANGEROUS WOMEN
PART I

DANGEROUS WOMEN PART I

EDITED BY

GEORGE R.R. MARTIN

AND

GARDNER DOZOIS

HARPER
Voyager

HarperCollins*Publishers*
1 London Bridge Street,
London SE1 9GF

www. harpervoyagerbooks.co.uk

This paperback edition 2014

12

Published by Harper*Voyager*
An imprint of HarperCollins*Publishers* 2014

A catalogue record for this book
is available from the British Library

ISBN: 9780007549429

Set in Adobe Caslon Pro

Printed and bound by
CPI Group (UK) Ltd, Croydon, CR0 4YY

Copyright Acknowledgments

To Jo Playford, my dangerous minion.

[—George R.R. Martin]

Contents

Introduction   1

The Princess and the Queen by George R.R. Martin   7

Raisa Stepanova by Carrie Vaughn   91

Second Arabesque, Very Slowly by Nancy Kress   119

I Know How to Pick 'Em by Lawrence Block   149

My Heart Is Either Broken by Megan Abbott   171

Wrestling Jesus by Joe R. Lansdale   197

Shadows For Silence in the Forests of Hell by Brandon Sanderson   231

Introduction by Gardner Dozois

Genre fiction has always been divided over the question of just *how* dangerous women are.

In the real world, of course, the question has long been settled. Even if the Amazons are mythological (and almost certainly wouldn't have cut their right breasts off to make it easier to draw a bow if they *weren't*), their legend was inspired by memory of the ferocious warrior women of the Scythians, who were very much *not* mythological. Gladiatrix, women gladiators, fought other women—and sometimes men—to the death in the arenas of Ancient Rome. There were female pirates like Anne Bonny and Mary Read, and even female samurai. Women served as frontline combat troops, feared for their ferocity, in the Russian army during World War II, and serve so in Israel today. Until 2013, women in the U.S. forces were technically restricted to "noncombat" roles, but many brave women gave their lives in Iraq and Afghanistan anyway, since bullets and land mines have never cared whether you're a noncombatant or not. Women who served as Women Airforce Service Pilots for the United States during World War II were also limited to noncombat roles (where many of them were nevertheless killed in the performance of their duties), but Russian women took to the skies as fighter pilots, and sometimes became aces. A Russian female sniper during World War II was credited with more than fifty kills. Queen Boudicca of the Iceni tribe led one of the most fearsome revolts ever against Roman authority, one that was almost successful in driving the Roman invaders from Britain, and a young French peasant girl inspired and led the troops against the enemy so successfully that she became famous forever afterwards as Joan of Arc.

On the dark side, there have been female "highwaymen" like Mary Frith and Lady Katherine Ferrers and Pearl Hart (the last person to ever rob a stagecoach); notorious poisoners like Agrippina and Catherine de Medici, modern female outlaws like Ma Barker and Bonnie Parker, even female serial killers like Aileen Wuornos. Elizabeth Báthory was said to have bathed in the blood of virgins, and even though that has been called into question, there is no doubt that she tortured and killed dozens, perhaps hundreds, of children during her life. Queen Mary I of England had hundreds of Protestants burnt at the stake; Queen Elizabeth of England later responded by executing large numbers of Catholics. Mad Queen Ranavalona of Madagascar had so many people put to death that she wiped out one-third of the entire population of Madagascar during her reign; she would even have you executed if you appeared in her dreams.

Popular fiction, though, has always had a schizophrenic view of the dangerousness of women. In the science fiction of the 1930s, '40s, and '50s, women, if they appeared at all, were largely regulated to the role of the scientist's beautiful daughter, who might scream during the fight scenes but otherwise had little to do except hang adoringly on the arm of the hero afterwards. Legions of women swooned helplessly while waiting to be rescued by the intrepid jut-jawed hero from everything from dragons to the bug-eyed monsters who were always carrying them off for improbable purposes either dietary or romantic on the covers of pulp SF magazines. Hopelessly struggling women were tied to railroad tracks, with nothing to do but squeak in protest and hope that the Good Guy arrived in time to save them.

And yet, at the same time, warrior women like Edgar Rice Burroughs's Dejah Thoris and Thuvia, Maid of Mars, were every bit as good with the blade and every bit as deadly in battle as John Carter and their other male comrades, female adventuresses like C. L. Moore's Jirel of Joiry swashbuckled their way through the pages of *Weird Tales* magazine (and blazed a trail for later female swashbucklers like Joanna Russ's Alyx); James H. Schmitz sent Agents of Vega like Granny Wannatel and fearless teenagers like Telzey Amberdon and Trigger Argee out to battle the sinister menaces and monsters of the spaceways; and Robert A. Heinlein's dangerous women were capable of being the captain of a spaceship or killing enemies in hand-to-hand combat. Arthur Conan Doyle's sly, shady Irene Adler was one of the only people ever to outwit his Sherlock Holmes, and probably one of the inspirations for the legions of tricky, dangerous, seductive, and treacherous "femmes fatale" who featured in the works of Dashiell Hammett and James M. Cain and later went on to appear in dozens of films noir, and who still turn up in the movies and on television to this day. Later television heroines such as Buffy the Vampire Slayer and Xena, Warrior Princess, firmly established women as being formidable and deadly enough to battle hordes of fearsome supernatural menaces, and helped to inspire the whole subgenre of paranormal romance, which is sometimes unofficially known as the "kick-ass heroine" genre.

Like our anthology *Warriors*, *Dangerous Women* was conceived of as a cross-genre anthology, one that would mingle every kind of fiction, so we asked writers from every genre—science fiction, fantasy, mystery, historical, horror, paranormal romance, men and women alike—to tackle the theme of "dangerous women," and that call was answered by some of the best writers in the business, including both new writers and giants of their fields like Diana Gabaldon, Jim Butcher, Sharon Kay Penman, Joe Abercrombie, Carrie Vaughn, Joe R. Lansdale, Lawrence Block, Cecelia Holland, Brandon Sanderson, Sherilynn Kenyon, S. M. Stirling, Nancy Kress, and George R.R. Martin.

Here you'll find no hapless victims who stand by whimpering in dread while the male hero fights the monster or clashes swords with the villain, and if you want to tie *these* women to the railroad tracks, you'll find you have a real fight on your hands. Instead, you will find sword-wielding women warriors; intrepid women fighter pilots and far-ranging spacewomen; deadly female serial killers; formidable female superheroes; sly and seductive femmes fatale; female wizards; hard-living bad girls; female bandits and rebels; embattled survivors in postapocalyptic futures; female private investigators; stern female hanging judges; haughty queens who rule nations and whose jealousies and ambitions send thousands to grisly deaths; daring dragonriders; and many more.

Enjoy!

George R.R. Martin

Hugo, Nebula, and World Fantasy Award–winner George R.R. Martin, *New York Times* bestselling author of the landmark A Song of Ice and Fire fantasy series, has been called "the American Tolkien."

Born in Bayonne, New Jersey, George R.R. Martin made his first sale in 1971, and soon established himself as one of the most popular SF writers of the seventies. He quickly became a mainstay of the Ben Bova *Analog* with stories such as "With Morning Comes Mistfall," "And Seven Times Never Kill Man," "The Second Kind of Loneliness," "The Storms of Windhaven" (in collaboration with Lisa Tuttle, and later expanded by them into the novel *Windhaven*), "Override," and others, although he also sold to *Amazing, Fantastic, Galaxy, Orbit,* and other markets. One of his *Analog* stories, the striking novella "A Song for Lya," won him his first Hugo Award, in 1974.

By the end of the seventies he had reached the height of his influence as a science fiction writer, and was producing his best work in that category with stories such as the famous "Sandkings," his best-known story, which won both the Nebula and the Hugo in 1980 (he'd later win another Nebula in 1985 for his story "Portraits of His Children"); "The Way of Cross and Dragon," which won a Hugo Award in the same year (making Martin the first author ever to receive two Hugo Awards for fiction in the same year): "Bitterblooms"; "The Stone City"; "Starlady"; and others. These stories would be collected in *Sandkings,* one of the strongest collections of the period. By now he had mostly moved away from *Analog,* although he would have a long sequence of stories about the droll interstellar adventures of Haviland Tuf (later collected in *Tuf Voyaging*) running throughout the eighties in the Stanley Schmidt *Analog,* as well as a few strong individual pieces such as the novella "Nightflyers." Most of his major work of the late seventies and early eighties, though, would appear in *Omni.* The late seventies and eighties also saw the publication of his memorable novel *Dying of the Light,* his only solo SF novel, while his stories were collected in *A Song for Lya, Sandkings, Songs of Stars and Shadows, Songs the Dead Men Sing, Nightflyers,* and *Portraits of His Children.* By the beginning of the eighties he'd moved away from SF and into the horror genre, publishing the big horror novel *Fevre Dream,* and winning the Bram Stoker Award for his horror story "The Pear-Shaped Man" and the World Fantasy Award for his werewolf novella "The Skin Trade." By the end of that decade, though, the crash of the horror market and the commercial failure of his ambitious horror novel *The Armageddon Rag* had driven him out of the print world and to a successful career in television instead, where for more than a decade he worked as story editor or producer on such shows as the new *Twilight Zone* and *Beauty and the Beast.*

After years away, Martin made a triumphant return to the print world in 1996 with the publication of the immensely successful fantasy novel *A Game of Thrones,* the start of his Song of Ice and Fire sequence. A freestanding novella taken from that work, "Blood of the Dragon," won Martin another Hugo Award in 1997. Further books in the Song of Ice and Fire series—*A Clash of Kings, A Storm of Swords, A Feast for Crows,* and *A Dance with Dragons,* have made it one of the most popular, acclaimed, and bestselling series in all of modern fantasy. Recently, the books were made into an HBO TV series, *Game of Thrones,* which has become one of the most popular and acclaimed shows on television, and made Martin a recognizable figure well outside of the usual genre boundaries, even inspiring a satirical version of him on *Saturday Night Live.* Martin's most recent books are the latest book in the Ice and Fire series, *A Dance with Dragons;* a massive retrospective collection spanning the entire spectrum of his career, *GRRM: A RRetrospective;* a novella collection, *Starlady and Fast-Friend;* a novel written in collaboration with Gardner Dozois and Daniel Abraham, *Hunter's Run;* and, as editor, several anthologies edited in collaboration with Gardner Dozois, including *Warriors, Songs of the Dying Earth, Songs of Love and Death,* and *Down These Strange Streets,* and several new volumes in his long-running Wild Cards anthology series, including *Suicide Kings* and *Fort Freak.* In 2012, Martin was given the Life Achievement Award by the World Fantasy Convention.

Here he takes us to the turbulent land of Westeros, home to his Ice and Fire series, for the bloody story of a clash between two very dangerous women whose bitter rivalry and ambition plunges all of Westeros disastrously into war.

THE PRINCESS AND THE QUEEN,
OR,
THE BLACKS AND THE GREENS

Being A History of the Causes, Origins, Battles, and
Betrayals of that Most Tragic Bloodletting Known as the Dance
of the Dragons, as set down by Archmaester Gyldayn
of the Citadel of Oldtown

(here transcribed by GEORGE R.R. MARTIN)

The Dance of the Dragons is the flowery name bestowed upon the savage internecine struggle for the Iron Throne of Westeros fought between two rival branches of House Targaryen during the years 129 to 131 AC. To characterize the dark, turbulent, bloody doings of this period as a "dance" strikes us as grotesquely inappropriate. No doubt the phrase originated with some singer. "The Dying of the Dragons" would be altogether more fitting, but tradition and time have burned the more poetic usage into the pages of history, so we must dance along with the rest.

There were two principal claimants to the Iron Throne upon the death of King Viserys I Targaryen: his daughter Rhaenyra, the only surviving child of his first marriage, and Aegon, his eldest son by his second wife. Amidst the chaos and carnage brought on by their rivalry, other would-be kings would stake claims as well, strutting about like mummers on a stage for a fortnight or a moon's turn, only to fall as swiftly as they had arisen.

The Dance split the Seven Kingdoms in two, as lords, knights, and smallfolk declared for one side or the other and took up arms against each other. Even House Targaryen itself became divided, when the kith, kin, and children of each of the claimants became embroiled in the fighting. Over the two years of struggle, a terrible toll was taken of the great lords of Westeros, together with their bannermen, knights, and smallfolk. Whilst the dynasty survived, the end of the fighting saw Targaryen power much diminished, and the world's last dragons vastly reduced in number.

The Dance was a war unlike any other ever fought in the long history of the Seven Kingdoms. Though armies marched and met in savage battle, much of the slaughter took place on water, and . . . especially . . . in the air, as dragon fought dragon with tooth and claw and flame. It was a war marked by stealth, murder, and betrayal as well, a war fought in shadows and stairwells, council chambers and castle yards, with knives and lies and poison.

Long simmering, the conflict burst into the open on the third day of third moon of 129 AC, when the ailing, bedridden King Viserys I Targaryen closed his eyes for a nap in the Red Keep of King's Landing, and died without waking. His body was discovered by a serving man at the hour of the bat, when it was the king's custom to take a cup of hippocras. The servant ran to inform Queen Alicent, whose apartments were on the floor below the king's.

The manservant delivered his dire tidings directly to the queen, and her alone, without raising a general alarum; the king's death had been anticipated for some time, and Queen Alicent and her party, the so-called greens*, had taken care to instruct all of Viserys's guards and servants in what to do when the day came.

Queen Alicent went at once to the king's bedchamber, accompanied by Ser Criston Cole, Lord Commander of the Kingsguard. Once they had confirmed that Viserys was dead, Her Grace ordered his room sealed and placed under guard. The serving man who had found the king's body was taken into

---

* In 111 AC, a great tourney was held at King's Landing on the fifth anniversary of the king's marriage to Queen Alicent. At the opening feast, the queen wore a green gown, whilst the princess dressed dramatically in Targaryen red and black. Note was taken, and thereafter it became the custom to refer to "greens" and "blacks" when talking of the queen's party and the party of the princess, respectively. In the tourney itself, the blacks had much the better of it when Ser Criston Cole, wearing Princess Rhaenyra's favor unhorsed all of the queen's champions, including two of her cousins and her youngest brother, Ser Gwayne Hightower.

custody, to make certain he did not spread the tale. Ser Criston returned to White Sword Tower and sent his brothers of the Kingsguard to summon the members of the king's small council. It was the hour of the owl.

Then as now, the Sworn Brotherhood of the Kingsguard consisted of seven knights, men of proven loyalty and undoubted prowess who had taken solemn oaths to devote their lives to defending the king's person and kin. Only five of the white cloaks were in King's Landing at the time of Viserys's death; Ser Criston himself, Ser Arryk Cargyll, Ser Rickard Thorne, Ser Steffon Darklyn, and Ser Willis Fell. Ser Erryk Cargyll (twin to Ser Arryk) and Ser Lorent Marbrand, with Princess Rhaenyra on Dragonstone, remained unaware and uninvolved as their brothers-in-arms went forth into the night to rouse the members of the small council from their beds.

Gathering in the queen's chambers as the body of her lord husband grew cold above were Queen Alicent herself; her father Ser Otto Hightower, Hand of the King; Ser Criston Cole, Lord Commander of the Kingsguard; Grand Maester Orwyle; Lord Lyman Beesbury, master of coin, a man of eighty; Ser Tyland Lannister, master of ships, brother to the Lord of Casterly Rock; Larys Strong, called Larys Clubfoot, Lord of Harrenhal, master of whisperers; and Lord Jasper Wylde, called Ironrod, master of laws.

Grand Maester Orwyle opened the meeting by reviewing the customary tasks and procedures required at the death of a king. He said, "Septon Eustace should be summoned to perform the last rites and pray for the king's soul. A raven must needs be sent to Dragonstone at once to inform Princess Rhaenyra of her father's passing. Mayhaps Her Grace the queen would care to write the message, so as to soften these sad tidings with some words of condolence? The bells are always rung to announce the death of a king, someone should see to that, and of course we must begin to make our preparations for Queen Rhaenyra's coronation—"

Ser Otto Hightower cut him off. "All this must needs wait," he declared, "until the question of succession is settled." As the King's Hand, he was empowered to speak with the king's voice, even to sit the Iron Throne in the king's absence. Viserys had granted him the authority to rule over the Seven Kingdoms, and "until such time as our new king is crowned," that rule would continue.

"Until our new *queen* is crowned," Lord Beesbury said, in a waspish tone.

"*King*," insisted Queen Alicent. "The Iron Throne by rights must pass to His Grace's eldest trueborn son."

The discussion that followed lasted nigh unto dawn. Lord Beesbury spoke on behalf of Princess Rhaenyra. The ancient master of coin, who had served King Viserys for his entire reign, and his grandfather Jaehaerys the Old King before him, reminded the council that Rhaenyra was older than her brothers and had more Targaryen blood, that the late king had chosen her as his successor, that he had repeatedly refused to alter the succession despite the pleadings of Queen Alicent and her greens, that hundreds of lords and landed knights had done obeisance to the princess in 105 AC, and sworn solemn oaths to defend her rights.

But these words fell on ears made of stone. Ser Tyland pointed out that many of the lords who had sworn to defend the succession of Princess Rhaenyra were long dead. "It has been twenty-four years," he said. "I myself swore no such oath. I was a child at the time." Ironrod, the master of laws, cited the Great Council of 101 and the Old King's choice of Baelon rather than Rhaenys in 92, then discoursed at length about Aegon the Conquerer and his sisters, and the hallowed Andal tradition wherein the rights of a trueborn son always came before the rights of a mere daughter. Ser Otto reminded them that Rhaenyra's husband was none other than Prince Daemon, and "we all know that one's nature. Make no mistake, should Rhaenyra ever sit the Iron Throne, it will be Daemon who rules us, a king consort as cruel and unforgiving as Maegor ever was. My own head will be the first cut off, I do not doubt, but your queen, my daughter, will soon follow."

Queen Alicent echoed him. "Nor will they spare my children," she declared. "Aegon and his brothers are the king's trueborn sons, with a better claim to the throne than her brood of bastards. Daemon will find some pretext to put them all to death. Even Helaena and her little ones. One of these Strongs put out Aemond's eye, never forget. He was a boy, aye, but the boy is the father to the man, and bastards are monstrous by nature."

Ser Criston Cole spoke up. Should the princess reign, he reminded them, Jacaerys Velaryon would rule after her. "Seven save this realm if we seat a bastard on the Iron Throne." He spoke of Rhaenyra's wanton ways and the infamy of her husband. "They will turn the Red Keep into a brothel. No man's daughter will be safe, nor any man's wife. Even the boys . . . we know what Laenor was."

It is not recorded that Lord Larys Strong spoke a word during this debate, but that was not unusual. Though glib of tongue when need be, the master of whisperers hoarded his words like a miser hoarding coins, preferring to listen rather than talk.

"If we do this," Grand Maester Orwyle cautioned the council, "it must surely lead to war. The princess will not meekly stand aside, and she has dragons."

"And friends," Lord Beesbury declared. "Men of honor, who will not forget the vows they swore to her and her father. I am an old man, but not so old that I will sit here meekly whilst the likes of you plot to steal her crown." And so saying, he rose to go.

But Ser Criston Cole forced Lord Beesbury back into his seat and opened his throat with a dagger.

And so the first blood shed in the Dance of the Dragons belonged to Lord Lyman Beesbury, master of coin and lord treasurer of the Seven Kingdoms.

No further dissent was heard after the death of Lord Beesbury. The rest of the night was spent making plans for the new king's coronation (it must be done quickly, all agreed), and drawing up lists of possible allies and potential enemies, should Princess Rhaenyra refuse to accept King Aegon's ascension. With the princess in confinement on Dragonstone, about to give birth, Queen Alicent's greens enjoyed an advantage; the longer Rhaenyra remained ignorant of the king's death, the slower she would be to move. "Mayhaps the whore will die in childbirth," Queen Alicent said.

No ravens flew that night. No bells rang. Those servants who knew of the king's passing were sent to the dungeons. Ser Criston Cole was given the task of taking into custody such "blacks" who remained at court, those lords and knights who might be inclined to favor Princess Rhaenyra. "Do them no violence, unless they resist," Ser Otto Hightower commanded. "Such men as bend the knee and swear fealty to King Aegon shall suffer no harm at our hands."

"And those who will not?" asked Grand Maester Orwyle.

"Are traitors," said Ironrod, "and must die a traitor's death."

Lord Larys Strong, master of whisperers, then spoke for the first and only time. "Let us be the first to swear," he said, "lest there be traitors here amongst us." Drawing his dagger, the Clubfoot drew it across his palm. "A blood oath," he urged, "to bind us all together, brothers unto death." And so each of the conspirators slashed their palms and clasped hands with one another, swearing brotherhood. Queen Alicent alone amongst them was excused from the oath, on the account of her womanhood.

Dawn was breaking over the city before Queen Alicent dispatched the Kingsguard to bring her sons to the council. Prince Daeron, the gentlest of her children, wept for his grandsire's passing. One-eyed Prince Aemond, nineteen, was found in the armory, donning plate and mail for his morning practice in the castle yard. "Is Aegon king," he asked Ser Willis Fell, "or must we kneel and kiss the old whore's cunny?" Princess Helaena was breaking her fast with her children when the Kingsguard came to her . . . but when asked the whereabouts of Prince Aegon, her brother and husband, said only, "He is not in my bed, you may be sure. Feel free to search beneath the blankets."

Prince Aegon was with a paramour when he was found. At first, the prince refused to be a part of his mother's plans. "My sister is the heir, not me," he said. "What sort of brother steals his sister's birthright?" Only when Ser Criston convinced him that the princess must surely execute him and his brothers should she don the crown did Aegon waver. "Whilst any trueborn Targaryen yet lives, no Strong can ever hope to sit the Iron Throne," Cole said. "Rhaenyra has no choice but to take your heads if she wishes her bastards to rule after her." It was this, and only this, that persuaded Aegon to accept the crown that the small council was offering him,

Ser Tyland Lannister was named master of coin in place of the late Lord Beesbury, and acted at once to seize the royal treasury. The crown's gold was divided into four parts. One part was entrusted to the care of the Iron Bank of Braavos for safekeeping, another sent under strong guard to Casterly Rock, a third to Oldtown. The remaining wealth was to be used for bribes and gifts, and to hire sellswords if needed. To take Ser Tyland's place as master of ships, Ser Otto looked to the Iron Islands, dispatching a raven to Dalton Greyjoy, the Red Kraken, the daring and bloodthirsty sixteen-year-old Lord Reaper of Pyke, offering him the admiralty and a seat on the council for his allegiance.

A day passed, then another. Neither septons nor silent sisters were summoned to the bedchamber where King Viserys lay, swollen and rotting. No bells rang. Ravens flew, but not to Dragonstone. They went instead to Oldtown, to Casterly Rock, to Riverrun, to Highgarden, and to many other lords and knights whom Queen Alicent had cause to think might be sympathetic to her son.

The annals of the Great Council of 101 were brought forth and examined, and note was made of which lords had spoken for Viserys, and which for Rhaenys, Laena, or Laenor. The lords assembled had favored the male claimant over the female by twenty to one, but there had been dissenters, and those same houses were most like to lend Princess Rhaenyra their support should it come to war. The princess would have the Sea Snake and his fleets, Ser Otto judged, and like as not the other lords of the eastern shores as well: Lords Bar Emmon, Massey, Celtigar, and Crabb most like, perhaps even the Evenstar of Tarth. All were lesser powers, save for the Velaryons. The northmen were a greater concern: Winterfell had spoken for Rhaenys at Harrenhal, as had Lord Stark's bannermen, Dustin of Barrowton and Manderly of White Harbor. Nor could House Arryn be relied upon, for the Eyrie was presently ruled by a woman, Lady Jeyne, the Maiden of the Vale, whose own rights might be called into question should Princess Rhaenyra be put aside.

The greatest danger was deemed to be Storm's End, for House Baratheon had always been staunch in support of the claims of Princess Rhaenys and her children. Though old Lord Boremund had died, his son Borros was even more belligerent than his father, and the lesser storm lords would surely follow wherever he led. "Then we must see that he leads them to our king," Queen Alicent declared. Whereupon she sent for her second son.

Thus it was not a raven who took flight for Storm's End that day, but Vhagar, oldest and largest of the dragons of Westeros. On her back rode Prince Aemond Targaryen, with a sapphire in the place of his missing eye. "Your purpose is to win the hand of one of Lord Baratheon's daughters," his grandsire Ser Otto told him, before he flew. "Any of the four will do. Woo her and wed her, and Lord Borros will deliver the stormlands for your brother. Fail—"

"I will not fail," Prince Aemond blustered. "Aegon will have Storm's End, and I will have this girl."

By the time Prince Aemond took his leave, the stink from the dead king's bedchamber had wafted all through Maegor's Holdfast, and many wild tales and rumors were spreading through the court and castle. The dungeons under the Red Keep had swallowed up so many men suspected of disloyalty that even the High Septon had begun to wonder at these disappearances, and sent word from the Starry Sept of Oldtown asking after some of the missing. Ser Otto Hightower, as methodical a man as ever served as Hand, wanted more time to make preparations, but Queen Alicent knew they could delay no longer. Prince Aegon had grown weary of secrecy. "Am I a king, or no?" he demanded of his mother. "If I am king, then crown me."

The bells began to ring on the tenth day of the third moon of 129 AC, tolling the end of a reign. Grand Maester Orwyle was at last allowed to send forth his ravens, and the black birds took to the air by the hundreds, spreading the word of Aegon's ascension to every far corner of the realm. The silent sisters were sent for, to prepare the corpse for burning, and riders went forth on pale horses to spread the word to the people of King's Landing, crying, "King Viserys is dead, long live King Aegon." Hearing the cries, some wept whilst others cheered, but most of the smallfolk stared in silence, confused and wary, and now and again a voice cried out, "Long live our queen."

Meanwhile, hurried preparations were made for the coronation. The Dragonpit was chosen as the site. Under its mighty dome were stone benches sufficient to seat eighty thousand, and the pit's thick walls, strong roof, and towering bronze doors made it defensible, should traitors attempt to disrupt the ceremony.

On the appointed day Ser Criston Cole placed the iron-and-ruby crown of Aegon the Conquerer upon the brow of the eldest son of King Viserys and Queen Alicent, proclaiming him Aegon of House Targaryen, Second of His Name, King of the Andals and the Rhoynar and the First Men, Lord of the Seven Kingdoms, and Protector of the Realm. His mother Queen Alicent, beloved of the smallfolk, placed her own crown upon the head of her daughter Helaena, Aegon's wife and sister. After kissing her cheeks, the mother knelt before the daughter, bowed her head, and said, "My queen."

With the High Septon in Oldtown, too old and frail to journey to King's Landing, it fell to Septon Eustace to anoint King Aegon's brow with holy oils, and bless him in the seven names of god. A few of those in attendance, with sharper eyes than most, may have noticed that there were but four white cloaks in attendance on the new king, not five as heretofore. Aegon II had suffered his first defections the night before, when Ser Steffon Darklyn of the Kingsguard had slipped from the city with his squire, two stewards, and four guardsmen. Under the cover of darkness they made their way out a postern gate to where a fisherman's skiff awaited to take them to Dragonstone. They brought with them a stolen crown: a band of yellow gold ornamented with seven gems of different colors. This was the crown King Viserys had worn, and the Old King Jaehaerys before him. When Prince Aegon had decided to wear the iron-and-ruby crown of his namesake, the Conquerer, Queen Alicent had ordered Viserys's crown locked away, but the steward entrusted with the task had made off with it instead.

After the coronation, the remaining Kingsguard escorted Aegon to his mount, a splendid creature with gleaming golden scales and pale pink wing membranes. Sunfyre was the name given this dragon of the golden dawn. Munkun tells us the king flew thrice around the city before landing inside the walls of the Red Keep. Ser Arryk Cargyll led His Grace into the torchlit throne room, where Aegon II mounted the steps of the Iron Throne before a thousand lords and knights. Shouts rang through the hall.

On Dragonstone, no cheers were heard. Instead, screams echoed through the halls and stairwells of Sea Dragon Tower, down from the queen's apartments where Rhaenyra Targaryen strained and shuddered in her third day of labor. The child had not been due for another turn of the moon, but the tidings from King's Landing had driven the princess into a black fury, and her rage seemed to bring on the birth, as if the babe inside her were angry too, and fighting to get out. The princess shrieked curses all through her labor, calling down the wroth of the gods upon her half brothers and their mother the queen, and detailing the torments she would inflict upon them before she would let them die. She cursed the child inside her too. "*Get out,*" she screamed, clawing at her swollen belly as her maester and her midwife tried to restrain her. "*Monster, monster, get out, get out, GET OUT!*"

When the babe at last came forth, she proved indeed a monster: a stillborn girl, twisted and malformed, with a hole in her chest where her heart should have been and a stubby, scaled tail. The dead girl had been named Visenya, Princess Rhaenyra announced the next day, when milk of the poppy had blunted the edge of her pain. "She was my only daughter, and they killed her. They stole my crown and murdered my daughter, and they shall answer for it."

And so the dance began, as the princess called a council of her own. "The black council," setting it against the "green council" of King's Landing. Rhaenyra herself presided, with her uncle and husband Prince Daemon. Her three sons were present with them, though none had reached the age of manhood (Jace was fifteen, Luke fourteen, Joffrey twelve). Two Kingsguard stood with them: Ser Erryk Cargyll, twin to Ser Arryk, and

the westerman, Ser Lorent Marbrand. Thirty knights, a hundred crossbowmen, and three hundred men-at-arms made up the rest of Dragonstone's garrison. That had always been deemed sufficient for a fortress of
such strength. "As an instrument of conquest, however, our army leaves
somewhat to be desired," Prince Daemon observed sourly.

A dozen lesser lords, bannermen and vassals to Dragonstone, sat at the
black council as well: Celtigar of Claw Isle, Staunton of Rook's Rest, Massey
of Stonedance, Bar Emmon of Sharp Point, and Darklyn of Duskendale
amongst them. But the greatest lord to pledge his strength to the princess
was Corlys Velaryon of Driftmark. Though the Sea Snake had grown old,
he liked to say that he was clinging to life "like a drowning sailor clinging
to the wreckage of a sunken ship. Mayhaps the Seven have preserved me
for this one last fight." With Lord Corlys came his wife Princess Rhaenys,
five-and-fifty, her face lean and lined, her silver hair streaked with white,
yet fierce and fearless as she had been at two-and-twenty—a woman
sometimes known among the smallfolk as "The Queen Who Never Was."

Those who sat at the black council counted themselves loyalists, but
knew full well that King Aegon II would name them traitors. Each had
already received a summons from King's Landing, demanding they present themselves at the Red Keep to swear oaths of loyalty to the new king.
All their hosts combined could not match the power the Hightowers
alone could field. Aegon's greens enjoyed other advantages as well. Oldtown, King's Landing, and Lannisport were the largest and richest cities
in the realm; all three were held by greens. Every visible symbol of legiti-
macy belonged to Aegon. He sat the Iron Throne. He lived in the Red
Keep. He wore the Conquerer's crown, wielded the Conquerer's sword,
and had been anointed by a septon of the Faith before the eyes of tens of
thousands. Grand Maester Orwyle sat in his councils, and the Lord
Commander of the Kingsguard had placed the crown upon his princely
head. And he was male, which in the eyes of many made him the rightful
king, his half sister the usurper.

Against all that, Rhaenyra's advantages were few. Some older lords
might yet recall the oaths they had sworn when she was made Princess of
Dragonstone and named her father's heir. There had been a time when she
had been well loved by highborn and commons alike, when they had
cheered her as the Realm's Delight. Many a young lord and noble knight
had sought her favor then . . . though how many would still fight for her,

now that she was a woman wed, her body aged and thickened by six childbirths, was a question none could answer. Though her half brother had looted their father's treasury, the princess had at her disposal the wealth of House Velaryon, and the Sea Snake's fleets gave her superiority at sea. And her consort Prince Daemon, tried and tempered in the Stepstones, had more experience of warfare than all their foes combined. Last, but far from least, Rhaenyra had her dragons.

"As does Aegon," Lord Staunton pointed out.

"We have more," said Princess Rhaenys, the Queen Who Never Was, who had been a dragonrider longer than all of them. "And ours are larger and stronger, but for Vhagar. Dragons thrive best here on Dragonstone." She enumerated for the council. King Aegon had his Sunfyre. A splendid beast, though young. Aemond One-Eye rode Vhagar, and the peril posed by Queen Visenya's mount could not be gainsaid. Queen Helaena's mount was Dreamfyre, the she-dragon who had once borne the Old King's sister Rhaena through the clouds. Prince Daeron's dragon was Tessarion, with her wings dark as cobalt and her claws and crest and belly scales as bright as beaten copper. "That makes four dragons of fighting size," said Rhaenys. Queen Helaena's twins had their own dragons too, but no more than hatchlings; the usurper's youngest son, Maelor, was possessed only of an egg.

Against that, Prince Daemon had Caraxes and Princess Rhaenyra Syrax, both huge and formidable beasts. Caraxes especially was fearsome, and no stranger to blood and fire after the Stepstones. Rhaenyra's three sons by Laenor Velaryon were all dragonriders; Vermax, Arrax, and Tyraxes were thriving, and growing larger every year. Aegon the Younger, eldest of Rhaenyra's two sons by Prince Daemon, commanded the young dragon Stormcloud, though he had yet to mount him; his little brother Viserys went everywhere with his egg. Rhaenys's own she-dragon, Meleys the Red Queen, had grown lazy, but remained fearsome when roused. Prince Daemon's twins by Laena Velaryon might yet be dragonriders too. Baela's dragon, the slender pale green Moondancer, would soon be large enough to bear the girl upon her back . . . and though her sister Rhaena's egg had hatched a broken thing that died within hours of emerging from the egg, Syrax had recently produced another clutch. One of her eggs had been given to Rhaena, and it was said that the girl slept with it every night, and prayed for a dragon to match her sister's.

Moreover, six other dragons made their lairs in the smoky caverns of the Dragonmont above the castle. There was Silverwing, Good Queen Alysanne's mount of old; Seasmoke, the pale grey beast that had been the pride and passion of Ser Laenor Velaryon; hoary old Vermithor, unridden since the death of King Jaehaerys. And back of the mountain dwelled three wild dragons, never claimed nor ridden by any man, living or dead. The smallfolk had named them Sheepstealer, Grey Ghost, and the Cannibal. "Find riders to master Silverwing, Vermithor, and Seasmoke, and we will have nine dragons against Aegon's four. Mount and fly their wild kin, and we will number twelve, even without Stormcloud," Princess Rhaenys pointed out. "That is how we shall win this war."

Lords Celtigar and Staunton agreed. Aegon the Conquerer and his sisters had proved that knights and armies could not stand against the fire of dragons. Celtigar urged the princess to fly against King's Landing at once, and reduce the city to ash and bone. "And how will that serve us, my lord?" the Sea Snake demanded of him. "We want to rule the city, not burn it to the ground."

"It will never come to that," Celtigar insisted. "The usurper will have no choice but to oppose us with his own dragons. Our nine must surely overwhelm his four."

"At what cost?" Princess Rhaenyra wondered. "My sons would be riding three of those dragons, I remind you. And it would not be nine against four. I will not be strong enough to fly for some time yet. And who is to ride Silverwing, Vermithor, and Seasmoke? You, my lord? I hardly think so. It will be five against four, and one of their four will be Vhagar. That is no advantage."

Surprisingly, Prince Daemon agreed with his wife. "In the Stepstones, my enemies learned to run and hide when they saw Caraxes's wings or heard his roar . . . but they had no dragons of their own. It is no easy thing for a man to be a dragonslayer. But *dragons* can kill dragons, and have. Any maester who has ever studied the history of Valyria can tell you that. I will not throw our dragons against the usurper's unless I have no other choice. There are other ways to use them, better ways." Then the prince laid his own strategies before the black council. Rhaenyra must have a coronation of her own, to answer Aegon's. Afterward they would send out ravens, calling on the lords of the Seven Kingdoms to declare their allegiance to their true queen.

"We must fight this war with words before we go to battle," the prince declared. The lords of the Great Houses held the key to victory, Daemon insisted; their bannermen and vassals would follow where they led. Aegon the Usurper had won the allegiance of the Lannisters of Casterly Rock, and Lord Tyrell of Highgarden was a mewling boy in swaddling clothes whose mother, acting as his regent, would most like align the Reach with her overmighty bannermen, the Hightowers ... but the rest of the realm's great lords had yet to declare.

"Storm's End will stand with us," Princess Rhaenys declared. She herself was of that blood on her mother's side, and the late Lord Boremund had always been the staunchest of friends.

Prince Daemon had good reason to hope that the Maid of the Vale might bring the Eyrie to their side as well. Aegon would surely seek the support of Pyke, he judged; only the Iron Islands could hope to match the strength of House Velaryon at sea. But the ironmen were notoriously fickle, and Dalton Greyjoy loved blood and battle; he might easily be persuaded to support the princess.

The north was too remote to be of much import in the fight, the council judged; by the time the Starks gathered their banners and marched south, the war might well be over. Which left only the riverlords, a notoriously quarrelsome lot ruled over, in name at least, by House Tully of Riverrun. "We have friends in the riverlands," the prince said, "though not all of them dare show their colors yet. We need a place where they can gather, a toehold on the mainland large enough to house a sizeable host, and strong enough to hold against whatever forces the usurper can send against us." He showed the lords a map. "Here. Harrenhal."

And so it was decided. Prince Daemon would lead the assault on Harrenhal, riding Caraxes. Princess Rhaenyra would remain on Dragonstone until she had recovered her strength. The Velaryon fleet would close off the Gullet, sallying forth from Dragonstone and Driftmark to block all shipping entering or leaving Blackwater Bay. "We do not have the strength to take King's Landing by storm," Prince Daemon said, "no more than our foes could hope to capture Dragonstone. But Aegon is a green boy, and green boys are easily provoked. Mayhaps we can goad him into a rash attack." The Sea Snake would command the fleet, whilst Princess Rhaenys flew overhead to keep their foes from attacking their ships with dragons. Meanwhile, ravens would go forth to Riverrun, the Eyrie, Pyke, and Storm's End, to gain the allegiance of their lords.

Then up spoke the queen's eldest son, Jacaerys. "*We* should bear those messages," he said. "Dragons will win the lords over quicker than ravens." His brother Lucerys agreed, insisting that he and Jace were men, or near enough to make no matter. "Our uncle calls us Strongs, and claims that we are bastards, but when the lords see us on dragonback they will know that for a lie. Only *Targaryens* ride dragons." Even young Joffrey chimed in, offering to mount his own dragon Tyraxes and join his brothers.

Princess Rhaenyra forbade that; Joff was but twelve. But Jacaerys was fifteen, Lucerys fourteen; strong and strapping lads, skilled in arms, who had long served as squires. "If you go, you go as messengers, not as knights," she told them. "You must take no part in any fighting." Not until both boys had sworn solemn oaths upon a copy of *The Seven-Pointed Star* would Her Grace consent to using them as her envoys. It was decided that Jace, being the older of the two, would take the longer, more dangerous task, flying first to the Eyrie to treat with the Lady of the Vale, then to White Harbor to win over Lord Manderly, and lastly to Winterfell to meet with Lord Stark. Luke's mission would be shorter and safer; he was to fly to Storm's End, where it was expected that Borros Baratheon would give him a warm welcome.

A hasty coronation was held the next day. The arrival of Ser Steffon Darklyn, late of Aegon's Kingsguard, was an occasion of much joy on Dragonstone, especially when it was learned that he and his fellow loyalists ("turncloaks," Ser Otto would name them, when offering a reward for their capture) had brought the stolen crown of King Jaehaerys the Conciliator. Three hundred sets of eyes looked on as Prince Daemon Targaryen placed the Old King's crown on the head of his wife, proclaiming her Rhaenyra of House Targaryen, First of Her Name, Queen of the Andals, the Rhoynar, and the First Men. The prince claimed for himself the style Protector of the Realm, and Rhaenyra named her eldest son, Jacaerys, the Prince of Dragonstone and heir to the Iron Throne.

Her first act as queen was to declare Ser Otto Hightower and Queen Alicent traitors and rebels. "As for my half brothers, and my sweet sister Helaena," she announced, "they have been led astray by the counsel of evil men. Let them come to Dragonstone, bend the knee, and ask my forgiveness, and I shall gladly spare their lives and take them back into my heart, for they are of my own blood, and no man or woman is as accursed as the kinslayer."

Word of Rhaenyra's coronation reached the Red Keep the next day, to the great displeasure of Aegon II. "My half sister and my uncle are guilty of high treason," the young king declared. "I want them attainted, I want them arrested, and I want them dead."

Cooler heads on the green council wished to parlay. "The princess must be made to see that her cause is hopeless," Grand Maester Orwyle said. "Brother should not war against sister. Send me to her, that we may talk and reach an amicable accord."

Aegon would not hear of it. Septon Eustace tells us that His Grace accused the grand maester of disloyalty and spoke of having him thrown into a black cell "with your black friends." But when the two queens—his mother Queen Alicent and his wife Queen Helaena—spoke in favor of Orwyle's proposal, the king gave way reluctantly. So Grand Maester Orwyle was dispatched across Blackwater Bay under a peace banner, leading a retinue that included Ser Arryk Cargyll of the Kingsguard and Ser Gwayne Hightower of the gold cloaks, along with a score of scribes and septons.

The terms offered by the king were generous. If the princess would acknowledge him as king and make obeisance before the Iron Throne, Aegon II would confirm her in her possession of Dragonstone, and allow the island and castle to pass to her son Jacaerys upon her death. Her second son, Lucerys, would be recognized as the rightful heir to Driftmark, and the lands and holdings of House Velaryon; her boys by Prince Daemon, Aegon the Younger and Viserys, would be given places of honor at court, the former as the king's squire, the latter as his cupbearer. Pardons would be granted to those lords and knights who had conspired treasonously with her against their true king.

Rhaenyra heard these terms in stony silence, then asked Orwyle if he remembered her father, King Viserys. "Of course, Your Grace," the maester answered. "Perhaps you can tell us who he named as his heir and successor," the queen said, her crown upon her head. "You, Your Grace," Orwyle replied. And Rhaenyra nodded and said, "With your own tongue you admit I am your lawful queen. Why then do you serve my half brother, the pretender? Tell my half brother that I will have my throne, or I will have his head," she said, sending the envoys on their way.

Aegon II was two-and-twenty, quick to anger and slow to forgive. Rhaenyra's refusal to accept his rule enraged him. "I offered her an honorable peace, and the whore spat in my face," he declared. "What happens now is on her own head."

Even as he spoke, the Dance began. On Driftmark, the Sea Snake's ships set sail from Hull and Spicetown to close the Gullet, choking off trade to and from King's Landing. Soon after, Jacaerys Velaryon was flying north upon his dragon, Vermax, his brother Lucerys south on Arrax, whilst Prince Daemon rode Caraxes to the Trident.

Harrenhal had already once proved vulnerable from the sky, when Aegon the Dragon had overthrown it. Its elderly castellan Ser Simon Strong was quick to strike his banners when Caraxes lighted atop Kingspyre Tower. In addition to the castle, Prince Daemon at a stroke had captured the not-inconsiderable wealth of House Strong and a dozen valuable hostages, amongst them Ser Simon and his grandsons.

Meanwhile, Prince Jacaerys flew north on his dragon, calling upon Lady Arryn of the Vale, Lord Manderly of White Harbor, Lord Borrell and Lord Sunderland of Sisterton, and Cregan Stark of Winterfell. So charming was the prince, and so fearsome his dragon, that each of the lords he visited pledged their support for his mother.

Had his brother's "shorter, safer" flight gone as well, much bloodshed and grief might well have been averted.

The tragedy that befell Lucerys Velaryon at Storm's End was never planned, on this all of our sources agree. The first battles in the Dance of the Dragons were fought with quills and ravens, with threats and promises, decrees and blandishments. The murder of Lord Beesbury at the green council was not yet widely known; most believed his lordship to be languishing in some dungeon. Whilst sundry familiar faces were no longer seen about court, no heads had appeared above the castle gates, and many still hoped that that the question of succession might be resolved peaceably.

The Stranger had other plans. For surely it was his dread hand behind the ill chance that brought the two princelings together at Storm's End, when the dragon Arrax raced before a gathering storm to deliver Lucerys Velaryon to the safety of the castle yard, only to find Aemond Targaryen there before him.

Prince Aemond's mighty dragon Vhagar sensed his coming first. Guardsman walking the battlements of the castle's mighty curtain walls clutched their spears in sudden terror when she woke, with a roar that shook the very foundations of Durran's Defiance. Even Arrax quailed before that sound, we are told, and Luke plied his whip freely as he forced him down.

Lightning was flashing to the east and a heavy rain falling as Lucerys leapt off his dragon, his mother's message clutched in his hand. He must surely have known what Vhagar's presence meant, so it would have come as no surprise when Aemond Targaryen confronted him in the Round Hall, before the eyes of Lord Borros, his four daughters, septon, and maester, and two score knights, guards, and servants.

"Look at this sad creature, my lord," Prince Aemond called out. "Little Luke Strong, the bastard." To Luke he said, "You are wet, bastard. Is it raining, or did you piss yourself in fear?"

Lucerys Velaryon addressed himself only to Lord Baratheon. "Lord Borros, I have brought you a message from my mother, the queen."

"The whore of Dragonstone, he means." Prince Aemond strode forward, and made to snatch the letter from Lucerys's hand, but Lord Borros roared a command and his knights intervened, pulling the princelings apart. One brought Rhaenyra's letter to the dais, where his lordship sat upon the throne of the Storm Kings of old.

No man can truly know what Borros Baratheon was feeling at that moment. The accounts of those who were there differ markedly one from the other. Some say his lordship was red-faced and abashed, as a man might be if his lawful wife found him abed with another woman. Others declare that Borros appeared to be relishing the moment, for it pleased his vanity to have both king and queen seeking his support.

Yet all the witnesses agree on what Lord Borros said and did. Never a man of letters, he handed the queen's letter to his maester, who cracked the seal and whispered the message into his lordship's ear. A frown stole across Lord Borros's face. He stroked his beard, scowled at Lucerys Velaryon, and said, "And if I do as your mother bids, which one of my daughters will you marry, boy?" He gestured at the four girls. "Pick one."

Prince Lucerys could only blush. "My lord, I am not free to marry," he replied. "I am betrothed to my cousin Rhaena."

"I thought as much," Lord Borros said. "Go home, pup, and tell the bitch your mother that the Lord of Storm's End is not a dog that she can whistle up at need to set against her foes." And Prince Lucerys turned to take his leave of the Round Hall.

But Prince Aemond drew his sword and said, "Hold, Strong!"

Prince Lucerys recalled his promise to his mother. "I will not fight you. I came here as an envoy, not a knight."

"You came here as a craven and a traitor," Prince Aemond answered. "I will have your life, Strong."

At that Lord Borros grew uneasy. "Not here," he grumbled. "He came an envoy. I want no blood shed beneath my roof." So his guards put themselves between the princelings and escorted Lucerys Velaryon from the Round Hall, back to the castle yard where his dragon Arrax was hunched down in the rain, awaiting his return.

Aemond Targaryen's mouth twisted in rage, and he turned once more to Lord Borros, asking for his leave. The Lord of Storm's End shrugged and answered, "It is not for me to tell you what to do when you are not beneath my roof." And his knights moved aside as Prince Aemond rushed to the doors.

Outside, the storm was raging. Thunder rolled across the castle, the rain fell in blinding sheets, and from time to time great bolts of blue-white lightning lit the world as bright as day. It was bad weather for flying, even for a dragon, and Arrax was struggling to stay aloft when Prince Aemon mounted Vhagar and went after him. Had the sky been calm, Prince Lucerys might have been able to outfly his pursuer, for Arrax was younger and swifter . . . but the day was black, and so it came to pass that the dragons met above Shipbreaker Bay. Watchers on the castle walls saw distant blasts of flame, and heard a shriek cut the thunder. Then the two beasts were locked together, lightning crackling around them. Vhagar was five times the size of her foe, the hardened survivor of a hundred battles. If there was a fight, it could not have lasted long.

Arrax fell, broken, to be swallowed by the storm-lashed waters of the bay. His head and neck washed up beneath the cliffs below Storm's End three days later, to make a feast for crabs and seagulls. Prince Lucerys's corpse washed up as well.

And with his death, the war of ravens and envoys and marriage pacts came to an end, and the war of fire and blood began in earnest.

On Dragonstone, Queen Rhaenyra collapsed when told of Luke's death. Luke's young brother Joffrey (Jace was still away on his mission north) swore a terrible oath of vengeance against Prince Aemond and Lord Borros. Only the intervention of the Sea Snake and Princess Rhaenys kept the boy from mounting his own dragon at once. As the black council sat to consider how to strike back, a raven arrived from Harrenhal. "An eye for an eye, a son for a son," Prince Daemon wrote. "Lucerys shall be avenged."

In his youth, Daemon Targaryen's face and laugh were familiar to every cut-purse, whore, and gambler in Flea Bottom. The prince still had friends in the low places of King's Landing, and followers amongst the gold cloaks. Unbeknownest to King Aegon, the Hand, or the Queen Dowager, he had allies at court as well, even on the green council . . . and one other go-between, a special friend he trusted utterly, who knew the wine sinks and rat pits that festered in the shadow of the Red Keep as well as Daemon himself once had, and moved easily through the shadows of the city. To this pale stranger he reached out now, by secret ways, to set a terrible vengeance into motion.

Amidst the stews of Flea Bottom, Prince Daemon's go-between found suitable instruments. One had been a serjeant in the City Watch; big and brutal, he had lost his gold cloak for beating a whore to death whilst in a drunken rage. The other was a rat-catcher in the Red Keep. Their true names are lost to history. They are remembered as Blood and Cheese.

The hidden doors and secret tunnels that Maegor the Cruel had built were as familiar to the rat-catcher as to the rats he hunted. Using a forgotten passageway, Cheese led Blood into the heart of the castle, unseen by any guard. Some say their quarry was the king himself, but Aegon was accompanied by the Kingsguard wherever he went, and even Cheese knew of no way in and out of Maegor's Holdfast save over the drawbridge that spanned the dry moat and its formidable iron spikes.

The Tower of the Hand was less secure. The two men crept up through the walls, bypassing the spearmen posted at the tower doors. Ser Otto's rooms were of no interest to them. Instead they slipped into his daughter's chambers, one floor below. Queen Alicent had taken up residence there after the death of King Viserys, when her son Aegon moved into Maegor's Holdfast with his own queen. Once inside, Cheese bound and gagged the Dowager Queen whilst Blood strangled her bedmaid. Then they settled down to wait, for they knew it was the custom of Queen Helaena to bring her children to see their grandmother every evening before bed.

Blind to her danger, the queen appeared as dusk was settling over the castle, accompanied by her three children. Jaehaerys and Jaehaera were six, Maelor two. As they entered the apartments, Helaena was holding his little hand and calling out her mother's name. Blood barred the door and slew the queen's guardsman, whilst Cheese appeared to snatch up Maelor. "Scream and you all die," Blood told Her Grace. Queen Helaena kept her calm, it is said. "Who are you?" she demanded of the two. "Debt collectors,"

said Cheese. "An eye for an eye, a son for a son. We only want the one, t'
square things. Won't hurt the rest o' you fine folks, not one lil' hair. Which
one you want t' lose, Your Grace?"

Once she realized what he meant, Queen Helaena pleaded with the
men to kill her instead. "A wife's not a son," said Blood. "It has to be a
boy." Cheese warned the queen to make a choice soon, before Blood grew
bored and raped her little girl. "Pick," he said, "or we kill them all." On
her knees, weeping, Helaena named her youngest, Maelor. Perhaps she
thought the boy was too young to understand, or perhaps it was because
the older boy, Jaehaerys, was King Aegon's firstborn son and heir, next in
line to the Iron Throne. "You hear that, little boy?" Cheese whispered to
Maelor. "Your momma wants you dead." Then he gave Blood a grin, and
the hulking swordsman slew Prince Jaehaerys, striking off the boy's head
with a single blow. The queen began to scream.

Strange to say, the rat-catcher and the butcher were true to their word.
They did no further harm to Queen Helaena or her surviving children,
but rather fled with the prince's head in hand.

Though Blood and Cheese had spared her life, Queen Helaena cannot
be said to have survived that fateful dusk. Afterward she would not eat, nor
bathe, nor leave her chambers, and she could no longer stand to look upon
her son Maelor, knowing that she had named him to die. The king had no
recourse but to take the boy from her and give him over to his mother, the
Dowager Queen Alicent, to raise as if he were her own. Aegon and his wife
slept separately thereafter, and Queen Helaena sank deeper and deeper into
madness, whilst the king raged, and drank, and raged.

Now the bloodletting began in earnest.

The fall of Harrenhal to Prince Daemon came as a great shock to His
Grace. Until that moment, Aegon II had believed his half sister's cause to
be hopeless. Harrenhal left His Grace feeling vulnerable for the first time.
Subsequent rapid defeats at the Burning Mill and Stone Hedge came as
further blows, and made the king realize that his situation was more per-
ilous than it had seemed. These fears deepened as ravens returned from
the Reach, where the greens had believed themselves strongest. House
Hightower and Oldtown were solidly behind King Aegon, and His Grace
had the Arbor too . . . but elsewhere in the south, other lords were declaring for Rhaenyra, amongst them Lord Costayne of Three Towers, Lord

Mullendore of Uplands, Lord Tarly of Horn Hill, Lord Rowan of Gold-engrove, and Lord Grimm of Greyshield.

Other blows followed: the Vale, White Harbor, Winterfell. The Black-woods and the other river lords streamed toward Harrenhal and Prince Daemon's banners. The Sea Snake's fleets closed Blackwater Bay, and every morning King Aegon had merchants whining at him. His Grace had no answer for their complaints, beyond another cup of strongwine. "Do something," he demanded of Ser Otto. The Hand assured him that something *was* being done; he had hatched a plan to break the Velaryon blockade. One of the chief pillars of support for Rhaenyra's claim was her consort, yet Prince Daemon represented one of her greatest weaknesses as well. The prince had made more foes than friends during the course of his adventures. Ser Otto Hightower, who had been amongst the first of those foes, was reaching across the narrow sea to another of the prince's ene-mies, the Kingdom of the Three Daughters, hoping to persuade them to move against the Sea Snake.

The delay did not sit well with the young king. Aegon II had run short of patience with his grandfather's prevarications. Though his mother the Dowager Queen Alicent spoke up in Ser Otto's defense, His Grace turned a deaf ear to her pleading. Summoning Ser Otto to the throne room, he tore the chain of office from his neck and tossed it to Ser Criston Cole. "My new Hand is a steel fist," he boasted. "We are done with writing let-ters." Ser Criston wasted no time in proving his mettle. "It is not for you to plead for support from your lords, like a beggar pleading for alms," he told Aegon. "You are the lawful king of Westeros, and those who deny it are traitors. It is past time they learned the price of treason."

King Aegon's master of whisperers, Larys Strong the Clubfoot, had drawn up a list of all those lords who gathered on Dragonstone to attend Queen Rhaenyra's coronation and sit on her black council. Lords Celtigar and Velaryon had their seats on islands; as Aegon II had no strength at sea, they were beyond the reach of his wroth. Those "black" lords whose lands were on the mainland enjoyed no such protection, however.

Duskendale fell easily, taken by surprise by the King's forces, the town sacked, the ships in the harbor set afire, Lord Darklyn beheaded. Rook's Rest was Ser Criston's next objective. Forewarned of their coming, Lord Staunton closed his gates and defied the attackers. Behind his walls, his lordship could only watch as his fields and woods and villages were burned, his sheep and cattle and smallfolk put to the sword. When provisions inside the castle began to run low, he dispatched a raven to Dragonstone, pleading for succor.

Nine days after Lord Staunton dispatched his plea for help, the sound of leathern wings was heard across the sea, and the dragon Meleys appeared above Rook's Rest. The Red Queen, she was called, for the scarlet scales that covered her. The membranes of her wings were pink, her crest, horns, and claws bright as copper. And on her back, in steel and copper armor that flashed in the sun, rode Rhaenys Targaryen, the Queen Who Never Was.

Ser Criston Cole was not dismayed. Aegon's Hand had expected this, counted on it. Drums beat out a command, and archers rushed forward, longbowmen and crossbowmen both, filling the air with arrows and quarrels. Scorpions were cranked upwards to loose iron bolts of the sort that had once felled Meraxes in Dorne. Meleys suffered a score of hits, but the arrows only served to make her angry. She swept down, spitting fire to right and left. Knights burned in their saddles as the hair and hide and harness of their horses went up in flames. Men-at-arms dropped their spears and scattered. Some tried to hide behind their shields, but neither oak nor iron could withstand dragon's breath. Ser Criston sat on his white horse shouting, "Aim for the rider," through the smoke and flame. Meleys roared, smoke swirling from her nostrils, a stallion kicking in her jaws as tongues of fire engulfed him.

Then came an answering roar. Two more winged shapes appeared: the king astride Sunfyre the Golden, and his brother Aemond upon Vhagar. Criston Cole had sprung his trap, and Rhaenys had come snatching at the bait. Now the teeth closed round her.

Princess Rhaenys made no attempt to flee. With a glad cry and a crack of her whip, she turned Meleys toward the foe. Against Vhagar alone she might have had some chance, for the Red Queen was old and cunning, and no stranger to battle. Against Vhagar and Sunfyre together, doom was certain. The dragons met violently a thousand feet above the field of battle, as balls of fire burst and blossomed, so bright that men swore later that the sky was full of suns. The crimson jaws of Meleys closed round Sunfyre's golden neck for a moment, till Vhagar fell upon them from above. All three beasts went spinning toward the ground. They struck so hard that stones fell from the battlements of Rook's Rest half a league away.

Those closest to the dragons did not live to tell the tale. Those farther off could not see, for the flame and smoke. It was hours before the fires guttered out. But from those ashes, only Vhagar rose unharmed. Meleys was dead, broken by the fall and ripped to pieces upon the ground. And Sunfyre, that splendid golden beast, had one wing half torn from his body, whilst his royal rider had suffered broken ribs, a broken hip, and burns that covered half his body. His left arm was the worst. The dragonflame had burned so hot that the king's armor had melted into his flesh.

A body believed to be Rhaenys Targaryen was later found beside the carcass of her dragon, but so blackened that no one could be sure it was her. Beloved daughter of Lady Jocelyn Baratheon and Prince Aemon Targaryen, faithful wife to Lord Corlys Velaryon, mother and grandmother, the Queen Who Never Was lived fearlessly, and died amidst blood and fire. She was fifty-five years old.

Eight hundred knights and squires and common men lost their lives that day as well. Another hundred perished not long after, when Prince Aemond and Ser Criston Cole took Rook's Rest and put its garrison to death. Lord Staunton's head was carried back to King's Landing and mounted above the Old Gate . . . but it was the head of the dragon Meleys, drawn through the city on a cart, that awed the crowds of smallfolk into silence. Thousands fled King's Landing afterward, until the Dowager Queen Alicent ordered the city gates closed and barred.

King Aegon II did not die, though his burns brought him such pain that some say he prayed for death. Carried back to King's Landing in a closed litter to hide the extent of his injuries, His Grace did not rise from his bed for the rest of the year. Septons prayed for him, maesters attended him with potions and milk of the poppy, but Aegon slept nine hours out of every ten, waking only long enough to take some meagre nourishment before he slept again. None was allowed to disturb his rest, save his mother the Queen Dowager and his Hand, Ser Criston Cole. His wife never so much as made the attempt, so lost was Helaena in her own grief and madness.

The king's dragon, Sunfyre, too huge and heavy to be moved, and unable to fly with his injured wing, remained in the fields beyond Rook's Rest, crawling through the ashes like some great golden wyrm. In the early days, he fed himself upon the burned carcasses of the slain. When those were gone, the men Ser Criston had left behind to guard him brought him calves and sheep.

"You must rule the realm now, until your brother is strong enough to take the crown again," the King's Hand told Prince Aemond. Nor did Ser Criston need to say it twice. And so one-eyed Aemond the Kinslayer took up the iron-and-ruby crown of Aegon the Conquerer. "It looks better on me than it ever did on him," the prince proclaimed. Yet Aemond did not assume the style of king, but named himself only Protector of the Realm and Prince Regent. Ser Criston Cole remained Hand of the King.

Meanwhile, the seeds Jacaerys Velaryon had planted on his flight north had begun to bear fruit, and men were gathering at White Harbor, Winterfell, Barrowton, Sisterton, Gulltown, and the Gates of the Moon. Should they join their strength with that of the river lords assembling at Harrenhal with Prince Daemon, even the strong walls of King's Landing might not be able to withstand them, Ser Criston warned the new Prince Regent.

Supremely confident in his own prowess as a warrior and the might of his dragon Vhagar, Aemond was eager to take the battle to the foe. "The whore on Dragonstone is not the threat," he said. "No more than Rowan and these traitors in the Reach. The danger is my uncle. Once Daemon is dead, all these fools flying our sister's banners will run back to their castles and trouble us no more."

East of Blackwater Bay, Queen Rhaenyra was also faring badly. The death of her son Lucerys had been a crushing blow to a woman already broken by pregnancy, labor, and stillbirth. When word reached Dragonstone that Princess Rhaenys had fallen, angry words were exchanged between the queen and Lord Velaryon, who blamed her for his wife's death. "It should have been *you*," the Sea Snake shouted at Her Grace. "Staunton sent to you, yet you left it to my wife to answer, and forbade your sons to join her!" For as all the castle knew, the princes Jace and Joff had been eager to fly with Princess Rhaenys to Rook's Rest with their own dragons.

It was Jace who came to the fore now, late in the year 129 AC. First he brought the Lord of the Tides back into the fold by naming him the Hand of the Queen. Together he and Lord Corlys began to plan an assault upon King's Landing.

Mindful of the promise he had made to the Maiden of the Vale, Jace ordered Prince Joffrey to fly to Gulltown with Tyraxes. Munkun suggests that Jace's desire to keep his brother far from the fighting was paramount in this decision. This did not sit well with Joffrey, who was determined to prove himself in battle. Only when told that he was being sent to defend the Vale against King Aegon's dragons did he grudgingly consent to go. Rhaena, the thirteen-year-old daughter of Prince Daemon by Laena Velaryon, was chosen to accompany him. Known as Rhaena of Pentos, for the city of her birth, she was no dragonrider, her hatchling having died some years before, but she brought three dragon's eggs with her to the Vale, where she prayed nightly for their hatching. The Prince of Dragonstone also had a care for the safety of his half brothers, Aegon the Younger and Viserys, aged nine and seven. Their father Prince Daemon had made many friends in the Free City of Pentos during his visits there, so Jacaerys reached across the narrow sea to the prince of that city, who agreed to foster the two boys until Rhaenyra had secured the Iron Throne. In the waning days of 129 AC, the young princes boarded the cog *Gay Abandon*— Aegon with Stormcloud, Viserys clutching his egg—to set sail for Essos. The Sea Snake sent seven of his warships with them as escort, to see that they reached Pentos safely.

With Sunfyre wounded and unable to fly near Rook's Rest, and Tessarion with Prince Daeron in Oldtown, only two mature dragons remained to defend King's Landing ... and Dreamfyre's rider, Queen Helaena, spent her days in darkness, weeping, and surely could not be counted as threat. That left only Vhagar. No living dragon could match Vhagar for size or ferocity, but Jace reasoned that if Vermax, Syrax, and Caraxes were to descend on King's Landing all at once, even "that hoary old bitch" would be unable to withstand them. Yet so great was Vhagar's repute that the prince hesitated, considering how he might add more dragons to his attack.

House Targaryen had ruled Dragonstone for more than two hundred years, since Lord Aenar Targaryen first arrived from Valyria with his dragons. Though it had always been their custom to wed brother to sister and cousin to cousin, young blood runs hot, and it was not unknown for men of the House to seek their pleasures amongst the daughters (and even the wives) of their subjects, the smallfolk who lived in the villages below the Dragonmont, tillers of the land and fishers of the sea. Indeed, until the reign of King Jaehaerys and Good Queen Alysanne, the ancient law of the first night had prevailed on Dragonstone, as it did throughout Westeros, whereby it was the right of a lord to bed any maiden in his domain upon her wedding night.

Though this custom was greatly resented elsewhere in the Seven King-doms, by men of a jealous temperament who did not grasp the honor be-ing conferred upon them, such feelings were muted upon Dragonstone, where Targaryens were rightly regarded as being closer to gods than the common run of men. Here, brides thus blessed upon their wedding nights were envied, and the children born of such unions were esteemed above all others, for the Lords of Dragonstone oft celebrated the birth of such with lavish gifts of gold and silk and land to the mother. These happy bastards were said to have been "born of dragonseed," and in time became known simply as "seeds." Even after the end of the right of the first night, certain Targaryens continued to dally with the daughters of innkeeps and the wives of fishermen, so seeds and the sons of seeds were plentiful on Dragonstone.

Prince Jacaerys needed more dragonriders, and more dragons, and it was to those born of dragonseed that he turned, vowing that any man who could master a dragon would be granted lands and riches and dubbed a knight. His sons would be ennobled, his daughters wed to lords, and he himself would have the honor of fighting beside the Prince of Dragon-stone against the pretender Aegon II Targaryen and his treasonous sup-porters.

Not all those who came forward in answer to the prince's call were seeds, nor even the sons or grandsons of seeds. A score of the queen's own household knights offered themselves as dragonriders, amongst them the Lord Commander of her Kingsguard, Ser Steffon Darklyn, along with squires, scullions, sailors, men-at-arms, mummers, and two maids.

Dragons are not horses. They do not easily accept men upon their backs, and when angered or threatened, they attack. Sixteen men lost their lives during an attempt to become dragonriders. Three times that number were burned or maimed. Steffon Darklyn was burned to death whilst attempt-ing to mount the dragon Seasmoke. Lord Gormon Massey suffered the same fate when approaching Vermithor. A man called Silver Denys, whose hair and eyes lent credence to his claim to be a bastard son of King Mae-gor the Cruel, had an arm torn off by Sheepstealer. As his sons struggled to staunch the wound, the Cannibal descended on them, drove off Sheep-stealer, and devoured father and sons alike.

Yet Seasmoke, Vermithor, and Silverwing were accustomed to men and tolerant of their presence. Having once been ridden, they were more accepting of new riders. Vermithor, the Old King's own dragon, bent his neck to a blacksmith's bastard, a towering man called Hugh the Hammer or Hard Hugh, whilst a pale-haired man-at-arms named Ulf the White (for his hair) or Ulf the Sot (for his drinking) mounted Silverwing, beloved of Good Queen Alysanne.

And Seasmoke, who had once borne Laenor Velaryon, took onto his back a boy of ten-and-five known as Addam of Hull, whose origins remain a matter of dispute amongst historians to this day. Not long after Addam of Hull had proved himself by flying Seasmoke, Lord Corlys went so far as to petition Queen Rhaenyra to remove the taint of bastardy from him and his brother. When Prince Jacaerys added his voice to the request, the queen complied. Addam of Hull, dragonseed and bastard, became Addam Velaryon, heir to Driftmark.

Dragonstone's three wild dragons were less easily claimed than those that had known previous riders, yet attempts were made upon them all the same. Sheepstealer, a notably ugly "mud brown" dragon hatched when the Old King was still young, had a taste for mutton, swooping down on shepherd's flocks from Driftmark to the Wendwater. He seldom harmed the shepherds, unless they attempted to interfere with him, but had been known to devour the occasional sheepdog. Grey Ghost dwelt in a smoking vent high on the eastern side of the Dragonmont, preferred fish, and was most oft glimpsed flying low over the narrow sea, snatching prey from the waters. A pale grey-white beast the color of morning mist, he was a notably shy dragon who avoided men and their works for years at a time.

The largest and oldest of the wild dragons was the Cannibal, so named because he had been known to feed on the carcasses of dead dragons, and descend upon the hatcheries of Dragonstone to gorge himself on newborn hatchlings and eggs. Would-be dragontamers had made attempts to ride him a dozen times; his lair was littered with their bones.

None of the dragonseeds were fool enough to disturb the Cannibal (any who were did not return to tell their tales). Some sought the Grey Ghost, but could not find him, for he was ever an elusive creature. Sheepstealer proved easier to flush out, but he remained a vicious, ill-tempered beast, who killed more seeds than the three "castle dragons" together. One who hoped to tame him (after his quest for Grey Ghost proved fruitless) was Alyn of Hull. Sheepstealer would have none of him. When he stumbled from the dragon's lair with his cloak aflame, only his brother's swift action saved his life. Seasmoke drove the wild dragon off as Addam used his own cloak to beat out the flames. Alyn Velaryon would carry the scars of the encounter on his back and legs for the rest of his long life. Yet he counted himself fortunate, for he lived. Many of the other seeds and seekers who aspired to ride upon Sheepstealer's back ended in Sheep-stealer's belly instead.

In the end, the brown dragon was brought to heel by the cunning and persistence of a "small brown girl" of six-and-ten, named Netty, who de-livered him a freshly slaughtered sheep every morning, until Sheepstealer learned to accept and expect her. She was black-haired, brown-eyed, brown-skinned, skinny, foul-mouthed, filthy, and fearless . . . and the first and last rider of the dragon Sheepstealer.

Thus did Prince Jacaerys achieve his goal. For all the death and pain it caused, the widows left behind, the burned men who would carry their scars until the day they died, four new dragonriders had been found. As 129 AC drew to a close, the prince prepared to fly against King's Landing. The date he chose for the attack was the first full moon of the new year.

Yet the plans of men are but playthings to the gods. For even as Jace laid his plans, a new threat was closing from the east. The schemes of Otto Hightower had borne fruit; meeting in Tyrosh, the High Council of the Triarchy had accepted his offer of alliance. Ninety warships swept from the Stepstones under the banners of the Three Daughters, bending their oars for the Gullet . . . and as chance and the gods would have it, the Pentoshi cog *Gay Abandon,* carrying two Targaryen princes, sailed straight into their teeth. The escorts sent to protect the cog were sunk or taken, the *Gay Abandon* captured.

The tale reached Dragonstone only when Prince Aegon arrived desper-ately clinging to the neck of his dragon, Stormcloud. The boy was white with terror, shaking like a leaf and stinking of piss. Only nine, he had never flown before . . . and would never fly again, for Stormcloud had been terribly wounded as he fled, arriving with the stubs of countless ar-rows embedded in his belly and a scorpion bolt through his neck. He died within the hour, hissing as the hot blood gushed black and smoking from his wounds. Aegon's younger brother, Prince Viserys, had no way of es-caping from the cog. A clever boy, he hid his dragon's egg and changed into ragged, salt-stained clothing, pretending to be no more than a com-mon ship's boy, but one of the real ship's boys betrayed him, and he was made a captive. It was a Tyroshi captain who first realized who he had, but the admiral of the fleet, Sharako Lohar of Lys, soon relieved him of his prize.

When Prince Jacaerys swept down upon a line of Lysene galleys on Vermax, a rain of spears and arrows rose up to meet him. The sailors of the Triarchy had faced dragons before whilst warring against Prince Daemon in the Stepstones. No man could fault their courage; they were prepared to meet dragonflame with such weapons as they had. "Kill the rider and the dragon will depart," their captains and commanders had told them. One ship took fire, and then another. Still the men of the Free Cities fought on ... until a shout rang out, and they looked up to see more winged shapes coming around the Dragonmont and turning toward them.

It is one thing to face a dragon, another to face five. As Silverwing, Sheepstealer, Seasmoke, and Vermithor descended upon them, the men of the Triarchy felt their courage desert them. The line of warships shattered as one galley after another turned away. The dragons fell like thunderbolts, spitting balls of fire, blue and orange, red and gold, each brighter than the next. Ship after ship burst asunder or was consumed by flames. Screaming men leapt into the sea, shrouded in fire. Tall columns of black smoke rose up from the water. All seemed lost ... all *was* lost ...

... till Vermax flew too low, and went crashing down into the sea.

Several differing tales were told afterward of how and why the dragon fell. Some claimed a crossbowman put an iron bolt through his eye, but this version seems suspiciously similar to the way Meraxes met her end, long ago in Dorne. Another account tells us that a sailor in the crow's nest of a Myrish galley cast a grapnel as Vermax was swooping through the fleet. One of its prongs found purchase between two scales, and was driven deep by the dragon's own considerable speed. The sailor had coiled his end of the chain about the mast, and the weight of the ship and the power of Vermax's wings tore a long jagged gash in the dragon's belly. The dragon's shriek of rage was heard as far off as Spicetown, even through the clangor of battle. His flight jerked to a violent end, Vermax went down smoking and screaming, clawing at the water. Survivors said he struggled to rise, only to crash headlong into a burning galley. Wood splintered, the mast came tumbling down, and the dragon, thrashing, became entangled in the rigging. When the ship heeled over and sank, Vermax sank with her.

It is said that Jacaerys Velaryon leapt free and clung to a piece of smoking wreckage for a few heartbeats, until some crossbowmen on the nearest Myrish ship began loosing quarrels at him. The prince was struck once, and then again. More and more Myrmen brought crossbows to bear. Finally one quarrel took him through the neck, and Jace was swallowed by the sea.

The Battle in the Gullet raged into the night north and south of Dragonstone, and remains amongst the bloodiest sea battles in all of history. The Triarchy's admiral Sharako Lohar had taken a combined fleet of ninety Myrish, Lysene, and Tyroshi warships from the Stepstones; only twenty-eight survived to limp home.

Though the attackers bypassed Dragonstone, no doubt believing that the ancient Targaryen stronghold was too strong to assault, they exacted a grievous toll on Driftmark. Spicetown was brutally sacked, the bodies of men, women, and children butchered in the streets and left as fodder for gulls and rats and carrion crows, its buildings burned. The town would never be rebuilt. High Tide was put to the torch as well. All the treasures the Sea Snake had brought back from the east were consumed by fire, his servants cut down as they tried to flee the flames. The Velaryon fleet lost almost a third of its strength. Thousands died. Yet none of these losses were felt so deeply as that of Jacaerys Velaryon, Prince of Dragonstone and heir to the Iron Throne.

A fortnight later, in the Reach, Ormund Hightower found himself caught between two armies. Thaddeus Rowan, Lord of Goldengrove, and Tom Flowers, Bastard of Bitterbridge, were bearing down on him from the northeast with a great host of mounted knights, whilst Ser Alan Beesbury, Lord Alan Tarly, and Lord Owen Costayne had joined their power to cut off his retreat to Oldtown. When their hosts closed around him on the banks of the river Honeywine, attacking front and rear at once, Lord Hightower saw his lines crumble. Defeat seemed imminent . . . until a shadow swept across the battlefield, and a terrible roar resounded overhead, slicing through the sound of steel on steel. A dragon had come.

The dragon was Tessarion, the Blue Queen, cobalt and copper. On her back rode the youngest of Queen Alicent's three sons, Daeron Targaryen, fifteen, Lord Ormund's squire.

The arrival of Prince Daeron and his dragon reversed the tide of battle. Now it was Lord Ormond's men attacking, screaming curses at their foes, whilst the queen's men fled. By day's end, Lord Rowan was retreating north with the remnants of his host, Tom Flowers lay dead and burned amongst the reeds, the two Alans had been taken captive, and Lord Costayne was dying slowly from a wound given him by Bold Jon Roxton's black blade, the Orphan-Maker. As wolves and ravens fed upon the bodies of the slain, Lord Hightower feasted Prince Daeron on aurochs and strongwine, and dubbed him a knight with the storied Valryian longsword Vigilance, naming him "Ser Daeron the Daring." The prince modestly replied, "My lord is kind to say so, but the victory belongs to Tessarion."

On Dragonstone, an air of despondence and defeat hung over the black court when the disaster on the Honeywine became known to them. Lord Bar Emmon went so far as to suggest that mayhaps the time had come to bend their knees to Aegon II. The queen would have none of it, however. Only the gods truly know the hearts of men, and women are full as strange. Broken by the loss of one son, Rhaenyra Targaryen seemed to find new strength after the loss of a second. Jace's death hardened her, burning away her fears, leaving only her anger and her hatred. Still possessed of more dragons than her half brother, Her Grace now resolved to use them, no matter the cost. She would rain down fire and death upon Aegon and all those who supported him, she told the black council, and either tear him from the Iron Throne or die in the attempt.

A similar resolve had taken root across the bay in the breast of Aemond Targaryen, ruling in his brother's name whilst Aegon lay abed. Contemptuous of his half sister Rhaenyra, Aemond One-Eye saw a greater threat in his uncle, Prince Daemon, and the great host he had gathered at Harrenhal. Summoning his bannermen and council, the prince announced his intent to bring the battle to his uncle and chastise the rebellious river lords.

Not all the members of the green council favored the prince's bold stroke. Aemond had the support of Ser Criston Cole, the Hand, and that of Ser Tyland Lannister, but Grand Maester Orwyle urged him to send word to Storm's End and add the power of House Baratheon to his own before proceeding, and Ironrod, Lord Jasper Wylde, declared that he should summon Lord Hightower and Prince Daeron from the south, on the grounds that "two dragons are better than one." The Queen Dowager favored caution as well, urging her son to wait until his brother the king and his dragon Sunfyre the Golden were healed, so they might join the attack.

Prince Aemond had no taste for such delays, however. He had no need of his brothers or their dragons, he declared; Aegon was too badly hurt, Daeron too young. Aye, Caraxes was a fearsome beast, savage and cunning and battle-tested . . . but Vhagar was older, fiercer, and twice as large. Septon Eustace tells us that the Kinslayer was determined that this should be his victory; he had no wish to share the glory with his brothers, nor any other man.

Nor could he be gainsaid, for until Aegon II rose from his bed to take up his sword again, the regency and rule were Aemond's. True to his resolve, the prince rode forth from the Gate of the Gods within a fortnight, at the head of a host four thousand strong.

Daemon Targaryen was too old and seasoned a battler to sit idly by and let himself be penned up inside walls, even walls as massive as Harrenhal's. The prince still had friends in King's Landing, and word of his nephew's plans had reached him even before Aemond had set out. When told that Aemond and Ser Criston Cole had left King's Landing, it is said that Prince Daemon laughed and said, "Past time," for he had long anticipated this moment. A murder of ravens took flight from the twisted towers of Harrenhal.

Elsewhere in the realm, Lord Walys Mooton led a hundred knights out of Maidenpool to join with the half-wild Crabbs and Brunes of Crackclaw Point and the Celtigars of Claw Isle. Through piney woods and mist-shrouded hills they hastened, to Rook's Rest, where their sudden appearance took the garrison by surprise. After retaking the castle, Lord Mooton led his bravest men to the field of ashes west of the castle, to put an end to the dragon Sunfyre.

The would-be dragonslayers easily drove off the cordon of guards who had been left to feed, serve, and protect the dragon, but Sunfyre himself proved more formidable than expected. Dragons are awkward creatures on the ground, and his torn wing left the great golden wyrm unable to take to the air. The attackers expected to find the beast near death. Instead they found him sleeping, but the clash of swords and thunder of horses soon roused him, and the first spear to strike him provoked him to fury. Slimy with mud, twisting amongst the bones of countless sheep, Sunfyre writhed and coiled like a serpent, his tail lashing, sending blasts of golden flame at his attackers as he struggled to fly. Thrice he rose, and thrice fell back to earth. Mooton's men swarmed him with swords and spears and axes, dealing him many grievous wounds . . . yet each blow only seemed to enrage him further. The number of the dead reached three score before the survivors fled.

Amongst the slain was Walys Mooton, Lord of Maidenpool. When his body was found a fortnight later by his brother Manfyrd, nought remained but charred flesh in melted armor, crawling with maggots. Yet nowhere on that field of ashes, littered with the bodies of brave men and the burned and bloated carcasses of a hundred horses, did Lord Manfyrd find King Aegon's dragon. Sunfyre was gone. Nor were there tracks, as surely there would have been had the dragon dragged himself away. Sunfyre the Golden had taken wing again, it seemed . . . but to where, no living man could say.

Meanwhile, Prince Daemon Targaryen himself hastened south on the wings of his dragon, Caraxes. Flying above the western shore of the Gods Eye, well away from Ser Criston's line of march, he evaded the enemy host, crossed the Blackwater, then turned east, following the river downstream to King's Landing. And on Dragonstone, Rhaenyra Targaryen donned a suit of gleaming black scale, mounted Syrax, and took flight as a rainstorm lashed the waters of Blackwater Bay. High above the city the queen and her prince consort came together, circling over Aegon's High Hill.

The sight of them incited terror in the streets the city below, for the smallfolk were not slow to realize that the attack they had dreaded was at last at hand. Prince Aemond and Ser Criston had denuded King's Landing of defenders when they set forth to retake Harrenhal . . . and the Kinslayer had taken Vhagar, that fearsome beast, leaving only Dreamfyre and a handful of half-grown hatchlings to oppose the queen's dragons. The young dragons had never been ridden, and Dreamfyre's rider, Queen Helaena, was a broken woman; the city had as well been dragonless.

Thousands of smallfolk streamed out the city gates, carrying their children and worldly possessions on their backs, to seek safety in the countryside. Others dug pits and tunnels under their hovels, dark dank holes where they hoped to hide whilst the city burned. Rioting broke out in Flea Bottom. When the sails of the Sea Snake's ships were seen to the east in Blackwater Bay, making for the river, the bells of every sept in the city began to ring, and mobs surged through the streets, looting as they went. Dozens died before the gold cloaks could restore the peace.

With both the Lord Protector and the King's Hand absent, and King Aegon himself burned, bedridden, and lost in poppy dreams, it fell to his mother the Queen Dowager to see to the city's defenses. Queen Alicent rose to the challenge, closing the gates of castle and city, sending the gold cloaks to the walls, and dispatching riders on swift horses to find Prince Aemond and fetch him back.

As well, she commanded Grand Maester Orwyle to send ravens to "all our leal lords," summoning them to the defense of their true king. When Orywle hastened back to his chambers, however, he found four gold cloaks waiting for him. One man muffled his cries as the others beat and bound him. With a bag pulled down over his head, the grand maester was escorted down to the black cells.

Queen Alicent's riders got no farther than the gates, where more gold cloaks took them into custody. Unbeknownest to Her Grace, the seven captains commanding the gates, chosen for their loyalty to King Aegon, had been imprisoned or murdered the moment Caraxes appeared in the sky above the Red Keep . . . for the rank and file of the City Watch still loved Daemon Targaryen, who had commanded them of old.

The queen's brother Ser Gwayne Hightower, second in command of the gold cloaks, rushed to the stables intending to sound the warning; he was seized, disarmed, and dragged before his commander, Luthor Largent. When Hightower denounced him as a turncloak, Ser Luthor laughed. "Daemon gave us these cloaks," he said, "and they're gold no matter how you turn them." Then he drove his sword through Ser Gwayne's belly and ordered the city gates opened to the men pouring off the Sea Snake's ships.

For all the vaunted strength of its walls, King's Landing fell in less than a day. A short, bloody fight was waged at the River Gate, where thirteen Hightower knights and a hundred men-at-arms drove off the gold cloaks and held out for nigh on eight hours against attacks from both within and without the city, but their heroics were in vain, for Rhaenyra's soldiers poured in through the other six gates unmolested. The sight of the queen's dragons in the sky above took the heart out of the opposition, and King Aegon's remaining loyalists hid or fled or bent the knee.

One by one, the dragons made their descent. Sheepstealer lighted atop Visenya's Hill, Silverwing and Vermithor on the Hill of Rhaenys, outside the Dragonpit. Prince Daemon circled the towers of the Red Keep before bringing Caraxes down in the outer ward. Only when he was certain that the defenders would offer him no harm did he signal for his wife the queen to descend upon Syrax. Addam Velaryon remained aloft, flying Seasmoke around the city walls, the beat of his dragon's wide leathern wings a caution to those below that any defiance would be met with fire.

Upon seeing that resistance was hopeless, the Dowager Queen Alicent emerged from Maegor's Holdfast with her father Ser Otto Hightower, Ser Tyland Lannister, and Lord Jasper Wylde the Ironrod. (Lord Larys Strong was not with them. The master of whisperers had somehow contrived to disappear.) Queen Alicent attempted to treat with her stepdaughter. "Let us together summon a great council, as the Old King did in days of old," said the Dowager Queen, "and lay the matter of succession before the lords of the realm." But Queen Rhaenyra rejected the proposal with scorn. "We both know how this council would rule." Then she bid her stepmother choose: yield, or burn.

Bowing her head in defeat, Queen Alicent surrendered the keys to the castle, and ordered her knights and men-at-arms to lay down their swords. "The city is yours, princess," she is reported to have said, "but you will not hold it long. The rats play when the cat is gone, but my son Aemond will return with fire and blood."

Yet Rhaenyra's triumph was far from complete. Her men found her rival's wife, the mad Queen Helaena, locked in her bedchamber . . . but when they broke down the doors of the king's apartments, they discovered only "his bed, empty, and his chamber pot, full." King Aegon II had fled. So had his children, the six-year-old Princess Jaehaera and two-year-old Prince Maelor, along with the knights Willis Fell and Rickard Thorne of the Kingsguard. Not even the Dowager Queen herself seemed to know where they had gone, and Luthor Largent swore none had passed through the city gates.

There was no way to spirit away the Iron Throne, however. Nor would Queen Rhaenyra sleep until she claimed her father's seat. So the torches were lit in the throne room, and the queen climbed the iron steps and seated herself where King Viserys had sat before her, and the Old King before him, and Maegor and Aenys and Aegon the Dragon in days of old. Stern-faced, still in her armor, she sat on high as every man and woman in the Red Keep was brought forth and made to kneel before her, to plead for her forgiveness and swear their lives and swords and honor to her as their queen.

The ceremony went on all through that night. It was well past dawn when Rhaenyra Targaryen rose and made her descent. "And as her lord husband Prince Daemon escorted her from the hall, cuts were seen upon Her Grace's legs and the palm of her left hand. Drops of blood fell to the floor as she went past, and wise men looked at one another, though none dared speak the truth aloud: the Iron Throne had spurned her, and her days upon it would be few."

All this came to pass even as Prince Aemond and Ser Criston Cole advanced upon the riverlands. After nineteen days on the march, they reached Harrenhal . . . and found the castle gates open, with Prince Daemon and all his people gone.

Prince Aemond had kept Vhagar with the main column throughout the march, thinking that his uncle might attempt to attack them on Caraxes. He reached Harrenhal a day after Cole, and that night celebrated a great victory; Daemon and his "river scum" had fled rather than face his wroth, Aemond proclaimed. Small wonder then that when word of the fall of King's Landing reached him, the prince felt thrice the fool. His fury was fearsome to behold.

West of Harrenhal, fighting continued in the riverlands as the Lannister host slogged onward. The age and infirmity of their commander, Lord Lefford, had slowed their march to a crawl, but as they neared the western shores of the Gods Eye, they found a huge new army athwart their path.

Roddy the Ruin and his Winter Wolves had joined with Forrest Frey, Lord of the Crossing, and Red Robb Rivers, known as the Bowman of Raventree. The northmen numbered two thousand, Frey commanded two hundred knights and thrice as many foot, Rivers brought three hundred archers to the fray. And scarce had Lord Lefford halted to confront the foe in front of him when more enemies appeared to the south, where Longleaf the Lionslayer and a ragged band of survivors from the earlier battles had been joined by the Lords Bigglestone, Chambers, and Perryn.

Caught between these two foes, Lefford hesitated to move against either, for fear of the other falling on his rear. Instead he put his back to the lake, dug in, and send ravens to Prince Aemond at Harrenhal, begging his aid. Though a dozen birds took wing, not one ever reached the prince; Red Robb Rivers, said to be the finest archer in all Westeros, took them down on the wing.

More rivermen turned up the next day, led by Ser Garibald Grey, Lord Jon Charlton, and the new Lord of Raventree, the eleven-year-old Benjicot Blackwood. With their numbers augmented by these fresh levies, the queen's men agreed that the time had come to attack. "Best make an end to these lions before the dragons come," said Roddy the Ruin.

The bloodiest land battle of the Dance of the Dragons began the next day, with the rising of the sun. In the annals of the Citadel it is known as the Battle by the Lakeshore, but to those men who lived to tell of it, it was always the Fishfeed.

Attacked from three sides, the westermen were driven back foot by foot into the waters of the Gods Eye. Hundreds died there, cut down whilst fighting in the reeds; hundreds more drowned as they tried to flee. By nightfall two thousand men were dead, amongst them many notables, including Lord Frey, Lord Lefford, Lord Bigglestone, Lord Charlton, Lord Swyft, Lord Reyne, Ser Clarent Crakehall, and Ser Tyler Hill, the Bastard of Lannisport. The Lannister host was shattered and slaughtered, but at such cost that young Ben Blackwood, the boy Lord of Raventree, wept when he saw the heaps of the dead. The most grievous losses were suffered by the northmen, for the Winter Wolves had begged the honor of leading the attack, and had charged five times into the ranks of Lannister spears. More than two thirds of the men who had ridden south with Lord Dustin were dead or wounded.

At Harrenhal, Aemond Targaryen and Criston Cole debated how best to answer the queen's attacks. Though Black Harren's seat was too strong to be taken by storm, and the river lords dared not lay siege for fear of Vhagar, the king's men were running short of food and fodder, and losing men and horses to hunger and sickness. Only blackened fields and burned villages remained within sight of the castle's massive walls, and those foraging parties that ventured further did not return. Ser Criston urged a withdrawal to the south, where Aegon's support was strongest, but the prince refused, saying "Only a craven runs from traitors." The loss of King's Landing and the Iron Throne had enraged him, and when word of the Fishfeed reached Harrenhal, the Lord Protector had almost strangled the squire who delivered the news. Only the incession of his bedmate, Alys Rivers, had saved the boy's life. Prince Aemond favored an immediate attack upon King's Landing. None of the queen's dragons were a match for Vhagar, he insisted.

Ser Criston called that folly. "One against six is a fight for fools, my prince," he declared. Let them march south, he urged once more, and join their strength to Lord Hightower's. Prince Aemond could reunite with his brother Daeron and his dragon. King Aegon had escaped Rhaenyra's grasp, this they knew, surely he would reclaim Sunfyre and join his brothers. And perhaps their friends inside the city might find a way to free Queen Helaena as well, so she could bring Dreamfyre to the battle. Four dragons could perhaps prevail against six, if one was Vhagar.

Prince Aemond refused to consider this "craven course."

Ser Criston and Prince Aemond decided to part ways. Cole would take command of their host and lead them south to join Ormund Hightower and Prince Daeron, but the Prince Regent would not accompany them. Instead he meant to fight his own war, raining fire on the traitors from the air. Soon or late, "the bitch queen" would send a dragon or two out to stop him, and Vhagar would destroy them. "She dare not send *all* her dragons," Aemond insisted. "That would leave King's Landing naked and vulnerable. Nor will she risk Syrax, or that last sweet son of hers. Rhaenyra may call herself a queen, but she has a woman's parts, a woman's faint heart, and a mother's fears."

And thus did the Kingmaker and the Kinslayer part, each to their own fate, whilst at the Red Keep, Queen Rhaenyra Targaryen set about rewarding her friends and inflicting savage punishments on those who had served her half brother.

Huge rewards were posted for information leading to the capture of "the usurper styling himself Aegon II," his daughter Jaehaera, his son Maelor, the "false knights" Willis Fell and Rickard Thorne, and Larys Strong, the Clubfoot. When that failed to produce the desired result, Her Grace sent forth hunting parties of "knights inquisitor" to seek after the "traitors and villains" who had escaped her, and punish any man found to have assisted them.

Queen Alicent was fettered at wrist and ankle with golden chains, though her stepdaughter spared her life "for the sake of our father, who loved you once." Her own father was less fortunate. Ser Otto Hightower, who had served three kings as Hand, was the first traitor to be beheaded. Ironrod followed him to the block, still insisting that by law a king's son must come before his daughter. Ser Tyland Lannister was given to the torturers instead, in hopes of recovering some of the crown's treasure.

Neither Aegon nor his brother Aemond had ever been much loved by the people of the city, and many kingslanders had welcomed the queen's return . . . but love and hate are two faces of the same coin, as fresh heads began appearing daily upon the spikes above the city gates, accompanied by ever more exacting taxes, the coin turned. The girl that they once cheered as the Realm's Delight had grown into a grasping and vindictive woman, men said, a queen as cruel as any king before her. One wit named Rhaenyra "King Maegor with teats," and for a hundred years thereafter "Maegor's Teats" was a common curse amongst kingslanders.

With the city, castle, and throne in her possession, defended by no fewer than six dragons, Rhaenyra felt secure enough to send for her sons. A dozen ships set sail from Dragonstone, carrying the queen's ladies and her son Aegon the Younger. Rhaenyra made the boy her cupbearer, so he might never be far from her side. Another fleet set out from Gulltown with Prince Joffrey, the last of the queen's three sons by Laenor Velaryon, together with his dragon Tyraxes. Her Grace began to make plans for a lavish celebration to mark Joffrey's formal installation as Prince of Dragonstone and heir to the Iron Throne.

In the fullness of her victory, Rhaenyra Targaryen did not suspect how few days remained to her. Yet every time she sat the Iron Throne, its cruel blades drew fresh blood from her hands and arms and legs, a sign that all could read.

Beyond the city walls, fighting continued throughout the Seven Kingdoms. In the riverlands, Ser Criston Cole abandoned Harrenhal, striking south along the western shore of the Gods Eye, with thirty-six hundred men behind him (death, disease, and desertion had thinned the ranks that had ridden forth from King's Landing). Prince Aemon had already departed, flying Vhagar. No longer tied to castle or host, the one-eyed prince was free to fly where he would. It was war as Aegon the Conquerer and his sisters had once waged it, fought with dragonflame, as Vhagar descended from the autumn sky again and again to lay waste to the lands and villages and castles of the river lords. House Darry was the first to know the prince's wroth. The men bringing in the harvest burned or fled as the crops went up in flame, and Castle Darry was consumed in a firestorm. Lady Darry and her younger children survived by taking shelter in vaults under the keep, but her lord husband and his heir died on their battlements, together with two score of his sworn swords and bowmen.

Three days later, it was Lord Harroway's Town left smoking. Lord's Mill, Blackbuckle, Buckle, Claypool, Swynford, Spiderwood . . . Vhagar's fury fell on each in turn, until half the riverlands seemed ablaze.

Ser Criston Cole faced fires as well. As he drove his men south through the riverlands, smoke rose up before him and behind him. Every village that he came to he found burned and abandoned. His column moved through forests of dead trees where living woods had been just days before, as the river lords set blazes all along his line of march. In every brook and pool and village well, he found death: dead horses, dead cows, dead men, swollen and stinking, befouling the waters. Elsewhere his scouts came across ghastly tableaux where armored corpses sat beneath the trees in rotting raiment, in a grotesque mockery of a feast. The feasters were men who had fallen in battle, skulls grinning under rusted helms as their green and rotted flesh sloughed off their bones.

Four days out of Harrenhall, the attacks began. Archers hid amongst the trees, picking off outriders and stragglers with their longbows. Men died. Men fell behind the rearguard and were never seen again. Men fled, abandoning their shields and spears to fade into the woods. Men went over to the enemy. In the village commons at Crossed Elms, another of the ghastly feasts was found. Familiar with such sights by now, Ser Criston's outriders grimaced and rode past, paying no heed to the rotting dead . . . until the corpses sprang up and fell upon them. A dozen died before they realized it had all been a ploy.

All this was but prelude, for the Lords of the Trident had been gathering their forces. When Ser Criston left the lake behind, striking out overland for the Blackwater, he found them waiting atop a stony ridge; three hundred mounted knights in armor, as many longbowmen, three thousand archers, three thousand ragged rivermen with spears, hundreds of northmen brandishing axes, mauls, spiked maces, and ancient iron swords. Above their heads flew Queen Rhaenyra's banners.

The battle that followed was as one-sided as any in the Dance. Lord Roderick Dustin raised a warhorn to his lips and sounded the charge, and the queen's men came screaming down the ridge, led by the Winter Wolves on their shaggy northern horses and the knights on their armored destriers. When Ser Criston was struck down and fell dead upon the ground, the men who had followed him from Harrenhal lost heart. They broke and fled, casting aside their shields as they ran. Their foes came after, cutting them down by the hundreds.

On Maiden's Day in the year 130 AC, the Citadel of Oldtown sent forth three hundred white ravens to herald the coming of winter, but this was high summer for Queen Rhaenyra Targaryen. Despite the disaffection of the Kingslanders, the city and crown were hers. Across the narrow sea, the Triarchy had begun to tear itself to pieces. The waves belonged to House Velaryon. Though snows had closed the passes through the Mountains of the Moon, the Maiden of the Vale had proven true to her word, sending men by sea to join the queen's hosts. Other fleets brought warriors from White Harbor, led by Lord Manderly's own sons, Medrick and Torrhen. On every hand Queen Rhaenyra's power swelled whilst King Aegon's dwindled.

Yet no war can be counted as won whilst foes remain unconquered. The Kingmaker, Ser Criston Cole, had been brought down, but somewhere in the realm Aegon II, the king he had made, remained alive and free. Aegon's daughter, Jaehaera, was likewise at large. Larys Strong the Clubfoot, the most enigmatic and cunning member of the green council, had vanished. Storm's End was still held by Lord Borros Baratheon, no friend of the queen. The Lannisters had to be counted amongst Rhaenyra's enemies as well, though with Lord Jason dead, the greater part of the chivalry of the west slain or scattered, Casterly Rock was in considerable disarray.

Prince Aemond had become the terror of the Trident, descending from the sky to rain fire and death upon the riverlands, then vanishing, only to strike again the next day fifty leagues away. Vhagar's flames reduced Old Willow and White Willow to ash, and Hogg Hall to blackened stone. At Merrydown Dell, thirty men and three hundred sheep died by dragon-flame. The Kinslayer then returned unexpectedly to Harrenhal, where he burned every wooden structure in the castle. Six knights and two score men-at-arms perished trying to slay his dragon. As word of these attacks spread, other lords looked skyward in fear, wondering who might be next. Lord Mooton of Maidenpool, Lady Darklyn of Duskendale, and Lord Blackwood of Raventree sent urgent messages to the queen, begging her to send them dragons to defend their holdings.

Yet the greatest threat to Rhaenyra's reign was not Aemond One-Eye, but his younger brother, Prince Daeron the Daring, and the great southron army led by Lord Ormund Hightower.

Hightower's host had crossed the Mander, and was advancing slowly on King's Landing, smashing the queen's loyalists wherever and whenever they sought to hinder him, and forcing every lord who bent the knee to add their strength to his own. Flying Tessarion ahead of the main column, Prince Daeron had proved invaluable as a scout, warning Lord Ormund of enemy movements and entrenchments. Oft as not, the queen's men would melt away at the first glimpse of the Blue Queen's wings rather than face dragonflame in battle.

Cognizant of all these threats, Queen Rhaenyra's Hand, old Lord Corlys Velaryon, suggested to Her Grace that the time had come to talk. He urged the queen to offer pardons to Lords Baratheon, Hightower, and Lannister if they would bend their knees, swear fealty, and offer hostages to the Iron Throne. The Sea Snake proposed to let the Faith take charge of Queen Alicent and Queen Helaena, so that they might spend the remainder of their lives in prayer and contemplation. Helaena's daughter, Jaehaera, could be made his own ward, and in due time married to Prince Aegon the Younger, binding the two halves of House Targaryen together once again. "And what of my half brothers?" Rhaenyra demanded, when the Sea Snake put this plan before her. "What of this false king Aegon, and the kinslayer Aemond? Would you have me pardon them as well, them who stole my throne and slew my sons?"

"Spare them, and send them to the Wall," Lord Corlys answered. "Let them take the black and live out their lives as men of the Night's Watch, bound by sacred vows."

"What are vows to oathbreakers?" Queen Rhaenyra demanded to know. "Their vows did not trouble them when they took my throne."

Prince Daemon echoed the queen's misgivings. Giving pardons to rebels and traitors only sowed the seeds for fresh rebellions, he insisted. "The war will end when the heads of the traitors are mounted on spikes above the King's Gate, and not before." Aegon II would be found in time, "hiding under some rock," but they could and should bring the war to Aemond and Daeron. The Lannisters and Baratheons should be destroyed as well, so their lands and castles might be given to men who had proved more loyal. Grant Storm's End to Ulf White and Casterly Rock to Hard Hugh Hammer, the prince proposed . . . to the horror of the Sea Snake. "Half the lords of Westeros will turn against us if we are so cruel as to destroy two such ancient and noble houses," Lord Corlys said.

It fell to the queen herself to choose between her consort and her Hand. Rhaenyra decided to steer a middle course. She would send envoys to Storm's End and Casterly Rock, offering "fair terms" and pardons . . . *after* she had put an end to the usurper's brothers, who were in the field against her. "Once they are dead, the rest will bend the knee. Slay their dragons, that I might mount their heads upon the walls of my throne room. Let men look upon them in the years to come, that they might know the cost of treason."

King's Landing must not be left undefended, to be sure. Queen Rhaenyra would remain in the city with Syrax, and her sons Aegon and Joffrey, whose persons could not be put as risk. Joffrey, not quite three-and-ten, was eager to prove himself a warrior, but when told that Tyraxes was needed to help his mother hold the Red Keep in the event of an attack, the boy swore solemnly to do so. Addam Velaryon, the Sea Snake's heir, would also remain in the city, with Seasmoke. Three dragons should suffice for the defense of King's Landing; the rest would be going into battle.

Prince Daemon himself would take Caraxes to the Trident, together with the girl Nettles and Sheepstealer, to find Prince Aemond and Vhagar and put an end to them. Ulf White and Hard Hugh Hammer would fly to Tumbleton, some fifty leagues southwest of King's Landing, the last leal stronghold between Lord Hightower and the city, to assist in the defense of the town and castle and destroy Prince Daeron and Tessarion.

Prince Daemon Targaryen and the small brown girl called Nettles long hunted Aemond One-Eye without success. They had based themselves at Maidenpool, at the invitation of Lord Manfryd Mooton, who lived in terror of Vhagar descending on his town. Instead Prince Aemond struck at Stonyhead, in the foothills of the Mountains of the Moon; at Sweetwillow on the Green Fork and Sallydance on the Red Fork; he reduced Bowshot Bridge to embers, burned Old Ferry and Crone's Mill, destroyed the motherhouse at Bechester, always vanishing back into the sky before the hunters could arrive. Vhagar never lingered, nor did the survivors oft agree on which way the dragon had flown.

Each dawn Caraxes and Sheepstealer flew from Maidenpool, climbing high above the riverlands in ever-widening circles in hopes of espying Vhagar below . . . only to return defeated at dusk. Lord Mooton made so bold as to suggest that the dragonriders divide their search, so as to cover twice the ground. Prince Daemon refused. Vhagar was the last of the three dragons that had come to Westeros with Aegon the Conquerer and his sisters, he reminded his lordship. Though slower than she had been a century before, she had grown nigh as large as the Black Dread of old. Her fires burned hot enough to melt stone, and neither Caraxes nor Sheepstealer could match her ferocity. Only together could they hope to withstand her. And so he kept the girl Nettles by his side, day and night, in sky and castle.

Meanwhile, to the south, battle was joined at Tumbleton, a thriving market town on the Mander. The castle overlooking the town was stout but small, garrisoned by no more than forty men, but thousands more had come upriver from Bitterbridge, Longtable, and farther south. The arrival of a strong force of river lords swelled their numbers further, and stiffened their resolve. All told, the forces gathered under Queen Rhaenyra's banners at Tumbleton numbered near nine thousand. The queen's men were greatly outnumbered by Lord Hightower's. No doubt the arrival of the dragons Vermithor and Silverwing with their riders was most welcome by the defenders of Tumbleton. Little could they know the horrors that awaited them.

The how and when and why of what has become known as the Treasons of Tumbleton remain a matter of much dispute, and the truth of all that happened will likely never be known. It does appear that certain of those who flooded into the town, fleeing before Lord Hightower's army, were actually part of that army, sent ahead to infiltrate the ranks of the defenders. Yet their betrayals would have counted for little, had not Ser Ulf White and Ser Hugh Hammer also chosen this moment to change their allegiance.

As neither man could read nor write, we shall never know what drove the Two Betrayers (as history has named them) to do what they did. Of the Battle of Tumbleton we know much and more, however. Six thousand of the queen's men formed up to face Lord Hightower in the field, and fought bravely for a time, but a withering rain of arrows from Lord Ormund's archers thinned their ranks, and a thunderous charge by his heavy horse broke them, sending the survivors running back toward the town walls. When most of the survivors were safe inside the gates, Roddy the Ruin and his Winter Wolves sallied forth from a postern gate, screaming their terrifying northern war cries as they swept around the left flank of the attackers. In the chaos that ensued, the northmen fought their way through ten times their own number to where Lord Ormund Hightower sat his warhorse beneath King Aegon's golden dragon and the banners of Oldtown and the Hightower. As the singers tell it, Lord Roderick was blood from head to heel as he came on, with splintered shield and cracked helm, yet so drunk with battle that he did not even seem to feel his wounds. Ser Bryndon Hightower, Lord Ormund's cousin, put himself between the northman and his liege, taking off the Ruin's shield arm at the shoulder with one terrible blow of his longaxe ... yet the savage Lord of Barrowton fought on, slaying both Ser Bryndon and Lord Ormund before he died. Lord Hightower's banners toppled, and the townfolk gave a great cheer, thinking the tide of battle turned. Even the appearance of Tessarion across the field did not dismay them, for they knew they had two dragons of their own ... but when Vermithor and Silverwing climbed into the sky and loosed their fires upon Tumbleton, those cheers changed to screams.

Tumbleton went up in flame: shops, homes, septs, people, all. Men fell burning from gatehouse and battlements, or stumbled shrieking through the streets like so many living torches. The Two Betrayers scourged the town with whips of flame from one end to the other. The sack that followed was as savage as any in the history of Westeros. Tumbleton, that prosperous market town, was reduced to ash and embers, never to be rebuilt. Thousands burned, and as many died by drowning as they tried to swim the river. Some would later say they were the fortunate ones, for no mercy was shown the survivors. Lord Footly's men threw down their swords and yielded, only to be bound and beheaded. Such townswomen as survived the fires were raped repeatedly, even girls as young as eight and ten. Old men and boys were put to the sword, whilst the dragons fed upon the twisted, smoking carcasses of their victims.

It was about this time that a battered merchant cog named *Nessaria* came limping into the harbor beneath Dragonstone to make repairs and take on provisions. She had been returning from Pentos to Old Volantis when a storm drove her off course, her crew said ... but to this common song of peril at sea, the Volantenes added a queer note. As *Nessaria* beat westward, the Dragonmont loomed up before them, huge against the setting sun ... and the sailors spied two dragons fighting, their roars echoing off the sheer black cliffs of the smoking mountain's eastern flanks. In every tavern, inn, and whorehouse along the waterfront the tale was told, retold, and embroidered, till every man on Dragonstone had heard it.

Dragons were a wonder to the men of Old Volantis; the sight of two in battle was one the men of *Nessaria* would never forget. Those born and bred on Dragonstone had grown up with such beasts . . . yet even so, the sailors' story excited interest. The next morning some local fisherfolk took their boats around the Dragonmont, and returned to report seeing the burned and broken remains of a dead dragon at the mountain's base. From the color of its wings and scales, the carcass was that of Grey Ghost. The dragon lay in two pieces, and had been torn apart and partially devoured.

On hearing this news Ser Robert Quince, the amiable and famously obese knight whom the queen had named castellan of Dragonstone upon her departure, was quick to name the Cannibal as the killer. Most agreed, for the Cannibal had been known to attack smaller dragons in the past, though seldom so savagely. Some amongst the fisherfolk, fearing that the killer might turn upon them next, urged Quince to dispatch knights to the beast's lair to put an end to him, but the castellan refused. "If we do not trouble him, the Cannibal will not trouble us," he declared. To be certain of that, he forbade fishing in the waters beneath the Dragonmont's eastern face, where the dragon's body lay rotting.

Meanwhile, on the western shore of Blackwater Bay, word of battle and betrayal at Tumbleton had reached King's Landing. It is said the Dowager Queen Alicent laughed when she heard. "All they have sowed, now shall they reap," she promised. On the Iron Throne, Queen Rhaenyra grew pale and faint, and ordered the city gates closed and barred; henceforth, no one was to be allowed to enter or leave King's Landing. "I will have no turncloaks stealing into my city to open my gates to rebels," she proclaimed. Lord Ormund's host could be outside their walls by the morrow or the day after; the betrayers, dragonborne, could arrive even sooner than that.

This prospect excited Prince Joffrey. "Let them come," the boy announced, "I will meet them on Tyraxes." Such talk alarmed his mother. "You will not," she declared. "You are too young for battle." Even so, she allowed the boy to remain as the black council discussed how best to deal with the approaching foe.

Six dragons remained in King's Landing, but only one within the walls of the Red Keep: the queen's own she-dragon, Syrax. A stable in the outer ward had emptied of horses and given over for her use. Heavy chains bound her to the ground. Though long enough to allow her to move from stable to yard, the chains kept her from flying off riderless. Syrax had long grown accustomed to chains; exceedingly well fed, she had not hunted for years.

The other dragons were all kept in the Dragonpit, the colossal structure that King Maegor the Cruel had built for just that purpose. Beneath its great dome, forty huge undervaults had been carved from the bones of the Hill of Rhaenys in a great ring. Thick iron doors closed these man-made caves at either end, the inner doors fronting on the sands of the pit, the outer opening to the hillside. Caraxes, Vermithor, Silverwing, and Sheepstealer had made their lairs there before flying off to battle. Five dragons remained: Prince Joffrey's Tyraxes, Addam Velaryon's pale grey Seasmoke, the young dragons Morghul and Shrykos, bound to Princess Jaehaera (fled) and her twin Prince Jaehaerys (dead) . . . and Dreamfyre, beloved of Queen Helaena. It had long been the custom for at least one dragonrider to reside at the pit, so as to be able to rise to the defense of the city should the need arise. As Queen Rhaenyrs preferred to keep her sons by her side, that duty fell to Addam Velaryon.

But now voices on the black council were raised to question Ser Addam's loyalty. The dragonseeds Ulf White and Hugh Hammer had gone over to the enemy . . . but were they the only traitors in their midst? What of Addam of Hull and the girl Nettles? They had been born of bastard stock as well. Could they be trusted?

Lord Bartimos Celtigar thought not. "Bastards are treacherous by nature," he said. "It is in their blood. Betrayal comes as easily to a bastard as loyalty to trueborn men." He urged Her Grace to have the two baseborn dragonriders seized immediately, before they too could join the enemy with their dragons. Others echoed his views, amongst them Ser Luthor Largent, commander of her City Watch, and Ser Lorent Marbrand, Lord Commander of her Queensguard. Even the two White Harbor men, that fearsome knight Ser Medrick Manderly and his clever, corpulent brother Ser Torrhen, urged the queen to mistrust. "Best take no chances," Ser Torrhen said. "If the foe gains two more dragons, we are lost."

Only Lord Corlys spoke in defense of the dragonseed, declaring that Ser Addam and his brother Alyn were "true Velaryons," worthy heirs to Driftmark. As for the girl, though she might be dirty and ill-favored, she had fought valiantly in the Battle of the Gullet. "As did the two betrayers," Lord Celtigar countered.

The Hand's impassioned protests had been in vain. All the queen's fears and suspicions had been aroused. She had been betrayed so often, by so many, that she was quick to believe the worst of any man. Treachery no longer had the power to surprise her. She had come to expect it, even from those she loved the most.

Queen Rhaenyra command Ser Luthor Largent to take twenty gold cloaks to the Dragonpit and arrest Ser Addam Velaryon. And thus did betrayal beget more betrayal, to the queen's undoing. As Ser Luthor Largent and his gold cloaks rode up Rhaenys's Hill with the queen's warrant, the doors of the Dragonpit were thrown open above them, and Seasmoke spread his pale grey wings and took flight, smoke rising from his nostrils. Ser Addam Velaryon had been forewarned in time to make his escape. Balked and angry, Ser Luthor returned at once to the Red Keep, where he burst into the Tower of the Hand and laid rough hands on the aged Lord Corlys, accusing him of treachery. Nor did the old man deny it. Bound and beaten, but still silent, he was taken down into the dungeons and thrown into a black cell to await trial and execution.

All the while tales of the slaughter at Tumbleton were spreading through the city . . . and with them, terror. King's Landing would be next, men told one another. Dragon would fight dragon, and this time the city would surely burn. Fearful of the coming foe, hundreds tried to flee, only to be turned back at the gates by the gold cloaks. Trapped within the city walls, some sought shelter in deep cellars against the firestorm they feared was coming, whilst others turned to prayer, to drink, and the pleasures to be found between a woman's thighs. By nightfall, the city's taverns, brothels, and septs were full to bursting with men and women seeking solace or escape and trading tales of horror.

A different sort of chaos reigned in Tumbleton, sixty leagues to the southwest. Whilst King's Landing quailed in terror, the foes they feared had yet to advance a foot toward the city, for King Aegon's loyalists found themselves leaderless, beset by division, conflict, and doubt. Ormund Hightower lay dead, along with his cousin Ser Bryndon, the foremost knight of Oldtown. His sons remained back at the Hightower a thousand leagues away, and were green boys besides. And whilst Lord Ormund had dubbed Daeron Targaryen "Daeron the Daring" and praised his courage in battle, the prince was still a boy. The youngest of King Aegon's sons, he had grown up in the shadow of his elder brothers, and was more used to following commands than giving them. The most senior

Hightower remaining with the host was Ser Hobert, another of Lord Ormund's cousins, hitherto entrusted only with the baggage train. A man "as stout as he was slow," Hobert Hightower had lived sixty years without distinguishing himself, yet now he presumed to take command of the host by right of his kinship to Queen Alicent.

Seldom has any town or city in the history of the Seven Kingdoms been subject to as long or cruel or savage a sack as Tumbleton after the Treasons. Prince Daeron was sickened by all he saw and commanded Ser Hobert Hightower to put a stop to it, but Hightower's efforts proved as ineffectual as the man himself.

The worst crimes were those committed by the Two Betrayers, the baseborn dragonriders Hugh Hammer and Ulf White. Ser Ulf gave himself over entirely to drunkenness, drowning himself in wine and flesh. Those who failed to please were fed to his dragon. The knighthood that Queen Rhaenyra had conferred on him did not suffice. Nor was he surfeit when Prince Daemon named him Lord of Bitterbridge. White had a greater prize in mind: he desired no less a seat than Highgarden, declaring that the Tyrells had played no part in the Dance, and therefore should be attainted as traitors.

Ser Ulf's ambitions must be accounted modest when compared to those of his fellow turncloak, Hugh Hammer. The son of a common blacksmith, Hammer was a huge man, with hands so strong that he was said to be able to twist steel bars into torcs. Though largely untrained in the art of war, his size and strength made him a fearsome foe. His weapon of choice was the warhammer, with which he delivered crushing, killing blows. In battle he rode Vermithor, once the mount of the Old King himself; of all the dragons in Westeros, only Vhagar was older or larger. For all these reasons, Lord Hammer (as he now styled himself) began to dream of crowns. "Why be a lord when you can be a king?" he told the men who began to gather round him.

Neither of the Two Betrayers seemed eager to help Prince Daeron press an attack on King's Landing. They had a great host, and three dragons besides, yet the queen had three dragons as well (as best they knew), and would have five once Prince Daemon returned with Nettles. Lord Peake preferred to delay any advance until Lord Baratheon could bring up his power from Storm's End to join them, whilst Ser Hobert wished to fall back to the Reach to replenish their fast-dwindling supplies. None seemed concerned that their army was shrinking every day, melting away like morning dew as more and more men deserted, stealing off for home and harvest with all the plunder they could carry.

Long leagues to the north, in a castle overlooking the Bay of Crabs, another lord found himself sliding down a sword's edge as well. From King's Landing came a raven bearing the queen's message to Manfryd Mooton, Lord of Maidenpool: he was to deliver her the head of the bastard girl Nettles, who was said to have become Prince Daemon's lover and who the queen had therefore judged guilty of high treason. "No harm is to be done my lord husband, Prince Daemon of House Targaryen," Her Grace commanded. "Send him back to me when the deed is done, for we have urgent need of him."

Maester Norren, keeper of the *Chronicles of Maidenpool,* says that when his lordship read the queen's letter he was so shaken that he lost his voice. Nor did it return to him until he had drunk three cups of wine. Thereupon Lord Mooton sent for the captain of his guard, his brother, and his champion, Ser Florian Greysteel. He bade his maester to remain as well. When all had assembled, he read to them the letter and asked them for their counsel.

"This thing is easily done," said the captain of his guard. "The prince sleeps beside her, but he has grown old. Three men should be enough to subdue him should he try to interfere, but I will take six to be certain. Does my lord wish this done tonight?"

"Six men or sixty, he is still Daemon Targaryen," Lord Mooton's brother objected. "A sleeping draught in his evening wine would be the wiser course. Let him wake to find her dead."

"The girl is but a child, however foul her treasons," said Ser Florian, that old knight, grey and grizzled and stern. "The Old King would never have asked this, of any man of honor."

"These are foul times," Lord Mooton said, "and it is a foul choice this queen has given me. The girl is a guest beneath my roof. If I obey, Maidenpool shall be forever cursed. If I refuse, we shall be attainted and destroyed."

To which his brother answered, "It may be we shall be destroyed whatever choice we make. The prince is more than fond of this brown child, and his dragon is close at hand. A wise lord would kill them both, lest the prince burn Maidenpool in his wroth."

"The queen has forbidden any harm to come to him," Lord Mooton reminded them, "and murdering two guests in their beds is twice as foul as murdering one. I should be doubly cursed." Thereupon he sighed and said, "Would that I had never read this letter."

And up spoke Maester Norren, saying, "Mayhaps you never did."

What was said after that is unknown. All we know is that the maester, a young man of two-and-twenty, found Prince Daemon and the girl Nettles at their supper that night, and showed them the queen's letter. After reading the letter, Prince Daemon said, "A queen's words, a whore's work." Then he drew his sword and asked if Lord Mooton's men were waiting outside the door to take them captive. When told that the maester had come alone and in secret, Prince Daemon sheathed his sword, saying, "You are a bad maester, but a good man," and then bade him leave, commanding him to "speak no word of this to lord nor love until the morrow."

How the prince and his bastard girl spent their last night beneath Lord Mooton's roof is not recorded, but as dawn broke they appeared together in the yard, and Prince Daemon helped Nettles saddle Sheepstealer one last time. It was her custom to feed him each day before she flew; dragons bend easier to their rider's will when full. That morning she fed him a black ram, the largest in all Maidenpool, slitting the ram's throat herself. Her riding leathers were stained with blood when she mounted her dragon, Maester Norren records, and "her cheeks were stained with tears." No word of farewell was spoken betwixt man and maid, but as Sheepstealer beat his leathery brown wings and climbed into the dawn sky, Caraxes raised his head and gave a scream that shattered every window in Jonquil's Tower. High above the town, Nettles turned her dragon toward the Bay of Crabs, and vanished in the morning mists, never to be seen again at court or castle.

Daemon Targaryen returned to the castle just long enough to break his fast with Lord Mooton. "This is the last that you will see of me," he told his lordship. "I thank you for your hospitality. Let it be known through all your lands that I fly for Harrenhal. If my nephew Aemond dares face me, he shall find me there, alone."

Thus Prince Daemon departed Maidenpool for the last time. When he had gone, Maester Norren went to his lord to say, "Take the chain from my neck and bind my hands with it. You must need deliver me the queen. When I gave warning to a traitor and allowed her to escape, I became a traitor as well." Lord Mooton refused. "Keep your chain," his lordship said. "We are all traitors here." And that night, Queen Rhaenyra's quartered banners were taken down from where they flew above the gates of Maidenpool, and the golden dragons of King Aegon II raised in their stead.

No banners flew above the blackened towers and ruined keeps of Harrenhal when Prince Daemon descended from the sky to take up the castle for his own. A few squatters had found shelter in the castle's deep vaults and undercellars, but the sound of Caraxes's wings sent them fleeing. When the last of them was gone, Daemon Targaryen walked the cavernous halls of Harren's seat alone, with no companion but his dragon. Each night at dusk he slashed the heart tree in the godswood to mark the passing of another day. Thirteen marks can be seen upon that weirwood still; old wounds, deep and dark, yet the lords who have ruled Harrenhal since Daemon's day say they bleed afresh every spring.

On the fourteenth day of the prince's vigil, a shadow swept over the castle, blacker than any passing cloud. All the birds in the godswood took to the air in fright, and a hot wind whipped the fallen leaves across the yard. Vhagar had come at last, and on her back rode the one-eyed prince Aemond Targaryen, clad in night-black armor chased with gold.

He had not come alone. Alys Rivers flew with him, her long hair streaming black behind her, her belly swollen with child. Prince Aemond circled twice about the towers of Harrenhal, then brought Vhagar down in the outer ward, with Caraxes a hundred yards away. The dragons glared balefully at each other, and Caraxes spread his wings and hissed, flames dancing across his teeth.

The prince helped his woman down from Vhagar's back, then turned to face his uncle. "Nuncle, I hear you have been seeking us."

"Only you," Daemon replied. "Who told you where to find me?"

"My lady," Aemond answered. "She saw you in a storm cloud, in a mountain pool at dusk, in the fire we lit to cook our suppers. She sees much and more, my Alys. You were a fool to come alone."

"Were I not alone, you would not have come," said Daemon.

"Yet you are, and here I am. You have lived too long, nuncle."

"On that much we agree," Daemon replied. Then the old prince bid Caraxes bend his neck, and climbed stiffly onto his back, whilst the young prince kissed his woman and vaulted lightly onto Vhagar, taking care to fasten the four short chains between belt and saddle. Daemon left his own chains dangling. Caraxes hissed again, filling the air with flame, and Vhagar answered with a roar. As one the two dragons leapt into the sky.

Prince Daemon took Caraxes up swiftly, lashing him with a steel-tipped whip until they disappeared into a bank of clouds. Vhagar, older and much the larger, was also slower, made ponderous by her very size, and ascended more gradually, in ever widening circles that took her and her rider out over the waters of the Gods Eye. The hour was late, the sun was close to setting, and the lake was calm, its surface glimmering like a sheet of beaten copper. Up and up she soared, searching for Caraxes as Alys Rivers watched from atop Kingspyre Tower in Harrenhal below.

The attack came sudden as a thunderbolt. Caraxes dove down upon Vhagar with a piercing shriek that was heard a dozen miles away, cloaked by the glare of the setting sun on Prince Aemond's blind side. The Blood Wyrm slammed into the older dragon with terrible force. Their roars echoed across the Gods Eye as the two grappled and tore at one another, dark against a blood red sky. So bright did their flames burn that fisher-folk below feared the clouds themselves had caught fire. Locked together, the dragons tumbled toward the lake. The Blood Wyrm's jaws closed about Vhagar's neck, her black teeth sinking deep into the flesh of the larger dragon. Even as Vhagar's claws raked her belly open and Vhagar's own teeth ripped away a wing, Caraxes bit deeper, worrying at the wound as the lake rushed up below them with terrible speed.

And it was then, the tales tell us, that Prince Daemon Targaryen swung a leg over his saddle and leapt from one dragon to the other. In his hand was Dark Sister, the sword of Queen Visenya. As Aemond One-Eye looked up in terror, fumbling with the chains that bound him to his sad-dle, Daemon ripped off his nephew's helm and drove the sword down into his blind eye, so hard the point came out the back of the young prince's throat. Half a heartbeat later, the dragons struck the lake, sending up a gout of water so high that it was said to have been as tall as Kingspyre Tower.

Neither man nor dragon could have survived such an impact, the fisherfolk who saw it said. Nor did they. Caraxes lived long enough to crawl back onto the land. Gutted, with one wing torn from his body and the waters of the lake smoking about him, the Blood Wyrm found the strength to drag himself onto the lakeshore, expiring beneath the walls of

Harrenhal. Vhagar's carcass plunged to the lake floor, the hot blood from the gaping wound in her neck bringing the water to a boil over her last resting place. When she was found some years later, after the end of the Dance of the Dragons, Prince Aemond's armored bones remained chained to her saddle, with Dark Sister thrust hilt-deep through his eye socket.

That Prince Daemon died as well we cannot doubt. His remains were never found, but there are queer currents in that lake, and hungry fish as well. The singers tell us that the old prince survived the fall and afterward made his way back to the girl Nettles, to spend the remainder of his days at her side. Such stories make for charming songs, but poor history.

It was upon the twenty-second day of the fifth moon of the year 130 AC when the dragons danced and died above the Gods Eye. Daemon Targaryen was nine-and-forty at his death; Prince Aemond had only turned twenty. Vhagar, the greatest of the Targaryen dragons since the passing of Balerion the Black Dread, had counted one hundred eighty-one years upon the earth. Thus passed the last living creature from the days of Aegon's Conquest, as dusk and darkness swallowed Black Harren's accursed seat. Yet so few were on hand to bear witness that it would be some time before word of Prince Daemon's last battle became widely known.

Back in King's Landing, Queen Rhaenyra was finding herself ever more isolated with every new betrayal. The suspected turncloak Addam Velaryon had fled before he could be put to the question. By ordering the arrest of Addam Velaryon, she had lost not only a dragon and a dragonrider, but her Queen's Hand as well . . . and more than half the army that had sailed from Dragonstone to seize the Iron Throne was made up of men sworn to House Velaryon. When it became known that Lord Corlys languished in a dungeon under the Red Keep, they began to abandon her cause by the hundreds. Some made their way to Cobbler's Square to join the throngs gathered there, whilst others slipped through postern gates or over the walls, intent on making their way back to Driftmark. Nor could those who remained be trusted.

That very day, not long after sunset, another horror visited the queen's court. Helaena Targaryen, sister, wife, and queen to King Aegon II and mother of his children, threw herself from her window in Maegor's Holdfast to die impaled upon the iron spikes that lined the dry moat below. She was but one-and-twenty.

By nightfall, a darker tale was being told in the streets and alleys of King's Landing, in inns and brothels and pot shops, even holy septs. Queen Helaena had been murdered, the whispers went, as her sons had been before her. Prince Daeron and his dragons would soon be at the gates, and with them the end of Rhaenyra's reign. The old queen was determined that her young half sister should not live to revel in her downfall, so she had sent Ser Luthor Largent to seize Helaena with his huge rough hands and fling her from the window onto the spikes below.

The rumor of Queen Helaena's "murder" was soon on the lips of half King's Landing. That it was so quickly believed shows how utterly the city had turned against their once-beloved queen. Rhaenyra was hated; Helaena had been loved. Nor had the common folk of the city forgotten the cruel murder of Prince Jaehaerys by Blood and Cheese. Helaena's end had been mercifully swift; one of the spikes took her through the throat and she died without a sound. At the moment of her death, across the city atop the Hill of Rhaenys, her dragon Dreamfyre rose suddenly with a roar that shook the Dragonpit, snapping two of the chains that bound her. When Queen Alicent was informed of her daughter's passing, she rent her garments and pronounced a dire curse upon her rival.

That night King's Landing rose in bloody riot.

The rioting began amidst the alleys and wynds of Flea Bottom, as men and women poured from the wine sinks, rat pits, and pot shops by the hundreds, angry, drunken, and afraid. From there the rioters spread throughout the city, shouting for justice for the dead princes and their murdered mother. Carts and wagons were overturned, shops looted, homes plundered and set afire. Gold cloaks attempting to quell the disturbances were set upon and beaten bloody. No one was spared, of high birth or low. Lords were pelted with rubbish, knights pulled from their saddles. Lady Darla Deddings saw her brother Davos stabbed through the eye when he tried to defend her from three drunken ostlers intent on raping her. Sailors unable to return to their ships attacked the River Gate and fought a pitched battle with the City Watch. It took Ser Luthor Largent and four hundred spears to disperse them. By then the gate had been hacked half to pieces and a hundred men were dead or dying, a quarter of them gold cloaks.

At Cobbler's Square the sounds of the riot could be heard from every quarter. The City Watch had come in strength, five hundred men clad in black ringmail, steel caps, and long golden cloaks, armed with short swords, spears, and spiked cudgels. They formed up on the south side of the square, behind a wall of shields and spears. At their head rode Ser Luthor Largent upon an armored warhorse, a longsword in his hand. The mere sight of him was enough to send hundreds streaming away into the wynds and alleys and side streets. Hundreds more fled when Ser Luthor ordered the gold cloaks to advance.

Ten thousand remained, however. The press was so thick that many who might gladly have fled found themselves unable to move, pushed and shoved and trod upon. Others surged forward, locked arms, and began to shout and curse, as the spears advanced to the slow beat of a drum. "Make way, you bloody fools," Ser Luthor roared. "Go home. No harm will come to you. Go home!"

Some say the first man to die was a baker, who grunted in surprise when a spearpoint pierced his flesh and he saw his apron turning red. Others claim it was a little girl, trodden under by Ser Luthor's warhorse. A rock came flying from the crowd, striking a spearman on the brow. Shouts and curses were heard, sticks and stones and chamber pots came raining down from rooftops, an archer across the square began to loose his shafts. A torch was thrust at a watchman, and quick as that his golden cloak was burning.

The gold cloaks were large men, young, strong, disciplined, well armed and well armored. For twenty yards or more their shield wall held, and they cut a bloody road through the crowd, leaving dead and dying all around them. But they numbered only five hundred, and tens of thousands of rioters had gathered. One watchman went down, then another. Suddenly smallfolk were slipping through the gaps in the line, attacking with knives and stones, even teeth, swarming over the City Watch and around their flanks, attacking from behind, flinging tiles down from roofs and balconies.

Battle turned to riot turned to slaughter. Surrounded on all sides, the gold cloaks found themselves hemmed in and swept under, with no room to wield their weapons. Many died on the points of their own swords. Others were torn to pieces, kicked to death, trampled underfoot, hacked apart with hoes and butcher's cleavers. Even the fearsome Ser Luthor Largent could not escape the carnage. His sword torn from his grasp, Largent was pulled from his saddle, stabbed in the belly, and bludgeoned to death with a cobblestone, his helm and head so crushed that it was only by its size that his body was recognized when the corpse wagons came the next day.

During that long night, chaos held sway over half the city, whilst strange lords and kings of misrule squabbled o'er the rest. A hedge knight named Ser Perkin the Flea crowned his own squire Trystane, a stripling of sixteen years, declaring him to be a natural son of the late King Viserys. Any knight can make a knight, and when Ser Perkin began dubbing every sellsword, thief, and butcher's boy who flocked to Trystane's ragged banner, men and boys appeared by the hundreds to pledge themselves to his cause.

By dawn, fires were burning throughout the city, Cobbler's Square was littered with corpses, and bands of lawless men roamed Flea Bottom, breaking into shops and homes and laying rough hands on every honest person they encountered. The surviving gold cloaks had retreated to their barracks, whilst gutter knights, mummer kings, and mad prophets ruled the streets. Like the roaches they resembled, the worst of these fled before the light, retreating to hidey-holes and cellars to sleep off their drunks, divvy up their plunder, and wash the blood off their hands. The gold cloaks at the Old Gate and the Dragon Gate sallied forth under the command of their captains, Ser Balon Byrch and Ser Garth the Harelip, and by midday had managed to restore some semblance of order to the streets north and east of Rhaenys's Hill. Ser Medrick Manderly, leading a hundred White Harbor men, did the same for the area northeast of Aegon's High Hill, down to the Iron Gate.

The rest of King's Landing remained in chaos. When Ser Torrhen Manderly led his northmen down the Hook, they found Fishermonger's Square and River Row swarming with Ser Perkin's gutter knights. At the River Gate, "King" Trystane's ragged banner flew above the battlements, whilst the bodies of the captain and three of his serjeants hung from the gatehouse. The remainder of the "Mudfoot" garrison had gone over to Ser Perkin. Ser Torrhen lost a quarter of his men fighting his way back to the Red Keep . . . yet escaped lightly compared to Ser Lorent Marbrand, who led a hundred knights and men-at-arms into Flea Bottom. Sixteen returned. Ser Lorent, Lord Commander of the Queensguard, was not amongst them.

By evenfall, Rhaenyra Targaryen found herself sore beset on every side, her reign in ruins. The queen raged when she learned that Maidenpool had gone over to the foe, that the girl Nettles had escaped, that her own beloved consort had betrayed her, and she trembled when Lady Mysaria warned her against the coming dark, that this night would be worse than the last. At dawn, a hundred men attended her in the throne room, but one by one they slipped away.

Her Grace swung from rage to despair and back again, clutching so desperately at the Iron Throne that both her hands were bloody by the time the sun set. She gave command of the gold cloaks to Ser Balon Byrch, captain at the Iron Gate, sent ravens to Winterfell and the Eyrie pleading for more aid, ordered that a decree of attainder be drawn up against the Mootons of Maidenpool, and named the young Ser Glendon Goode lord commander of the Queensguard. (Though only twenty, and a member of the White Swords for less than a moon's turn, Goode had distinguished himself during the fighting in Flea Bottom earlier that day. It was he who brought back Ser Lorent's body, to keep the rioters from despoiling it.)

Aegon the Younger was ever at his mother's side, yet seldom spoke a word. Prince Joffrey, ten-and-three, donned squire's armor and begged the queen to let him ride to the Dragonpit and mount Tyraxes. "I want to fight for you, Mother, as my brothers did. Let me prove that I am as brave as they were." His words only deepened Rhaenyra's resolve, however. "Brave they were, and dead they are, the both of them. My sweet boys." And once more, Her Grace forbade the prince to leave the castle.

With the setting of the sun, the vermin of King's Landing emerged once more from their rat pits, hidey-holes, and cellars, in even greater numbers than the night before.

At the River Gate, Ser Perkin feasted his gutter knights on stolen food and led them down the riverfront, looting wharfs and warehouses and any ship that had not put to sea. Though King's Landing boasted massive walls and stout towers, they had been designed to repel attacks from outside the city, not from within its walls. The garrison at the Gate of the Gods was especially weak, as their captain and a third their number had died with Ser Luthor Largent in Cobbler's Square. Those who remained, many wounded, were easily overcome by Ser Perkin's hordes.

Before an hour had passed, the King's Gate and the Lion Gate were open as well. The gold cloaks at the first had fled, whilst the "lions" at the other had thrown in with the mobs. Three of the seven gates of King's Landing were open to Rhaenyra's foes.

The most dire threat to the queen's rule proved to be within the city, however. By nightfall, another crowd had gathered in Cobbler's Square, twice as large and thrice as fearful as the night before. Like the queen they so despised, the mob was looking to the sky with dread, fearing that King Aegon's dragons would arrive before the night was out, with an army close behind them. They no longer believed that the queen could protect them.

When a crazed one-handed prophet called the Shepherd began to rant against dragons, not just the ones who were coming to attack them, but all dragons everywhere, the crowd, half-crazed themselves, listened. "When the dragons come," he shrieked, "your flesh will burn and blister and turn to ash. Your wives will dance in gowns of fire, shrieking as they burn, lewd and naked underneath the flames. And you shall see your little children weeping, weeping till their eyes do melt and slide like jelly down their faces, till their pink flesh falls black and crackling from their bones. The Stranger comes, *he comes, he comes,* to scourge us for our sins. Prayers cannot stay his wroth, no more than tears can quench the flame of dragons. Only blood can do that. Your blood, my blood, *their* blood." Then he raised the stump of his right arm, and pointed at Rhaenys's Hill behind him, at the Dragonpit black against the stars. "There the demons dwell, up *there*. This is their city. If you would make it yours, first must you destroy them! If you would cleanse yourself of sin, first must you bathe in dragon's blood! For only blood can quench the fires of hell!"

From ten thousand throats a cry went up. *"Kill them! Kill them!"* And like some vast beast with ten thousand legs, the Shepherd's lambs began to move, shoving and pushing, waving their torches, brandishing swords and knives and other, cruder weapons, walking and running through the streets and alleys toward the Dragonpit. Some thought better and slipped away to home, but for every man who left, three more appeared to join these dragonslayers. By the time they reached the Hill of Rhaenys, their numbers had doubled.

High atop Aegon's High Hill across the city, the Queen watched the attack unfold from the roof of Maegor's Holdfast with her sons and members of her court. The night was black and overcast, the torches so numerous that it was as if all the stars had come down from the sky to storm the

Dragonpit. As soon as word had reached her that the enraged crowd was on the march, Rhaenyra sent riders to Ser Balon at the Old Gate and Ser Garth at the Dragon Gate, commanding them to disperse the mob and defend the royal dragons . . . but with the city in such turmoil, it was far from certain that the riders had won through. Even if they had, what loyal gold cloaks remained were too few to have any hope of success. When Prince Joffrey pleaded with his mother to let him ride forth with their own knights and those from White Harbor, the queen refused. "If they take that hill, this one will be next," she said. "We will need every sword here to defend the castle."

"They will kill the *dragons*," Prince Joffrey said, anguished.

"Or the dragons will kill them," his mother said, unmoved. "Let them burn. The realm will not long miss them."

"Mother, what if they kill *Tyraxes*?" the young prince said.

The queen did not believe it. "They are vermin. Drunks and fools and gutter rats. One taste of dragonflame and they will run."

At that the court fool Mushroom spoke up, saying, "Drunks they may be, but a drunken man knows not fear. Fools, aye, but a fool can kill a king. Rats, that too, but a thousand rats can bring down a bear. I saw it happen once, down there in Flea Bottom." Her Grace turned back to the parapets.

It was only when the watchers on the roof heard Syrax roar that it was noticed that the prince had slunk sullenly away. "No," the queen was heard to say, "I forbid it, I *forbid* it," but even as she spoke, her dragon flapped up from the yard, perched for half a heartbeat atop the castle battlements, then launched herself into the night with the queen's son clinging to her back, a sword in hand. "After him," Rhaenyra shouted, "all of you, every man, every boy, to horse, *to horse*, go after him. Bring him back, bring him back, he does not know. My son, my sweet, my son . . ."

But it was too late.

We shall not pretend to any understanding of the bond between dragon and dragonrider; wiser heads have pondered that mystery for centuries. We do know, however, that dragons are not horses, to be ridden by any man who throws a saddle on their back. Syrax was the queen's dragon. She had never known another rider. Though Prince Joffrey was known to her by sight and scent, a familiar presence whose fumbling at her chains excited no alarm, the great yellow she-dragon wanted no part of him astride her. In his haste to be away before he could be stopped, the prince had vaulted onto Syrax without benefit of saddle or whip. His intent, we must presume, was either to fly Syrax into battle or, more likely, to cross the city to the Dragonpit and his own Tyraxes. Mayhaps he meant to loose the other pit dragons as well.

Joffrey never reached the Hill of Rhaenys. Once in the air, Syrax twisted beneath him, fighting to be free of this unfamiliar rider. And from below, stones and spears and arrows flew at him from the hands of the rioters below, maddening the dragon even further. Two hundred feet above Flea Bottom, Prince Joffrey slid from the dragon's back and plunged to the earth.

Near a juncture where five alleys came together, the prince's fall came to its bloody end. He crashed first onto a steep-pitched roof before rolling off to fall another forty feet amidst a shower of broken tiles. We are told that the fall broke his back, that shards of slate rained down about him like knives, that his own sword tore loose of his hand and pierced him through the belly. In Flea Bottom, men still speak of a candlemaker's daughter named Robin who cradled the broken prince in her arms and gave him comfort as he died, but there is more of legend than of history in that tale. "Mother, forgive me," Joffrey supposedly said, with his last breath ... though men still argue whether he was speaking of his mother the queen, or praying to the Mother Above.

Thus perished Joffrey Velaryon, Prince of Dragonstone and heir to the Iron Throne, the last of Queen Rhaenyra's sons by Laenor Velaryon ... or the last of her bastards by Ser Harwin Strong, depending on which truth one chooses to believe.

And even as blood flowed in the alleys of Flea Bottom, another battle raged round the Dragonpit above, atop the Hill of Rhaenys.

Mushroom was not wrong: swarms of starving rats do indeed bring down bulls and bears and lions, when there are enough of them. No matter how many the bull or bear might kill, there are always more, biting at the great beast's legs, clinging to its belly, running up its back. So it was that night. These human rats were armed with spears, longaxes, spiked clubs, and half a hundred other kinds of weapons, including both longbows and crossbows.

Gold cloaks from the Dragon Gate, obedient to the queen's command, issued forth from their barracks to defend the hill, but found themselves unable to cut through the mobs, and turned back, whilst the messenger sent to the Old Gate never arrived. The Dragonpit had its own contingent of guards, but they were few in number, and were soon overwhelmed and slaughtered when the mob smashed through the doors (the towering main gates, sheathed in bronze and iron, were too strong to assault, but the building had a score of lesser entrances) and came clambering through windows.

Mayhaps the attackers hoped to take the dragons within whilst they slept, but the clangor of the assault made that impossible. Those who lived to tell tales afterward spoke of shouts and screams, the smell of blood in the air, the splintering of oak-and-iron doors beneath crude rams and the blows of countless axes. "Seldom have so many men rushed so eagerly onto their funeral pyres," Grand Maester Munkun later wrote, "but a madness was upon them." There were four dragons housed within the Dragonpit. By the time the first of the attackers came pouring out onto the sands, all four were roused, awake, and angry.

No two chronicles agree on how many men and women died that night beneath the Dragonpit's great dome: two hundred or two thousand, be that as it may. For every man who perished, ten suffered burns and yet survived. Trapped within the pit, hemmed in by walls and dome and bound by heavy chains, the dragons could not fly away, or use their wings to evade attacks and swoop down on their foes. Instead they fought with horns and claws and teeth, turning this way and that like bulls in a Flea Bottom rat pit . . . but these bulls could breathe fire. The Dragonpit was transformed into a fiery hell where burning men staggered screaming through the smoke, the flesh sloughing from their blackened bones, but for every man who died, ten more appeared, shouting that the dragons must need die. One by one, they did.

Shrykos was the first dragon to succumb, slain by a woodsman known as Hobb the Hewer, who leapt onto her neck, driving his axe down into the beast's skull as Shrykos roared and twisted, trying to throw him off. Seven blows did Hobb deliver with his legs locked round the dragon's neck, and each time his axe came down he roared out the name of one of the Seven. It was the seventh blow, the Stranger's blow, that slew the dragon, crashing through scale and bones into the beast's brain.

Morghul, it is written, was slain by the Burning Knight, a huge brute of a man in heavy armor who rushed headlong into the dragon's flame with spear in hand, thrusting its point into the beast's eye repeatedly even as the dragonflame melted the steel plate that encased him and devoured the flesh within.

Prince Joffrey's Tyraxes retreated back into his lair, we are told, roasting so many would-be dragonslayers as they rushed after him that its entrance was soon made impassable by their corpses. But it must be recalled that each of these man-made caves had two entrances, one fronting on the sands of the pit, the other opening onto the hillside, and soon the rioters broke in by the "back door," howling through the smoke with swords and spears and axes. As Tyraxes turned, his chains fouled, entangling him in a web of steel that fatally limited his movement. Half a dozen men (and one woman) would later claim to have dealt the dragon the mortal blow.

The last of the four pit dragons did not die so easily. Legend has it that Dreamfyre had broken free of two of her chains at Queen Helaena's death. The remaining bonds she burst now, tearing the stanchions from the walls as the mob rushed her, then plunging into them with tooth and claw, ripping men apart and tearing off their limbs even as she loosed her terrible fires. As others closed about her she took wing, circling the cavernous interior of the Dragonpit and swooping down to attack the men below. Tyraxes, Shrykos, and Morghul killed scores, there can be little doubt, but Dreamfyre slew more than all three of them combined.

Hundreds fled in terror from her flames . . . but hundreds more, drunk or mad or possessed of the Warrior's own courage, pushed through to the attack. Even at the apex of the dome, the dragon was within easy reach of archer and crossbowman, and arrows and quarrels flew at Dreamfyre wherever she turned, at such close range that some few even punched through her scales. Whenever she lighted, men swarmed to the attack, driving her back into the air. Twice the dragon flew at the Dragonpit's great bronze gates, only to find them closed and barred and defended by ranks of spears.

Unable to flee, Dreamfyre returned to the attack, savaging her tormenters until the sands of the pit were strewn with charred corpses, and the very air was thick with smoke and the smell of burned flesh, yet still the spears and arrows flew. The end came when a crossbow bolt nicked one of the dragon's eyes. Half-blind, and maddened by a dozen lesser wounds, Dreamfyre spread her wings and flew straight up at the great dome above in a last desperate attempt to break into the open sky. Already weakened by blasts of dragonflame, the dome cracked under the force of impact, and a moment later half of it came tumbling down, crushing both dragon and dragonslayers under tons of broken stone and rubble.

The Storming of the Dragonpit was done. Four of the Targaryen dragons lay dead, though at hideous cost. Yet the queen's own dragon remained alive and free . . . and as the burned and bloody survivors of the carnage in the pit came stumbling from the smoking ruins, Syrax descended upon them from above.

A thousand shrieks and shouts echoed across the city, mingling with the dragon's roar. Atop the Hill of Rhaenys, the Dragonpit wore a crown of yellow fire, burning so bright it seemed as if the sun was rising. Even the queen trembled as she watched, the tears glistening on her cheeks. Many of the queen's companions on the rooftop fled, fearing that the fires would soon engulf the entire city, even the Red Keep atop Aegon's High Hill. Others took themselves to the castle sept to pray for deliverance. Rhaenyra herself wrapped her arms about her last living son, Aegon the Younger, clutching him fiercely to her bosom. Nor would she loose her hold upon him . . . until that dread moment when Syrax fell.

Unchained and riderless, Syrax might have easily have flown away from the madness. The sky was hers. She could have returned to the Red Keep, left the city entirely, taken wing for Dragonstone. Was it the noise and fire that drew her to the Hill of Rhaenys, the roars and screams of dying dragons, the smell of burning flesh? We cannot know, no more than we can know why Syrax chose to descend upon the mobs, rending them with tooth and claw and devouring dozens, when she might as easily have rained fire on them from above, for in the sky no man could have harmed her. We can only report what happened.

Many a conflicting tale is told of the death of the queen's dragon. Some credit Hobb the Hewer and his axe, though this is almost certainly mistaken. Could the same man truly have slain two dragons on the same night and in the same manner? Some speak of an unnamed spearman, "a blood-soaked giant" who leapt from the Dragonpit's broken dome onto the dragon's back. Others relate how a knight named Ser Warrick Wheaton slashed a wing from Syrax with a Valyrian steel sword. A crossbowman named Bean would claim the kill afterward, boasting of it in many a wine sink and tavern, until one of the queen's loyalists grew tired of his wagging tongue and cut it out. The truth of the matter no one will ever know—except that Syrax died that night.

The loss of both her dragon and her son left Rhaenyra Targaryen ashen and inconsolable. She retreated to her chambers whilst her counselors conferred. King's Landing was lost, all agreed; they must need abandon the city. Reluctantly, Her Grace was persuaded to leave the next day, at dawn. With the Mud Gate in the hands of her foes, and all the ships along the river burned or sunk, Rhaenyra and a small band of followers slipped out through the Dragon Gate, intending to make their way up the coast to Duskendale. With her rode the brothers Manderly, four surviving Queensguard, Ser Balon Byrch and twenty gold cloaks, four of the queen's ladies-in-waiting, and her last surviving son, Aegon the Younger.

Much and more was happening at Tumbleton as well, and it is there we must next turn our gaze. As word of the unrest at King's Landing reached Prince Daeron's host, many younger lords grew anxious to advance upon the city at once. Chief amongst them was Ser Jon Roxton, Ser Roger Corne, and Lord Unwin Peake . . . but Ser Hobert Hightower counseled caution, and the Two Betrayers refused to join any attack unless their own demands were met. Ulf White, it will be recalled, wished to be granted the great castle of Highgarden with all its lands and incomes, whilst Hard Hugh Hammer desired nothing less than a crown for himself.

These conflicts came to a boil when Tumbleton learned belatedly of Aemond Targaryen's death at Harrenhal. King Aegon II had not been seen nor heard from since the fall of King's Landing to his half sister Rhaenyra, and there were many who feared that the queen had put him secretly to death, concealing the corpse so as not to be condemned as a kinslayer. With his brother Aemond slain as well, the greens found themselves kingless and leaderless. Prince Daeron stood next in the line of succession. Lord Peake declared that the boy should be proclaimed as Prince of Dragonstone at once; others, believing Aegon II dead, wished to crown him king.

The Two Betrayers felt the need of a king as well . . . but Daeron Targaryen was not the king they wanted. "We need a strong man to lead us, not a boy," declared Hard Hugh Hammer. "The throne should be mine."

When Bold Jon Roxton demanded to know by what right he presumed to name himself a king, Lord Hammer answered, "The same right as the Conquerer. A dragon." And truly, with Vhagar dead at last, the oldest and largest living dragon in all Westeros was Vermithor, once the mount of the Old King, now that of Hard Hugh the bastard. Vermithor was thrice the size of Prince Daeron's she-dragon Tessarion. No man who glimpsed them together could fail to see that Vermithor was a far more fearsome beast.

Though Hammer's ambition was unseemly in one born so low, the bastard undeniably possessed some Targaryen blood, and had proved himself fierce in battle and open-handed to those who followed him, displaying the sort of largesse that draws men to leaders as a corpse draws flies. They were the worst sort of men, to be sure: sellswords, robber knights, and like rabble, men of tainted blood and uncertain birth who loved battle for its own sake and lived for rapine and plunder.

The lords and knights of Oldtown and the Reach were offended by the arrogance of the Betrayer's claim, however, and none more so than Prince Daeron Targaryen himself, who grew so wroth that he threw a cup of wine into Hard Hugh's face. Whilst Lord White shrugged this off as a waste of good wine, Lord Hammer said, "Little boys should be more mannerly when men are speaking. I think your father did not beat you often enough. Take care I do not make up for his lack." The Two Betrayers took their leave together, and began to make plans for Hammer's coronation. When seen the next day, Hard Hugh was wearing a crown of black iron, to the fury of Prince Daeron and his trueborn lords and knights.

One such, Ser Roger Corne, made so bold as to knock the crown off Hammer's head. "A crown does not make a man a king," he said. "You should wear a horseshoe on your head, blacksmith." It was a foolish thing to do. Lord Hugh was not amused. At his command, his men forced Ser Roger to the ground, whereupon the blacksmith's bastard nailed not one but three horseshoes to the knight's skull. When Corne's friends tried to intervene, daggers were drawn and swords unsheathed, leaving three men dead and a dozen wounded.

That was more than Prince Daeron's loyalist lords were prepared to suffer. Lord Unwin Peake and a somewhat reluctant Hobert Hightower summoned eleven other lords and landed knights to a secret council in the cellar of a Tumbleton inn, to discuss what might be done to curb the arrogance of the baseborn dragonriders. The plotters agreed that it would be a simple matter to dispose of White, who was drunk more oft than not and had never shown any great prowess at arms. Hammer posed a greater danger, for of late he was surrounded day and night by lickspittles, camp followers, and sellswords eager for his favor. It would serve them little to kill White and leave Hammer alive, Lord Peake pointed out; Hard Hugh must needs die first. Long and loud were the arguments in the inn beneath the sign of the Bloody Caltrops, as the lords discussed how this might best be accomplished.

"Any man can be killed," declared Ser Hobert Hightower, "but what of the dragons?" Given the turmoil at King's Landing, Ser Tyler Norcross said, Tessarion alone should be enough to allow them to retake the Iron Throne. Lord Peake replied that victory would be a deal more certain with Vermithor and Silverwing. Marq Ambrose suggested that they take the city first, then dispose of White and Hammer after victory had been secured, but Richard Rodden insisted such a course would be dishonorable. "We cannot ask these men to shed blood with us, then kill them." Bold John Roxton settled the dispute. "We kill the bastards now," he said. "Afterward, let the bravest of us claim their dragons and fly them into battle." No man in that cellar doubted that Roxton was speaking of himself.

Though Prince Daeron was not present at the council, the Caltrops (as the conspirators became known) were loath to proceed without his consent and blessing. Owen Fossoway, Lord of Cider Hall, was dispatched under cover of darkness to wake the prince and bring him to the cellar, that the plotters might inform him of their plans. Nor did the once-gentle prince hesitate when Lord Unwin Peake presented him with warrants for the execution of Hard Hugh Hammer and Ulf White, but eagerly affixed his seal.

Men may plot and plan and scheme, but they had best pray as well, for no plan ever made by man has ever withstood the whims of the gods above. Two days later, on the very day the Caltrops planned to strike, Tumbleton woke in the black of night to screams and shouts. Outside the town walls, the camps were burning. Columns of armored knights were pouring in from north and west, wreaking slaughter, the clouds were raining arrows, and a dragon was swooping down upon them, terrible and fierce.

Thus began the Second Battle of Tumbleton.

The dragon was Seasmoke, his rider Ser Addam Velaryon, determined to prove that not all bastards need be turncloaks. How better to do that than by retaking Tumbleton from the Two Betrayers, whose treason had stained him? Singers say Ser Addam had flown from King's Landing to the Gods Eye, where he landed on the sacred Isle of Faces and took counsel with the Green Men. The scholar must confine himself to known fact, and what we know is that Ser Addam flew far and fast, descending on castles great and small whose lords were loyal to the queen, to piece together an army.

Many a battle and skirmish had already been fought in the lands watered by the Trident, and there was scarce a keep or village that had not paid its due in blood . . . but Addam Velaryon was relentless and determined and glib of tongue, and the river lords knew much and more of the horrors that had befallen Tumbleton. By the time Ser Addam was ready to descend on Tumbleton, he had near four thousand men at his back.

The great host encamped about the walls of Tumbleton outnumbered the attackers, but they had been too long in one place. Their discipline had grown lax, and disease had taken root as well; the death of Lord Ormund Hightower had left them without a leader, and the lords who wished to command in his place were at odds with one another. So intent were they upon their own conflicts and rivalries that they had all but forgotten their true foes. Ser Addam's night attack took them completely unawares. Before the men of Prince Daeron's army even knew they were in a battle, the enemy was amongst them, cutting them down as they staggered from their tents, as they were saddling their horses, struggling to don their armor, buckling their sword belts.

Most devastating of all was the dragon. Seasmoke came swooping down again and yet again, breathing flame. A hundred tents were soon afire, even the splendid silken pavilions of Ser Hobart Hightower, Lord Unwin Peake, and Prince Daeron himself. Nor was the town of Tumbleton reprieved. Those shops and homes and septs that had been spared the first time were eugulfed in dragonflame.

Daeron Targaryen was in his tent asleep when the attack began. Ulf White was inside Tumbleton, sleeping off a night of drinking at an inn called the Bawdy Badger that he had taken for his own. Hard Hugh

Hammer was within the town walls as well, in bed with the widow of a knight slain during the first battle. All three dragons were outside the town, in fields beyond the encampments.

Though attempts were made to wake Ulf White from his drunken slumber, he proved impossible to rouse. Infamously, he rolled under a table and snored through the entire battle. Hard Hugh Hammer was quicker to respond. Half-dressed, he rushed down the steps to the yard, calling for his hammer, his armor, and a horse, so he might ride out and mount Vermithor. His men rushed to obey, even as Seasmoke set the stables ablaze. But Lord Jon Roxton was already in the yard.

When he spied Hard Hugh, Roxton saw his chance, and said, "Lord Hammer, my condolences." Hammer turned, glowering. "For what?" he demanded. "You died in the battle," Bold Jon replied, drawing Orphan-Maker and thrusting it deep into Hammer's belly, before opening the bastard from groin to throat.

A dozen of Hard Hugh's men came running in time to see him die. Even a Valyrian steel blade like Orphan-Maker little avails a man when it is one against ten. Bold Jon Roxton slew three before he was slain in turn. It is said that he died when his foot slipped on a coil of Hugh Hammer's entrails, but perhaps that detail is too perfectly ironic to be true.

Three conflicting accounts exist as to the manner of death of Prince Daeron Targaryen. The best known claims that the prince stumbled from his pavilion with his night clothes afire, only to be cut down by the Myrish sellsword Black Trombo, who smashed his face in with a swing of his spiked morningstar. This version was the one preferred by Black Trombo, who told it far and wide. The second version is more or less the same, save that the prince was killed with a sword, not a morningstar, and his slayer was not Black Trombo, but some unknown man-at-arms who like as not did not even realize who he had killed. In the third alternative, the brave boy known as Daeron the Daring did not even make it out at all, but died when his burning pavilion collapsed upon him.

In the sky above, Addam Velaryon could see the battle turning into a rout below him. Two of the three enemy dragonriders were dead, but he would have had no way of knowing that. He could doubtless see the enemy dragons, however. Unchained, they were kept beyond the town walls, free to fly and hunt as they would; Silverwing and Vermithor oft coiled about one another in the fields south of Tumbleton, whilst Tessarion slept and fed in Prince Daeron's camp to the west of the town, not a hundred yards from his pavilion.

Dragons are creatures of fire and blood, and all three roused as the battle bloomed around them. A crossbowman let fly a bolt at Silverwing, we are told, and two score mounted knights closed on Vermithor with sword and lance and axe, hoping to dispatch the beast whilst he was still half-asleep and on the ground. They paid for that folly with their lives. Elsewhere on the field, Tessarion threw herself into the air, shrieking and spitting flame, and Addam Velaryon turned Seasmoke to meet her.

A dragon's scales are largely (though not entirely) impervious to flame; they protect the more vulnerable flesh and musculature beneath. As a dragon ages, its scales thicken and grow harder, affording even more protection, even as its flames burn hotter and fiercer (where the flames of a hatchling can set straw aflame, the flames of Balerion or Vhagar in the fullness of their power could and did melt steel and stone). When two dragons meet in mortal combat, therefore, they will oft employ weapons other than their flame: claws black as iron, long as swords, and sharp as razors, jaws so powerful they can crunch through even a knight's steel plate, tails like whips whose lashing blows have been known to smash wagons to splinters, break the spine of heavy destriers, and send men flying fifty feet in the air.

The battle between Tessarion and Seasmoke was different.

History calls the struggle between King Aegon II and his sister Rhaenyra the Dance of the Dragons, but only at Tumbleton did the dragons ever truly dance. Tessarion and Seasmoke were young dragons, nimbler in the air than their older brothers had been. Time and time again they rushed one another, only to have one or the other veer away at the last instant. Soaring like eagles, stooping like hawks, they circled, snapping and roaring, spitting fire, but never closing. Once the Blue Queen vanished into a bank of cloud, only to reappear an instant later, diving on Seasmoke from behind to scorch her tail with a burst of cobalt flame. Meanwhile, Seasmoke rolled and banked and looped. One instant he would be below his foe, and suddenly he would twist in the sky and come around behind her. Higher and higher the two dragons flew, as hundreds watched from the roofs of Tumbleton. One such said afterward that the flight of

Tessarion and Seasmoke seemed more mating dance than battle. Perhaps it was.

The dance ended when Vermithor rose roaring into the sky.

Almost a hundred years old and as large as the two young dragons put together, the bronze dragon with the great tan wings was in a rage as he took flight, with blood smoking from a dozen wounds. Riderless, he knew not friend from foe, so he loosed his wroth on all, spitting flame to right and left, turning savagely on any man who dared to fling a spear in his direction. One knight tried to flee before him, only to have Vermithor snatch him up in his jaws, even as his horse galloped on. Lords Piper and Deddings, seated together atop a low rise, burned with their squires, servants, and sworn shields when the Bronze Fury chanced to take note of them. An instant later, Seasmoke fell upon him.

Alone of the four dragons on the field that day, Seasmoke had a rider. Ser Addam Velaryon had come to prove his loyalty by destroying the Two Betrayers and their dragons, and here was one beneath him, attacking the men who had joined him for this fight. He must have felt duty-bound to protect them, though surely he knew in heart that his Seasmoke could not match the older dragon.

This was no dance, but a fight to the death. Vermithor had been flying no more than twenty feet above the battle when Seasmoke slammed into him from above, driving him shrieking into the mud. Men and boys ran in terror or were crushed as the two dragons rolled and tore at one another. Tails snapped and wings beat at the air, but the beasts were so entangled that neither was able to be able to break free. Benjicot Blackwood watched the struggle from atop his horse fifty yards away. Vermithor's size and weight were too much for Seasmoke to contend with, Lord Blackwood said many years later, and he would surely have torn the silver-grey dragon to pieces . . . if Tessarion had not fallen from the sky at that very moment to join the fight.

Who can know the heart of a dragon? Was it simple bloodlust that drove the Blue Queen to attack? Did the she-dragon come to help one of the combatants? If so, which? Some will claim that the bond between a dragon and dragonrider runs so deep that the beast shares his master's loves and hates. But who was the ally here, and who the enemy? Does a riderless dragon know friend from foe?

We shall never know the answers to those questions. All that history tells us is that three dragons fought amidst the mud and blood and smoke of Second Tumbleton. Seasmoke was first to die, when Vermithor locked his teeth into his neck and ripped his head off. Afterward the bronze dragon tried to take flight with his prize still in his jaws, but his tattered wings could not lift his weight. After a moment he collapsed and died. Tessarion, the Blue Queen, lasted until sunset. Thrice she tried to regain the sky, and thrice failed. By late afternoon she seemed to be in pain, so Lord Blackwood summoned his best archer, a longbowman known as Billy Burley, who took up a position a hundred yards away (beyond the range of the dying dragon's fires) and sent three shafts into her eye as she lay helpless on the ground.

By dusk, the fighting was done. Though the river lords lost less than a hundred men, whilst cutting down more than a thousand of the men from Oldtown and the Reach, Second Tumbleton could not be accounted a complete victory for the attackers, as they failed to take the town. Tumbleton's walls were still intact, and once the king's men had fallen back inside and closed their gates, the queen's forces had no way to make a breach, lacking both siege equipment and dragons. Even so, they wreaked great slaughter on their confused and disorganized foes, fired their tents, burned or captured almost all their wagons, fodder, and provisions, made off with three-quarters of their warhorses, slew their prince, and put an end to two of the king's dragons.

On the morning after the battle, the conquerers of Tumbleton looked out from the town walls to find their foes gone. The dead were strewn all around the city, and amongst them sprawled the carcasses of three dragons. One remained: Silverwing, Good Queen Alysanne's mount in days of old, had taken to the sky as the carnage began, circling the battlefield for hours, soaring on the hot winds rising from the fires below. Only after dark did she descend, to land beside her slain cousins. Later, singers would tell of how she thrice lifted Vermithor's wing with her nose, as if to make him fly again, but this is most like a fable. The rising sun would find her flapping listlessly across the field, feeding on the burned remains of horses, men, and oxen.

Eight of the thirteen Caltrops lay dead, amongst them Lord Owen Fossoway, Marq Ambrose, and Bold Jon Roxton. Richard Rodden had taken an arrow to the neck and would die the next day. Four of the plotters remained, amongst them Ser Hobert Hightower and Lord Unwin Peake. And though Hard Hugh Hammer had died, and his dreams of kingship with him, the second Betrayer remained. Ulf White had woken from his drunken sleep to find himself the last dragonrider, and possessed of the last dragon.

"The Hammer's dead, and your boy as well," he is purported to have told Lord Peake. "All you got left is me." When Lord Peake asked him his intentions, White replied, "We march, just how you wanted. You take the city, I'll take the bloody throne, how's that?"

The next morning, Ser Hobert Hightower called upon him, to thrash out the details of their assault upon King's Landing. He brought with him two casks of wine as a gift, one of Dornish red and one of Arbor gold. Though Ulf the Sot had never tasted a wine he did not like, he was known to be partial to the sweeter vintages. No doubt Ser Hobert hoped to sip the sour red whilst Lord Ulf quaffed down the Arbor gold. Yet something about Hightower's manner—he was sweating and stammering and too hearty by half, the squire who served them testified later—pricked White's suspicions. Wary, he commanded that the Dornish red be set aside for later, and insisted Ser Hobert share the Arbor gold with him.

History has little good to say about Ser Hobert Hightower, but no man can question the manner of his death. Rather than betray his fellow Caltrops, he let the squire fill his cup, drank deep, and asked for more. Once he saw Hightower drink, Ulf the Sot lived up to his name, putting down three cups before he began to yawn. The poison in the wine was a gentle one. When Lord Ulf went to sleep, never to awaken, Ser Hobert lurched to his feet and tried to make himself retch, but too late. His heart stopped within the hour.

Afterward, Lord Unwin Peake offered a thousand golden dragons to any knight of noble birth who could claim Silverwing. Three men came forth. When the first had his arm torn off and the second burned to death, the third man reconsidered. By that time Peake's army, the remnants of the great host that Prince Daeron and Lord Ormund Hightower had led all the way from Oldtown, was falling to pieces as deserters fled Tumbleton by the score with all the plunder they could carry. Bowing to defeat, Lord Unwin summoned his lords and serjeants and ordered a retreat. The accused turncloak Addam Velaryon, born Addam of Hull, had saved King's Landing from the queen's foes . . . at the cost of his own life.

Yet the queen knew nothing of his valor. Rhaenyra's flight from King's Landing had been beset with difficulty. At Rosby, she found the castle gates were barred at her approach. Young Lord Stokeworth's castellan granted her hospitality, but only for a night. Half of her gold cloaks deserted on the road, and one night her camp was attacked by broken men. Though her knights beat off the attackers, Ser Balon Byrch was felled by an arrow, and Ser Lyonel Bentley, a young knight of the Queensguard, suffered a blow to the head that cracked his helm. He perished raving the following day. The queen pressed on toward Duskendale.

House Darklyn had been amongst Rhaenyra's strongest supporters, but the cost of that loyalty had been high. Only the intercession of Ser Harrold Darke persuaded Lady Meredyth Darklyn to allow the queen within her walls at all (the Darkes were distant kin to the Darklyns, and Ser Harrold had once served as a squire to the late Ser Steffon), and only upon the condition that she would not remain for long.

Queen Rhaenyra had neither gold nor ships. When she had sent Lord Corlys to the dungeons she had lost her fleet, and she had fled King's Landing in terror of her life, without so much as a coin. Despairing and fearful, Her Grace grew ever more grey and haggard. She could not sleep and would not eat. Nor would she suffer to be parted from Prince Aegon, her last living son; day and night, the boy remained by her side, "like a small pale shadow."

Rhaenyra was forced to sell her crown to raise the coin to buy passage on a Braavosi merchantman, the *Violande*. Ser Harrold Darke urged her to seek refuge with Lady Arryn in the Vale, whilst Ser Medrick Manderly tried to persuade her to accompany him and his brother Ser Torrhen back to White Harbor, but Her Grace refused them both. She was adamant on returning to Dragonstone. There she would find dragon's eggs, she told her loyalists; she must have another dragon, or all was lost.

Strong winds pushed the *Violande* closer to the shores of Driftmark than the queen might have wished, and thrice she passed within hailing distance of the Sea Snake's warships, but Rhaenyra took care to keep well out of sight. Finally the Braavosi put into the harbor below the Dragon-mont on the eventide. The queen had sent a raven to give notice of her coming, and found an escort waiting as she disembarked with her son Aegon, her ladies, and three Queensguard knights, all that was left of her party.

It was raining when the queen's party came ashore, and hardly a face was to be seen about the port. Even the dockside brothels appeared dark and deserted, but Her Grace took no notice. Sick in body and spirit, broken by betrayal, Rhaenyra Targaryen wanted only to return to her own seat, where she imagined that she and her son would be safe. Little did the queen know that she was about to suffer her last and most grievous treachery.

Her escort, forty strong, was commanded by Ser Alfred Broome, one of the men left behind when Rhaenyra had launched her attack upon King's Landing. Broome was the most senior of the knights at Dragonstone, having joined the garrison during the reign of the Old King. As such, he had expected to be named as castellan when Rhaenyra went forth to seize the Iron Throne . . . but Ser Alfred's sullen disposition and sour manner inspired neither affection nor trust, so the queen had passed him over in favor of the more affable Ser Robert Quince.

When Rhaenyra asked why Ser Robert had not come himself to meet her, Ser Alfred replied that the queen would be seeing "our fat friend" at the castle. And so she did . . . though Quince's charred corpse was burned beyond all recognition when they came upon it, hanging from the battlements of the gatehouse beside Dragonstone's steward, master-at-arms, and captain of guards. Only by his size did they know him, for Ser Robert had been enormously fat.

It is said that the blood drained from the queen's cheeks when she beheld the bodies, but young Prince Aegon was the first to realize what they meant. "Mother, flee!" he shouted, but too late. Ser Alfred's men men fell upon the queen's protectors. An axe split Ser Harrold Darke's head before his sword could clear its scabbard, and Ser Adrian Redfort was stabbed through the back with a spear. Only Ser Loreth Lansdale moved quickly enough to strike a blow in the queen's defense, cutting down the first two men who came at him before being slain himself. With him died of the last of the Queensguard. When Prince Aegon snatched up Ser Harrold's sword, Ser Alfred knocked the blade aside contemptuously.

The boy, the queen, and her ladies were marched at spearpoint through the gates of Dragonstone to the castle ward. There they found themselves face-to-face with a dead man and a dying dragon.

Sunfyre's scales still shone like beaten gold in the sunlight, but as he sprawled across the fused black Valyrian stone of the yard, it was plain to see that he was a broken thing, he who had been the most magnificent dragon ever to fly the skies of Westeros. The wing all but torn from his body by Meleys jutted from his body at an awkward angle, whilst fresh scars along his back still smoked and bled when he moved. Sunfyre was coiled in a ball when the queen and her party first beheld him. As he stirred and raised his head, huge wounds were visible along his neck, where another dragon had torn chunks from his flesh. On his belly were places where scabs had replaced scales, and where his right eye should have been was only an empty hole, crusted with black blood.

One must ask, as Rhaenyra surely did, how this had come to pass.

We now know much and more that the queen did not. It was Lord Larys Strong, the Clubfoot, who spirited the king and his children out of the city when the queen's dragons first appeared in the skies above King's Landing. So as not to pass through any of the city gates, where they might be seen and remembered, Lord Larys led them out through some secret passage of Maegor the Cruel, of which only he had knowledge.

It was Lord Larys who decreed the fugitives should part company as well, so that even if one were taken, the others might win free. Ser Rickard Thorne was commanded to deliver two-year-old Prince Maelor to Lord Hightower. Princess Jaehaera, a sweet and simple girl of six, was put in the charge of Ser Willis Fell, who swore to bring her safely to Storm's End. Neither knew where the other was bound, so neither could betray the other if captured.

And only Larys himself knew that the king, stripped of his finery and clad in a salt-stained fisherman's cloak, had been concealed amongst a load of codfish on a fishing skiff in the care of a bastard knight with kin on Dragonstone. Once she learned the king was gone, the Clubfoot reasoned, Rhaenyra was sure to send men hunting after him . . . but a boat leaves no trail upon the waves, and few hunters would ever think to look for Aegon on his sister's own island, in the very shadow of her stronghold.

And there Aegon might have remained, hidden yet harmless, dulling his pain with wine and hiding his burn scars beneath a heavy cloak, had Sunfyre not made his way to Dragonstone. We may ask what drew him back to the Dragonmont, for many have. Was the wounded dragon, with his half-healed broken wing, driven by some primal instinct to return to his birthplace, the smoking mountain where he had emerged from his egg? Or did he somehow sense the presence of King Aegon on the island, across long leagues and stormy seas, and fly there to rejoin his rider? Some go so far as to suggest that Sunfyre sensed Aegon's desperate *need*. But who can presume to know the heart of a dragon?

After Lord Walys Mooton's ill-fated attack drove him from the field of ash and bone outside Rook's Rest, history loses sight of Sunfyre for more than half a year. (Certain tales told in the halls of the Crabbs and Brunes suggest the dragon may have taken refuge in the dark piney woods and caves of Crackclaw Point for some of that time.) Though his torn wing had mended enough for him to fly, it had healed at an ugly angle, and remained weak. Sunfyre could no longer soar, not remain in the air for long, but must needs struggle to fly even short distances. Yet somehow he had crossed the waters of Blackwater Bay . . . for it was Sunfyre that the sailors on the *Nessaria* had seen attacking Grey Ghost. Ser Robert Quince had blamed the Cannibal . . . but Tom Tangletongue, a stammerer who heard more than he said, had plied the Volantenes with ale, making note of all the times they mentioned the attacker's golden scales. The Cannibal, as he knew well, was black as coal. And so the Two Toms and their "cousins" (a half-truth, as only Ser Marston shared their blood, being the bastard son of Tom Tanglebeard's sister by the knight who took her maidenhead) set sail in their small boat to seek out Grey Ghost's killer.

The burned king and the maimed dragon each found new purpose in the other. From a hidden lair on the desolate eastern slopes of the Dragonmont, Aegon ventured forth each day at dawn, taking to the sky again for the first time since Rook's Rest, whilst the Two Toms and their cousin Marston Waters returned to the other side of the island to seek out men willing to help them take the castle. Even on Dragonstone, long Queen Rhaenyra's seat and stronghold, they found many who misliked the queen for reasons both good and ill. Some grieved for brothers, sons, and fathers slain during the Sowing or during the Battle of the Gullet, some hoped for plunder or advancement, whilst others believed a son must come before a daughter, giving Aegon the better claim.

The queen had taken her best men with her to King's Landing. On its island, protected by the Sea Snake's ships and its high Valyrian walls, Dragonstone seemed unassailable, so the garrison Her Grace left to defend it was small, made up largely of men judged to be of little other use: greybeards and green boys, the halt and slow and crippled, men recovering from wounds, men of doubtful loyalty, men suspected of cowardice.

Over them Rhaenyra placed Ser Robert Quince, an able man grown old and fat.

Quince was a steadfast supporter of the queen, all agree, but some of the men under him were less leal, harboring certain resentments and grudges for old wrongs real or imagined. Prominent amongst them was Ser Alfred Broome. Broome proved more than willing to betray his queen in return for a promise of lordship, lands, and gold should Aegon II regain the throne. His long service with the garrison allowed him to advise the king's men on Dragonstone's strengths and weaknesses, which guards could be bribed or won over, and which must need be killed or imprisoned.

When it came, the fall of Dragonstone took less than an hour. Men traduced by Broome opened a postern gate during the hour of ghosts to allow Ser Marston Waters, Tom Tangletongue, and their men to slip into the castle unobserved. While one band seized the armory and another took Dragonstone's leal guardsmen and master-at-arms into custody, Ser Marston surprised Maester Hunnimore in his rookery, so no word of the attack might escape by raven. Ser Alfred himself led the men who burst into the castellan's chambers to surprise Ser Robert Quince. As Quince struggled to rise from his bed, Broome drove a spear into his huge pale belly, the thrust delivered with such force that the spear went out Ser Robert's back, through the featherbed and straw mattress, and into the floor beneath.

Only in one respect did the plan go awry. As Tom Tangletongue and his ruffians smashed down the door of Lady Baela's bedchamber to take her prisoner, the girl slipped out her window, scrambling across rooftops and down walls until she reached the yard. The king's men had taken care to send guards to secure the stable where the castle dragons had been kept, but Baela had grown up in Dragonstone, and knew ways in and out that they did not. By the time her pursuers caught up with her, she had already loosed Moondancer's chains and strapped a saddle onto her.

So it came to pass that when King Aegon II flew Sunfyre over Dragonmont's smoking peak and made his descent, expecting to make a triumphant entrance into a castle safely in the hands of his own men, with the queen's loyalists slain or captured, up to meet him rose Baela Targaryen, Prince Daemon's daughter by the Lady Laena, and fearless as her father.

Moondancer was a young dragon, pale green, with horns and crest and wingbones of pearl. Aside from her great wings, she was no larger than a warhorse, and weighed less. She was very quick, however, and Sunfyre, though much larger, still struggled with a malformed wing, and had taken fresh wounds from Grey Ghost.

They met amidst the darkness that comes before the dawn, shadows in the sky lighting the night with their fires. Moondancer eluded Sunfyre's flames, eluded his jaws, darted beneath his grasping claws, then came around and raked the larger dragon from above, opening a long smoking wound down his back and tearing at his injured wing. Watchers below said that Sunfyre lurched drunkenly in the air, fighting to stay aloft, whilst Moondancer turned and came back at him, spitting fire. Sunfyre answered with a furnace blast of golden flame so bright it lit the yard below like a second sun, a blast that took Moondancer full in the eyes. Like as not, the young dragon was blinded in that instant, yet still she flew on, slamming into Sunfyre in a tangle of wings and claws. As they fell, Moondancer struck at Sunfyre's neck repeatedly, tearing out mouthfuls of flesh, whilst the elder dragon sank his claws into her underbelly. Robed in fire and smoke, blind and bleeding, Moondancer's wings beat desperately as she tried to break away, but all her efforts did was slow their fall.

The watchers in the yard scrambled for safety as the dragons slammed into the hard stone, still fighting. On the ground, Moondancer's quickness proved of little use against Sunfyre's size and weight. The green dragon soon lay still. The golden dragon screamed his victory and tried to rise again, only to collapse back to the ground with hot blood pouring from his wounds.

King Aegon had leapt from the saddle when the dragons were still twenty feet from the ground, shattering both legs. Lady Baela stayed with Moondancer all the way down. Burned and battered, the girl still found the strength to undo her saddle chains and crawl away as her dragon coiled in her final death throes. When Alfred Broome drew his sword to slay her, Martson Waters wrenched the blade from his hand. Tom Tangletongue carried her to the maester.

Thus did King Aegon II win the ancestral seat of House Targaryen, but the price he paid for it was dire. Sunfyre would never fly again. He remained in the yard where he had fallen, feeding on the carcass of Moondancer, and later on sheep slaughtered for him by the garrison. And

Aegon II lived the rest of his life in great pain . . . though to his honor, this time His Grace refused the milk of the poppy. "I shall not walk that road again," he said.

Not long after, as the king lay in the Stone Drum's great hall, his broken legs bound and splinted, the first of Queen Rhaenyra's ravens arrived from Duskendale. When Aegon learned that his half sister would be returning on the *Violande,* he commanded Ser Alfred Broome to prepare a "suitable welcome" for her homecoming.

All of this is known to us now. None of this was known to the queen, when she stepped ashore into her brother's trap.

Rhaenyra laughed when she beheld the ruin of Sunfyre the Golden. "Whose work is this?" she said. "We must thank him."

"Sister," the King called down from a balcony. Unable to walk, or even stand, he had been carried there in a chair. The hip shattered at Rook's Rest had left Aegon bent and twisted, his once-handsome features had grown puffy from milk of the poppy, and burn scars covered half his body. Yet Rhaenyra knew him at once, and said, "Dear brother. I had hoped that you were dead."

"After you," Aegon answered. "You are the elder."

"I am pleased to know that you remember that," Rhaenyra answered. "It would seem we are your prisoners . . . but do not think that you will hold us long. My leal lords will find me."

"If they search the seven hells, mayhaps," the King made answer, as his men tore Rhaenyra from her son's arms. Some accounts say it was Ser Alfred Broome who had hold of her arm, others name the two Toms, Tanglebeard the father and Tangletongue the son. Ser Marston Waters stood witness as well, clad in a white cloak, for King Aegon had named him to his Kingsguard for his valor.

Yet neither Waters nor any of the other knights and lords present in the yard spoke a word of protest as King Aegon II delivered his half sister to his dragon. Sunfyre, it is said, did not seem at first to take any interest in the offering, until Broome pricked the queen's breast with his dagger. The smell of blood roused the dragon, who sniffed at Her Grace, then bathed her in a blast of flame, so suddenly that Ser Alfred's cloak caught fire as he leapt away. Rhaenyra Targaryen had time to raise her head toward the sky and shriek out one last curse upon her half brother before Sunfyre's jaws closed round her, tearing off her arm and shoulder.

The golden dragon devoured the queen in six bites, leaving only her left leg below the shin "for the Stranger." The queen's son watched in horror, unable to move. Rhaenyra Targaryen, the Realm's Delight and Half-Year Queen, passed from this veil of tears upon the twenty-second day of tenth moon of the 130th year after Aegon's Conquest. She was thirty-three years of age.

Ser Alfred Broome argued for killing Prince Aegon as well, but King Aegon forbade it. Only ten, the boy might yet have value as a hostage, he declared. Though his half sister was dead, she still had supporters in the field who must need be dealt with before His Grace could hope to sit the Iron Throne again. So Prince Aegon was manacled at neck, wrist, and ankle, and led down to the dungeons under Dragonstone. The late queen's ladies-in-waiting, being of noble birth, were given cells in Sea Dragon Tower, there to await ransom. "The time for hiding is done," King Aegon II declared. "Let the ravens fly that the realm may know the pretender is dead, and their true king is coming home to reclaim his father's throne." Yet even true kings may find some things more easily proclaimed than accomplished.

In the days following his half sister's death, the king still clung to the hope that Sunfyre might recover enough strength to fly again. Instead the dragon only seemed to weaken further, and soon the wounds in his neck began to stink. Even the smoke he exhaled had a foul smell to it, and toward the end he would no longer eat. On the ninth day of the twelfth moon of 130 AC, the magnificent golden dragon that had been King Aegon's glory died in the yard of Dragonstone where he had fallen. His Grace wept.

When his grief had passed, King Aegon II summoned his loyalists and made plans for his return to King's Landing, to reclaim the Iron Throne and be reunited once again with his lady mother, the Queen Dowager, who had at last emerged triumphant over her great rival, if only by outliving her. "Rhaenyra was never a queen," the king declared, insisting that henceforth, in all chronicles and court records, his half sister be referred to only as "princess," the title of queen being reserved only for his mother Alicent and his late wife and sister Helaena, the "true queens." And so it was decreed.

Yet Aegon's triumph would prove to be as short-lived as it was bittersweet. Rhaenyra was dead, but her cause had not died with her, and new "black" armies were on the march even as the king returned to the Red Keep. Aegon II would sit the Iron Throne again, but he would never recover from his wounds, would know neither joy nor peace. His restoration would endure for only half a year.

The account of how of the Second Aegon fell and was succeeded by the Third is a tale for another time, however. The war for the throne would go on, but the rivalry that began at a court ball when a princess dressed in black and a queen in green has come to its red end, and with that concludes this portion of our history.

Carrie Vaughn

New York Times bestseller Carrie Vaughn is the author of a wildly popular series of novels detailing the adventures of Kitty Norville, a radio personality who also happens to be a werewolf and who runs a late-night call-in radio advice show for supernatural creatures. The Kitty books include *Kitty and the Midnight Hour, Kitty Goes to Washington, Kitty Takes a Holiday, Kitty and the Silver Bullet, Kitty and the Dead Man's Hand, Kitty Raises Hell, Kitty's House of Horrors, Kitty Goes to War,* and *Kitty's Big Trouble.* Her other novels include *Voices of Dragons,* her first venture into young adult territory, and a fantasy, *Discord's Apple.* Vaughn's short work has appeared in *Lightspeed, Asimov's Science Fiction, Subterranean, Inside Straight* (a Wild Cards novel), *Realms of Fantasy, Jim Baen's Universe, Paradox, Strange Horizons, Weird Tales, All-Star Zeppelin Adventure Stories,* and elsewhere. Her most recent books include the novels *After the Golden Age* and *Steel;* a collection, *Straying from the Path;* a new Kitty novel, *Kitty Steals the Show;* and a collection of her Kitty stories, *Kitty's Greatest Hits.* Coming up is another new Kitty novel, *Kitty Rocks the House.* She lives in Colorado.

In the vivid and compelling story that follows, she takes us to the front lines in Russia during the darkest days of World War II for the story of a young woman flying the most dangerous of combat missions, who is determined to do her duty as a soldier and keep flying them, even if it kills her—which it very well might.

RAISA STEPANOVA

My Dear Davidya:

If you are reading this, it means I have died. Most likely been killed fighting in service of the glorious homeland. At least I hope so. I have this terrible nightmare that I am killed, not in the air fighting Fascists, but because a propeller blade falls off just as I am walking under the nose of my Yak and cuts my head off. People would make a good show of pretending to mourn, but they'd be laughing behind my back. My dead back, so I won't notice, but still, it's the principle of the thing. There'd certainly be no Hero of the Soviet Union for me, would there? Never mind, we will assume I perished gloriously in battle.

Please tell all the usual to Mama and Da, that I am happy to give my life in defense of you and them and Nina and the homeland, as we all are, and that if I must die at all I'm very happy to do it while flying. So don't be sad for me. I love you.

Very Sincerely: Raisa

"Raisa!" Inna called from outside the dugout. "We're up! Let's *go!*"
"Just a minute!" She scribbled a last few lines.

P.S. My wingman, Inna, will be very upset if I am killed. She'll think it's her fault, that she didn't cover me. (It won't be true because she's a very good pilot and wingman.) I think you should make an effort to comfort her at the very first opportunity. She's a redhead. You'll like her. Really like her, I mean. I keep a picture of you in our dugout and she thinks you're handsome. She'll weep on your shoulder and it will be very romantic, trust me.

"Raisa!"

Raisa folded the page into eighths and stuffed it under the blanket on her cot, where it was sure to be found if she didn't come back. David's name and regiment were clearly written on the outside, and Inna would know what to do with it. She grabbed her coat and helmet and ran with her wingman to the airfield, where their planes waited.

The pair of them flew out of Voronezh on a routine patrol and spotted enemy planes even before reaching the front. Raisa breathed slow to keep her heart from racing, letting the calm spread to her hands to steady them, where they rested on the stick.

"Raisa, you see that? Two o'clock?" Inna's voice cracked over the radio. She flew behind and to the right—Raisa didn't have to look to know she was there.

"Yes." Raisa squinted through the canopy and counted. More planes, dark spots gliding against a hazy sky, seemed to appear as she did so. They were meant to be patrolling for German reconnaissance planes, which only appeared one or two at a time. This—this was an entire squadron.

The profile of the planes clarified—twin propellers, topside canopy, long fuselage painted with black crosses. She radioed back to Inna, "Those are Junkers! That's a bombing run!"

She counted sixteen bombers—their target could have been any of the dozens of encampments, supply depots, or train stations along this section of the front. They probably weren't expecting any resistance at all.

"What do we do?" Inna said.

This was outside their mission parameters, and they were so far outnumbered as to be ridiculous. On the other hand, what else were they supposed to do? The Germans would have dropped their bombs before the 586th could scramble more fighters.

"What do you think?" Raisa answered. "We stop them!"

"With you!"

Raisa throttled up and pushed forward on the stick. The engine rumbled and shook the canopy around her. The Yak streaked forward, the sky a blur above her. A glance over her shoulder, and she saw Inna's fighter right behind her.

She aimed at the middle of the German swarm. Individual bombers became very large very quickly, filling the sky in front of her. She kept on, like an arrow, until she and Inna came within range.

The bombers scattered, as if they'd been blown apart by a wind. Planes at the edges of the formation peeled off, and ones in the middle climbed and dived at random. Clearly, they hadn't expected a couple of Russian fighters to shoot at them from nowhere.

She picked one that had the misfortune to evade right into her path, and focused her sights on it. She fired a series of rounds from the 20mm cannon, missed when the bomber juked out of range. She cursed.

Rounds blazed above her canopy; a gunner, shooting back. She banked hard, right and up, keeping a watch out for collisions. Dicey, maneuvering with all this traffic. The Yak was fast—she could fly circles around the Junkers and wasn't terribly worried about getting shot. But she could easily crash into one of them by not paying close enough attention. All she and Inna really had to do was stop the group from reaching its target, but if she could bring down one or two of them in the meantime . . . One second at a time, that was the only way to handle the situation. Stay alive so she could do some good.

The enemy gunner fired at her again, then Raisa recognized the sound of another cannon firing. A fireball expanded and burned out at the corner of her vision—a Junker, one of its engines breaking apart. The plane lurched, off balance until it fell in an arc, trailing smoke. It waggled once or twice, the pilot trying to regain control, but then the bomber started spinning and it was all over.

Inna cried over the radio, "Raisa! I got him, I got him!" It was her first kill in battle.

"Excellent! Only fifteen more to go!"

"Raisa Ivanovna, you're terrible."

The battle seemed to drag, but surely only seconds had passed since they scattered the formation. They couldn't engage for much longer before they'd run out of ammunition, not to mention fuel. The last few shots had to count, then she and Inna ought to run. *After* those last few shots, of course.

Raisa caught another target and banked hard to follow it. The bomber climbed, but it was slow, and she was right on it. By now her nerves were singing and instinct guided her more than reason. She squeezed hard on the trigger before the enemy was fully in her crosshairs, but it worked, because the Junker slid into the line of fire just as her shots reached it. She put holes across its wings and across its engine, which sparked and began pouring smoke. The plane could not survive, and sure enough, the nose tipped forward, the whole thing falling out of control.

Inna cheered for her over the radio, but Raisa was already hunting her next target. So many to choose from. The two fighters were surrounded, and Raisa should have been frightened, but she could only think about shooting the next bomber. And the next.

The Junkers struggled to return to formation. The loose, straggling collection had dropped five hundred meters from its original altitude. If the fighters could force down the entire squadron, what a prize that would be! But no, they were running, veering hard from the fighters, struggling to escape.

Bombs fell from the lead plane's belly, and the others followed suit. The bombs detonated on empty forest, their balloons of smoke rising harmlessly. They'd scared the bombers into dropping their loads early.

Raisa smiled at the image.

With nothing left in their bomb bays and no reason to continue, the Junkers peeled off and circled back to the west. Lighter and faster now, they'd be more difficult for the fighters to catch. But they wouldn't be killing any Russians today, either.

Raisa radioed, "Inna, let's get out of here."

"Got it."

With Inna back on her wing, she turned her Yak to the east, and home.

"That makes three confirmed kills total, Stepanova. Two more, and you'll be an ace."

Raisa was grinning so hard, she squinted. "We could hardly miss, with so many targets to pick from," she said. Inna rolled her eyes a little, but was also beaming. She'd bagged her first kill, and though she was doing a very good job of trying to act humble and dignified *now*, right after they'd landed and parked she'd run screaming up to Raisa and knocked her over with a big hug. Lots of dead Germans and they'd both walked away from the battle. They couldn't have been much more successful than that.

Commander Gridnev, a serious young man with a face like a bear, was reviewing a typed piece of paper at his desk in the largest dugout at the

101st Division's airfield. "The squadron's target was a rail station. A battalion of infantry was there, waiting for transport. They'd have been killed. You saved a lot of lives."

Even better. Tremendous. Maybe Davidya had been there and she'd saved him. She could brag about it in her next letter.

"Thank you, sir."

"Good work, girls. Dismissed."

Out of the commander's office, they ran back home, stumbling in their oversized men's flight suits and jackets and laughing.

A dozen women shared the dugout, which if you squinted in dim light seemed almost homelike, with wrought iron cots, wool bedding, whitewashed walls, and wooden tables with a few vases of wildflowers someone had picked for decorations. The things always wilted quickly—no sunlight reached inside. After a year of this—moving from base to base, from better conditions to worse and back again—they'd gotten used to the bugs and rats and rattling of distant bombing. You learned to pay attention to and enjoy the wilted wildflowers, or you went mad.

Though that happened sometimes, too.

The second best thing about being a pilot (the first being the flying itself) was the better housing and rations. And the vodka allotment for flying combat missions. Inna and Raisa pulled chairs up close to the stove to drive away the last of the chill from flying at altitude and tapped their glasses together in a toast.

"To victory," Inna said, because it was tradition and brought luck.

"To flying," Raisa said, because she meant it.

At dinner—runny stew and stale bread cooked over the stove—Raisa awaited the praise of her comrades and was ready to bask in their admiration—two more kills and she'd be an ace; who was a better fighter pilot, or a better shot, than she? But it didn't happen quite like that.

Katya and Tamara stumbled through the doorway, almost crashing into the table and tipping over the vase of flowers. They were flushed, gasping for breath as if they'd been running.

"You'll never guess what's happened!" Katya said.

Tamara talked over her: "We've just come from the radio operator; he told us the news!"

Raisa's eyes went round and she almost dropped the plate of bread she was holding. "We've pushed them back? They're retreating?"

"No, not that," Katya said, indignant, as if wondering how anyone could be so stupid.

"Liliia scored two kills today!" Tamara said. "She's got five now. She's an ace!"

Liliia Litviak. Beautiful, wonderful Liliia, who could do no wrong. Raisa remembered their first day with the battalion, and Liliia showed up, this tiny woman with the perfect face and bleached blond hair. After weeks of living in the dugouts, she still had a perfect face and bleached blond hair, looking like some American film star. She was so small, they thought she couldn't possibly pilot a Yak, she couldn't possibly serve on the front. Then she got in her plane and she *flew*. Better than any of them. Even Raisa had to admit that, but not out loud.

Liliia painted *flowers* on the nose of her fighter, and instead of making fun of her, everyone thought she was so *sweet*.

And now she was a fighter ace. Raisa stared. "Five kills. Really?"

"Indisputable! She had witnesses; the news is going out everywhere. Isn't it wonderful?"

It was wonderful, and Raisa did her best to act like it, smiling and raising a toast to Liliia and cursing the Fascists. They ate dinner and wondered when the weather would change, if winter had a last gasp of frigid cold for them or if they were well into the merely chilly damp of spring. No one talked about when, if ever, the war might be done. Two years now since the Germans invaded. They'd not gotten any farther in the last few months, and the Soviets had made progress—recapturing Voronezh for one, and moving forward operations there. That was something.

But Inna knew her too well to let her go. "You were frowning all the way through dinner," she said, when they were washing up outside, in darkness, before bed. "You didn't hide it very well."

Raisa sighed. "If I'd been sent to Stalingrad, I'd have just as many kills as she does. I'd have more. I'd have been an ace months ago."

"If you'd been sent to Stalingrad, you'd be dead," Inna said. "I'd rather have you here and alive."

Frowning, she bit off her words. "We're all dead. All of us on the front, we're all here to die; it's just a matter of when."

Inna wore a knit cap over her short hair, which curled up over the edges.

This, along with the freckles dotting her cheeks, made her look elfin. Her eyes were dark, her lips in a grim line. She was always solemn, serious. Always telling Raisa when her jokes had gone too far. Inna would never say a bad word about anyone.

"It'll be over soon," she said to Raisa under the overcast sky, not even a dim lantern to break the darkness, lest German reconnaissance flights find them. "It has to be over soon. With the Brits and Americans pounding on the one side and us on the other, Germany can't last for long."

Raisa nodded. "You're right, of course you're right. We just have to hold on as long as we can."

"Yes. That's exactly right."

Inna squeezed her arm, then turned back to the dugout and a cot with too-thin blankets and the skittering of rats. Sometimes Raisa looked around at the dirt and the worn boots, the tired faces and the lack of food, and believed she'd be living like this for the rest of her life.

Raisa arrived at the command dugout for a briefing—a combat mission, she hoped, and a chance for her next two kills—but one of the radio operators pulled her aside before she could go in.

She and Pavel often traded information. She'd give him the gossip from the flight line, and he'd pass on any news he'd heard from other regiments. He had the most reliable information from the front. More reliable than what they could get from command, even, because the official reports that trickled down were filtered, massaged, and manipulated until they said exactly what the higher-ups wanted people like her to know. Entire battalions had been wiped out and no one knew because the generals didn't want to damage morale, or some such nonsense.

Today Pavel seemed pale, and his frown was somber.

"What is it?" she asked, staring, because he could only have bad news. Very bad, to come seek her out. She thought of David, of course. It had to be about David.

"Raisa Ivanovna," he said. "I have news . . . about your brother."

Her head went light, as if she were flying a barrel roll, the world going upside down around her. But she stood firm, didn't waver, determined to get through the next few moments with her dignity intact. She could do this, for her brother's sake. Even though *she* was supposed to die first. The danger she faced in the air, flying these death traps against Messerschmitts, was so much greater. She'd always felt so sure that *she* would die, that David would have to be the one to stand firm while he heard the news.

"Tell me," she said, and her voice didn't waver.

"His squadron saw action. He . . . he's missing in action."

She blinked. Not the words she was expecting. But this . . . the phrase hardly made sense. How did a soldier just *disappear*, she wanted to demand. David wasn't like an earring or a slip of paper that one wandered the house searching for. She felt her face turn furrowed, quizzical, looking at Pavel for an explanation.

"Raisa—are you all right?" he said.

"Missing?" she repeated. The information and what it meant began to penetrate.

"Yes," the radio operator answered, his tone turning to despair.

"But that's . . . I don't even know what to say."

"I'm so sorry, Raisa. I won't tell Gridnev. I won't tell anyone until official word comes down. Maybe your brother will turn up before then and it won't mean anything."

Pavel's hangdog look of pity was almost too much to take. When she didn't reply, he walked away, trudging through the mud.

She knew what he was thinking, what everyone would think, and what would happen next. No one would say it out loud—they didn't dare—but she knew. Missing in action; how much better for everyone if he had simply died.

Comrade Stalin had given the order soon after the war began: "We have no prisoners of war, only traitors of the motherland." Prisoners were collaborators, because if they had been true patriots they would have died rather than be taken. Likewise, soldiers missing in action were presumed to have deserted. If David did not somehow reappear in the Soviet army, he would be declared a traitor, and his family would suffer. Their parents and younger sister would get no rations or aid. Raisa herself would most likely be barred from flying at the very least. They'd all suffer, even though David was probably lying dead at the bottom of a bog somewhere.

She pinched her nose to hold the tears back and went into the dugout for whatever briefing the commander had for the flight. She mustn't let on that anything was wrong. But she had a hard time listening that morning.

David wasn't a traitor, but no matter how much she screamed that truth from the mountaintops, it didn't matter. Unless he appeared—or a body were found, proving that he'd been killed in action—he'd be a traitor forever.

Terrible, to wish a body would be found.

She had a sudden urge to take up a gun—in her own two hands, even, and not in the cockpit of her plane—and murder someone. Stalin, perhaps.

If anyone here could read her mind, hear her thoughts, she'd be barred from flying, sent to a work camp, if not executed outright. Then her parents and sister would be even worse off, with *two* traitors in the family. So, she should not think ill of Stalin. She should channel her anger toward the real enemy, the ones who'd really killed David. If he were dead. Perhaps he wasn't dead, only missing, like the report said.

Inna sat beside her and took her arm. "Raisa, what's wrong? You look like you're going to explode."

"It's nothing," Raisa answered in a whisper.

She kept writing letters to David as if nothing had happened. The writing calmed her.

> *Dear Davidya:*
>
> *Did I mention I have three kills now? Three. How many Germans have you killed? Don't answer that, I know you'll tell me, and it'll be more, and I know it's harder for you because you have to face them with nothing but bullets and bayonets, while I have my beautiful Yak to help me. But still, I feel like I'm doing some good. I'm saving the lives of your fellow infantry. Inna and I stopped a whole squadron from completing its bombing run, and that's something to be proud of.*
>
> *I'm so worried about you, Davidya. I try not to be, but it's hard.*
>
> *Two more kills and I'll be an ace. Not the first woman ace, though. That's Liliia Litviak. Amazing Liliia, who fought at Stalingrad. I don't begrudge her that at all. She's a very good pilot, I've seen her fly. I won't even claim to be better. But I'm just as good, I know I am. By the way, you should know that if you see a picture of Litviak in the papers (I hear the papers are making much of her, so that she can inspire the troops or some such thing) that Inna is much*

prettier. Hard to believe, I know, but true. After my next two kills, I wonder if they'll put my picture in the paper? You could tell every-one you know me. If you're not too embarrassed by your mouse-faced little sister.

    I've gotten a letter from Mama, and I'm worried because she says Da is sick again. I thought he was better, but he's sick all the time, isn't he? And there isn't enough food. He's probably giving all his to Nina. It's what I would do. I'm afraid Mama isn't telling me everything, because she's worried that I can't take it. You'd tell me, wouldn't you?

    You'd think I had enough to worry about, that I wouldn't worry about home, too. They can take care of themselves. As I can take care of myself, so do not worry about me. We have food, and I get plenty of sleep. Well, I get some *sleep. I hear the bombing sometimes, and it's hard to think they won't be here next. But never mind.*

    Until I see you again, Raisa

Like dozens of other girls, Raisa had written a letter to the famous pilot Marina Raskova asking her how she could fly for the war. Comrade Raskova had written back: I am organizing a battalion for women. Come. Of course Raisa did.

Da had been angry: he wanted her to stay home and work in a factory—good, proud, noble work that would support the war effort just as much as flying a Yak would. But her mother had looked at him and quietly spoken: Let her have her wings while she can. Da couldn't argue with that. Her older brother, David, made her promise to write him every day, or at least every week, so he could keep an eye on her. She did.

Raisa was assigned to the fighter regiment, and for the first time met other girls like herself who'd joined a local flying club, who had to fight for the privilege of learning to fly. At her club, Raisa had been the only girl. The boys didn't take her seriously at first, laughed when she showed up wanting to take the classes to get her license. But she kept showing up to every session, every meeting, and every class. They had to let her join. Truth to tell, they didn't take her seriously even after she soloed and scored better on her navigation test than any of the boys. She never said it out loud, but what made Raisa particularly angry was the hypocrisy of it all. The great Soviet experiment with its noble egalitarian principles that was meant to bring equality to all, even between men and women, and here the boys were, telling her she should go home, work in a factory with other women, get married, and have babies, because that was what women were supposed to do. They weren't meant to fly. They *couldn't* fly. She had to prove them wrong over and over again.

Thank goodness for Marina Raskova, who proved so much for all of them. When she died—a stupid crash in bad weather, from what Raisa heard—the women pilots were afraid they'd be disbanded and sent to factories, building the planes they ought to be flying. Raskova and her connections to the very highest levels—to Stalin himself—were the only things keeping the women flying at the front. But it seemed the women had proven themselves, and they weren't disbanded. They kept flying, and fighting. Raisa pinned a picture of Raskova from a newspaper to the wall of their dugout. Most of the women paused by it now and then, offering it a smile, or sometimes a frown of quiet grief. More dead pilots had lined up behind her since.

"I want a combat mission, not scut work," Raisa told Gridnev. Didn't salute, didn't say "sir." They were all equal Soviet citizens, weren't they?

He'd handed her flight its next mission outside the dugout, in a blustery spring wind that Raisa hardly noticed. They were supposed to report to their planes immediately, but she held back to argue. Inna hovered a few yards away, nervous and worried.

"Stepanova. I need pilots for escort duty. You're it."

"The flight plan takes us a hundred miles away from the front lines. Your VIP doesn't need escorting, he needs babysitting!"

"Then you'll do the babysitting."

"Commander, I just need those next two kills—"

"You need to serve the homeland in whatever fashion the homeland sees fit."

"But—"

"This isn't about you. I need escort pilots; you're a pilot. Now go."

Gridnev walked away before she did. She looked after him, fuming, wanting to shout. She wouldn't get to kill anything flying as an *escort*.

She marched to the flight line.

Inna ran after her. "Raisa, what's gotten into you?"

Her partner had asked that every hour for the last day, it seemed like. Raisa couldn't hide. And if she couldn't trust Inna, she couldn't trust anyone.

"David's missing in action," Raisa said, and kept walking.

She opened her mouth, properly shocked and pitying, as Pavel had done. "Oh—oh no. I'm so sorry."

"It's nothing. But I have to work twice as hard, right?"

They continued to their planes in silence.

Raisa's hands itched. They lay lightly on the stick, and she didn't have to do much to keep steady. The air was calm, and they—Inna, Katya, and Tamara were in the other fighters—were flying in a straight line, practically. But she wanted to shoot something. They weren't told who it was in the Li-2 they guarded, not that it would have mattered. But she imagined it might be Stalin himself. She wondered if she'd have the courage to radio to him, "Comrade, let me tell you about my brother . . ." But the higher-ups wouldn't tap a flight of women pilots from the front to protect the premier. It wasn't him.

Not that their VIP needing guarding. Out here, the most dangerous thing she faced was the other pilots slipping out of formation and crashing into her. *That* would be embarrassing.

Just before they'd left, the radio operator had brought news that Liliia had scored another kill. *Six* confirmed kills. The Germans seemed to be lining up for the privilege of being shot down by beautiful Liliia. And here Raisa was, miles and miles from battle, playing at guarding.

If she died in battle, heroically, with lots of witnesses, leaving behind an indisputable body, perhaps she might help recover David's reputation. If she were a hero—an ace, even—he could not be a traitor, right?

She stretched her legs and scratched her hair under her leather helmet. Another couple of hours and they'd land and get a hot meal. That was one consolation—they were flying their charge to a real base with real food, and they'd been promised a meal before they had to fly back to Voronezh. Raisa wondered if they'd be able to wrap some up to stuff in their pockets and take back with them.

Scanning the sky around her, out to the horizon, she didn't see so much as a goose in flight. The other planes—the bullet-shaped Yaks and the big Lisunov with its two wing-mounted engines and stocky frame—hummed around her, in a formation that was rather stately. It always amazed her, these great beasts of steel and grease soaring through the air, in impossible defiance of gravity. The world spread out below her, wide plains splotched in beige and green, trimmed by forests, cut through with the winding path of a creek. She could believe that nothing existed down there—a clean, new land, and she was queen of everything she could see, for hundreds and hundreds of miles. She sailed over it without effort. Then she'd spot a farm, rows of square fields that should have been green with the new growth of crops but instead held blackened craters and scraps of destroyed tanks.

If she focused on the sound of the engine, a comforting rattle that flowed through the skin of the fuselage around her, she wouldn't think so much about the rest of it. If she tipped her head back, she could watch blue sky passing overhead and squint into the sun. The day was beautiful, and she had an urge to open her canopy and drink in the sky. The freezing wind would thrash her at this altitude, so she resisted. The cockpit was warm and safe as an egg.

Something outside caught her eye. Far off, across the flat plain they soared over, to where sky met earth. Dark specks moving against the blue. They were unnatural—they flew too straight, too smoothly to be birds. They seemed far away, which meant they had to be big—hard to tell, without a point of reference. But several of them flew together in the unmistakable shape of airplanes in formation.

She turned on the radio channel. "Stepanova here. Ten o'clock, toward the horizon, do you see it?"

Inna answered. "Yes. Are those bombers?"

They were, Raisa thought. They had a heavy look about them, droning steadily on rather than racing. The formation was coming closer, but still not close enough to see if they had crosses or stars painted on them.

"Theirs or ours?" Katya said.

"I'll find out," Raisa said, banking out of formation and opening the throttle. She'd take a look, and if she saw that black cross, she'd fire.

A male voice intruded, the pilot of the Li-2. "Osipov here. Get back here, Stepanova!"

"But—"

"Return to formation!"

The planes were *right there,* it would just take a *second* to check—

Inna came on the channel, pleading, "Raisa, you can't take them on your own!"

She could certainly try. . . .

Osipov said, "A squadron has been notified and will intercept the unknown flight. We're to continue on."

They couldn't stop her . . . but they could charge her with disobeying orders once she landed, and that wouldn't help anyone. So she circled around and returned to formation. Litviak was probably getting to shoot someone today. Raisa frowned at her washed-out reflection in the canopy glass.

> *Dear Davidya:*
>
> *I promised to write you every day, so I continue to do so.*
>
> *How are you this time? I hope you're well. Not sick, not hungry. We've taken to talking about eating the rats that swarm the dugouts here, but we haven't gotten to the point of actually trying it. Mostly because I think it would be far too much work for too little reward. The horrid beasts are as skinny as the rest of us. I'm not complaining, though. We've gotten some crates of canned goods—fruits, meat, milk—from an American supply drop and are savoring the windfall. It's like a taste of what we're fighting for, and what we can look forward to when this mess is all over. It was Inna who said that. Beautiful thought, yes? She keeps the whole battalion in good spirits all by herself.*
>
> *I ought to warn you, I've written a letter to be sent to you in case I die. It's quite grotesque, and now you'll be terrified that every letter you get from me will be that one. Have you done that, written me a letter that I'll only read if you die? I haven't gotten one, which gives me hope.*
>
> *I'm very grateful Nina isn't old enough to be on the front with us, or I'd be writing double the grotesque letters. I got a letter from her talking about what she'll do when she's old enough to come to the front, and she wants to fly like me and if she can't be a pilot she'll be a mechanic—my mechanic, even. She was very excited. I wrote her*

*back the same day telling her the war will be over before she's old
enough. I hope I'm right.*

Love and kisses, Raisa

Another week passed with no news of David. Most likely he was dead. Officially, he had deserted, and Raisa supposed she had to consider that he actually had, except that that made no sense. Where would he go? Or maybe he was simply lost and hadn't made his way back to his regiment yet. She wanted to believe that.

Gridnev called her to the operations dugout, and she presented herself at his desk. A man, a stranger in a starched army uniform, stood with him.

The air commander was grim and stone-faced as he announced, "Stepanova, this is Captain Sofin." Then Gridnev left the room.

Raisa knew what was coming. Sofin put a file folder on the desk and sat behind it. He didn't invite her to sit.

She wasn't nervous, speaking to him. But she had to tamp down on a slow, tight anger.

"Your brother is David Ivanovich Stepanov?"

"Yes."

"Are you aware that he has been declared missing in action?"

She shouldn't have known, officially, but it was no good hiding it. "Yes, I am."

"Do you have any information regarding his whereabouts?"

Don't you have a war you ought to be fighting? she thought. "I assume he was killed. So many are, after all."

"You have received no communication from him?"

And what if he found all those letters she'd been writing *him* and thought them real? "None at all."

"I must tell you that if you receive any news of him at all, it's your duty to inform command."

"Yes, sir."

"We will be watching closely, Raisa Stepanova."

She wanted to leap across the table in the operations dugout and strangle the little man with the thin moustache. Barring that, she wanted to cry, but didn't. Her brother was dead, and they'd convicted him without evidence or trial.

What was she fighting for, again? Nina and her parents, and even Davidya. Certainly not this man.

He dismissed her without ever raising his gaze from the file folder he studied, and she left the dugout.

Gridnev stood right outside the door, lurking like a schoolboy, though a serious one who worried too much. No doubt he had heard everything. She wilted, blushing, face to the ground, like a kicked dog.

"You have a place here at the 586th, Stepanova. You always will."

She smiled a thanks but didn't trust her voice to say anything. Like observing that Gridnev would have little to say in the matter, in the end.

No, she had to earn her innocence. If she gathered enough kills, if she became an ace, they couldn't touch her, any more than they could tarnish the reputation of Liliia Litviak. If she became enough of a hero, she could even redeem David.

Winter ended, but that only meant the insects came out in force, mosquitoes and biting flies that left them all miserable and snappish. Rumors abounded that the Allied forces in Britain and America were planning a massive invasion, that the Germans had a secret weapon they'd use to level Moscow and London. Living in a camp on the front, news was scarce. They got orders, not news, and could only follow those orders.

It made her tired.

"Stepanova, you all right?"

She'd parked her plane after flying a patrol, tracing a route along the front, searching for imminent attacks and troops on the move—perfectly routine, no Germans spotted. The motor had grumbled to stillness and the propeller had stopped turning long ago, but she remained in her cockpit, just sitting. The thought of pulling herself, her bulky gear, her parachute, logbook, helmet, all the rest of it, out of the cockpit and onto the wing left her feeling exhausted. She'd done this for months, and now, finally, she wasn't sure she had anything left. She couldn't read any numbers on the dials, no matter how much she blinked at the instrument panel.

"Stepanova!" Martya, her mechanic, called to her again, and Raisa shook herself awake.

"Yes, I'm fine, I'm coming." She slid open the canopy, gathered her things, and hauled herself over the edge.

Martya was waiting for her on the wing in shirt and overalls, sleeves rolled up, kerchief over her head. She couldn't have been more than twenty, but her hands were rough from years of working on engines.

"You look terrible," Martya said.

"Nothing a shot of vodka and a month in a feather bed won't fix," Raisa said, and the mechanic laughed.

"How's your fuel?"

"Low. You think she's burning more than she should?"

"Wouldn't surprise me. She's been working hard. I'll look her over."

"You're the best, Martya." The mechanic gave her a hand off the wing, and Raisa pulled her into a hug.

Martya said, "Are you sure you're all right?" Raisa didn't answer.

"Raisa!" That was Inna, walking over from her own plane, dragging her parachute with one arm, her helmet tucked under her other. "You all right?"

She wished people would stop asking that.

"Tired, I think," Martya answered for her. "You know what we need? A party or a dance or something. There are enough handsome boys around here to flirt with." She was right: the base was filled with male pilots, mechanics, and soldiers, and they were all dashing and handsome. The odds were certainly in the women's favor. Raisa hadn't really thought of it before.

Inna sighed. "Hard to think of flirting when you're getting bombed and shot at."

Martya leaned on the wing and looked wistful. "After the war, we'll be able to get dressed up. Wash our hair with real soap and go dancing."

"After the war. Yes," Inna said.

"After we *win* the war," Raisa said. "We won't be dancing much if the Fascists win."

They went quiet, and Raisa regretted saying anything. It was the unspoken assumption when people talked about "after the war": of course they'd win. If they lost, there wouldn't be an "after" at all.

Not that Raisa expected to make it that far.

Davidya:

I've decided that I'd give up being a fighter ace if it meant we could both get through the war alive. Don't tell anyone I said that;

I'd lose my reputation for being fierce, and for being hideously jealous of Liliia Litviak. If there's a God, maybe he'll hear me, and you'll come walking out of the wilderness, alive and well. Not dead and not a traitor. We'll go home, and Mama and Da and Nina will be well, and we can forget that any of this ever happened. That's my dream now.

I've still got that letter, the hideous one I wrote for you in case I die. I ought to burn it, since Inna doesn't have anyone to send it to now.

Your sister, Raisa

An alarm came at dawn.

By reflex, she tumbled out of her cot, into trousers and shirt, coat and boots, grabbing gloves and helmet on the way out of the dugout. Inna was at her side, running toward the airstrip. Planes were already rumbling overhead—scouts returning from patrol.

Mechanics and armorers were at the planes—all of them. Refueling, running chains of ammunition into cannon and machine guns. This was big. Not just a sortie, but a battle.

There was Commander Gridnev addressing them right on the field. The mission: German heavy bombers had crossed the front. Fighters were being scrambled to intercept. He'd be flying this one himself, leading the first squadron. First squadron launched in ten minutes and would engage any fighters sent with the attack. Second squadron—the women's squadron—would launch in fifteen and stop the bombers.

The air filled with Yak fighters, the drone of their engines like the buzz of bees made large.

No time to think, only to do, as they'd done hundreds of times before. Martya helped Raisa into her cockpit, slapped the canopy twice after closing it over her, then jumped off the wing to yank the chocks out from under the tires. A dozen Yaks lined up, taxiing from the flight line to wait their turn on the runway. One after another after another . . .

Finally, Raisa's turn came, and she was airborne. It was a relief, being in the air again, where she could *do* something. Up here, when someone attacked, she could dodge. Not like being on the ground when the bombs fell. She'd rather have a stick in her hand, a trigger under her finger. It felt *right*.

Glancing back through the canopy, Raisa found Inna on her wing, right where she should be. Her friend gave her a broad salute, and Raisa waved back. Once the squadron was airborne, they settled into an echelon formation, following Gridnev's squadron up ahead. They'd all flown with Gridnev's men; they'd all had months to get used to each other. Men or women, didn't make a difference, and most men realized that sooner or later. Which was something of a revelation if she stopped to think about it. But no one had time to stop and think about it. All she needed to know was that Aleksei Borisov liked diving to the left and would loop above if he got into trouble; Sofia Mironova was a careful pilot and tended to hang back; Valentina Gushina was fast, very good in combat; Fedor Baurin had the keenest eyesight. He'd spot their target before anyone else.

The Yaks flew on in loose formation, ready to break and engage as soon as the target was sighted. Raisa scanned the skies in all directions, peering above and over her shoulders. The commander had the coordinates; he'd estimated twenty minutes until contact. They should be in sight of them any minute now. . . .

"There!" Baurin called over the radio. "One o'clock!"

Gridnev came on the channel. "Steady. Remain in formation."

She saw the enemy, sunlight flashing off canopies, airplanes suspended in the air. Hard to judge scale and distance; her own group was traveling fast enough that the enemy planes seemed to be standing still. But they were approaching, rapidly and inexorably.

While the heavy bombers continued on, straight and level, a handful of smaller planes broke off from the main group—a squadron of fighters as escort.

Well, this was going to be interesting.

On the commander's orders, they spread out and prepared to engage. Raisa opened the throttle and sped ahead, planning to overshoot the fighters entirely: Their goal was preventing those bombers from reaching their target. Her Yak dipped down, yawed to the left, roared onward.

A flight of Messerschmitts rocketed overhead. Gunfire sounded. Then they were gone.

Inna had followed her, and the bombers lay ahead of them, waiting. They had a short time to be as disruptive as they could before those Messers came back around, no matter how much the others were able to keep them occupied.

As soon as she was within range, she opened fire. The rattle from the cannon shook her fuselage. Nearby, another cannon fired; Raisa traced the smoke of the shells from behind her toward the Junkers: Inna had fired as well.

The bombers dropped back. And the fighters caught up with her and Inna. Then chaos.

She watched for stars and crosses painted on the fuselages, marking friend or foe. They chased each other in three dimensions, until it was impossible to track them all, and she began to focus on avoiding collision. The Messers were torpedo shaped, sleek and nimble. Formidable. Both sets of pilots had had two years of war to gain experience. The fight would end only when one side or the other ran out of ammunition.

They had to bring down those bombers, if nothing else.

The others had the same idea, and the commander ordered them to their primary target, until the bombers scattered, just to get out of the way of the dogfights. Now the Messers had to worry about hitting their charges by accident. That made them more careful; it might give the Yaks an edge.

The grumble of engines, of props beating the air, filled the sky around her. She'd never seen so many planes in the air at once, not even in her early days of training at the club.

She looped around to the outside and found a target. The pilot of the fighter had targeted a Yak—Katya's, she thought—and was so focused on catching her that he was flying straight and steady. First and worst mistake. She found him in her sights and held there a second, enough to get shots off before tipping and diving out of the way before someone else targeted her.

Her shells sliced across the cockpit—right through the pilot. The canopy shattered, and there was blood. She thought she saw his face, under goggles and flight cap, just for a moment—a look of shock, then nothing. Out of control now, the Me-109 tipped nose down and fell into a spiraling descent. The sight, black smoke trailing, the plane falling, was compelling. But her own trajectory carried her past in an instant, showing blue sky ahead.

"Four!" Raisa gave a shout. Four kills. And surely with all these targets around she could get her fifth. Both of them for David.

Other planes were falling from the sky. One of the bombers had been hit and still flew, with one engine pouring billows of smoke. Another fighter sputtered, fell back, then dropped, trailing fire and debris— Aleksei, that was Aleksei. Could he win back control of his injured plane? If not, did he have time to bail out? She saw no life in the cockpit; it was all moot. Rather than mourn, she set her jaw and found another target. So many of them, she hardly knew where to look first.

Over the radio, Gridnev was ordering a retreat. They'd done damage; time to get out while they could. But surely they'd only been engaged a few minutes. The motor of her Yak seemed tired; the spinning props in front of her seemed to sputter.

A Messerschmitt came out of the sun overhead like a dragon.

A rain of bullets struck the fuselage of her Yak, sounding like hail. Pain stabbed through her thigh, but that was less worrisome than the bang and grind screeching from the engine. And black smoke suddenly pouring from the nose in a thick stream. The engine coughed; the propeller stopped turning. Suddenly her beautiful streamlined Yak was a dead rock waiting to fall.

She held the nose up by brute force, choked the throttle again and again, but the engine was dead. She pumped the pedals, but the rudder was stuck. The nose tipped forward, ruining any chance she had of gliding toward earth.

"Raisa, get out! Get out!" Inna screamed over the radio.

Abandoning her post, no, never. Better to die in a ball of fire than go missing.

The nose tipped further forward, her left wing tipped up—the start of a dive and spin. Now or never. Dammit.

Her whole right leg throbbed with pain, and there was blood on her sleeve, blood spattered on the inside of the canopy, and she didn't know where it had come from. Maybe from that pilot whose face she'd seen, the one looking back at her with dead eyes behind his goggles. Instinct and training won over. Reaching up, she slammed open the canopy. Wind struck her like a fist. She unbuckled her harness, worked herself out of her seat; her leg didn't want to move. She didn't jump so much as let the Yak fall away from her, and she was floating. No—she was falling. She pulled the rip cord, and the parachute billowed above her, a cream-colored flower spreading its petals. It caught air and jerked her to a halt. She hung in the harness like so much deadweight. Deadweight, ha.

Her plane was on fire now, a flaming comet spinning to earth, trailing a corkscrew length of black smoke. Her poor plane. She wanted to weep, and she hadn't wept at all, this whole war, despite everything.

The battle had moved on. She's lost sight of Inna's plane but heard gunfire in the tangle of explosions and engine growls. Inna had covered her escape, protecting her from being shot in midair. Not that that would have been a tragedy—she'd die in combat, at least. Now she didn't know which side of the line the barren field below her was on. Who would find her, Russians or Nazis? *No prisoners of war, only traitors. . . .*

The worst part was not being able to do anything about it. Blood dripped from her leg and spattered in the wind. She'd been shot. The dizziness that struck her could have been the shock of realization or blood loss. She might not even reach the ground. Would her body ever be found?

The sky had suddenly gotten very quiet, and the fighters and bombers swarmed like crows in the distance. She squinted, trying to see them better.

Then Raisa blacked out.

Much later, opening her eyes, Raisa saw a low ceiling striped with rows of wooden roof beams. She was in a cot, part of a row of cots, in what must have been a makeshift field hospital bustling with people going back and forth, crossing rows and aisles on obviously important business. They were speaking Russian, and relief rushed through her. She'd been found. She was home.

She couldn't move, and decided she didn't much want to. Lying mindlessly on the cot and blankets, some distance from the pain she was sure she ought to be feeling, seemed the best way to exist, for at least the next few minutes.

"Raisa! You're awake!"

A chair scooted close on a concrete floor, and a familiar face came into view: David. Clean-shaven, dark hair trimmed, infantry uniform pressed and buttoned, as if he was going to a parade and not visiting his sister in hospital. Just as he was in the formal picture he'd sent home right after he signed up. This must be a dream. Maybe this wasn't a hospital. Maybe it was heaven. She wasn't sure she'd been good enough.

"Raisa, say something, please," he said, and with his face all pinched up he looked too worried to be in heaven.

"Davidya!" She needed to draw two breaths to get the word out, and her voice scratched surprisingly. She licked dry lips. "You're alive! What happened?"

He gave a sheepish shrug. "My squad got lost. We engaged a Panzer unit in the middle of the forest, and a sudden spring snowstorm pinned us down. Half of us got frostbite and had to drag the other half out. It took weeks, but we made it."

All this time . . . he really was just lost. She wished Sofin were here so she could punch him in the face.

"I'd laugh at all the trouble you caused, but my chest hurts," she said.

His smile slipped, and she imagined he'd had an interview with someone very much like Sofin after he and his squad limped back home. She wouldn't tell him about her own interview, and she would burn those letters she'd written him as soon as she got back to the airfield.

"It's so good to see you, Raisa." He clasped her hand, the one that wasn't bandaged, and she squeezed as hard as she could, which wasn't very, but it was enough. "Your Commander Gridnev got word to me that you'd been hurt, and I was able to take a day to come see you."

She swallowed and the words came slowly. "I was shot. I had to bail out. I don't know what happened next."

"Your wingman was able to radio your location. Ground forces moved in and found you. They tell me you were a mess."

"But I got my fourth kill, did they tell you that? One more and I'll be an ace." Maybe not the first woman fighter ace, or even the second. But she'd be one.

David didn't smile. She felt him draw away, as the pressure on her hand let up.

She frowned. "What?"

He didn't want to say. His face had scrunched up, his eyes glistening— as if *he* was about to start crying. And here she was, the girl, and she hadn't cried once. Well, almost once, for her plane.

"Raisa, you're being medically discharged," he said.

"What? No. I'm okay, I'll be okay—"

"Both your legs are broken, half your ribs are cracked, you've dislocated your shoulder, you have a concussion and been shot twice. You can't go back. Not for a long time, at least."

She really hadn't thought she'd been so badly hurt. Surely she'd have known if it was that bad. But her body still felt so far away. . . . She didn't know anything. "I'll get better—"

"Please, Raisa. Rest. Just rest for now."

One more kill, she only needed one more. . . . "Davidya, if I can't fly, what will I do?"

"Raisa!" A clear voice called from the end of the row of cots.

"Inna," Raisa answered, as loud as her voice would let her.

Her wingman rushed forward, and when she couldn't find a chair, she knelt by the cot. "Raisa. Oh, Raisa, look at you, wrapped up like a mummy." She fussed with the blankets, smoothed a lock of hair peeking out from the bandage around Raisa's head, and then fussed with the blankets some more. Good, sweet Inna.

"Inna, this is my brother, David."

Her eyes widened in shock, but Raisa didn't get a chance to explain that, yes, "missing" sometimes really meant missing, because David had stood in a rush and offered his chair to Inna, but she shook her head, which left them both standing on opposite sides of the cot, looking at each other across Raisa. Belatedly, Inna held out her hand. David wiped his on his trouser leg before shaking hers. What a David thing to do.

"Raisa's told me so much about you," Inna said.

"And she's told me about you in her letters."

Inna blushed. Good. Maybe something good would come out of all this.

She ought to be happy. She'd gotten her wish, after all.

Raisa stood on the platform, waiting for the train that would take her away from Voronezh. Her arm was still in a sling, and she leaned heavily on a cane. She couldn't lift her own bags.

Raisa had argued with the military about the discharge. They should have known she wouldn't give in—they didn't understand what she'd had to go through to get into the cockpit in the first place. That was the trick: she kept writing letters, kept showing up, over and over, and they couldn't tell her no. In a fit of fancy, she wondered if that was what had brought David home: She'd never stopped writing him letters, so he had to come home.

When they finally offered her a compromise—to teach navigation at a training field near Moscow—she took it. It meant that even with the cane and sling, even if she couldn't walk right or carry her own gear, she still wore her uniform, with all its medals and ribbons. She still held her chin up.

But in the end, even she had to admit she wouldn't fly again—at least, not in combat.

"Are you sure you'll be all right?" Inna had come with her to the station to see her off. David had returned to his regiment, but she'd overheard the two of them exchanging promises to write.

"I'm fine, really."

Inna's eyes shone as if she might cry. "You've gone so quiet. I'm so used to seeing you run around like an angry chicken."

Raisa smiled at the image. "You'll write?"

"Of course. Often. I'll keep you up to date on all the gossip."

"Yes, I want to know exactly how many planes Liliia Litviak shoots down."

"She'll win the war all by herself."

No, in a few months Raisa would read in the newspaper that Liliia was declared missing in action, shot down over enemy territory, her plane and body unrecovered. First woman fighter ace in history, and she'd be declared a deserter instead of a hero. But they didn't know that now.

The train's whistle keened, still some distance away, but they could hear it approach, clacking along its tracks.

"Are you *sure* you'll be okay?" Inna asked, with something like pleading in her eyes.

Raisa had been staring off into space, something she'd been doing a lot of lately. Wind played with her dark hair, and she looked out across the field and the ruins of the town to where the airfield lay. She thought she heard airplanes overhead.

She said, "I imagined dying in a terrible crash, or shot down in battle. I'd either walk away from this war or I'd die in some gloriously heroic way. I never imagined being . . . crippled. That the war would keep going on without me."

Inna touched her shoulder. "We're all glad you didn't die. Especially David."

"Yes, because he would have had to find a way to tell my parents."

She sighed. "You're so *morbid*."

The train arrived, and a porter came over to help with her luggage. "Be careful, Inna. Find yourself a good wingman to train."

"I'll miss you, my dear."

They hugged tightly but carefully, and Inna stayed to make sure Raisa limped her way onto the train and to her seat without trouble. She waved at Raisa from the platform until the train rolled out of sight.

Sitting in the train, staring out the window, Raisa caught sight of the planes she'd been looking for: a pair of Yaks streaking overhead, on their way to the airfield. But she couldn't hear their thrumming engines over the sound of the train. Probably just as well.

Nancy Kress

Nancy Kress began selling her elegant and incisive stories in the mid-seventies, and has since become a frequent contributor to *Asimov's Science Fiction, The Magazine of Fantasy & Science Fiction, Omni, Sci Fiction,* and elsewhere. Her books include the novel version of her Hugo- and Nebula-winning story, *Beggars in Spain,* and a sequel, *Beggars and Choosers,* as well as *The Prince of Morning Bells, The Golden Grove, The White Pipes, An Alien Light, Brainrose, Oaths and Miracles, Stinger, Maximum Light, Crossfire, Nothing Human, Crucible, Dogs, Steal Across the Sky,* and the Probability Trilogy, comprised of *Probability Moon, Probability Sun, and Probability Space.* Her short work has been collected in *Trinity and Other Stories, The Aliens of Earth, Beaker's Dozen,* and *Nano Comes to Clifford Falls and Other Stories.* Her most recent books are a new novel, *After the Fall, Before the Fall, During the Fall,* and two new collections, *Fountain of Age* and *Five Stories.* In addition to the awards for "Beggars in Spain," she has also won Nebula Awards for her stories "Out of All Them Bright Stars" and "The Flowers of Aulit Prison," the John W. Campbell Memorial Award in 2003 for her novel *Probability Space,* and another Hugo in 2009 for "The Erdmann Nexus." She lives in Seattle, Washington, with her husband, writer Jack Skillingstead.

Here she takes us to a ruined future America to ask the question, in a world where only basic brute survival counts, is there any room left for beauty? And would you be willing to kill for it if you found it?

SECOND ARABESQUE, VERY SLOWLY

When we came to the new place it was already night and I couldn't see anything. It wasn't like Mike to move us after dark. But our pack had taken longer than he'd expected, or longer than the scouts had said, to travel south. That was partly my fault. I can't walk as fast or long as I once could. And neither could Pretty, because that day turned out to be her Beginning.

"My belly hurts, it does," the girl moaned.

"Just a little farther," I said, hoping that was true. Hoping, too, that I wouldn't have to threaten her. Pretty turned ugly when she felt bad and whined when she didn't, although never in Mike's presence. "A little farther, and tomorrow you'll have your ceremony."

"With candy?"

"With candy."

So Pretty trudged through the dark, broken, rubble-choked streets with me and the other six girls, behind a swinging lantern. The night was cold for July. The men closest to us—although I don't call fifteen-year-olds men, even if Mike does—walked bent over with the weight of our belongings. The men on the perimeter carried weapons. The danger was partly from other packs wanting foraging territory, although there are fewer territorial firefights than when I was young. Still, we have desirable assets: seven young women, at least two of them fertile, plus three children and me. And then there are the dogs. Cities are full of wild dogs.

I could hear them, howling in the distance. As that distance grew smaller and Mike still had us stumbling along by patchy moonlight and one lantern, I left the girls in Bonnie's charge and walked double time to find Mike.

"What be you doing here?" he demanded, gaze and rifle both focused outward. "Get back to them girls!"

"It's the girls I'm concerned about. How much farther?"

"Get back there, Nurse!"

"I'm asking because Pretty is in some pain. She's at her Beginning."

That took his attention from any dangers in the darkness. "Yeah? You sure?"

"Yes," I said, although I wasn't.

Mike gave his slow, rare smile. He wasn't a bad pack leader. Huge, strong, illiterate—well, they all were, and I needed them to be—he cared about his people, and wasn't any more brutal to us than discipline required. A big improvement on Lew, our previous leader. Sometimes Mike could even lurch into moments of grace, as he did now. "She be okay?"

"Yes." Nothing that the start of her monthlies and a little candy wouldn't cure.

And then, even more surprising, "You be okay, Nurse?"

"Yes."

"How old you be now?"

"Sixty," I said, shaving off four years. I was under no illusions what Mike would do once I could no longer keep up with the pack. Already Bonnie had learned half of what I had to teach her. Not even a Nurse would be allowed to slow down the nomadic moving that meant food.

We had kept walking as we talked. Mike said, "I be first, with Pretty."

"She knows that."

He grunted, not asking her thoughts about it. If Pretty were fertile, she must be mated with a fertile male, and no one knew which of the pack men that might be. Nor did we have any idea how to find out. So Pretty, like Junie and Lula before her, would be mated with all of them in turn. Already Pretty, a natural flirt when she wasn't a natural whiner, tossed her long blond hair and flashed her shapely legs at all of them.

The dogs were closer now, and I had lost Mike's attention. I stood still, waiting for the center of the pack to reach me, and rejoined my charges.

By the time we reached our new building, the moon had vanished behind the clouds, a drizzle had started, and I could see nothing. The men led us past some large structures—the city was full of large structures, most ruined but mostly on the insides—and through a metal door. Steps downward. Cold, damp. A featureless corridor. Still, this place would be easy to defend, since it was underground and nearly windowless. The scouts had prepared the women's room, which did have a small window, to which they'd vented our propane stove. The room was warm and blanketed. Junie and Lula bedded down their children, who were already half-asleep. So were the girls. I stayed awake long enough to prepare Pretty a hot tisane—only herbs, not drugs—to ease her cramps, and then fell into sleep.

In the morning I woke first and made my way outside to pee. The guard, a gentle sixteen-year-old named Guy, nodded at me. "Morning, Nurse."

"Good morrow to you, sir," I said, and Guy grinned. He was one of the few that was interested in the learning—history, literature—I sometimes tossed out. He could even read; I was teaching him. "Where is the piss pit?"

He told me. I continued outside, blinking a little in the bright sunshine, along the side of the building and around a corner, where I stopped dead.

I knew this place. I had never been here before, but I knew it.

Three large buildings set around a vast square of now broken and weedy stone, with steps at the far end leading down to a deserted street. On the tallest building, five wide, immensely tall arches looked down on a sea of smashed glass. The other two buildings, glass fronts also smashed, bristled with balconies, with marble, with stone sculptures too large to break or carry away. Inside, still visible, were remnants of ancient, tattered carpet.

I said aloud, "This is Lincoln Center." But the perimeter guard, sitting with his rifle on the edge of what had once been a fountain, was too far away to hear. I wasn't talking to him, anyway. I was talking to my grandmother.

"My best job, Susan," she'd said to me, "was when I was on the cleaning crew at Lincoln Center."

"Tell me," I said, although I'd heard all this so many times before that I could recite it. I never tired of it.

"I was young, before I went to nursing school. We deep-cleaned the Metropolitan Opera House the last two weeks in August and the first two weeks in September, when there were no performances," she always began. "It was way before the Infertility Plague, you know."

I knew. My grandmother was very old then, older than I am now, and dying. I was twelve. Grandmother was frantically teaching me to Nurse, in case I should prove infertile, which the following year, I did. Packs not desperate for bedmates have no use for infertile women unless a girl can prove herself as a fighter. I was no fighter.

"We lowered all twenty-one electric chandeliers at the Met—think of that, Susan, *twenty-one*—and cleaned each crystal drop individually. Every other year all the red carpet was completely replaced, at a cost of $700,000. In 1990s dollars! Every five years the seats were replaced in the New York State Theater—that's what it was called then, although later they changed the name, I forget to what. Five window washers worked every day of the year, constantly keeping the windows bright. At night, when all the buildings were lit up, they shone out on the plaza like liquid gold. People laughed and talked and lined up by the hundreds to hear opera and see ballet and watch plays and listen to concerts. And such rich performances as I saw . . . you can't imagine!"

No liquid gold now. No performances, no electricity, no opera nor ballet nor plays nor concerts. Grandmother had been talking about a time gone when I was born, and I am old.

I went back inside. Pretty was awake, her huge blue eyes filled with awe at herself. "Nurse! It started—my blood! I'm at my Beginning!"

"Congratulations," I said. "We'll have your ceremony today."

"I am a woman now," she said, with pride. I looked at her round, childish, simple face; at her skinny arms and legs; at her concave belly, not even distended with fluid retention. She was thirteen, early for our girls to Begin. Kara was a year older, with no sign of her monthlies. I said gently, "Yes, Pretty. You're a woman now. You can bear the pack a child."

"You other childless," Pretty said importantly, "you have to obey me now!"

The younger girls, Seela and Tiny, scowled ferociously.

My grandmother taught me a great deal more than nursing. And I read. Books might have survived the destruction and stupid rioting when the world realized that 99 percent of its women had contracted a virus that destroyed their eggs. Most books had not, however, survived time and damp and rats and insects. But some did.

How many other people are left in the world? There is no way to tell.

Census organizations, radio and TV stations, central governments—all that vanished decades ago. Too few people left to sustain them. The world now—or at least this part of it—consists of the communities and the packs. The communities live outside the city, and they farm. I have never seen one. I was born to a pack—although not this one—my mother and grandmother captive to it. The packs prefer to be hunter-gatherers in urban environments. We hunt meat—rabbits, deer, dogs—and gather canned goods. Not exactly what happened during the Stone Age, but we manage. Every once in a while rumors come of places that have preserved more of civilization, usually small cities north and west—"Endicott," "Bath," "Ithaca"—but I have no knowledge of them.

However, it turned out that among the others that *were* left in the world was a pack based just blocks away, in an old hotel on a street called "Central Park South," and Mike was furious with his scouts. "You don't *find this out?*"

The men hung their heads.

"You put us in danger 'cause you don't find this out? I deal with you later. Now we gotta parley."

I was startled. Parley, not move? But later Guy, off duty and cleaning his guns, explained it to me. "There be a big forest here, Nurse, with lotsa game. Mike wants to stay."

So Mike left with half his pack, all heavily armed, to parley for hunt-gather rights with the other pack. Meanwhile, guarded by Guy and his friend Jemmy, Bonnie and I looked for a good place to hold Pretty's ceremony.

Bonnie, my apprentice, might or might not make a good Nurse when I can no longer keep up with the pack. Smart and strong, she already knew more than I let Mike realize. She could use our dwindling supplies of pre-plague medicines, those miracles whose making is lost to us. More important, she could find, prepare, and administer the plant drugs we relied on: bilberry for diarrhea, horsetail to stop bleeding, elderberry for fever, primrose for rashes. She could set a bone, dig out a bullet, use maggots to clean a wound.

But Bonnie had neither warmth nor that brisk reassurance that, as much as drugs, brings men to healing. Bonnie was like stone. I'd never seen her smile, seldom heard her speak except in answer to a question, never sur-prised interest or delight on her face. Big, ungainly, painfully homely, she had colorless hair and almost no chin. I think she had a bad time when she Began, which was before I was taken into this pack. Her thighs and breasts bore permanent scars. Lew might have had her shot when she was declared infertile except it was about that time he was killed in a pack war. I persuaded Mike to let Bonnie become my apprentice. That also rescued her from the sex list, since Nurses—even apprentice Nurses—were the only women who got to invite men to bed. Bonnie never did.

She said nothing as she and I, Guy and Jemmy, went into all the ruined buildings of what had been Lincoln Center. From Grandmother's descriptions I recognized them all. Above us, in the New York State Theater, broken seats once supported the asses of people watching dancers. Our housing below had probably been practice rooms. In the Metropolitan Opera House, the building with five tall arches, the caved-in stage had once held opera singers. Here, in Somebody Hall (my memory wasn't what it had been), orchestras had played music. All the musicians wore black, with the women in long and sparkly dresses. Grandmother told me. In the Vivian Beaumont Theater, off to the side of the Met, the collapsed roof sheltered actors performing plays. The small library beside the Met had been burned and was now overgrown with weeds, wildflowers, and saplings.

But it was underneath the Vivian Beaumont, below street level and behind two locked doors that Guy shot open with his rifle, that we found it. I had brought a lantern, and now I lit it, although we'd left both doors open for light. The first door led to a downward-sloping ramp of concrete, the second to another small theater, eight rows of seats in a half circle, windowless and untouched except for time and rats. No looters had taken or destroyed the seats; no rain had rotted the wooden, uncurtained stage; no wild dogs nested in the tiny rooms beyond.

Jemmy let out a whoop and swung himself up to a booth on the back wall. Probably he hoped for undestroyed machinery, and his second whoop said he'd found it. A faint glow appeared in the booth.

"Jemmy!" I shouted up. "If you waste candles like that, Mike will flog you himself!"

No answer, and the light did not go off. Guy shrugged and laughed. "You know Jemmy."

"Help me up onto that stage," I said.

He did, leaping up gracefully to stand beside me, the lantern at our feet. I looked out over the darkened seats. What must it have been like, to stand here as an actor, a musician, a dancer? To perform in front of people who watched you with delight? To control an audience?

"Such rich performances as I saw . . . you can't imagine."

Boots on the corridor, and then a voice in the darkness: "Nurse? Get your ass back to them girls! Pretty waiting!"

"Is that you, Karl?"

"Yeah."

"Don't you ever again talk to me in that tone of voice, young man, or I will tell Mike that you're disrespecting a Nurse and you will go to the bottom of the sex list, if you even stay on it at all!"

Silence, then a sullen, "Yes'm."

"In fact, you bring all the girls here. This is where we'll have Pretty's ceremony, and we'll have it now."

"Here? Now?"

"You heard me."

"Yes'm." And then: "You tell Mike I disrespected you?"

"Not if you get those girls here right away."

Karl galloped off, his boots loud on the concrete ramp. Guy grinned at me. Then he gazed out into the darkness and I saw that he had been doing just what I had: imagining himself a performer in a vanished time. All at once he grabbed me around the waist and swung me into a dance.

I was never a dancer, and I am old. I stumbled, and Guy let me go. He danced alone, as he never would have done had anybody been present except me and his trusted friend Jemmy, who probably wasn't even looking away from his precious machinery. I watched Guy move gracefully through the two-step that packs danced at the rare gatherings, and sadness washed over me that Guy could never be anything but a low-level pack soldier. He was too kind and too dreamy to ever become a leader like Mike, too male to ever be as important as a fertile girl.

Bonnie watched, wooden-faced, before she turned away.

Pretty's ceremony was lit by thirteen candles, one for each year of her age, as was customary. No men present, of course, not even the two male children, year-old Davey and eight-year-old Rick, whose mother, Emma, died last year giving birth to a stillborn girl. Nothing I did saved either one of them, and if Lew had still been pack chief, I think I would have been shot then and there.

The two mothers, Junie and Lula, sat on chairs, with Lula's baby, Jaden, on her lap. Jaden started to fuss and Lula gave her the breast. Bonnie, as my apprentice but also as an infertile female, stood behind the mothers. The girls who had not yet had their Beginnings sat to one side on the floor, their hands full of wildflowers. Seela and Tiny, ten and nine, looked interested. Kara, her own Beginning only a few months off, judging from her buds of breasts, wore an expression I could not interpret.

Pretty, now neither child nor mother, sat in the center of the circle, on a sort of throne made of a chair covered with a blanket, which in turn was spread with towels. Old, as faded as everything else we take from abandoned buildings, the towels had once been sun-yellow. Pretty's legs were spread wide, the thighs smeared with the new blood she was so proud of. One by one, the unBegun girls laid flowers between Pretty's legs.

"May you be blessed with children," said Tiny, looking excited.

"May you be blessed with children." Seela, jealousy on her thin little face.

"May you be . . . blessed with . . . children." Kara could barely get the words out. Her face creased with anguish. Her fingers trembled.

Pretty looked at her in astonishment. "What be wrong with *you*?"

Bonnie pushed forward. "Be you sick, Kara? What be your symptoms?"

"I'm not sick! Leave me alone!"

"Come here, Kara," I said in the tone that all of the girls, and most of the younger men, obeyed instantly. I had been in charge of these girls since the pack acquired them, of Kara since she was four. Kara came to me. She had always been complicated, sweet-natured and hardworking (unlike lazy Pretty), but too excitable. Death distressed her too much, happiness elated her too much, beauty transported her too much. I have seen her in tears over a sunset.

"Do not spoil Pretty's ceremony," I said to her in a low voice, and she subsided.

Afterward, however, while the two mothers took Pretty aside for the traditional sex instruction that was hardly ever needed and the unBegun girls played with Jaden, I led Kara off the stage, to the back of the theater. "Sit."

"Yes, Nurse. What is this place?"

"It was a theater. Kara, what troubles you?"

She looked away, looked down, looked everywhere but at me until I took her chin in my hand and made her face me. Then she blurted, "I don't want to!"

"Don't want to what?"

"Any of it! Begin, have a ceremony, bed with Mike and all them. Have a baby—I don't want to!"

"Many girls are frightened at first." I remembered my own first bedding, with a pack leader much less gentle than I suspected Mike would be. So long ago. Yet I had come to like sex, and right up until a few years ago, I had sometimes gone with Buddy off-list, until he was killed by that wild dog.

"I be frightened, yes. But I also don't want to!"

"Is there something you want to do instead?" I was afraid she would say "nurse." I already had Bonnie, and anyway, even if she proved infertile, Kara would not make a Nurse. No amount of hard work would make up for her lack of stability and brains.

"No."

"What, then?" For girls there was only mother, nurse, or infertile bed-mate, and the last became camp drudges with little respect, when packs kept infertile women at all. Our last such, Daisy, had run away. I didn't like to imagine what had happened to her. Kara knew all this.

"I don't know!" It was a wail of pure anguish. I had no time for this: a self-indulgent girl with no aim, merely obstruction of what was necessary. A woman did what she had to do, just as men did. I left her sitting in the tattered velvet chair and went back to Pretty. It was her day, not Kara's.

Bonnie still stood, stony, beside Pretty's flower-strewn chair.

Mike returned from the parley looking pleased, a rare look for him. The other pack, smaller than ours, was not only unwilling to go to war over the urban forest but was interested in trading, even in possible joint hunting and foraging trips. I knew without being told that Mike hoped to eventually unite the two packs and become chief of both. The men brought back gifts from the other pack. Evidently their base had heaps of things so sealed in plastic—blankets, pillows, even clothing—that no rats had gotten into them and they looked almost new. Each of the girls got a fluffy white robe stitched with "St. Regis Hotel."

"Can't we move to a hotel?" Lula cried, twirling around in hers.

"Too hard to defend," Karl said. He reached up to catch Lula and pull her onto his lap. She giggled. Lula has always liked Karl; she maintained that she "knows" he fathered Jaden. Jaden did have his bright blue eyes.

We were all at Pretty's ceremony feast in the common room, an underground room in what Grandmother remembered as the New York State Theater. The common room had a wooden floor, a curious wooden rail on three sides, and a smashed, unusable piano in one corner. The boys had swept up the huge amount of mirror glass that yesterday lay all around. Junie had spread blankets on the floor for the feast, which tasted wonderful. Rabbit shot that morning and roasted with wild onions over open fires built on the stone terrace in front of the Vivian Beaumont. Cans of beans that Eric had brought back from foraging. A salad of dandelion greens and the candy that Pretty so loved and I had been hoarding since winter: maple sap mixed with nuts. Every lantern we owned was lit, giving the room a romantic glow.

Mike eyed Pretty, who blushed and cast eyes at him. The younger men watched enviously. I didn't have much sympathy for them. They were at the bottom of the sex list, of course, and, they didn't get much. Too bad—they should have treated Bonnie better when they had her.

Besides Bonnie, two of the young men seemed unaware of the heavy scent of sex filling the common room. Guy and Jemmy kept giving me significant looks, and eventually I got up from my dinner and went to them. "Do you need me?"

"I have a pain," Jemmy said, loud enough for Mike to hear. Jemmy was a terrible actor. His eyes shone, and every muscle in his body tensed with excitement. I had never seen anybody less in pain.

I went to Mike. "Jemmy is ill. I'm taking him to the sickroom to examine, in case it's contagious."

Mike nodded, too absorbed by Pretty to pay much attention.

Jemmy and I slipped out. Guy followed with a lantern. As soon as we were beyond earshot of the sullen guard—he was missing the feast—I said to Jemmy, "Well?"

"We want to show you something. Please come, Nurse!"

The pack had raised Jemmy since he was six and his mother died. He had a lively curiosity but, unlike Guy, Jemmy had never learned to read, although not because he shared the men's usual scorn for reading as useless and feminine. Jemmy said that the letters jumped places in front of his eyes, which made no sense but seemed to be true, since otherwise he was intelligent. Too delicately built to ever be of much use to Mike, he could make any mechanical equipment function again. It was Jemmy who figured out how to get the generators we sometimes found to run on the fuel we also sometimes found. The generators never lasted long, and most of the machinery they were supposed to power had decayed or rusted beyond use, but every once in a while we got lucky. Until the fuel ran out.

"Is it another generator?" I asked.

"Half be that!" Jemmy said.

Guy added mysteriously, "No, one-third."

But this arithmetic was too much for Jemmy, whose instincts about machinery were just that: instincts. He ignored Guy and pulled me along.

We went outside the building, across the square to the Vivian Beaumont, and to the rear of the building. It was dark out and there was a light drizzle, but the boys ignored it. I didn't get much choice. In the little underground theater our single lantern cast a forlorn glow.

"You climb up there," Jemmy said, pointing to the booth halfway up the wall. "The steps be gone, but I found a ladder."

"I'm not going up a ladder," I said, but of course I did. Their excitement was contagious. Also worrying: This was not the way Mike wanted his pack men to behave. In Mike's mind, fighters spoke little and showed less.

I was no longer young nor agile, and the ladder was a trial. But, lit from above by the lantern Guy carried, I heaved myself into the small space. The first thing I saw was a pile of books. "Oh!"

"That's not first," Guy said gleefully, preventing me from snatching at one. "The other things first!"

I said, "Let go of those books!"

Jemmy, scampering up the ladder like a skinny squirrel, echoed, "The other things first!"

I demanded of Guy, "Where did you find the books?"

"Here."

A noise filled the small space: another of Jemmy's generators. I was far more interested in the books.

Jemmy said, "I can't believe this still works! It be already connected or I don't know how to do. Look!"

A flat window standing on a table flickered and glowed. A moment of surprise, and then the word came to me: *teevee*. Grandmother had told me about them. I never saw one work before, and when I was a child I confused *teevee* and *teepee*, so that I thought tiny people must live in the window, as we sometimes lived in teepees on summer forages.

They did.

She started out alone on the stage, except for words that appeared briefly below her:

PAS DE DEUX FROM THE FOUR TEMPERAMENTS
MUSIC BY PAUL HINDEMITH
CHOREOGRAPHY BY GEORGE BALANCHINE

The girl wore tight, clinging clothes that Mike would never have permitted on his women: too inflaming for men far down the sex list. On her feet were flimsy pink shoes with pink ribbons and square toes. The girl raised one arm in a curve above her head and then raised her body up onto the ends of those pink shoes—how could she do that? Music started. She began to dance.

I heard myself gasp.

A man came onto the screen and they moved toward each other. She turned away from him, turned back, moved toward him. He lifted her then, waist-high, and carried her so that she seemed to float, legs stretched in a beautiful arch, across the stage. They danced together, all their movements light and precise and swift—so swift! It was achingly beautiful. Coiling around each other, the girl lifting her leg as high as her head, standing on her other on the ends of her toes. They flowed from one graceful pose to another, defying gravity. I had never seen anything so fragile, so moving. Never.

It lasted only a short time. Then the teevee went black.

"I can't believe the cube still works!" Jemmy said gleefully. "Want to see the other one?"

But Guy said nothing. In the shadows cast upward from the lantern, his face looked much older, and almost in pain. He said, "What is it? What is it called?"

"Ballet," I said.

Silently he handed me the pile of books. Three, four, five of them. The top one read in large gold letters: *The Story of Giselle*. The others were *A Ballet Companion: The Joy of Classical Dance, Basic Ballet Positions, Dancing for Mr. B.*, and a very small *2016 Tour Schedule*.

Guy shivered. Jemmy, oblivious to all but his mechanical miracle, said, "The other one be longer. See, these cubes fit into this slot. Only two cubes still work, though."

White words on a black screen: TAKING CLASS ON VIDEO. Then a whole roomful of women and men standing—oh! at wooden railings before mirrors; the place might be our common room, long ago. Music from a piano and then a woman's voice said, "Plié . . . and *one* two three four. Martine, less tense in your hand. Carolyn, breathe with the movement. . . ."

They were not on the ends of their toes, not until partway through "class." Before that came strange commands from the unseen woman: *battement tendu, rondes de jambs a terre, porte de bras.* After they rose on the ends of their toes—but only the women, I noticed—came more commands: "Jorge, your hand looks like a dead chicken—hold the fingers loosely!" "No, no, Terry—you are doing *this,* and you should be doing *this.*" Then the woman herself appeared, and she looked as old or older than I, although much slimmer.

"Now center work. . . . No, that is too slow, John, and one and one and one . . . good. Now an *arabesque penchée.* . . . Breathe with it, softly, softly . . ."

On the teevee, dancers doing impossible, bewitching things with their bodies.

"Again. . . . Timon, please start just before the arabesque. . . ."

A roomful of dancers, each with one leg rising slowly behind, arms curved forward, to balance on one foot and make a body line so exquisite that my eyes blurred.

The teevee again went black. Jemmy said, "Let's not play it again—I want to save fuel." Guy, to my astonishment, knelt before me, as if he were doing atonement to Mike.

"Nurse, I need your help," he said.

"Get up, you young idiot!"

"I need your help," he repeated. "I want to bring Kara here, and I can't without you."

Kara. All at once, certain speculative looks he has given her sprang into my mind. I pushed him away, scandalized. "Guy! You can't bed Kara! Why, she hasn't Begun, and even if she had, Mike would kill you!"

"I don't want to bed her!" He rose, looking no less desperate but much more determined. "I want to dance with her."

"Dance with her!"

"Like that." He gestured toward the blank teevee and tried out his new word, with reverence. "Ballet."

Even Jemmy looked shocked. "Guy—you can't do that!"

"I can learn. So can Kara."

I said the first thing that came into my mind, which, like most first things, was idiotic. "The Nurse on the teevee said it takes years of work to become a dancer!"

"I know," Guy said, "years to be like them be. But we could learn *some*, Kara and me, and maybe dance for the pack. Mike might like that."

"Mike like a girl who has not yet Begun to be handled by you? You're crazy, Guy!"

"I have to dance," he said doggedly. "Ballet. With Kara. She be the only one possible!"

He was right about that. Pretty, spoiled and conventional, would never learn the hard things which that dance Nurse had demanded. Tiny and Seela were too young, Lula and Junie busy with children, Bonnie big and ungainly—what was I thinking? The whole thing was not only ridiculous, but dangerous.

"Put ballet out of your mind," I said severely. "If you don't, I will tell Mike."

I climbed ponderously down the ladder and made my way alone through the dark little theater to the door. But I carried the five books, and in my bare room in the underground of the David H. Koch Theater (I had finally found a faded sign with the correct name), I used an entire precious candle, reading them for most of the night.

Two days later, the chief of the St. Regis pack returned Mike's visit. This was a risk for him, since he arrived with only two lieutenants. It was a clear gesture of cooperation, not war, and it put everyone in a good mood. We ate at noon under a bright summer sky on a not-too-cracked terrace, beside a long shallow pool filled with both debris and two huge jutting pieces of stone that, looked at from certain directions, might be a person lying down. A sentence from my grandmother floated into my troubled mind: "Every autumn they had trouble with leaves in the Vivian Beaumont reflecting pool."

My girls built fires at first light and cooked all morning. None of the girls were present at the meal, of course; Mike would not let anyone but sworn pack men see how many women the pack possessed, nor which ones might be fertile. But I was there, serving the dishes, and the only one not cheerful.

Mike had made a bad mistake.

I knew it as soon as the chief of the other pack, Keither, began to talk. No, before—when I watched him as he studied Mike, studied our pack, studied the way the guards were set, studied everything he could see. Keither had a long, intelligent face and continuously darting eyes. He spoke well; I would bet my medicine box that this man could, and did, read. More, he had the ability to say whatever would be well received, without slipping into outright flattery. Mike, of much simpler mind, saw none of this. He had a leader's nose for treachery but not for subtlety. He could not see that Keither, with a smaller and more lightly armed pack than Mike's, aspired to the leadership of ours. There would be trouble. Not yet, maybe not even soon, but eventually.

It would do no good to tell Mike this, of course. He would not listen. I was Nurse, but I was a woman.

"I brought you a gift," Keither said, when the food had been consumed and praised. From his sack he pulled out a bottle of Jack Daniel's. Mike already knew it was there, of course—no sack could be brought unexamined beyond our perimeter. But if the men were not surprised, they were enormously pleased. Cups were passed around, toasts made, jokes exchanged. The younger men drank too much. Neither Mike nor Keither took more than a courtesy sip.

Still, the liquor prolonged the meeting. Talk grew louder. The men agreed to a joint hunting expedition, to leave the next morning. Both chiefs would go—a much greater risk on their part than on ours, since their pack was so much smaller. We would also send twice as many men as they did, further lessening our risk. Keither had been based in Manhattan for months and offered to show Mike good and bad foraging areas, boundaries of other packs' territories, and other useful information.

"We have no Nurse," Keither said. "Is yours up for trade? Or does she have an apprentice who is?"

"No," Mike said, with courtesy but without explanation. Keither didn't mention it again.

I was tired. Serving sixteen men, sitting cross-legged for hours on the concrete terrace, is hard on a body of my age. When the first tinges of sunset touched the sky, I caught Mike's eye. He nodded and let me go.

In the women's room, the girls crowded around me. "What be they like?" "Did they bring any more gifts?" "Did you find out how many women they have?" The girls sounded too insistent, crowded too close; they were hiding something. And: "Be you tired, Nurse? Maybe you go to your room and rest?"

I pushed off the wave of white robes. "Where's Kara?"

She sat alone in a corner. But the minute she raised her face, shining with exaltation, I knew. Or maybe I had known all along. After all, I could have left the feast hours earlier, and had not.

This way, I was innocent. So far.

My false innocence did not last past the next afternoon. Mike and nine other men departed on the hunting trip, leaving his first lieutenant, Joe, in command. Joe sent me with a guard of three men to the ruins of a nearby drugstore to see if there were any medicines I could use. There weren't; the place had been picked over long ago. Most of my medicines came from homes, left in ruined bathrooms, stored in drawers beside beds crawling with vermin. The expiration dates on the drugs have long since passed. However, a surprising number of them were still effective, and scalpels, scissors, gauze, and alcohol swabs don't decay.

By the time we got back, it was mid-afternoon of a gorgeous July day. Men sat in the sunshine, weapons on their knees, talking and laughing. Lula and Junie had the babies on blankets to kick their fat little legs. Pretty sat combing her hair in full view of the lounging men. She had taken to sex like a squirrel to trees, and with Mike gone her list was due for variety.

I didn't ask anyone where the other girls were. Tiny and Seela would be playing together, under guard. Bonnie would be preparing medicinal plants, pounding leaves and boiling bark and drying berries. I slipped around the back of the Vivian Beaumont, pushed open the door to the underground corridor, and made my way in the dark to the theater. That door was locked. I pounded on it, and eventually Jemmy opened it.

"Nurse—"

I slapped him across the face and strode down the aisle.

They were onstage and had not even heard me over the music. Over their intense concentration. Over their wonder, visible on both faces.

Guy noticed me first. "Nurse!"

Kara turned ashen and clutched what I now knew was called a barre. The boys must have brought it from the base building: a heavy-looking length of wood fastened not to a wall, as in the common room, but to heavy metal poles on either end. They had lugged the generator and the teevee down from the booth—I couldn't imagine how—and installed both onstage. On the teevee the music abruptly stopped and the older woman said, "No, no—drop your right shoulder, Alicia!"

Kara dropped her right shoulder.

Guy's face turned stony, such a good imitation of Mike that I was startled. I said, "What are you doing?"

"We're taking class."

Taking class. Following the movements of the dancers on the screen. All at once my anger was swamped by pity. They were so young. Growing up in such a barren world (my grandmother saying, "*Such rich performances as I saw!*"), but they hadn't know how barren it was. Now they did, and they thought things could be changed.

"Children, you *can't*. If Mike ever finds out that you put your hands on a girl who hasn't Begun—"

"I didn't touch her!" Guy said.

"—you know you'd be shot. Instantly. Guy, *think!*"

He came to the edge of the stage and knelt, looking down at me. "Nurse, I have to do this. I *have* to. And I can't dance alone. 'Ballet is woman.'"

I had read that just last night. Some famous ballet maker whose name I had never heard. I said, "You stole my books."

"I borrowed one. It has pictures that— Nurse, I have to."

"So do I," Kara said.

"Kara, come with me this minute."

"No," she said. Her defiance shocked me even more than their stupid notion that they could teach themselves to dance. I turned on Jemmy.

"And what about *you*? Is this insane love of machinery worth getting yourself shot?"

I saw from his face that Jemmy hadn't even considered this. He looked from me to Guy, back again, then at the ground. I had him.

"Go, Jemmy. Now. None of us will ever tell anyone you were here."

He scuttled down the aisle like a rabbit pursued by dogs. One mis-guided idiot down.

"If Mike ever finds out you were alone with her—"

"We're not alone!" Kara said. "We have a chaperone!"

"Who? If you mean Jemmy—"

"Me," Bonnie said, stepping from the shadows at the side of the stage.

If Kara had been a shock, Bonnie was an earthquake. Bonnie, who did not break rules and who had always treated Kara with faint disdain: for her high-strung emotion, for her fragile beauty. Bonnie had no command over Guy, but she had a borrowed—from me—authority over Kara.

"Bonnie? You *allowed* this?"

Bonnie said nothing. In the dimness onstage I couldn't see her face.

"Nurse," Guy said again, "we *have* to."

"No, you don't. Kara, come with me."

"No." And then, in a rush, "I won't be like Pretty! I won't let men touch me and sex with me and stick themselves up me until I get swollen and pregnant and maybe die like Emma did! I won't, I won't, *I won't!*" Her voice rose to a shriek, surprising Guy. Kara had just broken the strongest rule among the pack: loyalty. You followed the chief, you obeyed those above you, you did not cause trouble. And you kept your fear to yourself.

I made my voice soothing. "Kara, you heard what the woman on the teevee said. It takes years to become a real dancer. *Years.* This isn't possible, dear heart."

"We know that," Guy said. "We don't be stupid enough to think we can do everything they do. But we can do *some*."

"And that's worth dying for?"

"Nobody will die if you tell Joe that you give us reading lessons here. Everybody knows Kara and me are learning to read off you!"

"No," I repeated. "It's too great a risk, for nothing."

And then Bonnie—Bonnie!—spoke up. "Not for nothing. Nurse, first watch the dancing."

Guy seized on this. "Yes! Watch just once! It's so beautiful!"

It wasn't beautiful. Kara and Guy took their places beside the railing, and he turned on Jemmy's teevee. The woman said, *"Battement tendu,"* and Guy and Kara swung their legs forward, down, to the side, down, to the back down. Their legs reached neither the height nor the purity of line of the dancers on-screen, but they were not without grace. Guy showed a flexibility and power I had not expected, and Kara a flowing delicacy. None of it made any difference.

They went through a few more steps and Guy turned off the screen. "We have to learn all we can before the generator fuel runs out. But we have the books, too. And later on in class there be combinations of steps!"

Five window washers worked every day of the year, constantly keeping the windows bright. At night, when all the buildings were lit up, they shone out on the plaza like liquid gold. So little in this hard life was bright, and nothing was liquid gold. But not at risk of our lives.

"No," I said.

Two days later, I fell in the forest—which I had learned from an old map was called "Central Park"—and tore my knee open on a pointed rock.

"Oh!" The pain was immediate and sharp, but not as sharp as my fear. I was old; if I couldn't walk when the pack moved on, I would be finished.

Bonnie was instantly beside me. "Nurse?"

I tried to rise, could not, was caught in her strong arms. I blinked back tears as we both stared at the white bone below my leathery flesh.

Then I fainted.

The sickroom under the New York State Theater, bare and dark, was no larger than a big closet. Lula sat beside me nursing Jaden, Madonna and child by a single smoky candle. "Grandmother . . ." I whispered, or maybe it was another word, I couldn't be sure. Everything felt blurry, as if I'd opened my eyes underwater.

"Nurse?" Lula said. She put down the baby, who immediately began to scream, and picked up a cup. "Here, drink this now, you be needing to sleep—"

A smell of mint, a bitter taste beneath the sweetness of honey. I slept.

The sickroom still, and I lay alone. Complete darkness. I groped for my leg and felt the hump of bandages, the wooden splint over the knee. Pain, muted. How long had I lain here?

Hours went by until Bonnie came with breakfast, with hot tea, with her wooden, unrevealing face.

"How bad is it, Bonnie? Will I walk again?"

"Can't say until you can stand."

"Is Mike back?"

"Not yet. Drink this."

"What is—"

"Just tea."

I needed more than just tea. I needed to be able to walk.

"Nurse? Nurse, you hear me?"

I did, dragging myself back from far away, or maybe it was Pretty who was far away. Only she was not. She crouched beside me, except that now there were two of her, and then three. How could that be? One Pretty was enough. Unless she was fertile and had given birth to herself again and yet again. . . .

"I be pregnant!" one of the Prettys shouted triumphantly. And then: "Can she hear me?"

"I don't know," Bonnie said.

"It be Mike's! I know! Bonnie, can she hear me?"

"I don't know."

And then, all of a sudden, I couldn't.

I was Grandmother, walking through Lincoln Center, watching the light spill from high arched windows, liquid gold. I took down twenty-one chandeliers and polished each crystal so bright that it burned my hand. The burning spread to the Library for the Performing Arts and charred it to the ground. Windows shattered and pieces of glass pierced me. "Lincoln Kirstein won't like that!" my grandmother cried. "He spent a fortune to build this place!" I laughed and kept on tacking down red carpet.

Finally, clarity returned. I knew who I was and where I was, and it was not Bonnie standing beside my bedroll but Joe, Mike's lieutenant, who'd been left in charge for—how long now?

"How be you, Nurse?" Joe said awkwardly.

I had known Joe since he was ten. A ferocious fighter, loyal, careful about guarding our camps but easygoing about what happened within the perimeter. However, he didn't look easy now.

I said, "My head is clear."

It wasn't my head he was interested in. "Can you walk?"

"I don't know."

"Find out." He left, abrupt and unsmiling. Cold slid down my spine.

Junie arrived a few minutes later, breathless with running, carrying Davey. "Oh, Nurse, be you better?"

"Yes. Send Bonnie to me."

"I don't know where she be! I wanted her a while ago to give Jaden something for that teething, she fusses so, Lula said maybe Bonnie give her something to calm her down but—"

Junie prattled on while I put one palm flat against the wall and tried to stand. I could do so, but only barely.

"Junie, how long have I been here?"

"Be . . . let me think . . . be a month? More?"

More than a month. Drugged for more than a month for the pain of a torn kneecap.

I said, "Find Bonnie and send her to me."

"I will. But, Nurse, Joe says—no, Tony, he be back and he—"

"Tony?" Tony had gone on the joint hunting trip with Mike and Keither's pack. I looked more closely at Junie, and now I saw the fear on her face. Davey felt it, too; his fat little hands clutched her body. I said, "Is Mike dead?"

"Tony says not when he ran off. Tony, he escaped. They got ambushed two days out—Nurse, Keither's pack be big, he lied, most of them not at the hotel when our men went there. They going to trade Mike for somebody, I forget who or why, and Tony escaped and Joe says we move out tomorrow morning! It ain't safe here no more. Oh, Nurse, can you walk?"

"Find Jemmy. Tell him to cut me a stick—*this* long—to lean on. Tell him I want it this minute."

"But you told me to find Bonnie and—"

"Not Bonnie. Jemmy. Now."

By the time Jemmy arrived with the stick, I'd eased my weight onto my leg, fallen, discovered the splint would hold, and gotten up again. Bonnie's splint was heavy; the cane balanced it. Leaning on Jemmy's shoulder, I got myself into the corridor without injuring anything further. In the women's room, the girls worked frantically even though the pack would not move until dawn and there was little enough to gather up. Anything taken must be carried. Each girl had her backpack, and the mothers had baby slings. The pockets of winter coats were stuffed with food. The coats themselves must be worn, no matter how hot the day, because we couldn't afford to lose them. In the morning, blankets would be rolled up with cooking utensils and strapped to Rick, eight years old and not ready to fight, and to whichever of the other men Joe chose.

Outside the building, the first stars shone faintly in a deep blue sky, although on the western horizon clouds mounted high. The air smelled of rain to come and the trees swayed. The Met loomed dark against the cobalt sky. *At night, when all the buildings were lit up, they shone out on the plaza like liquid gold. People laughed and talked and lined up by the hundreds to hear opera and see ballet and watch plays and listen to concerts.*

Somewhere a dog bayed, then another. A pack, hunting.

I said to Jemmy, "Take me to them."

Shadows beside the Vivian Beaumont, shadows in the sloping underground corridor. Jemmy wedged open the door with a rock so that I could hear if the guards started shooting. Inside the theater, more shadows.

They didn't see me. The barre had been pushed to the back of the stage, out of the way. Guy, barefoot, was stripped to the waist. Kara, also barefoot, wore white tights and something filmy and clinging and dotted with holes, unearthed from who knows what ancient storage area. Music played. It wasn't the thin, slightly tinny music of the piano that played for "class." This was the full, glorious sound of the music from the other recording, *The Four Temperaments*. And I realized what Guy had done.

While he arranged steps and combinations for him and Kara, he had held Paul Hindemith's music in his mind. Their dancing perfectly matched the music, blended with it, *was* it. In that blending, Guy's and Kara's inexperience became less important, in part because he had chosen so well movements that they could perform with grace. From studying the ballet books, I could even name some of them: *bourrées, pas de chat, battements.*

The names were unimportant. What mattered was the dancing. They never touched, but Kara's young body, on demi-pointe, bent toward his with sorrow, with loss, with longing, without ever reaching him. He yearned toward her but I knew it was not her he yearned for, nor she for him. The sorrow was for the dancing itself, so briefly embraced, lost tomorrow. The loss was of all the beauty they once might have had, were the world different. Guy raised his leg, extended his arm, and balanced in a perfect arabesque. In the soft glow of lantern light, the dancing figures were liquid gold, and they lit up the bare stage with heartbreaking regret for vanished beauty.

But it was Bonnie who stunned me.

She stood to one side of the stage: chaperone, guard, and something more. Never had I imagined that her homely face could look like that. She was not just alive; she shone with the ferocity of the angel guarding the gate to Eden. I had not known, not even suspected.

"Bonnie," I said. It came out a whisper, heard only by Jemmy. Before I could find a louder voice, the door behind me jerked open and a man roared, "What the fuck!"

Mike.

I turned. Blood caked the left side of his face, matted his beard. His left arm was in a crude sling. Behind him crowded three or four men. Mike pushed past me and ran toward the stage.

I lurched after him as fast as I could, pushing through the pain in my knee. "Wait! Wait! Don't—"

The men rammed past me. Mike stood below the stage, on which Kara and Guy had frozen.

"—do anything!" I yelled. "Bonnie was here the whole time, they were never alone!"

One of the other men—his back to me, I couldn't see who—raised a second lantern high in the air beside Mike, and I saw what Mike saw: the blood on Kara's thighs, brilliant red on the white tights. She had Begun.

I grabbed Mike's good arm. "Never alone! Do you understand, they were never alone! He never touched her!"

If it had been Joe, he might have shot Guy right there on the stage. If it had been Lew, he might have shot them both. Mike gave Guy a look of profound disgust: at his bare chest, at the arabesque Mike had interrupted, at everything about Guy that Mike would never understand. To

me, apparently not even noticing my leg, Mike growled, "Take them girls
to where they belong."

Someone fired a rifle at the teevee screen, and the music stopped.

Bonnie would answer none of my questions. She sat, silent and wooden,
in the sickroom until Mike had time to send for her. "What did you give
me?" I demanded. "In what dosage? And, Bonnie—*why?*"

She said nothing.

Lincoln Kirstein, Grandmother once told me, *got this place built. He used
his own money and made others donate money and founded a great ballet company. He wasn't a dancer or a choreographer or a musician. He didn't make
ballets, but he made ballet happen.*

Kara was not with us. She had been sent to the women's room. In a
week or so, when she stopped bleeding, she would be sent to Mike's bed,
to Joe's, to Karl's, to every man who might prove her fertile. Even shrieking, she would be sent.

A few hours later, Mike sent for me. Two men carried me between
them to a room at the end of the corridor. Small, with concrete walls, it
still held the twisted and rusted remains of those big machines that once
gave out food and drink in exchange for coins. There was an ancient sofa
nested by rats, a sagging table, a few chairs. I could picture dancers coming here from the practice rooms, throwing themselves across the sofa,
resting for a moment with a candy bar or soda.

Mike's men sat me in a mostly intact chair and he said, "Why, Nurse?"

The same question I had asked Bonnie. My concern now was to shield
her as much as I could. "They wanted to dance, Mike, that's all. They were
never alone and he never—"

"You don't know that. You be unconscious the whole time." He eyed
my leg. Someone had cleaned up the blood from his eye and beard.

"Yes, that's true, but if Bonnie says she was always with them, then she
was. She obeys orders, Mike. I told her that I'd given Kara and Guy permission to dance and that she must stay with them."

"You? *You* gave permission?"

"Yes, me. I mean, you know Bonnie—does she seem the type of person
interested in dancing?"

Mike frowned; he was not used to considering what "type of person" a woman might be. "You did this, Nurse? Not Bonnie?"

"Not Bonnie. And she's a good Nurse, Mike. She can make medicines just as well as I did. And do everything else, too."

Finally his gaze lifted from my bandaged knee to my face. He said simply, "Do you want to be shot or left behind?"

Shooting would be kinder. But I said, "Left behind."

He shrugged, losing interest. He still had a Nurse; Kara had not been touched; there were fighting tactics to occupy his mind. Into that indifference I dared to ask, "Guy?"

Mike scowled. To his men he said, "Take her wherever she wants to be left, and bring me the new Nurse." He strode from the room, having already forgotten me.

Mike's men left me under the Vivian Beaumont, just inside the first door, at the top of the sloping corridor. In the dark I groped in my pocket for the candle and matches. It wasn't easy to keep one hand on the wall, hold the candle and my cane in the other, and hobble my painful way down the corridor and through the second door. By the time I reached the shallow steps at the far side of the stage, I was crawling.

My five ballet books lay neatly stacked in a corner, where Guy had studied them who knew how many nights while I lay drugged and Kara, locked in the women's room, flexed and pointed her toes and dreamed of pointe shoes. I opened *The Story of Giselle* and turned the pages by candlelight until I found a photograph of a dancer in a long, filmy skirt held impossibly high by her partner, soaring in an exquisite arc above him. There are worse ways to die than gazing at beauty. From my pocket, I drew my packet of distilled monkshood leaves. Fairly quick, and not as painful as most.

Something moaned somewhere behind me.

They had beaten him bloody and chained him to a concrete column in one of the tiny dressing rooms behind the stage. Guy breathed as if in pain, but I could find no broken bones. Mike had not wanted him to die too quickly. He would either starve or be found by Keither's pack when they came looking for revenge, or for our women, or just for war.

"Guy?"

He moaned again. I searched the room but found no key to his chains. Sitting beside him, I held in one hand that packet of monkshood that did not contain enough for both of us, and in the other *The Story of Giselle*. And then, because I am old and had broken my knee and had lain inactive for over a month while Guy and Kara reinvented the dangers of ballet, I fell asleep.

"Nurse? Nurse?" And then: "Susan!"

The candle had gone out. But the dressing room was lit by a lantern—two lanterns. Bonnie and Kara stood there, dressed in men's clothing and backpacks, and both carried semiautomatic machine guns. On Kara, it looked like a butterfly equipped with a machete. In the sudden light, Guy's eyelids fluttered open.

"Oh!" Kara said, one hand flying to her mouth. The gun wobbled.

Bonnie snapped, "Don't you dare fuss!" and I was startled at her tone, which was my own. Had been my own. "Nurse, can you—"

"No," I said.

Bonnie didn't argue. She dropped to her knees and ran her hands impersonally over Guy.

"I already did that," I said. "Nothing broken."

"Then he can walk. Kara, pull Nurse out of here, back to the stage. Guy, pull yourself as far from the post as you can."

He did, closing his swollen and blood-crusted eyes. Kara tugged me away. Even from the stage, the sound of Bonnie's gun—not the semiautomatic—was loud as she shot at the chain. Even the ricochets—surely dangerous!—made my ears ring. After a few moments Guy and Bonnie emerged, he leaning on her and dragging lengths of chain on both ankles. But he was able to bend and scoop them off the floor. I caught at Bonnie's knee.

"Bonnie—how—"

"In their stew. Kara and I were serving."

"Dead?"

"I don't know. Some, maybe."

"What did you use? Pokeweed? Cowbane? Snakeroot?"

"Skyweed. The seeds."

Kara said suddenly, "Not the other girls, though. We wouldn't do that." And then: "But I won't bed anybody!"

Bonnie said, "And you have to dance."

I gaped at her. Kara wanted to dance, Guy wanted to dance, but it was *Bonnie* who was determined that they would dance. Slowly I said, "Where will you go?"

"North. Away from the city. It's going to rain hard, and that will cover our tracks before the pack revives."

"Try to find a farm community. Or, if you can, places called 'Ithaca' or 'Endicott' or 'Bath.' I'm not sure they exist, but they might. Have you got that map I found? And my medicine sack?"

"Yes. Do you have—"

"Yes."

"We have to go now, Nurse. Jemmy is with us, too."

Jemmy. Perhaps they would find a generator. Bonnie extracted the two recording cubes, *The Four Temperaments* and *Taking Class on Video,* from the blasted teevee. Kara was helping Guy dress in warm coat, boots, a rain poncho. He swayed on his feet but remained upright. She handed him her rifle, which actually seemed to steady him. Kara turned to me and her lips trembled.

"Don't," I said in my harshest tone. Kara, not understanding, looked hurt. But Bonnie knew.

"Good-bye, Nurse," she said, without painful sentiment, and grasped the other two to lead them away.

I waited until the sound of their boots crossed the stage, until the door to the theater closed, until they had had enough time to leave camp. Then I crawled out of the Vivian Beaumont. The rain had just started, sweet on the summer night air. The cookfires on the plaza sputtered and hissed. Beside them lay the men. Farther out would be the perimeter, and then the guards who had gone from their hearty dinner to the outposts on nearby streets or rooftops.

Two of the men by the fire were already dead. I thought most of the others, including Mike, might recover, but skyweed seeds are tricky. So much depends on how they are dried, pounded, leached, and stored. Bonnie knew a lot, but not as much as I did. I gathered up the men's guns, made a pile of them under a rain poncho, and sat beside it under another poncho, a loaded semiautomatic beside me.

This could happen several ways. If Keither's pack showed up soon, the kindest thing would be to shoot Mike and the others before they revived.

Keither's pack would claim the girls, who would be no better nor worse off than they were now. Fertile women were precious.

If Mike and the others revived after I judged Bonnie to be far enough away, I would swallow my packet of monkshood and let Mike take on Keither.

But . . . with skyweed, more of these men should have vomited before their paralysis. If Bonnie had misjudged her preparation or dosages, and the pack regained their senses and strength soon enough to follow her, I would do what was necessary.

We lowered all twenty-one electric chandeliers at the Met—think of that, Susan, twenty-one—and cleaned each crystal drop individually. Every other year all the red carpet was completely replaced, at a cost of $700,000. Every five years the seats were replaced. Five window washers worked every day of the year, constantly keeping the windows bright. At night, when all the buildings were lit up, they shone out on the plaza like liquid gold. People laughed and talked and lined up by the hundreds to hear opera and see ballet and watch plays and listen to concerts. And such rich performances as I saw . . . you can't imagine!

No, I can't. No more than I can imagine what will happen to Guy, and Kara, and ballet. No more than I could have imagined Bonnie caught in an enchantment she had never expected: the enchantment of the lost past, rising from ruin like a dancer rising into arabesque. Had that storm lain in her all along, needing only something to passionately love?

There are all kinds of storms, and all kinds of performances. Under the poncho, I hold my gun, and listen to the rain falling on Lincoln Center, and wait.

Lawrence Block

Here's a chiller about a dangerous woman with a dangerous plan in mind and the worst of intentions who maybe should have given the whole matter a little more thought. . . .

New York Times bestseller Lawrence Block, one of the kings of the modern mystery genre, is a Grand Master of Mystery Writers of America, the winner of four Edgar Awards and six Shamus Awards, and the recipient of the Nero Award, the Philip Marlowe Award, a Lifetime Achievement Award from the Private Eye Writers of America, and a Cartier Diamond Dagger for Life Achievement from the Crime Writers' Association. He's written more than fifty books and numerous short stories. Block is perhaps best known for his long-running series about alcoholic ex-cop/private investigator Matthew Scudder, the protagonist of novels such as *The Sins of the Fathers, In the Midst of Death, A Stab in the Dark,* and fifteen others, but he's also the author of the bestselling four-book series about the assassin Keller, including *Hit Man, Hit List, Hit Parade,* and *Hit and Run;* the eight-book series about globe-trotting insomniac Evan Tanner, including *The Thief Who Couldn't Sleep* and *The Canceled Czech;* and the eleven-book series about burglar and antiquarian book dealer Bernie Rhodenbarr, including *Burglars Can't Be Choosers, The Burglar in the Closet,* and *The Burglar Who Liked to Quote Kipling.* He's also written stand-alone novels such as *Small Town, Death Pulls a Doublecross,* and sixteen others, as well as novels under the names Chip Harrison, Jill Emerson, and Paul Kavanagh. His many short stories have been collected in *Sometimes They Bite, Like a Lamb to Slaughter, Some Days You Get the Bear, By the Dawn's Early Light, The Collected Mystery Stories, Death Wish and Other Stories, Enough Rope,* and *One Night Stands and Lost Weekends.* He's also edited thirteen mystery anthologies, including *Murder on the Run, Blood on Their Hands, Speaking of Wrath,* and, with Otto Penzler, *The*

Best American Mystery Stories 2001, and produced seven books of writing advice and nonfiction, including *Telling Lies for Fun & Profit*. His most recent books are the new Matt Scudder novel, *A Drop of the Hard Stuff*, the new Bernie Rhodenbarr novel, *Like a Thief in the Night*, and, writing as Jill Emerson, the novel *Getting Off*. He lives in New York City.

I KNOW HOW TO PICK 'EM

I sure know how to pick 'em.

Except I don't know as I've got any credit coming for this one, because it's hard to make the case that it was me that picked her. She walked into that edge-of-town roadhouse with the script all worked out in her mind, and all that was left to do was cast the lead.

The male lead, that is. Far as the true leading role was concerned, well, that belonged to her. That much went without saying. Woman like her, she'd have to be the star in all of her productions.

They had a jukebox, of course. Loud one. Be nice if I recalled what was playing when she crossed the threshold, but I wasn't paying attention—to the music, or to who came through the door. I had a beer in front of me, surprise surprise, and I was looking into it like any minute now it would tell me a secret.

Yeah, right. All any beer ever said to me was *Drink me down, horse. I might make things better and I sure can't make 'em worse.*

It was a country jukebox, which you could have guessed from the parking lot, where the pickups outnumbered the Harleys by four or five to one. So if I can't say what was playing when she came in, or even when I looked up from my PBR and got a look at her, I can tell you what wasn't playing. "I Only Have Eyes for You."

That wasn't coming out of that jukebox. But it should have been.

She was the beauty. Her face was all high cheekbones and sharp angles, and a girl who was just plain pretty would get all washed out standing next to her. She wasn't pretty herself, and a quick first glance might lead you to think that she wasn't attractive at all, but you'd look again and that first thought would get so far lost you'd forget you ever had it. There are fashion models with that kind of face. Film actresses, too, and they're the ones who keep on getting the good parts in their forties and fifties, when the pretty girls start looking like soccer moms and nosy neighbors.

And she only had eyes for me. Large, well-spaced eyes, a rich brown in color, and I swear I felt them on me before I was otherwise aware of her presence. Looked up, caught her looking at me, and she saw me looking and didn't look away.

I suppose I was lost right there.

She was a blonde, with her hair cut to frame and flatter her face. She was tall, say five-ten, five-eleven. Slender but curvy. Her blouse was silk, with a bold geometric print. It was buttoned too high to show a lot of cleavage, but when she moved it would cling to her and let you know what it wasn't showing.

The way her jeans fit, well, you all at once understood why people paid big money for designer jeans.

The joint wasn't crowded, it was early, but there were people between her and me. She flowed through them and they melted away. The bartender, a hard-faced old girl with snake tattoos, came over to take a drink order.

The blonde had to think it over. "I don't know," she said to me. "What should I have?"

"Whatever you want."

She put her hand on my arm. I was wearing a long-sleeved shirt, so her skin and mine never touched, but they might as well.

"Pick a drink for me," she said.

I was looking down at her hand, resting there on my forearm. Her fingernails were medium-long, their polish the bright color of arterial bleeding.

Pick a drink for her? The ones that came quickest to mind were too fancy for the surroundings. Be insulting to order her a shot and a beer. Had to be a cocktail, but one that the snake lady would know how to make.

I said, "Lady'll have a Cuervo margarita." Her hand was on my right arm, so rather than move it I used my left hand to poke the change I'd left on the bar top, indicating that the margarita was on me.

"And the same for you? Or another Blue Ribbon?"

I shook my head. "But you could give me a Joey C. twice to keep it company."

"Thank you," my blonde said, while the bartender went to work. "That's a perfect choice, a margarita."

The drinks came, hers in a glass with a salted rim, my double Cuervo in an oversize shot glass. She let go of my arm and picked up her drink, raised the glass in a wordless toast. I left my Cuervo where it was and returned the toast with my beer.

She didn't throw her drink back like a sailor, but didn't take a little baby-bird sip, either. She drank some and put the glass on the bar and her hand on my arm.

Nice.

No wedding ring. I'd noticed that right away, and hadn't needed a second glance to see that there'd been a ring on that finger, that it had come off recently enough to show not only the untanned band where the ring had been but the depression it had caused in the flesh. It said a lot, that finger. That she was married, and that she'd deliberately taken off her ring before entering the bar.

Hey, didn't I say? I know how to pick 'em.

But didn't I also say she picked me?

And picked that low-down roadhouse for the same reason. If my type was what she was looking for, that was the place to find it.

My type: well, big. Built like a middle linebacker, or maybe a tight end. Six-five, 230, big in the shoulders, narrow in the waist. More muscles than a man needs, unless he's planning to lift a car out of a rut.

Which I don't make a habit of. Not that good at lifting my poor self out of a rut, let alone an automobile.

Clean-shaven, when I shave; I was a day away from a razor when she came in and put her hand on my arm. But no beard, no mustache. Hair's dark and straight, and I haven't lost any of it yet. But I haven't hit forty yet, either, so who's to say I'll get to keep it?

My type: a big outdoorsy galoot, more brawn than brains, more street smarts than book smarts. Someone who probably won't notice you were wearing a wedding ring until a few minutes ago.

Or, if he does, won't likely care.

"Like to dance, little lady?"

I'd spotted him earlier out of the corner of my eye, a cowboy type, my height or an inch or two more, but packing less weight. Long and lean, built to play wide receiver to my tight end.

And no, I never played football myself. Only watch it when a TV's showing it in a room I'm in. Never cared about sports, even as a boy. Had the size, had the quickness, and I got tired of hearing I should go out for this team, go out for that one.

It was a game. Why waste my time on a game?

And here was this wide receiver, hitting on a woman who'd declared herself to be mine. She tightened her grip on my arm, and I guessed she was liking the way this was shaping up. Two studs taking it to the lot out back, squaring off, then doing their best to kill each other. And she'd stand there watching, the blood singing in her veins, until it was settled and she went home with the winner.

No question he was ready to play. He'd sized me up half an hour ago, before she was in the picture. There's a type of guy who'll do that: check out a room, work out who he might wind up fighting and how he'd handle it. Could be I'd done some of that myself, getting the measure of him, guessing what moves he'd make, guessing what would work against him.

Or I could walk away from it. Turn my back on both of 'em, head out of the bar, take my act on down the road. Not that hard to find a place that'd sell you a shot of Cuervo and a beer to back it up.

Except, you know, I never do walk away from things. Just knowing I could don't mean I can.

"Oh, that's very kind of you," she said. "But we were just leaving. Perhaps another time."

Getting to her feet as she said it, using just the right tone of voice, so as to leave no doubt that she meant it. Not cold, not putting him down, but nowhere near warm enough to encourage the son of a bitch.

Handled it just right, really.

I left my beer where it was, left my change there to keep it company. She took hold of my arm on the way out. There were some eyes on us as we left, but I guess we were both used to that.

When we hit the parking lot I was still planning the fight. It wasn't going to happen, but my mind was working it out just the same.

Funny how you'll do that.

You want to win that kind of a fight; what you want to do is get the first punch in. Before he sees it coming. First you bomb Pearl Harbor, then you declare war.

Let him think you're backing out of it, even. *Hey, I don't want to fight you!* And when he's afraid you're gonna chicken out, you give him your best shot. Time it right, take him by surprise, and one punch is all you need.

Wouldn't have done that with old Lash LaRue, though. Oh, not because it wouldn't have done the job. Would have worked just fine, put him facedown on the gravel, Wranglers and snap-fastened dude shirt and silly pompadour and all.

But that'd cheat her out of the fight she was hoping to see.

So what I'd have done, once we're outside and good to go, was spread my hands in a can't-we-work-this-out gesture, leaving it for him to sucker punch me. But I'd be ready, even though I wouldn't look ready, and I'd duck when he swung. They're always headhunters, dudes like him, and I'd be ducking almost before he was swinging, and I'd bury a fist midway between his navel and his nuts.

I'd do the whole deal with body shots. Why hurt your hands bouncing 'em off jawbone? Tall as he was, there was a whole lot of middle to him, and that's where I'd hammer him, and the first shot would take the fight out of him, and the starch out of his punches, if he even got to throw a second one.

I'd be aiming lefts at his liver. That's on the right, pretty much on the beltline. It's a legal punch in a boxing ring, never mind a parking lot, and if you find the spot it's a one-punch finisher. I haven't done it, or seen it done, but I believe it would be possible to kill a man with a liver shot.

But I was running the script for a fight that wasn't gonna happen, because my blonde had already written her own script and it turned out there wasn't a fight scene in it. Sort of a pity, in a way, because there'd have been a certain satisfaction in taking that cowboy apart, but his liver would live to fight another day. Any damage it sustained would be from the shots and beers he threw at it, not from any fists of mine.

And, you know, that would have been too easy, if all she was after was getting two roughnecks to duke it out over her. She had something a lot worse in mind.

"I hope I wasn't out of line," she said. "Getting us out of there. But I was afraid."

She hadn't seemed afraid.

"That you'd hurt him," she explained. "Kill him, even."

Her car was a Ford, the model the rental outfits were apt to give you. It was tucked between a pair of pickups, both of them showing dinged fenders and a lot of rust. She pressed a button to unlock the doors and the headlights winked.

I played the gentleman, tagging along at her side, reaching to open the driver's-side door for her. She hesitated, turned toward me, and it would have been a hard cue to miss.

I took hold of her and kissed her.

And yes, it was there, the chemistry, the biology, whatever you want to call it. She kissed back, and started to push her hips forward, then stopped herself, then couldn't stop herself. I felt the warmth of her through her jeans and mine, and I thought of doing her right there, just throwing her down and doing her on the gravel, with the two pickups screening us from view. Throw her a fast hard one, pull out and stand up while she's still quivering, and be out of there before she can get her game up and running.

Good-bye, little lady, because we just did what we came here to do, so whatever you've got to say, well, why do I have to listen to it?

I let go of her. She slipped behind the wheel, and I walked around the car and got in next to her. She started the engine but paused before putting the Ford in gear.

She said, "My name's Claudia."

Maybe it was and maybe it wasn't.

"Gary," I said.

"I don't live around here."

Neither did I. Don't live anywhere, really. Or, looking at it from another way, I live everywhere.

"My motel is just up the road. Maybe half a mile."

She waited for me to say something. What? *Are the sheets clean? Do they get HBO?*

I didn't say anything.

"Should we pick up something to drink? Because I don't have anything in the room."

I said I was fine. She nodded, waited for a break in the traffic, pulled onto the road.

I paid attention to the passing scenery, so I'd be able to come back for my car. A quarter mile down the road she took her right hand off the wheel and put it on my crotch. Her eyes never left the road. Another quarter mile and her hand returned to the wheel.

Had to wonder what was the point of that. Making sure I had something for her? Keeping me from forgetting why we were going to the motel?

Maybe just trying to show me she was every inch a lady.

I suppose I just keep on getting what I keep on looking for.

Because, face it, you don't go prospecting for Susie Homemaker in a low-down joint with a lot full of pickups and hogs. Walk into a room where you hear Kitty Wells singing how it wasn't God who made honky-tonk angels, well, what are you gonna find but a honky-tonk angel yourself?

You want a one-man woman, you want someone who'll keep house and buy into the whole white-picket-fence trip, there's other places you can go hunting.

And I wasn't showing up at Methodist socials, or meetings of Parents Without Partners, or taking poetry workshops at a continuing education program. I was—another song—looking for love in all the wrong places, so why blame fate for sending me a woman like Claudia?

Or whatever her name was.

The motel was a one-story non-chain number, presentable enough, but not where a woman like her would stay if all she wanted was a place to sleep. She'd pick a Ramada or a Hampton Inn, but what we had here was your basic no-tell motel. Clean enough, and reasonably well maintained, and set back from the road for privacy. Her unit was around the back, where the little Ford couldn't be seen from the road. If it wasn't a rental, if it was her own car, well, no one driving by could spot the plate.

Like it mattered.

Inside, with the door shut and the lock set, she turned to me and for the first time looked the least bit uncertain. Like she was trying to think what to say, or waiting for me to say something.

Well, the hell with that. She'd already groped my crotch in the car, and that ought to be enough to break the ice. I reached for her and kissed her, and I got one hand on her ass and drew her in close.

I could have peeled those jeans off of her, could have ripped that fine silk blouse. I had the impulse.

More, I wanted to do some damage. Soften her up with a fist in her belly, see what a liver shot would do to her.

Fact: I have thoughts like that. They'll come to me, and when they do I always get a quick flash of my mother's face. Just the quickest flash, like the flash of green you'll sometimes get when you watch the sun go down over water. It's gone almost before it registers, and afterward you can't quite swear that you really saw it.

Like that.

I was gentle with her. Well, gentle enough. She didn't pick me out of the crowd because she wanted tender words and butterfly kisses. I gave her what I sensed she wanted, but I didn't take her any further than she wanted to go. It wasn't hard to find her rhythm, wasn't hard to build her up and hold her back and then let it all happen for her, staying with her all the way, coaxing the last little quiver out of the sweet machinery of her body.

Nothing to it, really. I'd been taught young. I knew what to do and how to do it.

"I knew it would be good."

I was lying there, eyes closed. I don't know what I'd been thinking about. Sometimes my mind just wanders, goes off by itself somewhere and thinks its own thoughts, and then a car backfires or something changes the energy in the room, and I'm back where I was, and whatever I was thinking about is gone without a trace.

Must be like that for everybody, I suppose. Can't be that I'm that special, me and my private thoughts.

This time it was her voice, bringing the present back as sure as a thunderclap. I rolled over and saw she was half sitting in the bed beside me.

She'd taken the pillow from under her ass and had it supporting her head and shoulders.

She had the air of a woman smoking a cigarette, but she wasn't a smoker and there weren't any cigarettes around. But it was like that, the cigarette afterward, whether or not there was a cigarette in the picture.

"All I wanted," she said, "was to come in here and close a door and shut the world out, and then make everything in the world go away."

"Did it work?"

"Like magic," she said. "You didn't come."

"No."

"Was there something—"

"Sometimes I hold back."

"Oh."

"It makes the second time better. More intense."

"I can see how it would. But doesn't it take remarkable control?"

I hadn't been trying to hold back. I'd been trying to throw her a fuck she wouldn't quickly forget, that's all. But I didn't need to tell her all that.

"We'll be able to have a second time, won't we? You don't have to leave?"

"I'll be here all night," she said. "We can even have breakfast in the morning, if you'd like."

"I thought you might have to get home to your husband."

Her hands moved, and the fingers of her right hand fastened on the base of her ring finger, assuring themselves there was no ring there.

"Not the ring," I said. "The mark of the ring. A depression in the skin, because you must have taken it off just before you came into the road-house. And the thin white line, showing where the sun don't shine."

"Sherlock Holmes," she said.

She paused so that I could say something, but why help her out? I waited, and she said, "You're not married."

"No."

"Have you ever been?"

"Same answer."

She held her hand up, palm out, as if to examine her ring. I guess she was studying the mark where it had been.

She said, "I thought I'd get married right after high school. Where I grew up, if you were pretty, that's what happened. Or if you weren't pretty, but if somebody got you pregnant anyway."

"You were pretty."

She nodded. Why pretend she didn't know it? "But I wasn't pregnant, and this girlfriend got this idea, let's get out of this town, let's go to Chicago and see what happens. So just like that I packed a bag and we went, and it took her three weeks to get homesick and go right back."

"But not you."

"No, I liked Chicago. Or I thought I did. What I liked was the person I got to be in Chicago, not because it was Chicago but because it wasn't home."

"So you stayed."

"Until I went someplace else. Another city. And I had jobs, and I had boyfriends, and I spent some time between boyfriends, and it was all fine. And I thought, well, some women have husbands and children, and some don't, and it looks like I'll be one of the ones who don't."

I let her talk but didn't listen too closely. She met this man, he wanted to marry her, she thought it was her last chance, she knew it was a mistake, she went ahead and did it anyway. It was her story, but hardly hers alone. I'd heard it often enough before.

Sometimes I suppose it was true. Maybe it was true this time, far as that goes.

Maybe not.

When I got tired of hearing her I put a hand on her belly and stroked her. Her sudden intake of breath showed she wasn't expecting it. I ran my hand down, and her legs parted in anticipation, and I put my hand on her and fingered her. Just that, just lay beside her and worked her with my fingers. She'd closed her eyes, and I watched her face while my fingers did what they did.

"Oh! Oh! *Oh!*"

I got hard doing this, but didn't feel the need to do anything about it. After she came I just lay where I was. I closed my eyes and got soft again and lay there listening to all the silence in the room.

My father moved away when I was still in diapers. At least, that was what I was told. I don't remember him, and I'm not convinced he was there. Somebody got her pregnant, it wasn't the Holy Ghost, but did he ever know it? Did she even know his last name?

So I was raised by a single mother, though I don't recall hearing the term back then. Early on she brought men home, and then she stopped doing that. She might come home smelling of where she'd been and what she'd been doing, but she'd come home alone.

Then she stopped that, too, and spent her evenings in front of the TV. One night we were watching some program, I forget what, and she said, "You're old enough now. I suppose you touch yourself."

I knew what she meant. What I didn't know was how to respond.

She said, "Don't be ashamed. Everybody does it, it's part of growing up. Let me see it." And, when confusion paralyzed me, "Take off your pajama bottoms and show me your dick."

I didn't want to. I did want to. I was embarrassed, I was excited, I was . . .

"It's getting bigger," she said. "You'll be a man soon. Show me how you touch yourself. Look how it grows! This is better than television. What do you think about when you touch it?"

Did I say anything? I don't believe I did.

"Titties?" She opened her robe. "You sucked on them when you were a baby. Do you remember?"

Wanting to look away. Wanting to stop touching myself.

"I'll tell you a secret. Touching your dick is nice, but it's nicer when someone else touches it for you. See? You can touch my titties while I do this for you. Doesn't that feel good? Doesn't it?"

I shot all over her hand. Thought she'd be angry. She put her hand to her face, licked it clean. Smiled at me.

"I don't know," she said.

Claudia, my blonde. I'd wondered, without much caring, just how natural that blondness might be. Still an open question, because the hair on her head was the only hair she had.

Had to wonder what my mother would have made of that. Shaving her legs was her concession to femininity, and one she accepted grudgingly.

Got so she'd have me do it. Come out of the bath, all warm from the tub, and I'd spread lather and wield the safety razor. I'd be growing whiskers in a couple of years, she told me. Might as well get in some practice for a lifetime of shaving.

I asked Claudia what she didn't know.

"I just wanted an adventure," she said.

"Shut the world out. Keep it on the other side of that door."

"But you've got a power," she said. "The same thing that drew me to you, pulled me right across the room to where you were standing—it scares me."

"Why's that?"

She closed her eyes, chose her words carefully. "What happens here stays here. Isn't that how it works?"

"Like Las Vegas?"

She opened her eyes, looked into mine. "I've done this sort of thing before," she said.

"I'm shocked."

"Not as often as you might think, but now and then."

"When the moon's full?"

"And left it behind me when I drove away. Like a massage, like a spa treatment."

"Then home to hubby."

"How was it hurting him? He never knew. And I was a better wife to him for having an outlet."

Taking her time getting to it. It was like watching a baseball pitcher going through an elaborate windup. Kind of interesting when you already knew what kind of curveball to expect.

"But this feels like more than that, doesn't it?"

She gave me a long look, like she wanted to say yes but was reluctant to speak the words.

Oh, she was good.

"You've thought of leaving him."

"Of course. But I have . . . oh, how to say this? He gives me a very comfortable life."

"That generally means money."

"His parents were wealthy," she said, "and he was an only child, and they're gone, and it's all come to him."

"I guess the Ford's a rental."

"The Ford? Oh, the car I'm driving. Yes, I picked it up at the airport. Why would you—oh, because I probably have a nicer car than that. Is that what you meant?"

"Something like that."

"We have several cars. There's a Lexus that I usually drive, and he bought me a vintage sports car as a present. An Aston Martin."

"Very nice."

"I suppose. I enjoyed driving it at first: the power, the responsiveness. Now I rarely take it out of the garage. It's an expensive toy. As am I."

"His toy. Does he take you out and play with you much?"

She didn't say anything.

I put my hand where she didn't have any hair. Not stroking her, just resting it there. Staking a claim.

I said, "If you divorced him—"

"I signed one of those things."

"A prenup."

"Yes."

"You'd probably get to keep the toys."

"Maybe."

"But the lush life would be over."

A nod.

"I suppose he's a lot older than you."

"Just a few years. He seems older, he's one of those men who act older than their years, but he's not that old."

"How's his health?"

"It's good. He doesn't exercise, he's substantially overweight, but he gets excellent reports at his annual physical."

"Still, anybody can stroke out or have a heart attack. Or a drunk driver runs a red light, hits him broadside."

"I don't even like to talk about something like that."

"Because it's almost like wishing for it."

"Yes."

"Still," I said, "it'd be convenient, wouldn't it?"

It wasn't like that with my mother. A stroke, a heart attack, a drunk driver. There one day and gone the next.

Not like that at all.

Two, three years after she showed me how much nicer it was to have someone else touch me. Two, three years when I went to school in the morning and came straight home in the afternoon and closed the door on the whole world.

She showed me all the things she knew. Plus things she'd heard or read about but never done.

And told me how to be with girls. "Like it's a sport and I'm your coach," she said. What to say, how to act, and how to get them to do things, or let me do things.

Then I'd come home and tell her about it. In bed, acting it out, fooling around.

Two, three years. And she started losing weight, and lost color in her face, and I must have noticed but it was day by day, and I was never conscious of it. And then I came home one day and she wasn't there, but there was a note, she'd be home soon. And an hour later she came in and I saw something in her face and I knew, but I didn't know what until she told me.

Ovarian cancer, and it had spread all through her, and they couldn't do anything. Nothing that would work.

Because of where it started, she wondered if it was punishment. For what we did.

"Except that's crap and I know it's crap. I was brought up believing in God, but I grew out of it, and I never raised you that way. And even if there was a God, he wouldn't work it that way. And what's wrong with what we did? Did it hurt anybody?"

And a little later, "All they can give me is chemo and all it'll do is hurt like fury and make my hair fall out and maybe stretch my life a few months longer. My sweet baby boy, I don't want you remembering a jaundiced old lady dying by inches and going crazy with the pain. I don't want to hang around that long, and you have to help me get out."

School. I didn't play sports, I didn't join clubs, I didn't have friends. But I knew who sold drugs; everybody knew that much. Anything you wanted, and what I wanted was downs, and that was easy.

She wanted to take them when I left for school, so that I'd be gone when it happened, but I talked her out of that. She took them at night, and I lay beside her and held her hand while sleep took her. And I stayed there, so I could tell when her breathing stopped, but I couldn't stay awake, I fell asleep myself, and when I woke up around dawn she was gone.

I straightened the house, went into my room and made the bed look as though it had been slept in. Went to school and kept myself from thinking about anything. Went home and, turning my key in the lock I had this flash, expecting her to be walking around when I opened the door.

Yeah, right. I found her where I'd left her, and I called the doctor, said I'd left in the morning without wanting to disturb her. He could tell it was pills, I could tell he could tell, but he wanted to spare me, said it was her heart giving out suddenly, said it happened a lot in cases like hers.

If she was alive, if she'd never gotten sick, I'd still be living there. With the two of us in that house, and the whole rest of the world locked out of it.

She said, "I can't pretend I never thought about it. But I never wished for it. He's not a bad man. He's been good to me."

"Takes good care of you."

"He cleans his golf clubs after he plays a round. Has this piece of flannel he uses to wipe the faces of the irons. Takes the cars in for their scheduled maintenance. And yes, he takes good care of me."

"Maybe that's all you want."

"I was willing to settle for it," she said.

"And now you're not?"

"I don't know," she said, and put her hand on me. For just a moment it was another hand, a firm but gentle hand, and I was a boy again. Just for an instant, and then that passed.

And she went on holding me, and she didn't say anything, but I could hear her voice in my head as clearly as if she'd spoken. *Willing to settle? Not anymore, my darling, because I've met you, and my world has changed forever. If only something could happen to him and we could be together forever. If only—*

"You want me to kill him," I said.

"Oh my God!"

"Isn't that where you were headed?"

She didn't answer, breathed deeply in and out, in and out. Then she said, "Have you ever—"

"Government puts you in a uniform, gives you a rifle, sends you halfway around the world. Man winds up doing a whole lot of things he might never do otherwise."

All of which was true, I suppose, but it had nothing much to do with me. I was never in the service.

Went to sign up once. You drift around, different things start looking good to you. Army shrink asked me a batch of questions, heard something he didn't like in my answers, and they thanked me for my time and sent me on my way.

Have to say that man was good at his job. I wouldn't have liked it there, and they wouldn't have liked me much, either.

She found something else to talk about, some rambling story about some neighbor of hers. I lay there and watched her lips move without taking in what she was saying.

Why bother? What she wasn't saying was more to the point.

Pleased with herself, I had to figure. Because she'd managed to get where she wanted to go without saying the words herself. Played it so neatly that I brought it up for her.

Like, I'm two steps ahead of you, missy. Knew where you were going, saw what a roundabout route you had mapped out for yourself, figured I'd save us some time.

Better now, looking without listening. And it was like I couldn't hear her if I wanted to, all I could hear was her voice speaking in my head, telling me what I knew she was thinking. How we could be together for the rest of our lives, how I was all she wanted and all she needed, how we'd have a life of luxury and glamour and travel. Her voice in my head, drawing pictures of her idea of my idea of paradise.

Voices.

She moved, lay on her side. Stopped talking, and I stopped hearing that other voice, and she ran a hand the length of my body. And kissed my face and my neck, and worked her way south.

Yeah, right. To give me a hint of the crazy pleasures on offer once her husband was dead and buried. Because every man loves that, right?

Thing is, I don't. Not since another woman took the pills I'd bought her and didn't wake up.

One time, I had this date with a girl in my class. And she was coaching me.

You can get her to suck it. She'll still be a virgin, she can't get pregnant from it, and she'll be making you happy. Plus deep down she's plain dying to do it.

But what you want to do is help her out, tell her when she's doing something wrong. Like you'll be her *coach, you know?*

Then she was gone, and since then I don't like having anybody doing that to me.

That army shrink? I guess he knew his business.

Still, she got it hard.

It plays by its own rules, doesn't it? The blood flows there or it doesn't, and you can't make it happen or keep it from happening. Didn't mean I enjoyed it, didn't mean I wanted her to keep it up. More she did it, less I liked it.

Took hold of her head, moved her away.

"Is something wrong?"

"My turn," I said, and spread her out on the bed, and tucked a pillow under her ass, and stuck a finger in to make sure she was wet. Stuck the finger in her mouth, gave her a taste of herself.

Got on her, rode her long and hard, long and hard. She had one of those rolling orgasms that won't quit, on and on and on, the gift that keeps on giving.

I don't know where my mind was while this was going on. Off somewhere, tuned in to something else. Watching HBO while she was getting fucked on Showtime.

When she was done I just stayed where I was, on her and in her. Looked down at her face, jaw slack, eyes shut, and saw what I hadn't seen earlier.

That she looked like a pig. Just had a real piggish quality to her features. Never saw it before.

Funny.

Her eyes opened. And her mouth started running, telling me it had never been like this before.

"Did you—"

"Not yet."

"My God, you're still hard! Is there anything—"

"Not just yet," I said. "Something I'd like to know first. When you walked into the bar?"

"A lifetime ago," she said. And relaxed into what she thought was going to be a stroll down memory lane. How we met, how we fell in love without a word being spoken.

I said, "What I wondered. How did you know?"

"How did I—"

"How'd you know I was the one man in there who'd be willing to kill your husband for you?"

Eyes wide. Speechless.

"What did you see? What did you think you saw?"

And my hips started working, slowly, short strokes.

"Had it all worked out in your mind," I said. I moved my elbows so they were on her shoulders, pinning her to the bed, and my hands found her neck, circled it.

"So you'd be out of town, maybe pick up some other lucky guy to make sure you'd have an alibi. Get off good with him, because all the while you're thinking about how I'm doing it, killing your husband. Wondering exactly how I'm doing it: Am I using a gun, a knife, a club? And you think of me doing him with my bare hands and that's what really gets you off, isn't it? Isn't it?"

She was saying something, but I couldn't hear it. Couldn't have heard a thunderclap, couldn't have heard the world ending.

"Filling my head with happily ever after, but once he's gone you don't need me anymore, do you? Maybe you'd find another sucker, get him to take me off the board."

Thrusting harder now. And my hands tightening on her throat. The terror in her eyes, Jesus, you could taste it.

Then the light went out of her eyes, and just like that she was gone.

Three, four more strokes and I got where I was going. What's funny is I didn't really feel it. The machinery worked, and I emptied myself into her, but you couldn't call it sensational, because, see, there wasn't a whole lot of sensation involved. There was a release, and that felt good, the way a piss does when you've been walking around with a full bladder.

Fact is, it's like that more often than not. I'd say the army shrink could explain it, but let's not make him into a genius. All he knew was the army was better off without me.

Most anybody's better off without me.

Claudia, for sure. Lying there now with her throat crushed and her eyes glassy. Minute I laid eyes on her, I knew she had the whole script worked out in her mind.

How'd she know? How'd she pick me?

And if I knew all that, if I could read her script and figure out a different ending than the one she had in mind, why'd I buy her a drink? All's said and done, how much real choice did I have in the matter once she'd gone and laid her hand on my arm?

Time to leave this town now, but who was I kidding? I'd find the same thing in the next town, or the town after that. Another roadhouse, where I might have to fight a guy or might not, but either way I'd walk out with a woman. She might not look as fine as this one, and she might have more hair besides what she had on her head, but she'd have the same plans for me.

And if I stayed out of the bars? If I went to some church socials, or Parents Without Partners, or some such?

Might work, but I wouldn't count on it. My luck, I'd wind up in the same damn place.

Like I said, I really know how to pick 'em.

Megan Abbott

Megan Abbott was born in the Detroit area, graduated from the University of Michigan with a B.A. in English literature, received her Ph.D. in English and American literature from New York University, and has taught literature, writing, and film at New York University and the State University of New York at Oswego. She published her first novel, *Die a Little*, in 2005, and has since come to be regarded as one of the foremost practitioners of modern noir mystery writing, with the *San Francisco Chronicle* saying that she was poised to "claim the throne as the finest prose stylist in crime fiction since Raymond Chandler." Her novels include *Queenpin*, which won the Edgar Award in 2008, *The Song Is You*, *Bury Me Deep*, and *The End of Everything*. Her most recent novel is *Dare Me*. Her other books include, as editor, the anthology *A Hell of a Woman: An Anthology of Female Noir* and a nonfiction study, *The Street Was Mine: White Masculinity in Hardboiled Fiction and Film Noir*. She lives in Forest Hills, New York, and maintains a website at meganabbott.com.

In the subtle yet harrowing story that follows, she shows us that there are some things that you just can't get over, no matter how hard you try—and some insights into the hearts of even those we love the most that you can't unsee once you see them.

MY HEART IS EITHER BROKEN

He waited in the car. He had parked under one of the big banks of lights. No one else wanted to park there. He could guess why. Three vehicles over, he saw a woman's back pressed against a window, her hair shaking. Once, she turned her head and he almost saw her face, the blue of her teeth as she smiled.

Fifteen minutes went by before Lorie came stumbling across the parking lot, heels clacking.

He had been working late and didn't even know she wasn't home until he got there. When she finally picked up her cell, she told him where she was, a bar he'd never heard of, a part of town he didn't know.

"I just wanted some noise and people," she had explained. "I didn't mean anything."

He asked if she wanted him to come get her.

"Okay," she said.

On the ride home, she was doing the laughing-crying thing she'd been doing lately. He wanted to help her but didn't know how. It reminded him of the kinds of girls he used to date in high school. The ones who wrote in ink all over their hands and cut themselves in the bathroom stalls at school.

"I hadn't been dancing in so long, and if I shut my eyes no one could see," she was saying, looking out the window, her head tilted against the window. "No one there knew me until someone did. A woman I didn't know. She kept shouting at me. Then she followed me into the bathroom stall and said she was glad my little girl couldn't see me now."

He knew what people would say. That she was out dancing at a grimy pickup bar. They wouldn't say she cried all the way home, that she didn't know what to do with herself, that no one knows how they'll act when something like this happens to them. Which it probably won't.

But he also wanted to hide, wanted to find a bathroom stall himself, in another city, another state, and never see anyone he knew again, especially his mother or his sister, who spent all day on the Internet trying to spread the word about Shelby, collecting tips for the police.

Shelby's hands—well, people always talk about baby's hands, don't they?—but they were like tight little flowers and he loved to put his palm over them. He never knew he'd feel like that. Never knew he'd be the kind of guy—that there even were kinds of guys—who would catch the milky scent of his daughter's baby blanket and feel warm inside. Even, sometimes, press his face against it.

It took him a long time to tug off the dark red cowboy boots she was wearing, ones he did not recognize.

When he pulled off her jeans, he didn't recognize her underwear either. The front was a black butterfly, its wings fluttering against her thighs with each tug.

He looked at her and a memory came to him of when they first dated, Lorie taking his hand and running it along her belly, her thighs. Telling him she once thought she'd be a dancer, that maybe she could be. And that if she ever had a baby she'd have a C-section, because everyone knew what happened to women's stomachs after, *not to mention what it does down there,* she'd said, laughing, and put his hand there next.

He'd forgotten all this, and other things too, but now the things kept coming back and making him crazy.

He poured a tall glass of water for her and made her drink it. Then he refilled it and set it beside her.

She didn't sleep like a drunk person but like a child, her lids twitching dreamily and a faint smile tugging at her mouth.

The moonlight coming in, it felt like he watched her all night, but at some point he must have fallen asleep.

When he woke, she had her head on his belly, was rubbing him drowsily.

"I was dreaming I was pregnant again," she murmured. "It was like Shelby all over again. Maybe we could adopt. There are so many babies out there that need love."

———

They had met six years ago. He was working for his mother, who owned a small apartment building on the north side of town.

Lorie lived on the first floor, where the window was high and you could see people walking on the sidewalk. His mother called it a "sunken garden apartment."

She lived with another girl and sometimes they came in very late, laughing and pressing up against each other in the way young girls do, whispering things, their legs bare and shiny in short skirts. He wondered what they said.

He was still in school then and would work evenings and weekends, changing washers on leaky faucets, taking out the trash.

Once, he was in front of the building, hosing down the garbage cans with bleach, and she rushed past him, her tiny coat bunched around her face. She was talking on the phone and she moved so quickly he almost didn't see her, almost splashed her with the hose. For a second he saw her eyes, smeary and wet.

"I wasn't lying," she was saying into the phone as she pushed her key into the front door, as she heaved her shoulders against it. "I'm not the liar here."

One evening not long after, he came home and there was a note under the door. It read:

My heart is either broken or I haven't paid the bill.
Thx, Lorie, #1-A

He'd read it four times before he figured it out.

She smiled when she opened the door, the security chain across her forehead.

He held up his pipe wrench.

"You're just in time," she said, pointing to the radiator.

No one ever thinks anything will ever happen to their baby girl. That's what Lorie kept saying. She'd been saying that to reporters, the police, for every day of the three weeks since it happened.

He watched her with the detectives. It was just like on TV except nothing like on TV. He wondered why nothing was ever like you thought it would be and then he realized it was because you never thought this would be you.

She couldn't sit still, her fingers twirling through the edges of her hair. Sometimes, at a traffic signal, she would pull nail scissors from her purse and trim the split ends. When the car began moving, she would wave her hand out the window, scattering the clippings into the wind.

It was the kind of careless, odd thing that made her so different from any girl he ever knew. Especially that she would do it front of him.

He was surprised how much he had liked it.

But now all of it seemed different and he could see the detectives watching her, looking at her like she was a girl in a short skirt, twirling on a bar stool and tossing her hair at men.

"We're gonna need you to start from the beginning again," the male one said, and that part was like on TV. "Everything you remember."

"She's gone over it so many times," he said, putting his hand over hers and looking at the detective wearily.

"I meant you, Mr. Ferguson," the detective said, looking at him. "Just you."

They took Lorie to the outer office and he could see her through the window, pouring long gulps of creamer into her coffee, licking her lips.

He knew how that looked too. The newspapers had just run a picture of her at a smoothie place. The caption was "What about Shelby?" They must have taken it through the front window. She was ordering something at the counter, and she was smiling. They always got her when she was smiling. They didn't understand that she smiled when she was sad. Sometimes she cried when she was happy, like at their wedding, when she cried all day, her face pink and gleaming, shuddering against his chest.

I never thought you would, she had said. *I never thought I would. That any of this could happen.*

He didn't know what she meant, but he loved feeling her huddled against him, her hips grinding against him like they did when she couldn't hold herself together and seemed to be holding on to him to keep from flying off the earth itself.

"So, Mr. Ferguson," the detective said, "you came home from work and there was no one home?"

"Right," he said. "Call me Tom."

"Tom," the detective started again, but the name seemed to fumble in his mouth like he'd rather not say it. Last week he'd called him Tom. "Was it unusual to find them gone at that time of day?"

"No," he said. "She liked to keep busy."

It was true, because Lorie never stayed put and sometimes would strap Shelby into the car seat and drive for hours, putting 100 or 200 miles on the car.

She would take her to Mineral Pointe and take photos of them in front of the water. He would get them on his phone at work and they always made him grin. He liked how she was never one of these women who stayed at home and watched court shows or the shopping channels.

She worked twenty-five hours a week at the Y while his mother stayed with Shelby. Every morning, she ran five miles, putting Shelby in the jogging stroller. She made dinner every night and sometimes even mowed the lawn when he was too busy. She never ever stopped moving.

This is what the newspapers and the TV people loved. They loved to take pictures of her jogging in her short shorts and talking on the phone in her car and looking at fashion magazines in line at the grocery store.

"What about Shelby?" the captions always read.

They never understood her at all. He was the only one.

"So," the detective asked him, rousing from his thoughts, "what did you do when you found the house empty?"

"I called her cell." He had. She hadn't answered, but that wasn't unusual either. He didn't bother to tell them that. That he'd called four or five times and the phone went straight to voice mail and it wasn't until the last time she picked up.

Her voice had been strange, small, like she might be in the doctor's office, or the ladies' room. Like she was trying to make herself quiet and small.

"Lorie? Are you okay? Where are you guys?"

There had been a long pause and the thought came that she had crashed the car. For a crazy second he thought she might be in the hospital, both of them broken and battered. Lorie was a careless driver, always sending him texts from the car. Bad pictures came into his head. He'd dated a girl once who had a baby shoe that hung on her rearview mirror. She said it was to remind her to drive carefully, all the time. No one ever told you that after you were sixteen.

"Lorie, just tell me." He had tried to make his voice firm but kind.

"Something happened."

"Lorie," he tried again, like after a fight with her brother or her boss, "just take a breath and tell me."

"Where did she go?" her voice came. "And how is she going to find me? She's a little girl. She doesn't know anything. They should put dog tags on them like they did when we were kids, remember that?"

. He didn't remember that at all, and there was a whirr in his head that was making it hard for him to hear.

"Lorie, you need to tell me what's going on."

So she did.

She said she'd been driving around all morning, looking at lawn mowers she'd found for sale on Craigslist. She was tired, decided to stop for coffee at the expensive place.

She saw the woman there all the time. They talked online about how expensive the coffee was but how they couldn't help it. And what was an Americano, anyway? And, yeah, they talked about their kids. She was pretty sure the woman said she had kids. Two, she thought. And it was only going to be two minutes, five at the most.

"What was going to be five minutes?" he had asked her.

"I don't know how it happened," she said, "but I spilled my coffee, and it was everywhere. All over my new white coat. The one you got me for Christmas."

He had remembered her opening the box, tissue paper flying. She had said he was the only person who'd ever bought her clothes that came in boxes, with tissue paper in gold seals.

She'd spun around in the coat and said, *Oh, how it sparkles.*

Crawling onto his lap, she'd smiled and said only a man would give the mother of a toddler a white coat.

"The coat was soaking," she said now. "I asked the woman if she could watch Shelby while I was in the restroom. It took a little while because I had to get the key. One of those heavy keys they give you."

When she came out of the restroom, the woman was gone, and so was Shelby.

———

He didn't remember ever feeling the story didn't make sense. It was what happened. It was what happened to them, and it was part of the whole impossible run of events that led to this. That led to Shelby being gone and no one knowing where.

But it seemed clear almost from the very start that the police didn't feel they were getting all the information, or that the information made sense.

"They don't like me," Lorie said. And he told her that wasn't true and had nothing to do with anything anyway, but maybe it did.

He wished they could have seen Lorie when she had pushed through the front door that day, her purse unzipped, her white coat still damp from the spilled coffee, her mouth open so wide, all he could see was the red inside her, raw and torn.

Hours later, their family around them, her body shuddering against him as her brother talked endlessly about Amber Alerts and Megan's Law and his criminal justice class and his cop buddies from the gym, he felt her pressing into him and saw the feathery curl tucked in her sweater collar, a strand of Shelby's angel-white hair.

By the end of the second week, the police hadn't found anything, or if they did they weren't telling. Something seemed to have shifted, or gotten worse.

"Anybody would do it," Lorie said. "People do it all the time."

He watched the detective watch her. This was the woman detective, the one with the severe ponytail who was always squinting at Lorie.

"Do what?" the woman detective asked.

"Ask someone to watch their kid, for just a minute," Lorie said, her back stiffening. "Not a guy. I wouldn't have left her with a man. I wouldn't have left her with some homeless woman waving a hairbrush at me. This was a woman I saw in there every day."

"Named?" They had asked her for the woman's name many times. They knew she didn't know it.

Lorie looked at the detective, and he could see those faint blue veins showing under her eyes. He wanted to put his arm around her, to make her feel him there, to calm her. But before he could do anything, she started talking again.

"Mrs. Caterpillar," she said, throwing her hands in the air. "Mrs. Linguini. Madame Lafarge."

The detective stared at her, not saying anything.

"Let's try looking her up on the Internet," Lorie said, her chin jutting and a kind of hard glint to her eyes. All the meds and the odd hours they were keeping, all the sleeping pills and sedatives and Lorie walking through the house all night, talking about nothing but afraid to lie still.

"Lorie," he said. "Don't—"

"Everything always happens to me," she said, her voice suddenly soft and strangely liquid, her body sinking. "It's so unfair."

He could see it happening, her limbs going limp, and he made a grab for her.

She nearly slipped from him, her eyes rolling back in her head.

"She's fainting," he said, grabbing her, her arms cold like frozen pipes. "Get someone."

The detective was watching.

"I can't talk about it because I'm still coping with it," Lorie told the reporters who were waiting outside the police station. "It's too hard to talk about."

He held her arm tightly and tried to move her through the crowd, bunched so tightly, like the knot in his throat.

"Is it true you're hiring at attorney?" one of the reporters asked.

Lorie looked at them. He could see her mouth open and there was no time to stop her.

"I didn't do anything wrong," she said, a hapless grin on her face. As if she had knocked someone's grocery cart with her own.

He looked at her. He knew what she meant—she meant leaving Shelby for that moment, that scattered moment. But he also knew how it sounded, and how she looked, that panicky smile she couldn't stop.

That was the only time he let her speak to reporters.

Later, at home, she saw herself on the nightly news

Walking slowly to the TV, she kneeled in front of it, her jeans skidding on the carpet, and did the oddest thing.

She put her arms around it, like it was a teddy bear, a child.

"Where is she?" she whispered. "Where is she?"

And he wished the reporters could see this, the mystifying way grief was settling into her like a fever.

But he was also glad they couldn't.

It was the middle of the night, close to dawn, and she wasn't next to him.

He looked all over the house, his chest pounding. He thought he must be dreaming, calling out her name, both their names.

He found her in the backyard, a lithe shadow in the middle of the yard. She was sitting on the grass, her phone lighting her face.

"I feel closer to her out here," she said. "I found this."

He could barely see, but moving closer saw the smallest of earrings, an enamel butterfly, caught between her fingers.

They had had a big fight when she came home with Shelby, her ears pierced, thick gold posts plugged in such tiny lobes. Her ears red, her face red, her eyes soft with tears.

"Where did she go, babe?" Lorie said to him now. "Where did she go?"

He was soaked with sweat and was pulling his T-shirt from his chest.

"Look, Mr. Ferguson," the detective said, "you've cooperated with us fully. I get that. But understand our position. No one can confirm her story. The employee who saw your wife spill her coffee remembers seeing her leave with Shelby. She doesn't remember another woman at all."

"How many people were in there? Did you talk to all of them?"

"There's something else too, Mr. Ferguson."

"What?"

"One of the other employees said Lorie was really mad about the coffee spill. She told Shelby it was her fault. That everything was her fault. And that Lorie then grabbed your daughter by the arm and shook her."

"That's not true," he said. He'd never seen Lorie touch Shelby roughly. Sometimes it seemed she barely knew she was there.

"Mr. Ferguson, I need to ask you: Has your wife had a history of emotional problems?"

"What kind of question is that?"

"It's a standard question in cases like this," the detective said. "And we've had some reports."

"Are you talking about the local news?"

"No, Mr. Ferguson. We don't collect evidence from TV."

"Collecting evidence? What kind of evidence would you need to collect about Lorie? It's Shelby who's missing. Aren't you—"

"Mr. Ferguson, did you know your wife spent three hours at Your Place Lounge on Charlevoix yesterday afternoon?"

"Are you following her?"

"Several patrons and one of the bartenders contacted us. They were concerned."

"Concerned? Is that what they were?" His head was throbbing.

"Shouldn't they be concerned, Mr. Ferguson? This is a woman whose baby is missing."

"If they were so concerned, why didn't they call me?"

"One of them asked Lorie if he could call you for her. Apparently, she told him not to."

He looked at the detective. "She didn't want to worry me."

The detective looked back at him. "Okay."

"You can't tell how people are going to act when something like this happens to you," he said, feeling his head dipping. Suddenly his shoulders felt very heavy and he had these pictures of Lorie in his head, at the far corner of the long black lacquered bar, eyes heavy with makeup and filled with dark feelings. Feelings he could never touch. Never once did he feel sure he knew what she was thinking. That was part of it. Part of the throb in his chest, the longing there that never left.

"No," he said, suddenly.

"What?" the detective asked, leaning forward.

"She has no history of emotional problems. My wife."

It was the fourth week, the fourth week of false leads and crying and sleeping pills and night terrors. And he had to go back to work or they wouldn't make the mortgage payment. They'd talked about Lorie returning to her part-time job at the candle store, but somebody needed to be home, to be waiting.

(Though what, really, were they waiting for? Did toddlers suddenly toddle home after twenty-seven days? That's what he could tell the cops were thinking.)

"I guess I'll call the office tomorrow," he said. "And make a plan."

"And I'll be here," she said. "You'll be there and I'll be here."

It was a terrible conversation, like a lot of those conversations couples have in dark bedrooms, late into the night, when you know the decisions you've been avoiding all day won't wait anymore.

After they talked, she took four big pills and pushed her face into her pillow.

He couldn't sleep and went into Shelby's room, which he only ever did at night. He leaned over the crib, which was too small for her but Lorie wouldn't use the bed yet, said it wasn't time, not nearly.

He put his fingers on the soft baby bumpers, festooned with bright yellow fish. He remembered telling Shelby they were goldfish, but she kept saying *Nana, nana,* which was what she called bananas.

Her hands were always covered with the pearly slime of bananas, holding on to the front of Lorie's shirt.

One night, sliding his hand under Lorie's bra clasp, between her breasts, he felt a daub of banana even there.

"It's everywhere," Lorie had sighed. "It's like she's made of bananas."

He loved that smell, and his daughter's forever-glazed hands.

At some point, remembering this, he started crying, but then he stopped and sat in the rocking chair until he fell asleep.

In part, he was relieved to go back to work, all those days with neighbors and families and friends huddling in the house, trading Internet rumors, organizing vigils and searches. But now there were fewer family members, only a couple friends who had no other place to go, and no neighbors left at all.

The woman from the corner house came late one evening and asked for her casserole dish back.

"I didn't know you'd keep it so long," she said, eyes narrowing.

She seemed to be trying to look over his shoulder, into the living room. Lorie was watching a show, loudly, about a group of blond women with tight lacquered faces and angry mouths. She watched it all the time; it seemed to be the only show on TV anymore.

"I didn't know," the woman said, taking her dish, inspecting it, "how things were going to turn out."

you sexy, sexy boy, Lorie's text said. *i want your hands on me. come home and handle me, rough as u like. rough me up.*

He swiveled at his desk chair hard, almost like he needed to cover the phone, cover his act of reading the text.

He left the office right away, driving as fast as he could. Telling himself that something was wrong with her. That this had to be some side effect of the pills the doctor had given her, or the way sorrow and longing could twist in her complicated little body.

But that wasn't really why he was driving so fast, or why he nearly tripped on the dangling seat belt as he hurried from the car.

Or why he felt, when he saw her lying on the bed, flat on her stomach and head turned, smiling, that he'd burst in two if he didn't have her. If he didn't have her then and there, the bed moaning beneath them and she not making a sound but, the blinds pulled down, her white teeth shining, shining from her open mouth.

It felt wrong but he wasn't sure why. He knew her, but he didn't. This was her, but a Lorie from long ago. Except different.

The reporters called all the time. And there were two that never seemed to leave their block. They had been there right at the start, but then seemed to go away, to move on to other stories.

They came back when the footage of Lorie coming out of Magnum Tattoo Parlor began appearing. Someone shot it with their cell phone.

Lorie was wearing those red cowboy boots again, and red lipstick, and she walked right up to the camera.

They ran photos of it in the newspaper with the headline: *A Mother's Grief?*

He looked at the tattoo.

The words *Mirame quemar* written in script, wrapping itself around her hip.

It covered just the spot where a stretch mark had been, the one she always covered with her fingers when she stood before him naked.

He looked at the tattoo in the dark bedroom, a band of light coming from the hallway. She turned her hip, kept turning it, spinning her torso so he could feel it, all of it.

"I needed it," she said. "I needed something. Something to put my fingers on. To remind me of me.

"Do you like it?" she asked, her breath in his ear. The ink looked like it was moving.

"I like it," he said, putting his fingers there. Feeling a little sick. He did like it. He liked it very much.

Late, late into that night, her voice shook him from a deep sleep.

"I never knew she was coming and then she was here," she was saying, her face pressed in her pillow. "And I never knew she was going and now she's gone."

He looked at her, her eyes shut, dappled with old makeup.

"But," she said, her voice grittier, strained, "she was always doing whatever she wanted."

That's what he thought she said. But she was sleeping, and didn't make any sense at all.

"You liked it until you thought about it," she said. "Until you looked close at it and then you decided you didn't want it anymore. Or didn't want to be the guy who wants it."

He was wearing the new shirt she had bought for him the day before. It was a deep, deep purple and beautiful and he felt good in it, like the unit manager who all the women in the office talked about. They talked about his shoes and he always wondered where people got shoes like that.

"No," he said. "I love it. But it's just . . . expensive."

That wasn't it, though. It didn't seem right buying things, buying anything, right now. But it was also how colorful the shirt was, the sheen on it. The bright, hard beauty of it. A shirt for going out, for nightclubs, for dancing. For those things they did when they still did things: vodka and pounding music and frenzied sex in her car.

The kind of drunken sex so messy and crazy that you were almost shy around each other after, driving home, screwed sober, feeling like you'd showed something very private and very bad.

Once, years ago, she did something to him no one had ever done and he couldn't look at her afterward at all. The next time he did something to her. For a while, it felt like it would never stop.

"I think someone should tell you about your wife," the e-mail said. That was the subject line. He didn't recognize the address, a series of letters and digits, and there was no text in the body of the e-mail. There was only a photo of a girl dancing in a bright green halter top, the ties loose and dangling.

It was Lorie, and he knew it must be an old picture. Weeks ago, the newspapers had gotten their hands on some snapshots of Lorie from her late teens, dancing on tabletops, kissing her girlfriends. Things girls did when they were drinking and someone had a camera.

In those shots, Lorie was always posing, vamping, trying to look like a model, a celebrity. It was a Lorie before he really knew her, a Lorie from what she called her "wild girl days."

But in this picture she didn't seem to be aware of the camera at all, seemed to be lost in the thrall of whatever music was playing, whatever sounds she was hearing in her crowded head. Her eyes were shut tight, her head thrown back, her neck long and brown and beautiful.

She looked happier than he had ever seen her.

A Lorie from long ago, or never.

But when he scrolled further down, he saw the halter top riding up her body, saw the pop of a hip bone. Saw the elegant script letters: *Mirame quemar.*

That night, he remembered a story she had told him long ago. It seemed impossible he'd forgotten it. Or maybe it just seemed different now, making it seem like something new. Something uncovered, an old sunken box you find in the basement smelling strong and you're afraid to open it.

It was back when they were dating, when her roommate was always around and they had no place to be alone. They would have thrilling bouts in his car, and she loved to crawl into the backseat and lie back, hoisting a leg high over the headrest and begging him for it.

It was after the first or second time, back when it was all so crazy and confusing and his head was pounding and starbursting, that Lorie curled against him and talked and talked about her life, and the time she stole four Revlon eyeslicks from CVS and how she had slept with a soggy-eared stuffed animal named Ears until she was twelve. She said she felt she could tell him anything.

Somewhere in the blur of those nights—nights when he, too, told her private things, stories about babysitter crushes and shoplifting Matchbox cars—that she told him the story.

How, when she was seven, her baby brother was born and she became so jealous.

"My mom spent all her time with him, and left me alone all day," she said. "So I hated him. Every night, I would pray that he would be taken away. That something awful would happen to him. At night, I'd sneak over to his crib and stare at him through the little bars. I think maybe I figured I could think it into happening. If I stared at him long enough and hard enough, it might happen."

He had nodded, because this is how kids could be, he guessed. He was the youngest and wondered if his older sister thought things like this about him. Once, she smashed his finger under a cymbal and said it was an accident.

But she wasn't done with her story and she snuggled closer to him and he could smell her powdery body and he thought of all its little corners and arcs, how he liked to find them with his hands, all the soft, hot places on her. Sometimes it felt like her body was never the same body, like it changed under his hands. *I'm a witch, a witch.*

"So one night," she said, her voice low and sneaky, "I was watching him through the crib bars and he was making this funny noise."

Her eyes glittered in the dark of the car.

"I leaned across, sticking my hands through the rails," she said, snaking her hand towards him. "And that's when I saw this piece of string dangling on his chin, from his pull toy. I starting pulling it, and pulling it."

He watched her tugging the imaginary string, her eyes getting bigger and bigger.

"Then he let out this gasp," she said, "and started breathing again."

She paused, her tongue clicking.

"My mom came in at just that moment. She said I saved his life," she said. "Everyone did. She bought me a new jumper and the hot-pink shoes I wanted. Everyone loved me."

A pair of headlights flashed across them and he saw her eyes, bright and brilliant.

"So no one ever knew the real story," she said. "I've never told anyone." She smiled, pushing herself against him.

"But now I'm telling you," she said. "Now I have someone to tell."

"Mr. Ferguson, you told us, and your cell phone records confirm, that you began calling your wife at 5:50 p.m. on the day of your daughter's disappearance. Finally, you reached her at 6:45. Is that right?"

"I don't know," he said, this the eighth, ninth, tenth time they'd called him in. "You would know better than me."

"Your wife said she was at the coffee place at around five. But we tracked down a record of your wife's transaction. It was at 3:45."

"I don't know," he said, rubbing at the back of his neck, the prickling there. He realized he had no idea what they might tell him. No idea what might be coming.

"So what do you think your wife was doing for three hours?"

"Looking for this woman. Trying to find her."

"She did make some other calls during that time. Not to the police, of course. Or even you. She made a call to a man named Leonard Drake. Another one named Jason Patrini."

One sounded like an old boyfriend—Lenny someone—the other he didn't even know. He felt something hollow out inside him. He didn't know who they were even talking about anymore, but it had nothing to do with him.

The female detective walked in, giving her partner a look.

"Since she was making all these calls, we could track her movements. She went to the Harbor View Mall."

"Would you like to see her on the security camera footage there?" the female detective asked. "We have it now. Did you know she bought a tank top."

He felt nothing.

"She also went to the quickie mart. The cashier just IDed her. She used the bathroom. He said she was in there a long time and when she came out, she had changed clothing.

"Would you like to see the footage there? She looks like a million bucks."

She slid a grainy photo across the desk. A young woman in a tank top and hoodie tugged low over her brow. She was smiling.

"That's not Lorie," he said softly. She looked too young, looked like she looked when he met her, a little elfin beauty with a flat stomach and pigtails and a pierced navel. A hoop he used to tug. He'd forgotten about that. She must have let it seal over.

"I'm sure this is tough to hear, Mr. Ferguson," the male detective said. "I'm sorry."

He looked up. The detective did look very sorry.

"What did you say to them?" he asked.

Lorie was sitting in the car with him, a half block from the police station.

"I don't know if you should say anything to them anymore," he said. "I think maybe we should call a lawyer."

Lorie was looking straight ahead, at the strobing lights from the intersection. Slowly, she lifted her hand to the edges of her hair, combing them thoughtfully.

"I explained," she said, her face dark except for a swoop of blue from the car dealership sign, like a tadpole up her cheek. "I told them the truth."

"What truth?" he asked. The car felt so cold. There was a smell coming from her, of someone who hasn't eaten. A raw smell of coffee and nail polish remover.

"They don't believe anything I say anymore," she said. "I explained how I'd been to the coffee place twice that day. Once to get a juice for Shelby and then later for coffee for me. They said they'd look into it, but I could see how it was on their faces. I told them so. I know what they think of me."

She turned and looked at him, the car moving fast, sending red lights streaking up her face. It reminded him of a picture he once saw in a *National Geographic* of an Amazon woman, her face painted crimson, a wooden peg through her lip.

"Now I know what everyone thinks of me," she said, and turned away again.

It was late that night, his eyes wide open, that he asked her. She was sound asleep, but he said it.

"Who's Leonard Drake? Who's Jason whatever?"

She stirred, shifted to face him, her face flat on the sheet.

"Who's Tom Ferguson? Who is he?

"Is that what you do?" he asked, his voice rising. "Go around calling men."

It was easier to ask her this than to ask her other things. To ask her if she had shaken Shelby, if she had lied about everything. Other things.

"Yes," she said. "I call men all day long, I go to their apartments. I leave my daughter in the car, especially if it's very hot. I sneak up their apartment stairs."

She had her hand on her chest, was moving it there, watching him.

"You should feel how much I want them by the time they open their doors."

Stop, he said, without saying it.

"I have my hands on their belts before they close the door behind me. I crawl onto their laps on their dirty bachelor's sofas and do everything."

He started shaking his head, but she wouldn't stop.

"You have a baby, your body changes. You need something else. So I let them do anything. I've done everything."

Her hand was moving, touching herself. She wouldn't stop.

"That's what I do while you're at work. I wasn't calling people on Craigslist, trying to replace your lawn mower. I wasn't doing something for you, always for you."

He'd forgotten about the lawn mower, forgotten that's what she'd said she'd been doing that day. Trying to get a secondhand one after he'd gotten blood blisters on both hands using it the last time. That's what she'd said she was doing.

"No," she was saying, "I was calling men, making dates for sex. That's what I do since I've had a baby and been at home. I don't know how to do anything else. It's amazing I haven't been caught before. If only I hadn't been caught."

He covered his face with his hand. "I'm sorry. I'm sorry."

"How could you?" she said, a strangle in her throat. She was tugging all the sheet into her hands, rolling it, pulling off him, wringing it. "How could you?"

He dreamt of Shelby that night.

He dreamt he was wandering through the blue-dark of the house and when he got to Shelby's room, there was no room at all and suddenly he was outside.

The yard was frost-tipped and lonely looking and he felt a sudden sadness. He felt suddenly like he had fallen into the loneliest place in the world, and the old toolshed in the middle seemed somehow the very center of that loneliness.

When they'd bought the house, they'd nearly torn it down—everyone said they should—but they decided they liked it; the "baby barn," they'd called it, with its sloping roof and faded red paint.

But it was too small for anything but a few rakes and that push lawn mower with the sagging left wheel.

It was the only old thing about their house, the only thing left from before he was there.

By day, it was a thing he never thought about at all anymore, didn't notice it other than the smell sometimes coming off it after rain.

But in the dream it seemed a living thing, neglected and pitiful.

It came to him suddenly that the lawn mower in the shed might still be fixed, and if it were, then everything would be okay and no one would need to look for lawn mowers and the thick tug of grass under his feet would not feel so heavy and all this loneliness would end.

He put his hand on the shed's cool, crooked handle and tugged it open.

Instead of the lawn mower, he saw a small black sack on the floor of the shed.

He thought to himself in the way you do in dreams: *I must have left the cuttings in here. They must be covered with mold and that must be the smell so strong it—*

Grabbing for the sack, it slipped open, and the bag itself began to come apart in his hands.

There was the sound, the feeling of something heavy dropping to the floor of the shed.

It was too dark to see what was slipping over his feet, tickling his ankles.

Too dark to be sure, but it felt like the sweet floss of his daughter's hair.

He woke already sitting up. A voice was hissing in his head: *Will you look in the shed? Will you?*

And that was when he remembered there was no shed in the backyard anymore. They'd torn it down when Lorie was pregnant because she said the smell of rot was giving her headaches, making her sick.

The next day the front page of the paper had a series of articles marking the two-month anniversary of Shelby's disappearance.

They had the picture of Lorie under the headline: *What Does She Know?* There was a picture of him, head down, walking from the police station yesterday. The caption read: "More unanswered questions."

He couldn't read any of it, and when his mother called he didn't pick up.

All day at work, he couldn't concentrate. He felt everyone looking at him. When his boss came to his desk, he could feel the careful way he was being talked to.

"Tom, if you want to leave early," he said, "that's fine."

Several times he caught the administrative assistant staring at his screen saver, the snapshot of Lorie with ten-month-old Shelby in her Halloween costume, a black spider with soft spider legs.

Finally he did leave, at three o'clock.

Lorie wasn't in the house and he was standing at the kitchen sink, drinking a glass of water, when he saw her through the window.

Though it was barely seventy degrees, she was lying on one of the summer loungers.

Headphones on, she was in a bright orange bikini with gold hoops in the straps and on either hip.

She had pushed the purple playhouse against the back fence, where it tilted under the elm tree.

He had never seen the bikini before, but he recognized the sunglasses, large ones with white frames she had bought on a trip Mexico she had taken with an old girlfriend right before she got pregnant.

Gleaming in the center of her slicked torso was a gold belly ring.

She was smiling, singing along to whatever music was playing in her head.

That night he couldn't bring himself to go to bed. He watched TV for hours without watching any of it. He drank four beers in a row, which he had not done since he was twenty years old.

Finally, the beer pulled on him, and the Benadryl he took after, and he found himself sinking at last onto their mattress.

At some point in the middle of the night, there was a stirring next to him, her body shifting hard. It felt like something was happening.

"Kirsten," she mumbled.

"What?" he asked. "What?"

Suddenly she half sat up, her elbows beneath her, looking straight ahead.

"Her daughter's name was Kirsten," she said, her voice soft and tentative. "I just remembered. Once, when we were talking, she said her daughter's name was Kirsten. Because she liked how it sounded with Krusie."

He felt something loosen inside him, then tighten again. What was this?

"Her last name was Krusie with a *K*," she said, her face growing more animated, her voice more urgent. "I don't know how it was spelled, but it was with a *K*. I can't believe I just remembered. It was a long time ago. She said she liked the two *K*s. Because she was two *K*s. Katie Krusie. That's her name."

He looked at her and didn't say anything.

"Katie Krusie," she said. "The woman at the coffee place. That's her name."

He couldn't seem to speak or even move.

"Are you going to call?" she said. "The police?"

He found he couldn't move. He was afraid somehow. So afraid he couldn't breathe.

She looked at him, paused, and then reached across him, grabbing for the phone herself.

As she talked to the police, told them, her voice now clear and firm, what she'd remembered, as she told them she would come to the station, would leave in five minutes, he watched her, his hand over his own heart, feeling it beating so hard it hurt.

———

"We believe we have located the Krusie woman," the female detective said. "We have officers heading there now."

He looked at both of them. He could feel Lorie beside him, breathing hard. It had been less than a day since Lorie first called.

"What are you saying?" he said, or tried to. No words came out.

Katie-Ann Krusie had no children, but told people she did, all the time. After a long history of emotional problems, she had spent a fourteen-month stint at the state hospital following a miscarriage.

For the past eight weeks she had been living in a rental in Torring, forty miles away with a little blond girl she called Kirsten.

After the police released a photo of Katie-Ann Krusie on Amber Alert, a woman who worked at a coffee chain in Torring recognized her as a regular customer, always ordering extra milk for her babies.

"She sure sounded like she loved her kids," the woman said. "Just talking about them made her so happy."

The first time he saw Shelby again, he couldn't speak at all.

She was wearing a shirt he'd never seen and shoes that didn't fit and she was holding a juice box the policeman had given her.

She watched him as he ran down the hall toward her.

There was something in her face that he had never seen before, knew hadn't been there before, and he knew in an instant he had to do everything he could to make it gone.

That was all he would do, if it took him the rest of his life to do it.

The next morning, after calling everyone, one by one, he walked into the kitchen to see Lorie sitting next to Shelby, who was eating apple slices, her pinkie finger curled out in that way she had.

He sat and watched her and Shelby asked him why he was shaking and he said because he was glad to see her.

It was hard to leave the room, even to answer the door when his mother and sister came, when everyone started coming.

Three nights later, at the big family dinner, the Welcome Home dinner for Shelby, Lorie drank a lot of wine and who could blame her, everyone was saying.

He couldn't either, and he watched her.

As the evening carried on, as his mother brought out an ice cream cake for Shelby, as everyone huddled around Shelby, who seemed confused and shy at first and slowly burst into something beautiful that made him want to cry again—as all these things were occurring—he had one eye on Lorie, her quiet, still face. On the smile there, which never grew or receded, even when she held Shelby in her lap, Shelby nuzzling her mother's wine-flushed neck.

At one point he found her standing in the kitchen and staring into the sink; it seemed to him she was staring down into the drain.

It was very late, or even early, and Lorie wasn't there.

He thought she had gotten sick from all the wine, but she wasn't in the bathroom either.

Something was turning in him, uncomfortably, as he walked into Shelby's room.

He saw her back, naked and white from the moonlight. The plum-colored underpants she'd slept in.

She was standing over Shelby's crib, looking down.

He felt something in his chest move.

Then, slowly, she kneeled, peeking through the crib rails, looking at Shelby.

It looked like she was waiting for something.

For a long time he stood there, five feet from the doorway, watching her watching their sleeping baby.

He listened close for his daughter's high breaths, the stop and start of them.

He couldn't see his wife's face, only that long white back of hers, the notches of her spine. *Mirame quemar* etched on her hip.

He watched her watching his daughter, and knew he could not ever leave this room. That he would have to be here forever now, on guard. There was no going back to bed.

Joe R. Lansdale

Prolific Texas writer Joe R. Lansdale has won the Edgar Award, the British Fantasy Award, the American Horror Award, the American Mystery Award, the International Crime Writer's Award, and six Bram Stoker Awards. Although perhaps best known for horror/thrillers such as *The Nightrunners, Bubba Ho-Tep, The Bottoms, The God of the Razor,* and *The Drive-In,* he also writes the popular Hap Collins and Leonard Pine mystery series—*Savage Season, Mucho Mojo, The Two-Bear Mambo, Bad Chili, Rumble Tumble, Captains Outrageous*—as well as Western novels such as *Texas Night Riders* and *Blood Dance,* and totally unclassifiable cross-genre novels such as *Zeppelins West, The Magic Wagon,* and *Flaming London.* His other novels include *Dead in the West, The Big Blow, Sunset and Sawdust, Act of Love, Freezer Burn, Waltz of Shadows, The Drive-In 2: Not Just One of Them Sequels,* and *Leather Maiden.* He has also contributed novels to series such as Batman and Tarzan. His many short stories have been collected in *By Bizarre Hands; Tight Little Stitches in a Dead Man's Back; The Shadows, Kith and Kin; The Long Ones; Stories by Mama Lansdale's Youngest Boy; Bestsellers Guaranteed; On the Far Side of the Cadillac Desert with Dead Folks; Electric Gumbo; Writer of the Purple Rage; A Fist Full of Stories; Steppin' Out, Summer, '68; Bumper Crop; The Good, the Bad, and the Indifferent; For a Few Stories More; Mad Dog Summer and Other Stories; The King and Other Stories; Deadman's Road;* an omnibus, *Flaming Zeppelins: The Adventures of Ned the Seal;* and *High Cotton: Selected Stories of Joe R. Lansdale.* As editor, he has produced the anthologies *The Best of the West, Retro Pulp Tales, Son of Retro Pulp Tales, Razored Saddles* (with Pat LoBrutto), *Dark at Heart: All New Tales of Dark Suspense from Today's Masters* (with his wife Karen Lansdale), *The Horror Hall of Fame: The Stoker Winners,* and the Robert E. Howard tribute anthology *Cross Plains Universe* (with Scott A. Cupp). An anthology in tribute to Lansdale's work is *Lords of the Razor.* His most recent books are two new Hap and Leonard novels, *Devil Red* and *Hyenas;* the novels *Deranged by Choice* and *Edge of Dark Water;* a new collection, *Shadows West* (with John L. Lansdale); and, as editor, two new anthologies, *Crucified Dreams* and *The Urban Fantasy Anthology* (with Peter S. Beagle). He lives with his family in Nacogdoches, Texas.

Here he introduces us to the best bad girl ever, a woman who has the mojo, the black doo-doo, and the silent dog whistle over every man she meets; a woman like a bright red apple with a worm in the center, one who could make a priest go home and cut his throat if he saw her walking down the street. In short, a character that only Lansdale could write.

WRESTLING JESUS

First they took Marvin's sack lunch, then his money, and then they kicked his ass. In fact, he felt the ass whipping, had it been put on a scale of one to ten, was probably about a fourteen. However, Marvin factored in that some of the beating had been inconsistent, as one of his attackers had paused to light a cigarette, and afterwards, two of them had appeared tired and out of breath.

Lying there, tasting blood, he liked to think that, taking in the pause for a smoke and the obvious exhaustion of a couple of his assailants, points could be taken away from their overall performance, and their rating would merely have been nine or ten instead of the full fourteen.

This, however, didn't help his ribs one little bit, and it didn't take away the spots swimming before his eyes just before he passed out from the pain. When he awoke, he was being slapped awake by one of the bullies, who wanted to know if he had any gold teeth. He said he didn't, and the thug insisted on seeing, and Marvin opened his mouth, and the mugger took a look.

Disappointed, the thug threatened to piss in his mouth or fuck him, but the thug and his gang were either too tired from beating him to fuck him, or weren't ready to make water, because they started walking away, splitting up his money in fourths as they walked. They had each made about three dollars and twenty cents, and from his backpack they had taken a pretty good ham sandwich and a little container of Jell-O. There was, however, only one plastic spoon.

Marvin was beginning to feel one with the concrete when a voice said, "You little shits think you're something, don't ya?"

Blinking, Marvin saw that the speaker was an old man, slightly stooped, bowlegged, with white hair and a face that looked as if it had once come apart and been puzzled back together by a drunk in a dark room with cheap glue. His ear—Marvin could see the right one—contained enough hair to knit a small dog sweater. It was the only visible hair the man had that was black. The hair on his head was the color of a fish belly. He was holding up his loose pants with one hand. His skin was dark as a walnut and his mouth was a bit overfull with dentures. One of his pants pockets was swollen with something. Marvin thought it might be his balls: a rupture.

The gang stopped in their tracks and turned. They were nasty-looking fellows with broad shoulders and muscles. One of them had a large belly, but it was hard, and Marvin knew for a fact they all of them had hard fists and harder shoes. The old man was about to wake up dead.

The one who had asked Marvin if he had any gold teeth, the hard belly, looked at the old man and said, as he put down Marvin's stolen backpack, "You talking to us, you old geezer?"

"You're the only shit I see," said the old man. "You think you're a real bad man, don't you? Anyone can beat up some pussy like this kid. My crippled grandma could, and she's been dead some twenty years. Kid's maybe sixteen; what are you fucks—twenty? You're a bunch of cunts without any hair on your slit."

Marvin tried to crawl backwards until he was out of sight, not wanting to revive their interest in him, and thinking he might get away while they were killing the old man. But he was too weak to crawl. Hard Belly started strutting toward the old man, grinning, preening.

When he was about six feet away, the old man said, "You gonna fight me by yourself, Little Shit? You don't need your gang to maybe hold me?"

"I'm gonna kick out any real teeth you got, you old spic," said Hard Belly.

"Ain't got no real ones, so have at it."

The boy stepped in and kicked at the old man, who slapped his leg aside with his left hand, never taking the right away from holding up his pants, and hit him with a hard left jab to the mouth that knocked him down and made his lips bleed. When Hard Belly tried to get up, the old man made with a sharp kick to the windpipe. Hard Belly dropped, gagging, clutching at his throat.

"How's about you girls? You up for it, you little cunts?"

The little cunts shook their heads.

"That's good," said the old man, and pulled a chain out of his pocket.

That had been the bulk in his pocket, not a ruptured nut. He was still holding his pants with his other hand.

"I got me an equalizer here. I'll wrap this motherfucker around your head like an anchor chain. Come over here and get Mr. Butt Hole and take him away from me, and fast."

The three boys pulled Mr. Butt Hole, aka Hard Belly, to his feet, and when they did, the old man pushed his face close to Hard Belly's and said, "Don't come back around here. I don't want to see you no more."

"You'll be sorry, spic," said Hard Belly, bubbling blood over his lips and down his chin.

The old man dropped the chain on the ground and popped Hard Belly with a left jab again, breaking Hard Belly's nose, spewing blood all over his face.

"What the fuck you got in your ears?" the old man said. "Mud? Huh? You got mud? You hear me talkin' to you? Adios, asshole."

The three boys, and Hard Belly, who was wobbling, made their way down the street and were gone.

The Old Man looked down at Marvin, who was still lying on the ground.

"I've had worse beatings than that from my old mother, and she was missing an arm. Get the hell up."

Marvin managed to get his feet under him, thinking it a feat equal with building one of the Great Pyramids—alone.

"What you come around here for?" the old man said. "Ain't nobody around here but shits. You look like a kid might come from someplace better."

Marvin shook his head. "No," he said. "I'm from around here."

"Since when?"

"Since a week ago."

"Yeah? You moved here on purpose, or you just lose your map?"

"On purpose."

"Well, kid, you maybe better think about moving away."

There was nothing Marvin wanted to do more than move. But his mother said no dice. They didn't have the money. Not since his father died. That had nipped them in the bud, and quite severely, that dying business. Marvin's dad had been doing all right at the factory, but then he died and since then their lives had gone downhill faster than a little red wagon stuffed full of bricks. He and his mom had to be where they were, and there was nothing else to be said about it. A downgrade for them would be a cardboard box with a view. An upgrade would be lifts in their shoes.

"I can't move. Mama doesn't have the money for it. She does laundry."

"Yeah, well, you better learn to stand up for yourself, then," said the old man. "You don't, you might just wake up with your pants down and your asshole big as a dinner plate."

"They'd really do that?"

"Wouldn't put it past them," said the old man. "You better learn to fight back."

"Can you teach me?"

"Teach you what?"

"To fight."

"I can't do it. I have to hold my pants up. Get yourself a stick."

"You could teach me, though."

"I don't want to, kid. I got a full-time job just trying to stay breathing. I'm nearly eighty fucking years old. I ought to been feeding the worms five years ago. Listen up. You stay away from here, and if you can't . . . well, good luck, boy."

Holding his pants with one hand, the old man shuffled away. Marvin watched him go for a moment, and then fled. It was his plan to make it through the week, when school would turn out for the summer, and then he'd just stay in the apartment and never leave until school started up in the fall. By then, maybe he could formulate a new plan.

He hoped that in that time the boys would have lost interest in punching him, or perhaps been killed in some dreadful manner, or moved off themselves. Started a career, though he had a pretty good idea they had already started one—professional thugs.

He told his mother he fell down. She believed him. She was too preoccupied with trying to keep food on the table to think otherwise, and he didn't want her to know anyway. Didn't want her to know he couldn't take care of himself, and that he was a walking punching bag. Thing was, she wasn't too alert to his problems. She had the job, and now she had a boyfriend, a housepainter. The painter was a tall, gangly guy that came over and watched TV and drank beer, then went to bed with his mother. Sometimes, when he was sleeping on the couch, he could hear them back there. He didn't remember ever hearing that kind of thing when his dad was alive, and he didn't know what to think about it. When it got really loud, he'd wrap his pillow around his ears and try to sleep.

During the summer he saw some ads online about how you could build your body, and he sent off for a DVD. He started doing push-ups and sit-ups and a number of other exercises. He didn't have money for the weights the DVD suggested. The DVD cost him what little money he had saved, mostly a nickel here, a quarter there. Change his mother gave him. But he figured if his savings kept him from an ass whipping, it was worth every penny.

Marvin was consistent in his workouts. He gave them everything he had, and pretty soon his mother mentioned that he seemed to be looking stronger. Marvin thought so too. In fact, he actually had muscles. His arms were knotted and his stomach was pretty flat, and his thighs and calves had grown. He could throw a jab and a cross now. He found a guide on-line for how to do it. He was planning on working on the uppercut next, maybe the hook, but right now he had the jab and the cross down.

"All right," he said to the mirror. "Let them come. I'm ready."

After the first day of school in the fall, Marvin went home the same way he had that fateful day he had taken a beating. He didn't know exactly how he felt about what he was doing. He hoped he would never see them again on one hand, and on the other, he felt strong now, felt he could handle himself.

Marvin stuck his hand in his pocket and felt for the money he had there. Not much. A dollar or so in change. More money saved up from what his mother gave him. And he had his pack on his back. They might want that. He had to remember to come out of it, put it aside if he had to fight. No hindrances.

When he was where it happened before, there was no one. He went home feeling a bit disappointed. He would have enjoyed banging their heads together.

On his third day after school, he got his chance.

There were only two of them this time: Hard Belly, and one of the weasels that had been with him before. When they spotted him, Hard Belly smiled and moved toward Marvin quickly, the weasel trailing behind as if looking for scraps.

"Well, now," Hard Belly said as he got closer. "You remember me?"

"Yes," Marvin said.

"You ain't too smart, are you, kid? Thought you had done moved off. Thought I'd never get a chance to hit you again. That old man, I want you to know, he caught me by surprise. I could have kicked his ass from Monday to next Sunday."

"You can't whip me, let alone him."

"Oh, so, during the summer, you grew a pair of balls."

"Big pair."

"Big pair, huh. I bet you I can take that pack away from you and make you kiss my shoes. I can make you kiss my ass."

"I'm going to whip your ass," Marvin said.

The bully's expression changed, and Marvin didn't remember much after that.

He didn't come awake until Hard Belly was bent over, saying, "Now kiss it. And pucker good. A little tongue would be nice. You don't, Pogo here, he's gonna take out his knife and cut your dick off. You hear?"

Marvin looked at Hard Belly. Hard Belly dropped his pants and bent over with his hands on his knees, his asshole winking at Marvin. The weasel was riffling through Marvin's backpack, strewing things left and right.

"Lick or get cut," Hard Belly said.

Marvin coughed out some blood and started to try and crawl away.

"Lick it," Hard Belly said. "Lick it till I feel good. Come on, boy. Taste some shit."

A foot flew out and went between Hard Belly's legs, caught his nuts with a sound like a beaver's tail slapping on water. Hard Belly screamed, went forward on his head, as if he were trying to do a headstand.

"Don't never do it, kid," a voice said. "It's better to get your throat cut."

It was the old man. He was standing close by. He wasn't holding his pants this time. He had on a belt.

Pogo came at the old man and swung a wild right at him. The old man didn't seem to move much but somehow he went under the punch, and when he came up, the uppercut that Marvin had not practiced was on exhibition. It hit Pogo under the chin and there was a snapping sound, and

Pogo, the weasel, seemed to lose his head for a moment. It stretched his neck like it was made of rubber. Spittle flew out of Pogo's mouth and Pogo collapsed on the cement in a wad.

The old man wobbled over to Hard Belly, who was on his hands and knees, trying to get up, his pants around his ankles. The old man kicked him between the legs a couple of times. The kicks weren't pretty, but they were solid. Hard Belly spewed a turd and fell on his face.

"You need to wipe up," the old man said. But Hard Belly wasn't listening. He was lying on the cement, making a sound like a truck trying to start.

The old man turned and looked at Marvin.

"I thought I was ready," Marvin said.

"You ain't even close, kid. If you can walk, come with me."

Marvin could walk, barely.

"You got some confidence somewhere," the old man said. "I seen that right off. But you didn't have no reason for it."

"I did some training."

"Yeah, well, swimming on dry land ain't the same as getting into it. There's things you can do that's just in the air, or with a partner that can make a real difference, but you don't get no feel for nothing. I hadn't come along, you'd have been licking some ass crack and calling it a snow cone. Let me tell you, son. Don't never do that. Not unless it's a lady's ass and you've been invited. Someone wants to make you do something like that, you die first. You do that kind of thing once, you'll have the taste of shit in your mouth for the rest of your life."

"I guess it's better than being dead," Marvin said.

"Naw, it ain't neither. Let me tell you. Once I had me a little dog. He wasn't no bigger than a minute, but he had heart big as all the outdoors. Me and him took walks. One day we was walking along—not far from here, actually—and there was this German shepherd out nosing in some garbage cans. Rough-looking old dog, and it took in after my little dog. Mike was his name. And it was a hell of a fight. Mike wouldn't give. He fought to the death."

"He got killed?"

"Naw. The shepherd got killed."

"Mike killed the shepherd?"

"Naw. 'Course not. I'm jerking you. I hit the shepherd with a board I picked up. But the lesson here is you got to do your best, and sometimes you got to hope there's someone around on your side with a board."

"You saying I'm Mike and you're the guy with the board?"

"I'm saying you can't fight for shit. That's what I'm saying."

"What happened to Mike?"

"Got hit by a truck he was chasing. He was tough and willing, but he didn't have no sense. Kind of like you. Except you ain't tough. And another drawback you got is you ain't a dog. Another thing, that's twice I saved you, so you owe me something."

"What's that?"

"Well, you want to learn to fight, right?"

Marvin nodded.

"And I need a workout partner."

The old man's place wasn't far from the fight scene. It was a big, two-story concrete building. The windows were boarded over. When they got to the front door, the old man pulled out a series of keys and went to work on several locks.

While he did that, he said, "You keep a lookout. I got to really be careful when I do this, 'cause there's always some asshole wanting to break in. I've had to hurt some jackasses more than once. Why I keep that two-by-four there in the can."

Marvin looked. There was indeed a two-by-four stuffed down inside a big trash can. The two-by-four was all that was in it.

The old man unlocked the door and they went inside. The old man flicked some lights and everything went bright. He then went to work on the locks, clicked them into place. They went along a narrow hall into a wide space—a very wide space.

What was there was a bed and a toilet out in the open on the far wall, and on the other wall was a long plank table and some chairs. There was a hot plate on the table, and above and behind it were some shelves stuffed with canned goods. There was an old refrigerator, one of those bullet-shaped things. It hummed loudly, like a child with a head injury. Next to the table was a sink, and not far from that was a shower, with a once-green curtain pulled around a metal scaffold. There was a TV under some posters on the wall and a few thick chairs with the stuffing leaking out.

There was a boxing ring in the middle of the room. In the ring was a thick mat, taped all over with duct tape. The sun-faded posters were of men in tights, crouched in boxing or wrestling positions. One of them said, "Danny Bacca, X-Man."

Marvin studied the poster. It was a little wrinkled at the corners, badly framed, and the glass was specked with dust.

"That's me," the old man said.

Marvin turned and looked at the old man, looked back at the poster.

"It's me before wrinkles and bad knees."

"You were a professional wrestler?" Marvin said.

"Naw, I was selling shoes. You're slow on the upbeat, kid. Good thing I was out taking my walk again or flies would be having you for lunch."

"Why were you called X-Man?"

"'Cause you got in the ring with me, they could cross you off the list. Put an X through your name. Shit, I think that was it. It's been so long ago, I ain't sure no more. What's your name, by the way?"

"Marvin."

"All right, Marvin, let's you and me go over to the ring."

The old man dodged through the ropes easily. Marvin found the ropes were pulled taut, and he had more trouble sliding between them than he thought. Once in the ring, the old man said, "Here's the thing. What I'm gonna do is I'm gonna give you a first lesson, and you're gonna listen to me."

"Okay."

"What I want—and I ain't fucking with you here—is I want you to come at me hard as you can. Try and hit me, take me down, bite my ear off. Whatever."

"I can't hurt you."

"I know that."

"I'm not saying I'm not willing," Marvin said. "I'm saying I know I can't. You've beat a guy twice I've had trouble with, and his friends, and I couldn't do nothing, so I know I can't hurt you."

"You got a point, kid. But I'm wantin' you to try. It's a lesson."

"You'll teach me how to defend myself?"

"Sure."

Marvin charged, ducking low, planning to try and take the old man's feet. The old man squatted, almost sitting on his ass, and threw a quick uppercut.

Marvin dreamed he was flying. Then falling. The lights in the place were spotted suddenly. Then the spots went away and there was only brightness. Marvin rolled over on the mat and tried to get up. His eye hurt something awful.

"You hit me," he said when he made a sitting position.

The old man was in a corner of the ring, leaning on the ropes.

"Don't listen to shit like someone saying 'Come and get me.' That's foolish. That's leading you into something you might not like. Play your game."

"You told me to."

"That's right, kid, I did. That's your first lesson. Think for yourself, and don't listen to some fool giving you advice, and like I said, play your own game."

"I don't have a game," Marvin said.

"We both know that, kid. But we can fix it."

Marvin gingerly touched his eye. "So, you're going to teach me?"

"Yeah, but the second lesson is this. Now, you got to listen to every goddamn word I say."

"But you said . . ."

"I know what I said, but part of lesson two is this: Life is full of all kinds of contradictions."

It was easy to get loose to go to practice, but it wasn't easy getting there. Marvin still had the bullies to worry about. He got up early and went, telling his mother he was exercising at the school track.

The old man's home turned out to be what was left of an old TB hospital, which was why the old man bought it cheap, sometime at the far end of the Jurassic, Marvin figured.

The old man taught him how to move, how to punch, how to wrestle, how to throw. When Marvin threw the X-Man, the old guy would land lightly and get up quickly and complain about how it was done. When the workout was done, Marvin showered in the big room behind the faded curtain and went home the long way, watching for bullies.

After a while, he began to feel safe, having figured out that whatever time schedule the delinquents kept, it wasn't early morning, and it didn't seem to be early evening.

When summer ended and school started up, Marvin went before and after school to train, told his mother he was studying boxing with some kids at the Y. She was all right with that. She had work and the housepainter on her mind. The guy would be sitting there when Marvin came home evenings. Sitting there looking at the TV, not even nodding when Marvin came in, sometimes sitting in the padded TV chair with Marvin's mother on his knee, his arm around her waist, her giggling like a schoolgirl. It was enough to gag a maggot.

It got so home was not a place Marvin wanted to be. He liked the old man's place. He liked the training. He threw lefts and rights, hooks and uppercuts, into a bag the old man hung up. He sparred with the old man, who, once he got tired—and considering his age, it seemed a long time—would just knock him down and go lean on the ropes and breathe heavily for a while.

One day, after they had finished, sitting in chairs near the ring, Marvin said, "So, how am I helping you train?"

"You're a warm body, for one thing. And I got this fight coming up."

"A fight?"

"What are you, an echo? Yeah. I got a fight coming up. Every five years me and Jesus the Bomb go at it. On Christmas Eve."

Marvin just looked at him. The old man looked back, said, "Think I'm too old? How old are you?"

"Seventeen."

"Can I whip your ass, kid?"

"Everyone can whip my ass."

"All right, that's a point you got there," the old man said.

"Why every five years?" Marvin asked. "Why this Jesus guy?"

"Maybe I'll tell you later," the old man said.

Things got bad at home.

Marvin hated the painter and the painter hated him. His mother loved the painter and stood by him. Everything Marvin tried to do was tainted by the painter. He couldn't take the trash out fast enough. He wasn't doing good enough in school for the painter, like the painter had ever graduated so much as kindergarten. Nothing satisfied the painter, and when Marvin complained to his mother, it was the painter she stood behind.

The painter was nothing like his dad, nothing, and he hated him. One day he told his mother he'd had enough. It was him or the painter.

She chose the painter.

"Well, I hope the crooked painting son of a bitch makes you happy," he said.

"Where did you learn such language?" she asked.

He had learned a lot of it from the old man, but he said, "The painter."

"Did not," his mother said.

"Did too."

Marvin put his stuff in a suitcase that belonged to the painter and left. He waited for his mother to come chasing after him, but she didn't. She called out as he went up the street, "You're old enough. You'll be all right."

He found himself at the old man's place.

Inside the doorway, suitcase in hand, the old man looked at him, nodded at the suitcase, said, "What you doing with that shit?"

"I got thrown out," Marvin said. Not quite the truth, but he felt it was close enough.

"You mean to stay here? That what you're after?"

"Just till I get on my feet."

"On your feet?" the X-Man said. "You ain't got no job. You ain't got dick. You're like a fucking vagabond."

"Yeah," Marvin said. "Well, all right."

Marvin turned around, thinking maybe he could go home and kiss some ass, maybe tell the painter he was a good guy or something. He got to the door and the old man said, "Where the fuck you going?"

"Leaving. You wanted me to, didn't you?"

"Did I say that? Did I say anything like that? I said you were a vagabond. I didn't say something about leaving. Here. Give me the goddamn suitcase."

Before Marvin could do anything, X-Man took it and started down the hall toward the great room. Marvin watched him go: a wiry, balding, white-haired old man with a slight bowlegged limp to his walk.

One night, watching wrestling on TV, the old man, having sucked down a six-pack, said, "This is shit. Bunch a fucking tough acrobats. This ain't wrestling. It ain't boxing, and it sure ain't fighting. It's like a movie show or something. When we wrestled in fairs, we really wrestled. These big-ass fuckers wouldn't know a wrist lock from a dick jerk. Look at that shit. Guy waits for the fucker to climb on the ropes and jump on him. And what kind of hit is that? That was a real hit, motherfucker would be dead, hitting him in the throat like that. He's slapping the guy's chest high up, that's all. Cocksuckers."

"When you wrestled, where did you do it?" Marvin asked.

The old man clicked off the TV. "I can't take no more of that shit. . . . Where did I wrestle? I rode the rails during the Great Depression. I was ten years old on them rails, and I'd go from town to town and watch guys wrestle at fairs, and I began to pick it up. When I was fifteen, I said I was eighteen, and they believed me, ugly as I was. I mean, who wants to think a kid can be so goddamn ugly, you know. So by the end of the Great Depression I'm wrestling all over the place. Let me see, it's 1992, so I been doing it awhile. Come the war, they wouldn't let me go because of a rupture. I used to wrap that sucker up with a bunch of sheet strips and go and wrestle. I could have fought Japs bundled up like that if they'd let me. Did have to stop now and then when my nuts stuck out of the rip in my balls. I'd cross my legs, suck it up and push them back in, cinch up those strips of sheet, and keep on keeping on. I could have done that in the war, but they was all prissy about it. Said it'd be a problem. So I didn't kill no Japs. I could have, though. Germans. Hungarians. Martians. I could kill anybody they put me in front of. 'Course, glad I didn't in one way. Ain't good to kill a man. But them son of a bitches were asking for it. Well, I don't know about the Hungarians or the Martians, but the rest of them bastards were.

"I learned fighting by hard knocks. Now and then I met some guys knew a thing or two, and I picked it up. Some of them Jap tricks and the like. I had folks down in Mexico. So when I was in my twenties, I went there and became a wrestler for money."

"Wasn't that fake?"

The old man gave Marvin a look that made the water inside Marvin's body boil.

"There was them that put on shows, but then there was us. Me and Jesus, and ones like us. We did the real thing. We was hitting and kicking and locking and throwing. Look at this."

The old man jerked up a sleeve on his sweatshirt. There was a mark there like a tire track. "See that. Jesus bit me. I had him in a clench and he bit me. Motherfucker. 'Course, that's what I'd have done. Anyway, he got loose on account of it. He had this technique—the Bomb, he called it, how he got his nickname. He'd grab you in a bear hug, front or back, lift you up and fall back and drive your head into the mat. You got that done to you once or twice, you felt like your ears were wiggling around your asshole. It was something. Me, I had me the step-over-toe-hold. That was my move, and still is."

"Did you use it on Jesus?"

"Nope. He got the Bomb on me. After the Bomb I thought I was in Africa fucking a gorilla. I didn't know my dick from a candlewick."

"But you're still wrestling him?"

"Haven't beat him yet. I've tried every hold there is, every move, every kind of psychology I know, and nothing. It's the woman. Felina Valdez. She's got the mojo on me, the juju, the black doo-doo, and the silent dog whistle. Whatever there is that makes you stupid, she's got it on me."

Marvin didn't follow any of that, but he didn't say anything. He drank his glass of tea while X-Man drank another beer. He knew he would come back to the subject eventually. That's how he worked.

"Let me tell you about Felina. She was a black-eyed maiden, had smooth, dark skin. A priest saw her walking down the street, he'd go home and cut his throat. First time I seen her, that stack of dynamite was in a blue dress so tight, you could count the hairs on her thingamajig.

"She was there in the crowd to watch the wrestling. She's in the front row with her legs crossed, and her dress is slithering up to her knee like a snake creeping, and I'm getting a pretty good look, you see. Not seeing the vine-covered canyon, but I'm in the neighborhood. And looking at that broad, I'm almost killed by this wrestler named Joey the Yank. Guy from Maine who takes my legs out from under me and butts me and gets me in an arm bar. I barely manage to work out of it, get him and throw him and latch on my step-over-toe-hold. I put that on you, you pass through

time, baby. Past and future, and finally you're looking at your own goddamn grave. He tapped out.

"Next thing I know, this blue-dress doll is sliding up next to me, taking
my arm, and, well, kid, from that point on I was a doomed man. She
could do more tricks with a dick than a magician could with a deck of
cards. I thought she was going to kill me, but I thought too it was one hell
of a good way to go. Hear what I'm saying?"

"Yes, sir," Marvin said.

"This is all kind of nasty talk for a kid, ain't it?"

"No, sir," Marvin said.

"Fuck it. You're damn near eighteen. By now you got to know about
pussy."

"I know what it is," Marvin said.

"No, kid. You talk like you know where it is, not what it is. Me, I was
lost in that stuff. I might as well have let her put my nuts in a vise and
crank it. She started going to all my fights. And I noticed something
pretty quick. I gave a great performance, won by a big margin, the loving
was great. It was a mediocre fight, so was the bedding. I had it figured.
She wasn't so much in love with me as she was a good fight and my fin-
ishing move, the step-over-toe-hold. She had me teach it to her. I let her
put it on me one time, and kid, I tell you, way she latched it, I suddenly
had some mercy for all them I'd used it on. I actually had to work my way
out of it, like I was in a match, 'cause she wasn't giving me no quarter.
That was a cheap price to pay, though, all that savage monkey love I was
getting, and then it all come apart.

"Jesus beat me. Put the Bomb on me. When I woke up I was out back of
the carnival, lying on the grass with ants biting me. When I came to myself,
Felina was gone. She went with Jesus. Took my money, left me with nothing
but ant bites on my nuts."

"She sounds shallow."

"As a saucer, kid. But once she slapped that hoodoo on me, I couldn't
cut myself loose. Let me tell you, it was like standing on the railroad tracks
in the dark of night, and you can see a train coming, the light sweeping
the tracks, and you can't step off. All you can do is stand there and wait
for it to hit you. One time when we were together, we're walking in Mexico City, where I had some bouts, and she sees a guy with a wooden cage
full of pigeons, six or seven of them. She has me buy all of them, like we're

gonna take them back to the States. But what she does is she takes them back to our hotel room. We had to sneak them in. She puts the cage on an end table and just looks at the birds. I give them some bread, you know, 'cause they got to eat, and I clean out their cage, and I think: this girl is one crazed bird lover. I go and take a shower, tell her to order up some dinner.

"I take my time in there. Shit and shave, good hot shower. When I come out, there she is, sitting at one of those little push tables room service brings up, and she's eating fried chicken. Didn't wait on me, didn't say boo. She was like that. Everything was about her. But right then I learned something else. I saw that cage of birds, and they were all dead. I asked her what happened to the birds, and she says, 'I got tired of them.'

"I went and looked, and their necks was wrung."

"But why?" Marvin asked.

The old man leaned back and sucked his beer, took his time before he spoke. "I don't know, kid. Right then I should have thrown my shit in a bag and got the hell out of there. But I didn't. It's like I told you about those train tracks. Christ, kid. You should have seen her. There wasn't never nothing like her, and I couldn't let her go. It's like you catch the finest fish in the world, and someone's telling you to throw it back, and all you can think about is that thing fried up and laid out on a bed of rice. Only it ain't really nothing like that. There ain't no describing it. And then, like I said, she went off with Jesus, and every day I get up my heart burns for her. My mind says I'm lucky to be shed of her, but my heart, it don't listen. I don't even blame Jesus for what he done. How could he not want her? She belonged to whoever could pin the other guy to the mat. Me and him, we don't fight nobody else anymore, just each other. Every five years. If I win, I get her back. I know that. He knows that. And Felina knows that. He wins, he keeps her. So far, he keeps her. Its best he does. I ought to let it go, kid, but I can't."

"She really that bad?"

"She's the best bad girl ever. She's a bright red apple with a worm in the center. Since that woman's been with Jesus, he left a wife, had two of his children die, one in a house fire that happened while he was out, and Felina gave birth to two babies that both died within a week. Some kind of thing happens now and then. Cradle death, something like that. On top of that, she's screwed just about everyone short of a couple of eunuchs, but she stays with Jesus, and he keeps her. He keeps her because she has a power, kid. She can hold you to her tight as liver cancer. Ain't no getting away from that bitch. She lets you go, you still want her like you want a drink when you're a drunk."

"The way you mentioned the fire and Jesus's kids, the two babies that died . . . you sounded like—"

"Like I didn't believe the fire was no accident? That the babies didn't die naturally? Yeah, kid. I was thinking about that cage full of pigeons. I was thinking about how she used to cut my hair, and how she had this little box she had with her, kept it in the purse she carried. I seen her wrap some hair into the knot of a couple twisted pipe cleaners. Oh, hell. You already think I'm nuts."

Marvin shook his head. "No. No, I don't."

"All right, then. I think she really did have the hoodoo on me. I read somewhere that people who know spells can get a piece of your hair and they can use that as part of that spell, and it can tie you to them. I read that."

"That doesn't mean it's true," Marvin said.

"I know that, kid. I know how I sound. And when it's midday I think thinking like that is so much dog shit, but it gets night, or it's early morning and the light's just starting to creep in, I believe it. And I guess I always believed it. I think she's got me in a spell. Ain't nothing else would explain why I would want that cheating, conniving, pigeon-killing, house-burning, baby-murdering bitch back. It don't make no sense, does it?"

"No, sir," Marvin said, and then after a moment he added, "She's pretty old now, isn't she?"

"'Course she is. You think time stood still? She ain't the same. But neither am I. Neither is Jesus. But it's me and him, and one of us gets the girl, and so far he always gets her. What I want is to have her back, die quick, and have one of those Greek funerals. That way I get the prize, but I don't have to put up with it."

"What's a Greek funeral?"

"Heroes like Hercules had them. When he died, they put him on a pile of sticks and such and burned up the body, let his smoke rise to the heavens. Beats being buried in the ground or cooked up in some oven, your ashes scraped into a sack. Or having to spend your last days out with that woman, though that's exactly what I'm trying to do."

"Do Jesus and Felina live here in the city?" Marvin asked.

"They don't live nowhere. They got a motor trailer. And they got some retirement money. Like me. Jesus and me worked other jobs as well as wrestled. You couldn't make it just on the wrestling circuit, especially the underground circuit, so we got some of that social security money coming, thank goodness. They drive around to different places. He trains, and he comes back every five years. Each time I see him, it's like there's this look in his eyes that says 'Beat me this time and take this bitch off my hands.' Only he always fights like a bear and I can't beat him."

"You win, sure she'll go with you?"

"It's me or him, and that's all there is to it. Ain't nobody else now. Me or him. It's us she's decided to suck dry and make miserable."

"Can't you let it go?" Marvin asked.

X-Man laughed. It was a dark laugh, like a dying man that suddenly understands an old joke. "Wish I could, kid, 'cause if I could, I would."

They trained for the fight.

X-Man would say: "This is what Jesus the Bomb does. He comes at you, and next thing you know, you're on your ass, 'cause he grabs you like this, or like this. And he can switch from this to this." And so on.

Marvin did what he was told. He tried Jesus' moves. Every time he did, he'd lose. The old man would twist him, throw him, lock him, punch him (lightly), and even when Marvin felt he was getting good at it, X-Man would outsmart him in the end and come out of something Marvin thought an oiled weasel couldn't slither out of. When it was over, it was Marvin panting in the corner, X-Man wiping sweat off his face with a towel.

"That how Jesus does it?" Marvin asked, after trying all of the moves he had been taught.

"Yeah," said the old man, "except he does it better."

This went on for months, getting closer and closer to the day when the X-Man and Jesus the Bomb were to go at it. Got so Marvin was so focused on the training, he forgot all about the bullies.

Until one day Marvin was by himself, coming out of the store two blocks from the old man's place, carrying a sack with milk and vanilla cookies in it, and there's Hard Belly. He spotted Marvin and started across the street, pulling his hands out of his pockets, smiling.

"Well, now," Hard Belly said when he was near Marvin. "I bet you forgot about me, didn't you? Like I wasn't gonna get even. This time you ain't got your fossil to protect you."

Marvin put the sack on the sidewalk. "I'm not asking for trouble."

"That don't mean you ain't gonna get some," Hard Belly said, standing right in front of Marvin. Marvin didn't really plan on anything—he wasn't thinking about it—but when Hard Belly moved closer, his left jab popped out and hit him in the nose. Down went Hard Belly like he had been hit with a baseball bat. Marvin couldn't believe it, couldn't believe how hard his punch was, how good it was. He knew right then and there it was over between him and Hard Belly, because he wasn't scared anymore. He picked up the sack and walked back to the old man's place, left Hard Belly napping.

One night, during the time school was out for the Thanksgiving holiday, Marvin woke up. He was sleeping in the boxing ring, a blanket over him, and he saw there was a light on by the old man's bed. The old man was sitting on the edge of it, bent over, pulling boxes out from beneath. He reached in one and pulled out a magazine, then another. He spread the magazines on the bed and looked at them.

Marvin got up and climbed out of the ring and went over to him. The old man looked up. "Damn, kid. I wake you?"

"Woke up on my own. What you doing?"

"Looking at these old magazines. They're underground fight magazines. Had to order them through the mail. Couldn't buy them off the stands."

Marvin looked at the open magazines on the bed. They had a lot of photographs in them. From the poster on the wall, he recognized photographs of X-Man.

"You were famous," Marvin said.

"In a way, I suppose," X-Man said. "I look at these, I got to hate getting old. I wasn't no peach to look at, but I was strong then, looked better than now. Ain't much of the young me left."

"Is Jesus in them?"

X-Man flipped a page on one of the open magazines, and there was a photograph of a squatty man with a black mop of hair. The man's chest was almost as hairy. He had legs like a tree trunks.

X-Man grinned. "I know what you're thinking: Couple mugs like me and Jesus, what kind of love magnets are we? Maybe Felina ain't the prime beaver I say she is?"

The old man went around to the head of the bed and dragged a small cardboard box out from under it. He sat it on the bed between them, popped the lid, and scrounged around in a pile of yellowed photographs. He pulled one out. It was slightly faded, but it was clear enough. The woman in it looked maybe mid-twenties. It was a full shot, and she was indeed a knockout. Black hair, high cheekbones, full lips, and black as the Pit eyes that jumped out of the photo and landed somewhere in the back of Marvin's head.

There were other photos of her, and he showed Marvin all of them. There were close shots and far shots, and sneaky camera shots that rested on her ass. She was indeed fabulous to look at.

"She ain't that way now, but she's still got it somehow. What I was gonna do, kid, was gather up all these photos and pile them and burn them, then I was gonna send word to Jesus he could forget the match. That Felina was his until the end of time. But I think that every few years or so, and then I don't do it. You know what Jesus told me once? He said she liked to catch flies. Use a drinking glass and trap them, then stick a needle through them, string them on thread. Bunches of them. She'd knot one end, fasten the other to a wall with a thumbtack, watch them try to fly. Swat a fly, that's one thing. But something like that, I don't get it, kid. And knowing that, I ought to not get her. But it don't work that way. . . . Tell you what, you go on to bed. Me, I'm gonna turn off the light and turn in."

Marvin went and crawled under his blanket, adjusted the pillow under his head. When he looked at the old man, he still had the light on and had the cardboard box with the pictures in his lap. He was holding up a photograph, looking at it like it was a hand-engraved invitation to the Second Coming.

As Marvin drifted off, all he could think about were those flies on the thread.

————

Next day the old man didn't wake him for the morning workout, and when Marvin finally opened his eyes it was nearly noon. The old man was nowhere to be seen. He got up and went to the refrigerator to have some milk. There was a note on the door.

DON'T EAT HEAVY. I'M BRINGING THANKSGIVING.

Marvin hadn't wanted to spend Thanksgiving with his mother and the painter, so he hadn't really thought about it at all. Once his mother dropped him out of her mind, he had dropped the holidays out of his. But right then he thought about them, and hoped the painter would choke on a turkey bone.

He poured a glass of milk and sat in a chair by the ring and sipped it.

Not long after, the old man came back with a sack of groceries. Marvin got up and went over to him. "I'm sorry. I missed the workout."

"You didn't miss nothing. It's a fucking holiday. Even someone needs as much training as you ought to have a day off."

The old man pulled things out of the sack. Turkey lunch meat, some cheese slices, and a loaf of good bread, the kind you had to cut with a knife. And there was a can of cranberry sauce.

"It ain't exactly a big carving turkey, but it'll be all right," the old man said.

They made sandwiches and sat in the TV chairs with a little table between them. They placed their plates there, the old man put a video in his aging machine, and they watched a movie. An old black-and-white one. Marvin liked color, and he was sure he would hate it. It was called Night and the City. It was about wrestling. Marvin didn't hate it. He loved it. He ate his sandwich. He looked at the old man, chewing without his dentures. Right then he knew he loved him as dearly as if he were his father.

Next day they trained hard. Marvin had gotten so he was more of a challenge for the old man, but he still couldn't beat him.

On the morning of the bout with Jesus, Marvin got up and went out to the store. He had some money X-Man gave him now and then for being a training partner, and he bought a few items and took them home.

One of them was a bottle of liniment, and when he got back he used it to give the old man a rubdown.

When that was done, the old man stretched out on the floor on an old mattress and fell asleep as easily as a kitten. While he slept, Marvin took the rest of the stuff he had bought into the bathroom and made a few arrangements. He brought the bag out and wadded it up and shoved it in the trash.

Then he did what the old man had instructed him to do. He got folding chairs out of the closet, twenty-five of them, and set them up near the ring. He put one of them in front of the others, close to the ring.

At four-fifteen, he gently spoke to the old man, called him awake.

The old man got up and showered and put on red tights and a T-shirt with a photograph of his younger self on it. The words under the photograph read: X-MAN.

It was Christmas Eve.

About seven that evening they began to arrive. On sticks, in wheelchairs, and on walkers, supported by each other and, in a couple of cases, walking unassisted. They came to the place in dribbles, and Marvin helped them locate a chair. The old man had stored away some cheap wine and beer, and had even gone all out for a few boxes of crackers and a suspicious-looking cheese ball. These he arranged on a long foldout table to the left of the chairs. The old people, mostly men, descended on it like vultures alighting on fresh roadkill. Marvin had to help some of them who were so old and decrepit they couldn't hold a paper plate and walk at the same time.

Marvin didn't see anyone that he thought looked like Jesus and Felina. If one of the four women was Felina, she was certainly way past any sex appeal, and if any one of them was Jesus, X-Man had it in the bag. But, of course, none of them were either.

About eight o'clock Marvin answered a hard knocking on the door. When he opened it, there was Jesus. He was wearing a dark robe with red trim. It was open in front, and Marvin could see he had on black tights and no shirt. He was gray-haired where he had hair left on his head, and there was a thick thatch of gray hair on his chest, nestled there like a carefully constructed bird's nest. He had the same simian build as in the photograph. The Bomb looked easily ten years younger than his age; he moved easily and well.

With him was a tall woman and it was easy to recognize her, even from ancient photos. Her hair was still black, though certainly it came out of a bottle now, and she had aged well, looked firm of face and high of bone. Marvin thought maybe she'd had some work. She looked like a movie star in her fifties that still gets work for her beauty. Her eyes were like wells, and Marvin had to be careful not to fall into them. She had on a long black dress with a black coat hanging off her shoulders in a sophisticated way. It had a fur collar that at first glance looked pretty good and at second glance showed signs of decay, like a sleeping animal with mange.

"I'm here to wrestle," Jesus said.

"Yes, sir," Marvin said.

The woman smiled at Marvin, and her teeth were white and magnificent, and looked as real as his own. Nothing was said, but in some way or another he knew he was to take her coat, and he did. He followed after her and Jesus, and, watching Felina walk, Marvin realized he was sexually aroused. She was pretty damn amazing, considering her age, and he was reminded of an old story he had read about a succubus, a female spirit that preyed on men, sexually depleted them, and took their souls.

When Felina sashayed in and the old man saw her, there was a change in his appearance. His face flushed and he stood erect. She owned him.

Marvin put Felina's coat away, and when he hung it in the closet, a smell came off it that was sweet and tantalizing. He thought some of it was perfume, but knew most of it was her.

Jesus and X-Man shook hands and smiled at each other, but X-Man couldn't take his eyes off of Felina. She moved past them both as if unaware of their presence, and without being told took the chair that had been placed in front of the others.

The old man called Marvin over and introduced him to Jesus. "This kid is my protégé, Jesus. He's pretty good. Like me, maybe, when I started out, if I'd had a broke leg."

They both laughed. Marvin even laughed. He had begun to understand this was wrestling humor and that he had in fact been given a great compliment.

"You think you're gonna beat me this year?" Jesus said. "I sometimes don't think you're really trying."

"Oh, I'm trying all right," X-Man said.

Jesus was still smiling, but now the smile look pinned there when he spoke. "You win, you know she'll go with you?"

The old man nodded.

"Why do we keep doing this?" Jesus said.

X-Man shook his head.

"Well," Jesus said. "Good luck. And I mean it. But you're in for a fight."

"I know that," X-Man said.

It was nine o'clock when X-Man and Jesus took out their teeth and climbed into the ring, took some time to stretch. The chairs in the audience were near half empty and those that were seated were spread apart like Dalmatian spots. Marvin stood on the outside of the ropes at the old man's corner.

The old man came and leaned on the ropes. One of the elders in the audience, wearing red pants pulled up nearly to his armpits, dragged his chair next to the side of the ring, scraping it across the floor as he went. He had a cowbell in his free hand. He wheezed himself into the seat, placed the bell on his knee. He produced a large watch from his pants pocket and placed it on his other knee. He looked sleepy.

"We do this five years from now," X-Man said to Marvin, "it'll be in hell somewhere, and the devil will be our timekeeper."

"All right," said the timekeeper. "Geezer rules. Two minutes rounds. Three minutes rests. Goes until it's best two out of three or someone quits. Everybody ready?"

Both parties said they were.

Marvin looked at Felina. She was sitting with her hands in her lap. She appeared confident and smug, like a spider waiting patiently on a fly.

The timekeeper hit the watch with his left thumb and rang the bell with his right hand. X-Man and Jesus came together with a smacking sound, grabbing at each other's knees for a throw, bobbing and weaving. And then X-Man came up from a bob and threw a quick left. To Marvin's amazement, Jesus slipped it over his shoulder and hooked X-Man in the ribs. It was a solid shot, and Marvin could tell X-Man felt it. X-man danced back, and one elderly man in the small crowd booed.

"Go fuck yourself," X-Man yelled out.

X-Man and the Bomb came together again. There was a clenching of hands on shoulders, and Jesus attempted to knee X-Man in the balls. X-man was able to turn enough to take it on the side of the leg, but not in the charley horse point. They whirled around and around like angry lovers at a dance.

Finally X-Man faked, dove for Jesus' knee, and got hold of it, but Jesus twisted on him, brought one leg over X-Man's head, hooked the leg under his neck and rolled, grabbed X-Man's arm, stretched it out, and lifted his pelvis against it. There was a sound like someone snapping a stick over their knee, and X-Man tapped out. That ended the round. It had gone less than forty-five seconds.

X-Man waddled over to his corner, nursing his arm a little. He leaned on the ropes. Marvin brought out the stool.

"Put it back," the old man said. "I don't want them to think I'm hurt." Marvin put it back, said, "Are you hurt?"

"Yeah, but that cracking you heard was just air bubbles in my arm. I'm fine. Fuck it. Put the stool back."

Marvin put the stool back. X-Man sat down. Across the way, Jesus was seated on his stool, his head hung. He and X-Man looked like two men who wouldn't have minded being shot.

"I know this," X-Man said. "This is my last match. After this, I ain't got no more in me. I can feel what's left of me running out of my feet."

Marvin glanced at Felina. One of the lights overhead was wearing out. It popped and went from light to dark and back to light again. Marvin thought for a moment, there in the shadow, Felina had looked older, and fouler, and her thick hair had resembled a bundle of snakes. But as he looked more closely, it was just the light.

The cowbell clattered. They had gotten some of their juice back. They moved around each other, hands outstretched. They finally clinched their fingers together, both hands. X-Man suddenly jutted his fingers forward in a way that allowed him to clench down on the back of Jesus' fingers, snap him to the floor in pain. It was a simple move, but it put the Bomb's face in front of X-Man's knee. X-man kneed him in the face so hard, blood spewed all over the matting, all over X-Man.

Still clutching Jesus's fingers, X-Man stepped back and squatted, pulled Jesus to his face. X-Man pulled free of the fingers, and as Jesus tried to rise, X-Man kicked him in the face. It was a hard kick. Jesus went unconscious.

The cowbell clattered. The timekeeper put the cowbell down and made his way to the ring. He climbed through and hitch-legged it over to Jesus. It took almost as much time as it would take for a blind man to find a needle in a haystack.

The timekeeper got down on one knee. Jesus groaned and sat up slowly. His face was a bloody mess.

The timekeeper looked him over. "You up for it?" he said.

"Hell, yeah," Jesus said.

"One to one!" yelled the timekeeper, and he made his slow pilgrimage back to his chair.

Jesus got up slowly, went back to his corner, trying to hold his head up high. X-Man was sitting on his stool, breathing heavily. "I hope I didn't break something inside the old cocksucker," he said.

X-Man closed his eyes and sat resting on his stool. Marvin was quiet. He thought the old man was asleep. Three minutes later, the cowbell clattered.

Jesus huffed loudly, creaked bones off the stool, stuttered-stepped to the center of the ring. X-Man came out in a slow shuffle.

They exchanged a few punches, none of which landed particularly well. Surprisingly, both seemed to have gotten a second wind. They tossed one another, and rolled, and jabbed, and gouged, and the bell rang again.

When X-Man was on his stool, he said, "My heart feels like a bird fluttering."

"You ought to quit," Marvin said. "It's not worth a heart attack."

"It ain't fluttering from the fight, but from seeing Felina."

Marvin looked. Felina was looking at X-Man the way a puppy looks at a dog treat.

"Don't fall for it," Marvin said. "She's evil. Goddamn evil."

"So you believe me?"

"I do. You think maybe she has those pipe cleaners with your hair with her?"

"How would I know?"

"In her coat, maybe?"

"Again, how would I know." And then it hit the old man. He knew what Marvin was getting at. "You mean if she did have, and you got them . . ."

"Yeah," Marvin said.

Marvin left X-Man sitting there, made a beeline for the closet. He opened the door and moved his hands around in there, trying to look like he was about natural business. He glanced back at X-Man, who had turned on his stool to look.

The cowbell rang. The two old gentlemen went at it again.

It was furious. Slamming punches to the head and ribs, the breadbasket. Clutching one another, kneeing in the balls. Jesus even bit the lobe off X-Man's ear. Blood was everywhere. It was a fight that would have been amazing if the two men in the ring were in their twenties, in top shape. At their age it was phenomenal.

Marvin was standing in the old man's corner now, trying to catch X-Man's eye, but not in a real obvious way. He didn't want him to lose focus, didn't want Jesus to come under him and lift him up and drive the old man's head into the ground like a lawn dart.

Finally the two clenched. They went around and around like that, breathing heavy as steam engines. Marvin caught X-Man's eye. Marvin lifted up two knotted pipe cleaners, dark hair in the middle of the knot. Marvin untwisted the pipe cleaners and the hair floated out like a puff of dark dandruff, drifted to the floor.

X-Man let out his breath, seemed to relax.

Jesus dove for him. It was like a hawk swooping down on a mouse. Next thing Marvin knew, Jesus had X-Man low on the hips in a two-arm clench, and was lifting him up, bending back at the same time so he could drive X-Man over his head, straight into the mat.

But as X-Man went over, he ducked his head under Jesus' buttocks, grasped the inside of Jesus' legs. Jesus flipped backwards, but X-Man came up on his back, not his head. Instead, his head was poking between Jesus' legs, and his toothless gums were buried in Jesus' tights, clamping down on his balls like a clutched fist. A cry went up from the crowd.

Jesus screamed. It was the kind of scream that went down your back and got hold of your tailbone and pulled at it. X-Man maintained the clamp. Jesus writhed and twisted and kicked and punched. The punches hit X-Man in the top of the head, but still he clung. When Jesus tried to roll out, X-Man rolled with him, his gums still buried deep in Jesus' balls.

Some of the oldsters were standing up from their seats, yelling with excitement. Felina hadn't moved or changed her expression.

Then it happened.

Jesus slapped out both hands on the mat, called, "Time." And it was over.

The elders left. Except Jesus and Felina.

Jesus stayed in the bathroom for a long time. When he came out, he was limping. The front of his tights were plumped out and dark with blood.

X-Man was standing, one hand on the back of a chair, breathing heavy.

Jesus said, "You about took my nuts, X-Man. I took one of your towels, shoved it down my pants to stop the blood. Them's some gums you got, X-man. Gums like that, you don't need teeth."

"All's fair in love and war," X-Man said. "Besides, old as you are, what you using your nuts for?"

"I hear that," Jesus said, and his whole demeanor was different. He was like a bird in a cage with the door left open. He was ready to fly out.

"She's all yours," Jesus said.

We all looked at Felina. She smiled slightly. She took X-Man's hand.

X-man turned and looked at her. He said, "I don't want her," and let go of her hand. "Hell, I done outlived my dick anyhow."

The look on Felina's face was one of amazement.

"You won her," Jesus said. "That's the rule."

"Naw," X-Man said. "Ain't no rule."

"No?" Jesus said, and you could almost see that cage door slam and lock.

"No," said X-Man, looking at Felina. "That hoodoo you done with the pipe cleaners. My boy here undid it."

"What the fuck are you talking about?" Felina said.

They just stared at each other for a long moment.

"Get out," X-Man said. "And Jesus. We ain't doing this no more."

"You don't want her?" Jesus said.

"No. Get out. Take the bitch with you. Get on out."

Out they went. When Felina turned the corner into the hallway, she paused and looked back. It was a look that said: You had me, and you let me go, and you'll have regrets.

X-Man just grinned at her. "Hit the road, you old bitch."

When they were gone, the old man stretched out on his bed, breathing heavily. Marvin pulled a chair nearby and sat. The old man looked at him and laughed.

"That pipe cleaner and hair wasn't in her coat, was it?"

"What do you mean?" Marvin said.

"That look on her face when I mentioned it. She didn't know what I was talking about. Look at me, boy. Tell me true."

Marvin took a moment, said, "I bought the pipe cleaners and some shoe polish. I cut a piece of my hair, made it dark with the shoe polish, twisted it up in the pipe cleaners."

X-Man let out a hoot. "You sneaky son of a bitch."

"I'm sorry," Marvin said.

"I'm not."

"You're not?"

"Nope. I learned something important. I'm a fucking dope. She didn't never have no power over me I didn't give her. Them pipe cleaners and the hair, hell, she forgot about that fast as she did it. Just some way to pass time for her, and I made it something special. It was just me giving myself an excuse to be in love with someone wasn't worth the gunpowder it would take to blow her ass up. She just liked having power over the both of us. Maybe Jesus will figure that out too. Maybe me and him figured a lot of things out today. It's all right, kid. You done good. Hell, it wasn't nothing I didn't know deep down, and now I'm out of excuses, and I'm done with her. It's like someone just let go of my throat and I can breathe again. All these years, and this thing with Felina, it wasn't nothing but me and my own bullshit."

About seven in the morning X-Man woke up Marvin.

"What's the matter?" Marvin asked.

X-Man was standing over him. Giving him a dentureless grin. "Nothing. It's Christmas. Merry Christmas."

"You too," Marvin said.

The old man had a T-shirt. He held it out with both hands. It said X-Man and had his photograph on it, just like the one he was wearing. "I want you to have it. I want you to be X-Man."

"I can't be X-Man. No one can."

"I know that. But I want you to try."

Marvin was sitting up now. He took the shirt.

"Put it on," said X-Man.

Marvin slipped off his shirt and, still sitting on the floor, pulled the X-Man shirt over his head. It fit good. He stood up. "But I didn't get you nothing."

"Yeah you did. You got me free."

Marvin nodded. "How do I look?"

"Like X-Man. You know, if I had had a son, I'd have been damn lucky if he'd been like you. Hell, if he'd *been* you. 'Course, that gets into me fucking your mother, and we don't want to talk about that. Now I'm going back to sleep. Maybe later we'll have something for Christmas dinner."

Later in the day Marvin got up, fixed coffee, made a couple of sandwiches, went to wake X-Man.

He didn't wake up. He was cold. He was gone. There were wrestling magazines lying on the bed with him.

"Damn," Marvin said, and sat down in the chair by the bed. He took the old man's hand to hold. There was something in it. A wadded-up photo of Felina. Marvin took it and tossed it on the floor and held the old man's hand for a long time.

After a while Marvin tore a page out of one of the wrestling magazines, got up, and put it to the hot plate. It blazed. He went over and held it burning in one hand while he used the other to pull out one of the boxes of magazines. He set fire to it and pushed it back under the bed. Flames licked around the edges of the bed. Other boxes beneath the bed caught fire. The bedclothes caught. After a moment the old man caught too. He smelled like pork cooking.

Like Hercules, Marvin thought. He's rising up to the gods.

Marvin, still wearing his X-Man shirt, got his coat out of the closet. The room was filling with smoke and the smell of burning flesh. He put his coat on and strolled around the corner, into the hallway. Just before he went outside, he could feel the heat of the fire warming his back.

Brandon Sanderson

Another of the fastest-rising stars in the fantasy genre, along with writers such as Joe Abercrombie, Patrick Rothfuss, Scott Lynch, Lev Grossman, and K. J. Parker, *New York Times* bestseller Brandon Sanderson was chosen to finish Robert Jordan's famous Wheel of Time sequence, left uncompleted on Jordan's death, an immense task that Sanderson tackled with volumes such as *The Gathering Storm, Towers of Midnight,* and *A Memory of Light.* He is also well-known for another fantasy series, the Mistborn sequence, which consists of *The Final Empire, The Well of Ascension, The Hero of Ages,* and *The Alloy of Law,* as well as the young adult fantasy series Alcatraz, consisting of *Alcatraz Versus the Evil Librarians, Alcatraz Versus the Scrivener's Bones, Alcatraz Versus the Knights of Crystallia,* and *Alcatraz Versus the Shattered Lens.* His other books include the novels *Elantris, Warbreaker,* and *Firstborn,* and the start of the new Stormlight Archive series, *The Way of Kings.* He lives in American Fork, Utah, and maintains a website at brandonsanderson.com.

Here he takes us deep into the sinister silence of the Forests for the tale of a desperate and dangerous woman who will risk anything, *do* anything, to save her family, even in a place where hungry ghosts wait unseen behind every tree, and one false move means instant death. . . .

SHADOWS FOR SILENCE
IN THE FORESTS OF HELL

"The one you have to watch for is the White Fox," Daggon said, sipping his beer. "They say he shook hands with the Evil itself, that he visited the Fallen World and came back with strange powers. He can kindle fire on even the deepest of nights, and no shade will dare come for his soul. Yes, the White Fox. Meanest bastard in these parts for sure. Pray he doesn't set his eyes on you, friend. If he does, you're dead."

Daggon's drinking companion had a neck like a slender wine bottle and a head like a potato stuck sideways on the top. He squeaked as he spoke, a Lastport accent, voice echoing in the eaves of the waystop's common room. "Why . . . why would he set his eyes on me?"

"That depends, friend," Daggon said, looking about as a few overdressed merchants sauntered in. They wore black coats, ruffled lace poking out the front, and the tall-topped, wide-brimmed hats of fortfolk. They wouldn't last two weeks out here, in the Forests.

"It depends?" Daggon's dining companion prompted. "It depends on what?"

"On a lot of things, friend. The White Fox is a bounty hunter, you know. What crimes have you committed? What have you done?"

"Nothing." That squeak was like a rusty wheel.

"Nothing? Men don't come out into the Forests to do 'nothing,' friend."

His companion glanced from side to side. He'd given his name as Earnest. But then, Daggon had given his name as Amity. Names didn't mean a whole lot in the Forests. Or maybe they meant everything. The right ones, that was.

Earnest leaned back, scrunching down that fishing-pole neck of his as if trying to disappear into his beer. He'd bite. People liked hearing about the White Fox, and Daggon considered himself an expert. At least, he was an expert at telling stories to get ratty men like Earnest to pay for his drinks.

I'll give him some time to stew, Daggon thought, smiling to himself. *Let him worry.* Earnest would pry him for more information in a bit.

While he waited, Daggon leaned back, surveying the room. The merchants were making a nuisance of themselves, calling for food, saying they meant to be on their way in an hour. That *proved* them to be fools. Traveling at night in the Forests? Good homesteader stock would do it. Men like these, though . . . they'd probably take less than an hour to violate one of the Simple Rules and bring the shades upon them. Daggon put the idiots out of his mind.

That fellow in the corner, though . . . dressed all in brown, still wearing his hat despite being indoors. That fellow looked truly dangerous. *I wonder if it's him,* Daggon thought. So far as he knew, nobody had ever seen the White Fox and lived. Ten years, over a hundred bounties turned in. Surely someone knew his name. The authorities in the forts paid him the bounties, after all.

The waystop's owner, Madam Silence, passed by the table and deposited Daggon's meal with an unceremonious thump. Scowling, she topped off his beer, spilling a sudsy dribble onto his hand, before limping off. She was a stout woman. Tough. Everyone in the Forests was tough. The ones that survived, at least.

He'd learned that a scowl from Silence was just her way of saying hello. She'd given him an extra helping of venison; she often did that. He liked to think that she had a fondness for him. Maybe someday . . .

Don't be a fool, he thought to himself as he dug into the heavily gravied food. Better to marry a stone than Silence Montane. A stone showed more affection. Likely, she gave him the extra slice because she recognized the value of a repeat customer. Fewer and fewer people came this way lately. Too many shades. And then there was Chesterton. Nasty business, that.

"So . . . he's a bounty hunter, this Fox?" The man who called himself Earnest seemed to be sweating.

Daggon smiled. Hooked right good, this one was. "He's not just a bounty hunter. He's *the* bounty hunter. Though, the White Fox doesn't go for the small-timers—and no offense, friend, but you seem pretty small-time."

His friend grew more nervous. What *had* he done? "But," the man stammered, "he wouldn't come for me—er, pretending I'd done something, of course—anyway, he wouldn't come in here, would he? I mean, Madam Silence's waystop, it's protected. Everyone knows that. Shade of her dead husband lurks here. I had a cousin who saw it, I did."

"The White Fox doesn't fear shades," Daggon said, leaning in. "Now, mind you, I don't *think* he'd risk coming in here—but not because of some shade. Everyone knows this is neutral ground. You've got to have some safe places, even in the Forests. But . . ."

Daggon smiled at Silence as she passed him by, on the way to the kitchens again. This time she didn't scowl at him. He was getting through to her for certain.

"But?" Earnest squeaked.

"Well . . ." Daggon said. "I could tell you a few things about how the White Fox takes men, but you see, my beer is nearly empty. A shame. I think you'd be very interested in how the White Fox caught Makepeace Hapshire. Great story, that."

Earnest squeaked for Silence to bring another beer, though she bustled into the kitchen and didn't hear. Daggon frowned, but Earnest put a coin on the side of the table, indicating he'd like a refill when Silence or her daughter returned. That would do. Daggon smiled to himself and launched into the story.

Silence Montane closed the door to the common room, then turned and pressed her back against it. She tried to still her racing heart by breathing in and out. Had she made any obvious signs? Did they know she'd recognized them?

William Ann passed by, wiping her hands on a cloth. "Mother?" the young woman asked, pausing. "Mother, are you—"

"Fetch the book. Quickly, child!"

William Ann's face went pale, then she hurried into the back pantry. Silence clutched her apron to still her nerves, then joined William Ann as the girl came out of the pantry with a thick, leather satchel. White flour dusted its cover and spine from the hiding place.

Silence took the satchel and opened it on the high kitchen counter, revealing a collection of loose-leaf papers. Most had faces drawn on them. As Silence rifled through the pages, William Ann moved to look through the peephole back into the common room.

For a few moments, the only sound to accompany Silence's thumping heart was that of hastily turned pages.

"It's the man with the long neck, isn't it?" William Ann asked. "I remember his face from one of the bounties."

"That's just Lamentation Winebare, a petty horse thief. He's barely worth two measures of silver."

"Who, then? The man in the back, with the hat?"

Silence shook her head, finding a sequence of pages at the bottom of her pile. She inspected the drawings. *God Beyond*, she thought. *I can't decide if I want it to be them or not.* At least her hands had stopped shaking.

William Ann scurried back and craned her neck over Silence's shoulder. At fourteen, the girl was already taller than her mother. A fine thing to suffer, a child taller than you. Though William Ann grumbled about being awkward and lanky, her slender build foreshadowed a beauty to come. She took after her father.

"Oh, God *Beyond*," William Ann said, raising a hand to her mouth. "You mean—"

"Chesterton Divide," Silence said. The shape of the chin, the look in the eyes . . . they were the same. "He walked right into our hands, with four of his men." The bounty on those five would be enough to pay her supply needs for a year. Maybe two.

Her eyes flickered to the words below the pictures, printed in harsh, bold letters. **Extremely dangerous. Wanted for murder, rape, extortion.** And, of course, there was the big one at the end: **And assassination.**

Silence had always wondered if Chesterton and his men had intended to kill the governor of the most powerful city on this continent, or if it had it been an accident. A simple robbery gone wrong. Either way, Chesterton understood what he'd done. Before the incident, he had been a common—if accomplished—highway bandit.

Now he was something greater, something far more dangerous. Chesterton knew that if he were captured, there would be no mercy, no quarter. Lastport had painted Chesterton as an anarchist, a menace, and a psychopath.

Chesterton had no reason to hold back. So he didn't.

Oh, God Beyond, Silence thought, looking at the continuing list of his crimes on the next page.

Beside her, William Ann whispered the words to herself. "He's out there?" she asked. "But where?"

"The merchants," Silence said.

"What?" William Ann rushed back to the peephole. The wood there—indeed, all around the kitchen—had been scrubbed so hard that it had been bleached white. Sebruki had been cleaning again.

"I can't see it," William Ann said.

"Look closer." Silence hadn't seen it at first either, even though she spent each night with the book, memorizing its faces.

A few moments later William Ann gasped, raising her hand to her mouth. "That seems so *foolish* of him. Why is he going about perfectly visible like this? Even in disguise."

"Everyone will remember just another band of fool merchants from the fort who thought they could brave the Forests. It's a clever disguise. When they vanish from the paths in a few days, it will be assumed—if anyone cares to wonder—that the shades got them. Besides, this way Chesterton can travel quickly and in the open, visiting waystops and listening for information."

Was this how Chesterton discovered good targets to hit? Had they come through her waystop before? The thought made her stomach turn. She had fed criminals many times; some were regulars. Every man was probably a criminal out in the Forests, if only for ignoring taxes imposed by the fortfolk.

Chesterton and his men were different. She didn't need the list of crimes to know what they were capable of doing.

"Where's Sebruki?" Silence said.

William Ann shook herself, as if coming out of a stupor. "She's feeding the pigs. Shadows! You don't think they'd recognize her, do you?"

"No," Silence said. "I'm worried she'll recognize them." Sebruki might only be eight, but she could be shockingly—disturbingly—observant.

Silence closed the book of bounties. She rested her fingers on its leather.

"We're going to kill them, aren't we?" William Ann asked.

"Yes."

"How much are they worth?"

"Sometimes, child, it's not about what a man is worth." Silence heard the faint lie in her voice. Times were increasingly tight, with the price of silver from both Bastion Hill and Lastport on the rise.

Sometimes it wasn't about what a man was worth. But this wasn't one of those times.

"I'll get the poison." William Ann left the peephole and crossed the room.

"Something light, child," Silence cautioned. "These are dangerous men. They'll notice if things are out of the ordinary."

"I'm not a fool, Mother," William Ann said dryly. "I'll use fenweed. They won't taste it in the beer."

"Half dose. I don't want them collapsing at the table."

William Ann nodded, entering the old storage room, where she closed the door and began prying up floorboards to get to the poisons. Fenweed would leave the men cloudy-headed and dizzy, but wouldn't kill them.

Silence didn't dare risk something more deadly. If suspicion ever came back to her waystop, her career—and likely her life—would end. She needed to remain, in the minds of travelers, the crotchety but fair innkeeper who didn't ask too many questions. Her waystop was a place of perceived safety, even for the roughest of criminals. She bedded down each night with a heart full of fear that someone would realize a suspicious number of the White Fox's bounties stayed at Silence's waystop in the days preceding their demise.

She went into the pantry to put away the bounty book. Here, too, the walls had been scrubbed clean, the shelves freshly sanded and dusted. That child. Who had heard of a child who would rather clean than play? Of course, given what Sebruki had been through . . .

Silence could not help reaching onto the top shelf and feeling the crossbow she kept there. Silver boltheads. She kept it for shades, and hadn't yet turned it against a man. Drawing blood was too dangerous in the Forests. It still comforted her to know that in a true emergency she had the weapon at hand.

Bounty book stowed, she went to check on Sebruki. The child was indeed caring for the pigs. Silence liked to keep a healthy stock, though of course not for eating. Pigs were said to ward away shades. She used any tool she could to make the waystop seem more safe.

Sebruki knelt inside the pig shack. The short girl had dark skin and long, black hair. Nobody would have taken her for Silence's daughter, even if they hadn't heard of Sebruki's unfortunate history. The child hummed to herself, scrubbing at the wall of the enclosure.

"Child?" Silence asked.

Sebruki turned to her and smiled. What a difference one year could make. Once, Silence would have sworn that this child would never smile again. Sebruki had spent her first three months at the waystop staring at walls. No matter where Silence had put her, the child had moved to the nearest wall, sat down, and stared at it all day. Never speaking a word. Eyes dead as those of a shade. . . .

"Aunt Silence?" Sebruki asked. "Are you well?"

"I'm fine, child. Just plagued by memories. You're . . . cleaning the *pig shack* now?"

"The walls need a good scrubbing," Sebruki said. "The pigs do so like it to be clean. Well, Jarom and Ezekiel prefer it that way. The others don't seem to care."

"You don't need to clean so hard, child."

"I like doing it," Sebruki said. "It feels good. It's something I can do. To help."

Well, it was better to clean the walls than stare blankly at them all day. Today, Silence was happy for anything that kept the child busy. Anything, so long as she didn't enter the common room.

"I think the pigs will like it," Silence said. "Why don't you keep at it in here for a while?"

Sebruki eyed her. "What's wrong?"

Shadows. She was so observant. "There are some men with rough tongues in the common room," Silence said. "I won't have you picking up their cussing."

"I'm not a child, Aunt Silence."

"Yes you are," Silence said firmly. "And you'll obey. Don't think I won't take a switch to your backside."

Sebruki rolled her eyes, but went back to work and began humming to herself. Silence let a little of her grandmother's ways out when she spoke with Sebruki. The child responded well to sternness. She seemed to crave it, perhaps as a symbol that someone was in control.

Silence wished she actually were in control. But she was a Forescout—the surname taken by her grandparents and the others who had left Homeland first and explored this continent. Yes, she was a Forescout, and she'd be damned before she'd let anyone know how absolutely powerless she felt much of the time.

Silence crossed the backyard of the large inn, noting William Ann inside the kitchen mixing a paste to dissolve in the beer. Silence passed her by and looked in on the stable. Unsurprisingly, Chesterton had said they'd be leaving after their meal. While a lot of folk sought the relative safety of a waystop at night, Chesterton and his men would be accustomed to sleeping in the Forests. Even with the shades about, they would feel more comfortable in a camp of their own devising than they would in a waystop bed.

Inside the stable, Dob, the old stable hand, had just finished brushing down the horses. He wouldn't have watered them. Silence had a standing order to not do that until last.

"This is well done, Dob," Silence said. "Why don't you take your break now?"

He nodded to her with a mumbled, "Thank'ya, mam." He'd find the front porch and his pipe, as always. Dob hadn't two wits to rub together, and he hadn't a clue about what she really did at the waystop, but he'd been with her since before William's death. He was as loyal a man as she'd ever found.

Silence shut the door after him, then fetched some pouches from the locked cabinet at the back of the stable. She checked each one in the dim light, then set them on the grooming table and heaved the first saddle back onto its owner's back.

She was near finished with the saddling when the door eased open. She froze, immediately thinking of the pouches on the table. Why hadn't she stuffed them in her apron? Sloppy!

"Silence Forescout," a smooth voice said from the doorway.

Silence stifled a groan and turned to confront her visitor. "Theopolis," she said. "It's not polite to sneak about on a woman's property. I should have you thrown out for trespassing."

"Now, now. That would be rather like . . . the horse kicking at the man who feeds him, hmmm?" Theopolis leaned his gangly frame against the doorway, folding his arms. He wore simple clothing, no markings of his station. A fort tax collector often didn't want random passers to know of his profession. Clean-shaven, his face always had that same patronizing smile on it. His clothing was too clean, too new to be that of one who lived out in the Forests. Not that he was a dandy, nor was he a fool. Theopolis was dangerous, just a different kind of dangerous from most.

"Why are you here, Theopolis?" she said, hefting the last saddle onto the back of a snorting roan gelding.

"Why do I always come to you, Silence? It's not because of your cheerful countenance, hmmm?"

"I'm paid up on taxes."

"That's because you're mostly exempt from taxes," Theopolis said. "But you haven't paid me for last month's shipment of silver."

"Things have been a little dry lately. It's coming."

"And the bolts for your crossbow?" Theopolis asked. "One wonders if you're trying to forget about the price of those silver boltheads, hmmm? And the shipment of replacement sections for your protection rings?"

His whining accent made her wince as she buckled the saddle on. Theopolis. Shadows, what a day!

"Oh my," Theopolis said, walking over to the grooming tale. He picked up one of the pouches. "What are these, now? That looks like wetleek sap. I've heard that it glows at night if you shine the right kind of light upon it. Is this one of the White Fox's mysterious secrets?"

She snatched the pouch away. "Don't say that name," she hissed.

He grinned. "You have a bounty! Delightful. I have always wondered how you tracked them. Poke a pinhole in that, attach it to the underside of the saddle, then follow the dripping trail it leaves? Hmmm? You could probably track them a long way, kill them far from here. Keep suspicion off the little waystop?"

Yes, Theopolis was dangerous, but she needed *someone* to turn in her bounties for her. Theopolis was a rat, and like all rats he knew the best holes, troughs, and crannies. He had connections in Lastport, and had managed to get her the money in the name of the White Fox without revealing her.

"I've been tempted to turn you in lately, you know," Theopolis said. "Many a group keeps a betting pool on the identity of the infamous Fox. I could be a rich man with this knowledge, hmmm?"

"You're already a rich man," she snapped. "And though you're many things, you are not an idiot. This has worked just fine for a decade. Don't tell me you'd trade wealth for a little notoriety?"

He smiled, but did not contradict her. He kept half of what she earned from each bounty. It was a fine arrangement for Theopolis. No danger to him, which was how she knew he liked it. He was a civil servant, not a bounty hunter. The only time she'd seen him kill, the man he'd murdered couldn't fight back.

"You know me too well, Silence," Theopolis said with a laugh. "Too well indeed. My, my. A bounty! I wonder who it is. I'll have to go look in the common room."

"You'll do nothing of the sort. Shadows! You think the face of a tax collector won't spook them? Don't you go walking in and spoiling things."

"Peace, Silence," he said, still grinning. "I obey your rules. I am careful not to show myself around here often, and I don't bring suspicion to you. I couldn't stay today anyway; I merely came to give you an offer. Only, now you probably won't need it! Ah, such a pity. After all the trouble I went to in your name, hmmm?"

She felt cold. "What help could you possibly give me?"

He took a sheet of paper from his satchel, then carefully unfolded it with too-long fingers. He moved to hold it up, but she snatched it from him.

"What is this?"

"A way to relieve you of your debt, Silence! A way to prevent you from ever having to worry again."

The paper was a writ of seizure, an authorization for Silence's creditors— Theopolis—to claim her property as payment. The forts claimed jurisdiction over the roadways and the land to either side of them. They did send soldiers out to patrol them. Occasionally.

"I take it back, Theopolis," she spat. "You most certainly *are* a fool. You'd give up everything we have for a greedy land snatch?"

"Of course not, Silence. This wouldn't be giving up anything at all! Why, I *do* so feel bad seeing you constantly in my debt. Wouldn't it be more efficient if I took over the finances of the waystop? You would remain working here, and hunting bounties, as you always have. Only, you would no longer have to worry about your debts, hmmm?"

She crumpled the paper in her hand. "You'd turn me and mine into slaves, Theopolis."

"Oh, don't be so dramatic. Those in Lastport have begun to worry that such an important waypoint as this is owned by an unknown element.

You are drawing attention, Silence. I should think that is the last thing you want."

Silence crumpled the paper further in her hand, fist tight. Horses shuffled in their stalls. Theopolis grinned.

"Well," he said. "Perhaps it won't be needed. Perhaps this bounty of yours is a big one, hmmm? Any clues to give me, so I don't sit wondering all day?"

"Get out," she whispered.

"Dear Silence," he said. "Forescout blood, stubborn to the last breath. They say your grandparents were the first of the first. The first people to come scout this continent, the first to homestead the Forests . . . first to stake a claim on hell itself."

"Don't call the Forests that. This is my home."

"But it is how men saw this land, before the Evil. Doesn't that make you curious? Hell, land of the damned, where the shadows of the dead made their home. I keep wondering: Is there really a shade of your departed husband guarding this place, or is it just another story you tell people? To make them feel safe, hmmm? You spend a fortune in silver. That offers the real protection, and I never *have* been able to find record of your marriage. Of course, if there wasn't one, that would make dear William Ann a—"

"*Go.*"

He grinned, but tipped his hat to her and stepped out. She heard him climb into the saddle, then ride off. Night would come before too long; it was probably too much to hope that the shades would take Theopolis. She'd long suspected that he had a hiding hole somewhere near, probably a cavern he kept lined with silver.

She breathed in and out, trying to calm herself. Theopolis was frustrating, but he didn't know everything. She forced her attention back to the horses and got out a bucket of water. She dumped the contents of the pouches into it, then gave a hearty dose to the horses, who each drank thirstily.

Pouches that dripped sap in the way Theopolis indicated would be too easy to spot. What would happen when her bounties removed their saddles at night and found the sap packets? They'd know someone was coming for them. No, she needed something less obvious.

"How am I going to manage this?" she whispered as a horse drank from her bucket. "Shadows. They're reaching for me on all sides."

Kill Theopolis. That was probably what Grandmother would have done. She considered it.

No, she thought. *I won't become that. I won't become her.* Theopolis was a thug and a scoundrel, but he had not broken any laws, nor had he done anyone direct harm that she knew. There had to be rules, even out here. There had to be lines. Perhaps, in that respect, she wasn't so different from the fortfolk.

She'd find another way. Theopolis only had a writ of debt; he had been required to show it to her. That meant she had a day or two to come up with his money. All neat and orderly. In the Fortress Towns, they claimed to have civilization. Those rules gave her a chance.

She left the stable. A glance through the window into the common room showed her William Ann delivering drinks to the "merchants" of Chesterton's gang. Silence stopped to watch.

Behind her, the Forests shivered in the wind.

Silence listened, then turned to face them. You could tell fortfolk by the way they refused to face the Forests. They averted their eyes, never looking into the depths. Those solemn trees covered almost every inch of this continent, those leaves shading the ground. Still. Silent. Animals lived out there, but fort surveyors declared that there were no predators. The shades had gotten those long ago, drawn by the shedding of blood.

Staring into the Forests seemed to make them . . . retreat. The darkness of their depths withdrew, the stillness give way to the sound of rodents picking through fallen leaves. A Forescout knew to look the Forests straight on. A Forescout knew that the surveyors were wrong. There *was* a predator out there. The Forest itself was one.

Silence turned and walked to the door into the kitchen. Keeping the waystop had to be her first goal, so she was committed to collecting Chesterton's bounty now. If she couldn't pay Theopolis, she had little faith that everything would stay the same. He'd have a hand around her throat, as she couldn't leave the waystop. She had no fort citizenship, and times were too tight for the local homesteaders to take her in. No, she'd *have* to stay and work the waystop for Theopolis, and he would squeeze her dry, taking larger and larger percentages of the bounties.

She pushed open the door to the kitchen. It—

Sebruki sat at the kitchen table holding the crossbow in her lap.

"God Beyond!" Silence gasped, pulling the door closed as she stepped inside. "Child, what are you—"

Sebruki looked up at her. Those haunted eyes were back, eyes void of life and emotion. Eyes like a shade.

"We have visitors, Aunt Silence," Sebruki said in a cold, monotone voice. The crossbow's winding crank sat next to her. She had managed to load the thing and cock it, all on her own. "I coated the bolt's tip with black blood. I did that right, didn't I? That way, the poison will kill him for sure."

"Child . . ." Silence stepped forward.

Sebruki turned the crossbow in her lap, holding it at an angle to support it, one small hand holding the trigger. The point turned toward Silence.

Sebruki stared ahead, eyes blank.

"This won't work, Sebruki," Silence said, stern. "Even if you were able to lift that thing into the common room, you wouldn't hit him—and even if you did, his men would kill us all in retribution!"

"I wouldn't mind," Sebruki said softly. "So long as I got to kill him. So long as I pulled the trigger."

"You care nothing for us?" Silence snapped. "I take you in, give you a home, and this is your payment? You steal a weapon? You *threaten* me?"

Sebruki blinked.

"What is wrong with you?" Silence said. "You'd shed blood in this place of sanctuary? Bring the shades down upon us, beating at our protections? If they got through, they'd kill everyone under my roof! People I've promised safety. How *dare* you!"

Sebruki shook, as if coming awake. Her mask broke and she dropped the crossbow. Silence heard a snap, and the catch released. She felt the bolt pass within an inch of her cheek, then break the window behind.

Shadows! Had the bolt grazed Silence? Had Sebruki *drawn blood*? Silence reached up with a shaking hand, but blessedly felt no blood. The bolt hadn't hit her.

A moment later Sebruki was in her arms, sobbing. Silence knelt down, holding the child close. "Hush, dear one. It's all right. It's all right."

"I heard it all," Sebruki whispered. "Mother never cried out. She knew I was there. She was strong, Aunt Silence. That was why I could be strong, even when the blood came down. Soaking my hair. I heard it. *I heard it all.*"

Silence closed her eyes, holding Sebruki tight. She herself had been the only one willing to investigate the smoking homestead. Sebruki's father had stayed at the waystop on occasion. A good man. As good a man as was left after the Evil took Homeland, that was.

In the smoldering remains of the homestead, Silence had found the corpses of a dozen people. Each family member had been slaughtered by Chesterton and his men, right down to the children. The only one left had been Sebruki, the youngest, who had been shoved into the crawl space under the floorboards in the bedroom.

She'd lain there, soaked in her mother's blood, soundless even as Silence found her. She'd only found the girl because Chesterton had been careful, lining the room with silver dust to protect against shades as he prepared to kill. Silence had tried to recover some of the dust that had trickled between the floorboards, and had run across eyes staring up at her through the slits.

Chesterton had burned thirteen different homesteads over the last year. Over fifty people murdered. Sebruki was the only one who had escaped him.

The girl trembled as she heaved with sobs. "Why . . . Why?"

"There is no reason. I'm sorry." What else could she do? Offer some foolish platitude or comfort about the God Beyond? These were the Forests. You didn't survive on platitudes.

Silence did hold the girl until her crying began to subside. William Ann entered, then stilled beside the kitchen table, holding a tray of empty mugs. Her eyes flickered toward the fallen crossbow, then at the broken window.

"You'll kill him?" Sebruki whispered. "You'll bring him to justice?"

"Justice died in Homeland," Silence said. "But yes, I'll kill him. I promise it to you, child."

Stepping timidly, William Ann picked up the crossbow, then turned it, displaying its now broken bow. Silence breathed out. She should never have left the thing where Sebruki could get to it.

"Care for the patrons, William Ann," Silence said. "I'll take Sebruki upstairs."

William Ann nodded, glancing at the broken window.

"No blood was shed," Silence said. "We will be fine. Though if you get a moment, see if you can find the bolt. The head is silver. . . ." This was hardly a time when they could afford to waste money.

William Ann stowed the crossbow in the pantry as Silence carefully set Sebruki on a kitchen stool. The girl clung to her, refusing to let go, so Silence relented and held her for a time longer.

William Ann took a few deep breaths, as if to calm herself, then pushed back out into the common room to distribute drinks.

Eventually, Sebruki let go long enough for Silence to mix a draught. She carried the girl up the stairs to the loft above the common room, where the three of them made their beds. Dob slept in the stable and the guests in the nicer rooms on the second floor.

"You're going to make me sleep," Sebruki said, regarding the cup with reddened eyes.

"The world will seem a brighter place in the morning," Silence said. *And I can't risk you sneaking out after me tonight.*

The girl reluctantly took the draught, then drank it down. "I'm sorry. About the crossbow."

"We will find a way for you to work off the cost of fixing it."

That seemed to comfort Sebruki. She was a homesteader, Forests born. "You used to sing to me at night," Sebruki said softly, closing her eyes, laying back. "When you first brought me here. After . . . after . . ." She swallowed.

"I wasn't certain you noticed." Silence hadn't been certain Sebruki noticed anything, during those times.

"I did."

Silence sat down on the stool beside Sebruki's cot. She didn't feel like singing, so she began humming. It was the lullaby she'd sung to William Ann during the hard times right after her birth.

Before long, the words came out, unbidden:

"Hush now, my dear one . . . be not afraid. Night comes upon us, but sunlight will break. Sleep now, my dear one . . . let your tears fade. Darkness surrounds us, but someday we'll wake. . . ."

She held Sebruki's hand until the child fell asleep. The window by the bed overlooked the courtyard, so Silence could see as Dob brought out Chesterton's horses. The five men in their fancy merchant clothing stomped down off the porch and climbed into their saddles.

They rode in a file out onto the roadway; then the Forests enveloped them.

One hour after nightfall, Silence packed her rucksack by the light of the hearth.

Her grandmother had kindled that hearth's flame, and it had been burning ever since. She'd nearly lost her life lighting the fire, but she hadn't been willing to pay any of the fire merchants for a start. Silence shook her head. Grandmother always had bucked convention. But then, was Silence any better?

Don't kindle flame, don't shed the blood of another, don't run at night. These things draw shades. The Simple Rules, by which every homesteader lived. She'd broken all three on more than on occasion. It was a wonder she hadn't been withered away into a shade by now.

The fire's warmth seemed a distant thing as she prepared to kill. Silence glanced at the old shrine, really just a closet, she kept locked. The flames reminded her of her grandmother. At times, she thought of the fire *as* her grandmother. Defiant of both the shades and the forts, right until the end. She'd purged the waystop of other reminders of Grandmother, all save the shrine to the God Beyond. That was set behind a locked door beside the pantry, and next to the door had once hung her grandmother's silver dagger, symbol of the old religion.

That dagger was etched with the symbols of divinity as a warding. Silence carried it, not for its wardings, but because it was silver. One could never have too much silver in the Forests.

She packed the sack carefully, first putting in her medicine kit and then a good-sized pouch of silver dust to heal withering. She followed that with ten empty sacks of thick burlap, tarred on the inside to prevent their contents from leaking. Finally, she added an oil lamp. She wouldn't want to use it, as she didn't trust fire. Fire could draw shades. However, she'd found it useful to have on prior outings, so she brought it. She'd only light it if she ran across someone who already had a fire started.

Once done, she hesitated, then went to the old storage room. She removed the floorboards and took out the small, dry-packed keg that lay beside the poisons.

Gunpowder.

"Mother?" William Ann asked, causing her to jump. She hadn't heard the girl enter the kitchen.

Silence nearly dropped the keg in her startlement, and that nearly stopped her heart. She cursed herself for a fool, tucking the keg under her arm. It couldn't explode without fire. She knew that much.

"Mother!" William Ann said, looking at the keg.

"I probably won't need it."

"But—"

"I know. Hush." She walked over and placed the keg into her sack. Attached to the side of the keg, with cloth stuffed between the metal arms, was her grandmother's firestarter. Igniting gunpowder counted as kindling flames, at least in the eyes of the shades. It drew them almost as quickly as blood did, day or night. The early refugees from Homeland had discovered that in short order.

In some ways, blood was easier to avoid. A simple nosebleed or issue of blood wouldn't draw the shades; they wouldn't even notice. It had to be the blood of another, shed by your hands—and they would go for the one who shed the blood first. Of course, after that person was dead, they often didn't care who they killed next. Once enraged, shades were dangerous to all nearby.

Only after Silence had the gunpowder packed did she notice that William Ann was dressed for traveling in trousers and boots. She carried a sack like Silence's.

"What do you think you're about, William Ann?" Silence asked.

"You intend to kill five men who had only half a dose of fenweed by yourself, Mother?"

"I've done similar before. I've learned to work on my own."

"Only because you didn't have anyone else to help." William Ann slung her sack onto her shoulder. "That's no longer the case."

"You're too young. Go back to bed; watch the waystop until I return."

William Ann remained firm.

"Child, I told you—"

"Mother," William Ann said, taking her arm firmly, "you aren't a *youth* anymore! You think I don't see your limp getting worse? You can't do everything by yourself! You're going to have to start letting me help you sometime, dammit!"

Silence regarded her daughter. Where had that fierceness come from?

It was hard to remember that William Ann, too, was Forescout stock. Grandmother would have been disgusted by her, and that made Silence proud. William Ann had actually had a childhood. She wasn't weak, she was just . . . normal. A woman could be strong without having the emotions of a brick.

"Don't you cuss at your mother," Silence finally told the girl.

William Ann raised an eyebrow.

"You may come," Silence said, prying her arm out of her daughter's grip. "But you *will* do as you are told."

William Ann let out a deep breath, then nodded eagerly. "I'll warn Dob we're going." She walked out, adopting the natural slow step of a Homesteader as she entered the darkness. Even though she was within the protection of the waystop's silver rings, she knew to follow the Simple Rules. Ignoring them when you were safe led to lapses when you weren't.

Silence got out two bowls, then mixed two different types of glowpaste. When finished, she poured them into separate jars, which she packed into her sack.

She stepped outside into the night. The air was crisp, chill. The Forests had gone silent.

The shades were out, of course.

A few of them moved across the grassy ground, visible by their own soft glow. Ethereal, translucent, the ones nearby right now were old shades; they barely had the forms of men any longer. The heads rippled, faces shifting like smoke rings. They trailed waves of whiteness about an arm's length behind them. Silence had always imagined that as tattered remains of their clothing.

No woman, not even a Forescout, looked upon shades without feeling a coldness inside of her. The shades were about during the day, of course; you just couldn't see them. Kindle fire, draw blood, and they'd come for you even then. At night, though, they were different. Quicker to respond to infractions. At night they also responded to quick motions, which they never did during the day.

Silence took out one of the glowpaste jars, bathing the area around her in a pale green light. The light was dim, but even and steady, unlike torchlight. Torches were unreliable, since you couldn't relight them if they went out.

William Ann waited at the front with the lantern poles. "We will need to move quietly," Silence told her while affixing the jars to the poles. "You may speak, but do so in a whisper. I said you will obey me. You will, in all things, immediately. These men we're after . . . they will kill you, or worse, without giving the deed a passing thought."

William Ann nodded.

"You're not scared enough," Silence said, slipping a black covering around the jar with the brighter glowpaste. That plunged them into darkness, but the Starbelt was high in the sky today. Some of that light would filter down through the leaves, particularly if they stayed near the road.

"I—" William Ann began.

"You remember when Harold's hound went mad last spring?" Silence asked. "Do you remember that look in the hound's eyes? No recognition? Eyes that lusted for the kill? Well, that's what these men are, William Ann. Rabid. They need to be put down, same as that hound. They won't see you as a person. They'll see you as meat. Do you understand?"

William Ann nodded. Silence could see that she was still more excited than afraid, but there was no helping that. Silence handed William Ann the pole with the darker glowpaste. It had a faintly blue light to it but didn't illuminate much. Silence put the other pole to her shoulder, sack over the other, then nodded toward the roadway.

Nearby, a shade drifted toward the boundary of the waystop. When it touched the thin barrier of silver on the ground, it crackled like sparks and drove the thing backward with a sudden jerk. The shade floated the other way.

Each touch like that cost Silence money. The touch of a shade ruined silver. That was what her patrons paid for: a waystop whose boundary had not been broke for over a hundred years, with a long-standing tradition that no unwanted shades were trapped within. Peace, of a sort. The best the Forests offered.

William Ann stepped across the boundary, which was marked by the curve of the large silver hoops jutting from the ground. They were anchored below by concrete so you couldn't just pull one up. Replacing an overlapping section from one of the rings—she had three concentric ones surrounding her waystop—required digging down and unchaining the section. It was a lot of work, which Silence knew intimately. A week didn't pass that they didn't rotate or replace one section or another.

The shade nearby drifted away. It didn't acknowledge them. Silence didn't know if regular people were invisible to them unless the rules were broken, or if the people just weren't worthy of attention until then.

She and William Ann moved out onto the dark roadway, which was somewhat overgrown. No road in the Forests was well maintained. Perhaps if the forts ever made good on their promises, that would change. Still, there was travel. Homesteaders traveling to one fort or another to trade food. The grains grown out in Forest clearings were richer, tastier than what could be produced up in the mountains. Rabbits and turkeys caught in snares or raised in hutches could be sold for good silver.

Not hogs. Only someone in one of the Forts would be so crass as to eat a pig.

Anyway, there *was* trade, and that kept the roadway worn, even if the trees around did have a tendency to reach down their boughs—like grasping arms—to try to cover up the pathway. Reclaim it. The Forests did not like that men had infested them.

The two women walked carefully and deliberately. No quick motions. Walking so, it seemed an eternity before something appeared on the road in front of them.

"There!" William Ann whispered.

Silence released her tension in a breath. Something glowing blue marked the roadway in the light of the glowpaste. Theopolis's guess at how she tracked her quarries had been a good one, but incomplete. Yes, the light of the paste known as Abraham's Fire did make drops of wetleek sap glow. By coincidence, wetleek sap *also* caused a horse's bladder to loosen.

Silence inspected the line of glowing sap and urine on the ground. She'd been worried that Chesterton and his men would cut into the Forests soon after leaving the waystop. That hadn't been likely, but still, she'd worried.

Now she was sure she had the trail. If Chesterton cut into the Forests, he'd do it a few hours after leaving the waystop, to be more certain their cover was safe. She closed her eyes and breathed a sigh of relief, then found herself offering a prayer of thanks by rote. She hesitated. Where had that come from? It had been a long time.

She shook her head, rising and continuing down the road. By drugging all five horses, she got a steady sequence of markings to follow.

The Forests felt . . . dark this night. The light of the Starbelt above didn't seem to filter through the branches as well as it should. And there seemed to be more shades than normal, prowling between the trunks of trees, glowing just faintly.

William Ann clung to her lantern pole. The child had been out in the night before, of course. No Homesteader looked forward to doing so, but none shied away from it, either. You couldn't spend your life trapped inside, frozen by fear of the darkness. Live like that, and . . . well, you were no better off than the people in the forts. Life in the Forests was hard, often deadly. But it was also free.

"Mother," William Ann whispered as they walked. "Why don't you believe in God anymore?"

"Is this really the time, girl?"

William Ann looked down as they passed another line of urine, glowing blue on the roadway. "You always say something like that."

"And I'm usually trying to avoid the question when you ask it," Silence said. "But I'm also not usually walking the Forests at night."

"It just seems important to me now. You're wrong about me not being afraid enough. I can hardly breathe, but I do know how much trouble the waystop is in. You're always so angry after Master Theopolis visits. You don't change our border silver as often as you used to. One out of two days, you don't eat anything but bread."

"And you think this has to do with God, why?"

William Ann kept looking down.

Oh, shadows, Silence thought. *She thinks we're being punished.* Fool girl. Foolish as her father.

They passed the Old Bridge, walking its rickety wooden planks. When the light was better, you could still pick out timbers from the New Bridge down in the chasm below, representing the promises of the forts and their gifts, which always looked pretty but frayed before long. Sebruki's father had been one of those who had come put the Old Bridge back up.

"I believe in the God Beyond," Silence said, after they reached the other side.

"But—"

"I don't worship," Silence said, "but that doesn't mean I don't believe. The old books, they called this land the home of the damned. I doubt that worshiping does any good if you're already damned. That's all."

William Ann didn't reply.

They walked another good two hours. Silence considered taking a shortcut thorough the woods, but the risk of losing the trail and having to double back felt too dangerous. Besides. Those markings, glowing a soft blue-white in the unseen light of the glowpaste . . . those were something *real*. A lifeline of light in the shadows all around. Those lines represented safety for her and her children.

With both of them counting the moments between urine markings, they didn't miss the turnoff by much. A few minutes walking without seeing a mark, and they turned back without a word, searching the sides of the path. Silence had worried this would be the most difficult part of the hunt, but they easily found where the men had turned into the Forests. A glowing hoofprint formed the sign; one of the horses had stepped in another's urine on the roadway, then tracked it into the Forests.

Silence set down her pack and opened it to retrieve her garrote, then held a finger to her lips and motioned for William Ann to wait by the road. The girl nodded. Silence couldn't make out much of her features in the darkness, but she did hear the girl's breathing grow more rapid. Being a Homesteader and accustomed to going out at night was one thing. Being alone in the Forests . . .

Silence took the blue glowpaste jar and covered it with her handkerchief. Then she took off her shoes and stockings and crept out into the night. Each time she did this, she felt like a child again, going into the Forests with her grandfather. Toes in the dirt, testing for crackling leaves or twigs that would snap and give her away.

She could almost hear his voice giving instructions, telling her how to judge the wind and use the sound of rustling leaves to mask her as she crossed noisy patches. He'd loved the Forests until the day they'd claimed him. *Never call this land hell,* he had said. *Respect the land as you would a dangerous beast, but do not hate it.*

Shades slid through the trees nearby, almost invisible with nothing to illuminate them. She kept her distance, but even so, she occasionally turned to see one of the things drifting past her. Stumbling into a shade could kill a man, but that kind of accident was uncommon. Unless enraged, shades moved away from men who got too close, as if blown by a soft breeze. So long as you were moving slowly—and you *should* be—you would be all right.

She kept the handkerchief around the jar except when she wanted to check specifically the markings nearby. Glowpaste illuminated shades, and shades that glowed too brightly might give warning of her approach.

A groan sounded nearby. Silence froze, heart practically bursting from her chest. Shades made no sound; that had been a man. Tense, silent, she searched until she caught sight of him, well hidden in the hollow of a tree. He moved, massaging his temples. The headaches from William Ann's poison were upon him.

Silence considered, then crept around the back of the tree. She crouched down, then waited a painful five minutes for him to move. He reached up again, rustling the leaves.

Silence snapped forward and looped her garrote around his neck, then pulled tight. Strangling wasn't the best way to kill a man in the Forests. It was so slow.

The guard started to thrash, clawing at his throat. Shades nearby halted.

Silence pulled tighter. The guard, weakened by the poison, tried to push back at her with his legs. She shuffled backward, still holding tightly, watching those shades. They looked around like animals sniffing the air. A few of them started to dim, their own faint natural luminescence fading, their forms bleeding from white to black.

Not a good sign. Silence felt her heartbeat like thunder inside. *Die, damn you!*

The man finally stopped jerking, motions growing more lethargic. After he trembled a last time and fell still, Silence waited there for a painful eternity, holding her breath. Finally, the shades nearby faded back to white, then drifted off in their meandering directions.

She unwound the garrote, breathing out in relief. After a moment to get her bearings, she left the corpse and crept back to William Ann.

The girl did her proud; she'd hidden herself so well that Silence didn't see her until she whispered, "Mother?"

"Yes," Silence said.

"Thank the God Beyond," William Ann said, crawling out of the hollow where she'd covered herself in leaves. She took Silence by the arm, trembling. "You found them?"

"Killed the man on watch," Silence said with a nod. "The other four should be sleeping. This is where I'll need you."

"I'm ready."

"Follow."

They moved back along the path Silence had taken. They passed the heap of the scout's corpse and William Ann inspected it, showing no pity. "It's one of them," she whispered. "I recognize him."

"Of course it's one of them."

"I just wanted to be sure. Since we're . . . you know."

Not far beyond the guard post, they found the camp. Four men in bedrolls slept amid the shades as only true Forestborn would ever try. They had set a small jar of glowpaste at the center of the camp, inside a pit so it wouldn't glow too brightly and give them away, but it was enough light to show the horses tethered a few feet away on the other side of the camp. The green light also showed William Ann's face, and Silence was shocked to see not fear but intense anger in the girl's expression. She had taken quickly to being a protective older sister to Sebruki. She was ready to kill after all.

Silence gestured toward the rightmost man, and William Ann nodded. This was the dangerous part. On only a half dose, any of these men could still wake to the noise of their partners dying.

Silence took one of the burlap sacks from her pack and handed it to William Ann, then removed her hammer. It wasn't some war weapon, like her grandfather had spoken of. Just a simple tool for pounding nails. Or other things.

Silence stooped over the first man. Seeing his sleeping face sent a shiver through her. A primal piece of her waited, tense, for those eyes to snap open.

She held up three fingers to William Ann, then lowered them one at a time. When the third finger went down, William Ann shoved the sack down over the man's head. As he jerked, Silence pounded him hard on the side of the temple with the hammer. The skull cracked and the head sank in a little. The man thrashed once, then grew limp.

Silence looked up, tense, watching the other men as William Ann pulled the sack tight. The shades nearby paused, but this didn't draw their attention as much as the strangling had. So long as the sack's lining of tar kept the blood from leaking out, they should be safe. Silence hit the man's head twice more, then checked for a pulse. There was none.

They carefully did the next man in the row. It was brutal work, like slaughtering animals. It helped to think of these men as rabid, as she'd told

William Ann earlier. It did not help to think of what the men had done to Sebruki. That would make her angry, and she couldn't afford to be angry. She needed to be cold, quiet, and efficient.

The second man took a few more knocks to the head to kill, but he woke more slowly than his friend. Fenweed made men groggy. It was an excellent drug for her purposes. She just needed them sleepy, a little disoriented. And—

The next man sat up in his bedroll. "What . . . ?" he asked in a slurred voice.

Silence leaped for him, grabbing him by the shoulders and slamming him to the ground. Nearby shades spun about as if at a loud noise. Silence pulled her garrote out as the man heaved at her, trying to push her aside, and William Ann gasped in shock.

Silence rolled around, wrapping the man's neck. She pulled tight, straining while the man thrashed, agitating the shades. She almost had him dead when the last man leaped from his bedroll. In his dazed alarm, he chose to dash away.

Shadows! That last one was Chesterton himself. If he drew the shades upon himself . . .

Silence left the third man gasping and threw caution aside, racing after Chesterton. If the shades withered him to dust, she'd have *nothing*. No corpse to turn in meant no bounty.

The shades around the campsite faded from view as Silence reached Chesterton, catching him at the perimeter of the camp by the horses. She desperately tackled him by the legs, throwing the groggy man to the ground.

"You bitch," he said in a slurred voice, kicking at her. "You're the innkeeper. You poisoned me, you *bitch*!"

In the forest, the shades had gone completely black. Green eyes burst alight as they opened their earthsight. The eyes trailed a misty light.

Silence battered aside Chesterton's hands as he struggled.

"I'll pay you," he said, clawing at her. "I'll pay you—"

Silence slammed her hammer into his arm, causing him to scream. Then she brought it down on his face with a crunch. She ripped off her sweater as he groaned and thrashed, somehow wrapping it around his head and the hammer.

"William Ann!" she screamed. "I need a bag. A bag, girl! Give me—"

William Ann knelt beside her, pulling a sack over Chesterton's head as the blood soaked through the sweater. Silence reached to the side with a frantic hand and grabbed a stone, then smashed it into the sack-covered head. The sweater muffled Chesterton's screams but also muffled the rock. She had to beat again and again.

He finally fell still. William Ann held the sack against his neck to keep the blood from flowing out, her breath coming in in quick gasps. "Oh, God Beyond. Oh, *God* . . ."

Silence dared look up. Dozens of green eyes hung in the forest, glowing like little fires in the blackness. William Ann squeezed her eyes shut and whispered a prayer, tears leaking down her cheeks.

Silence reached slowly to her side and took out her silver dagger. She remembered another night, another sea of glowing green eyes. Her grandmother's last night. *Run, girl! RUN!*

That night, running had been an option. They'd been close to safety. Even then, Grandmother hadn't made it. She might have, but she hadn't.

That night horrified Silence. What Grandmother had done. What Silence had done. . . . Well, tonight, she had one only hope. Running would not save them. Safety was too far away.

Slowly, blessedly, the eyes started to fade away. Silence sat back and let the silver knife slip out of her fingers to the ground.

William Ann opened her eyes. "Oh, God Beyond!" she said as the shades faded back into view. "A miracle!"

"Not a miracle," Silence said. "Just luck. We killed him in time. Another second and they'd have enraged."

William Ann wrapped her arms around herself. "Oh, shadows. Oh, shadows. I thought we were dead. Oh, shadows."

Suddenly, Silence remembered something. The third man. She hadn't finished strangling him before Chesterton ran. She stumbled to her feet, turning.

He lay there, immobile.

"I finished him off," William Ann said. "Had to strangle him with my hands. My hands . . ."

Silence glanced back at her. "You did well, girl. You probably saved our lives. If you hadn't been here, I'd never have killed Chesterton without enraging the shades."

The girl still stared out into the woods, watching the placid shades.

"What would it take?" she asked. "For you to see a miracle instead of a coincidence?"

"It would take a miracle, obviously," Silence said. "Instead of just a coincidence. Come on. Let's put a second sack on these fellows."

William Ann joined her, lethargic as she helped put sacks on the heads of the bandits. Two sacks each, just in case. Blood was the most dangerous. Running drew shades, but slowly. Fire enraged them immediately, but it also blinded and confused them.

Blood, though . . . blood shed in anger, exposed to the open air . . . a single drop could make the shades slaughter you, and then everything else within their sight.

Silence checked each man for a heartbeat, just in case, and found none. They saddled the horses and heaved the corpses, including the scout, into the saddles and tied them in place. They took the bedrolls and other equipment, too. Hopefully, the men would have some silver on them. Bounty laws let Silence keep what she found unless there was specific mention of something stolen. In this case, the forts just wanted Chesterton dead. Pretty much everyone did.

Silence pulled a rope tight, then paused.

"Mother!" William Ann said, noticing the same thing. Leaves rustling out in the Forests. They'd uncovered their jar of green glowpaste to join that of the bandits, so the small campsite was well illuminated as a gang of eight men and women on horseback rode in through the Forests.

They were from the forts. The nice clothing, the way they kept looking into the Forests at the shades . . . City people for certain. Silence stepped forward, wishing she had her hammer to look at least a little threatening. That was still tied in the sack around Chesterton's head. It would have blood on it, so she couldn't get it out until that dried or she was in someplace very, *very* safe.

"Now, look at this," said the man at the front of the newcomers. "I couldn't believe what Tobias told me when he came back from scouting, but it appears to be true. All five men in Chesterton's gang, killed by a couple of Forest Homesteaders?"

"Who are you?" Silence asked.

"Red Young," the man said with a tip of the hat. "I've been tracking this lot for the last four months. I can't thank you enough for taking care of them for me." He waved to a few of his people, who dismounted.

"Mother!" William Ann hissed.

Silence studied Red's eyes. He was armed with a cudgel, and one of the women behind him had one of those new crossbows with the blunt tips. They cranked fast and hit hard but didn't draw blood.

"Step away from the horses, child," Silence said.

"But—"

"Step away." Silence dropped the rope of the horse she was leading. Three fort people gathered up the ropes, one of the men leering at William Ann.

"You're a smart one," Red said, leaning down and studying Silence. One of his women walked past, towing Chesterton's horse with the man's corpse slumped over the saddle.

Silence stepped up, resting a hand on Chesterton's saddle. The woman towing it paused, then looked at her boss. Silence slipped her knife from its sheath.

"You'll give us something," Silence said to Red, knife hand hidden. "After what we did. One quarter, and I don't say a word."

"Sure," he said, tipping his hat to her. He had a fake kind of grin, like one in a painting. "One quarter it is."

Silence nodded. She slipped the knife against one of the thin ropes that held Chesterton in the saddle. That gave her a good cut on it as the woman pulled the horse away. Silence stepped back, resting her hand on William Ann's shoulder while covertly moving the knife back into its sheath.

Red tipped his hat to her again. In moments, the bounty hunters had retreated back through the trees toward the roadway.

"One quarter?" William Ann hissed. "You think he'll pay it?"

"Hardly," Silence said, picking up her pack. "We're lucky he didn't just kill us. Come on." She moved out into the Forests. William Ann walked with her, both moving with the careful steps the Forests demanded. "It might be time for you to return to the waystop, William Ann."

"And what are you going to do?"

"Get our bounty back." She was a Forescout, dammit. No prim fort man was going to steal from her.

"You mean to cut them off at the white span, I assume. But what will you do? We can't fight so many, Mother."

"I'll find a way." That corpse meant freedom—*life*—for her daughters.

She would not let it slip away, like smoke between the fingers. They entered the darkness, passing shades that had, just a short time before, been almost ready to wither them. Now the spirits drifted away, completely ambivalent toward the flesh that passed them.

Think, Silence. Something is very wrong here. How had those men found the camp? The light? Had they heard her and William Ann talking? They'd claimed to have been chasing Chesterton for months. Shouldn't she have heard of them before now? These men and women looked too crisp, too new to have been out in the Forests for months trailing killers.

It led to a conclusion she did not want to admit. One man had known she was hunting a bounty today and had seen how she was planning to track that bounty. One man had cause to see that bounty stolen from her.

Theopolis, I hope I'm wrong, she thought. *Because if you're behind this . . .*

Silence and William Ann trudged through the guts of the Forest, a place where the gluttonous canopy above drank in all of the light, leaving the ground below barren. Shades patrolled these wooden halls like blind sentries. Red and his bounty hunters were of the forts. They would keep to the roadways; that was her advantage. The Forests were no friend to a Homesteader, no more than a familiar chasm was any less dangerous a drop.

But Silence was a sailor on this abyss. She could ride its winds better than any fort dweller. Perhaps it was time to make a storm.

What Homesteaders called the "white span" was a section of roadway lined by mushroom fields. It took about an hour through the Forests to reach the span, and Silence was feeling the price of a night without sleep by the time she arrived. She ignored the fatigue, tromping through the field of mushrooms, holding her jar of green light and giving an ill cast to trees and furrows in the land.

The roadway bent around through the Forests, then came back this way. If the men were heading toward Lastport or any of the other nearby forts, they would come this direction. "You continue on," Silence said to William Ann. "It's only another hour's hike back to the waystop. Check on things there."

"I'm not leaving you, Mother."

"You promised to obey. Would you break your word?"

"And you promised to let me help you. Would you break yours?"

"I don't need you for this," Silence said. "And it will be dangerous."

"What are you going to do?"

Silence stopped beside the roadway, then knelt, fishing in her pack. She came out with the small keg of gunpowder. William Ann went as white as the mushrooms.

"Mother!"

Silence untied her grandmother's firestarter. She didn't know for certain if it still worked. She'd never dared compress the two metal arms, which looked like tongs. Squeezing them together would grind the ends against one another, making sparks, and a spring at the joint would make them come back apart.

Silence looked up at her daughter, then held the firestarter up beside her head. William Ann stepped back, then glanced to the sides, toward nearby shades.

"Are things really that bad?" the girl whispered. "For us, I mean?"

Silence nodded.

"All right, then."

Fool girl. Well, Silence wouldn't send her away. The truth was, she probably *would* need help. She intended to get that corpse. Bodies were heavy, and there wasn't any way she'd be able to cut off just the head. Not out in the Forests, with shades about.

She dug into her pack, pulling out her medical supplies. They were tied between two small boards, intended to be used as splints. It was not difficult to tie the two boards to either side of the firestarter. With her hand trowel, she dug a small hole in the roadway's soft earth, about the size of the powder keg.

She then opened the plug to the keg and set it into the hole. She soaked her handkerchief in the lamp oil, stuck one end in the keg, then positioned the firestarter boards on the road with the end of the kerchief next to the spark-making heads. After covering the contraption with some leaves, she had a rudimentary trap. If someone stepped on the top board, that would press it down and grind out sparks to light the kerchief. Hopefully.

She couldn't afford to light the fire herself. The shades would come first for the one who made the fire.

"What happens if they don't step on it?" William Ann asked.

"Then we move it to another place on the road and try again," Silence said.

"That could shed blood, you realize."

Silence didn't reply. If the trap was triggered by a footfall, the shades wouldn't see Silence as the one causing it. They'd come first for the one who triggered the trap. But if blood was drawn, they would enrage. Soon after, it wouldn't matter who had caused it. All would be in danger.

"We have hours of darkness left," Silence said. "Cover your glowpaste."

William Ann nodded, hastily putting the cover on her jar. Silence inspected her trap again, then took William Ann by the shoulder and pulled her to the side of the roadway. The underbrush was thicker there, as the road tended to wind through breaks in the canopy. Men sought out places in the Forests where they could see the sky.

The men came along eventually. Silent, illuminated by a jar of glowpaste each. Fortfolk didn't talk at night. They passed the trap, which Silence had placed on the narrowest section of roadway. She held her breath, watching the horses pass, step after step missing the lump that marked the board. William Ann covered her ears, hunkering down.

A hoof hit the trap. Nothing happened. Silence released an annoyed breath. What would she do if the firestarter was broken? Could she find another way to—

The explosion struck her, the wave of force shaking her body. Shades vanished in a blink, green eyes snapping open. Horses reared and whinnied, men yelling.

Silence shook off her stupefaction, grabbing William Ann by the shoulder and pulling her out of hiding. Her trap had worked better than she'd assumed; the burning rag had allowed the horse who had triggered the trap to take a few steps before the blast hit. No blood, just a lot of surprised horses and confused men. The little keg of gunpowder hadn't done as much damage as she'd anticipated—the stories of what gunpowder could do were often as fanciful as stories of the Homeland—but the sound had been incredible.

Silence's ears rang as she fought through the confused men, finding what she'd hoped to see. Chesterton's corpse lay on the ground, dumped from his saddleback by a bucking horse and a frayed rope. She grabbed the corpse under the arms and William Ann took the legs. They moved sideways into the Forests.

"Idiots!" Red bellowed from amid the confusion. "Stop her! It—"

He cut off as shades swarmed the roadway, descending upon the men. Red had managed to keep his horse under control, but now he had to dance it back from the shades. Enraged, they had turned pure black, though the blast of light and fire had obviously left them dazed. They fluttered about, like moths around a flame. Green eyes. A small blessing. If those turned red . . .

One bounty hunter, standing on the road and spinning about, was struck. His back arched, black-veined tendrils crisscrossing his skin. He dropped to his knees, screaming as the flesh of his face shrank around his skull.

Silence turned away. William Ann watched the fallen man with a horrified expression.

"Slowly, child," Silence said in what she hoped was a comforting voice. She hardly felt comforting. "Carefully. We can move away from them. William Ann. Look at me."

The girl turned to look at her.

"Hold my eyes. Move. That's right. Remember, the shades will go to the source of the fire first. They are confused, stunned. They can't smell fire like they do blood, and they'll look from it to the nearest sources of quick motion. Slowly, easily. Let the scrambling city men distract them."

The two of them eased into the Forests with excruciating deliberateness. In the face of so much chaos, so much danger, their pace felt like a crawl. Red organized a resistance. Fire-crazed shades could be fought, destroyed, with silver. More and more would come, but if the men were clever and lucky, they'd be able to destroy those nearby and then move slowly away from the source of the fire. They could hide, survive. Maybe.

Unless one of them accidentally drew blood.

Silence and William Ann stepped through a field of mushrooms that glowed like the skulls of rats and broke silently beneath their feet. Luck was not completely with them, for as the shades shook off their disorientation from the explosion, a pair of them on the outskirts turned and struck out toward the fleeing women.

William Ann gasped. Silence deliberately set down Chesterton's shoulders, then took out her knife. "Keep going," she whispered. "Pull him away. Slowly, girl. *Slowly.*"

"I won't leave you!"

"I will catch up," Silence said. "You aren't ready for this."

She didn't look to see if William Ann obeyed, for the shades—figures of jet black streaking across the white-knobbed ground—were upon her. Strength was meaningless against shades. They had no real substance.

Only two things mattered: moving quickly and not letting yourself be frightened.

Shades *were* dangerous, but so long as you had silver, you could fight. Many a man died because he ran, drawing even more shades, rather than standing his ground.

Silence swung at the shades as they reached her. *You want my daughter, hellbound?* she thought with a snarl. *You should have tried for the city men instead.*

She swept her knife through the first shade, as Grandmother had taught. *Never creep back and cower before shades. You're Forescout blood. You claim the Forests. You are their creature as much as any other. As am I. . . .*

Her knife passed through the shade with a slight tugging feeling, creating a shower of bright white sparks that sprayed out of the shade. The shade pulled back, its black tendrils writhing about one another.

Silence spun on the other. The pitch sky let her see only the thing's eyes, a horrid green, as it reached for her. She lunged.

Its spectral hands were upon her, the icy cold of its fingers gripping her arm below the elbow. She could feel it. Shade fingers had substance; they could grab you, hold you back. Only silver warded them away. Only with silver could you fight.

She rammed her arm in farther. Sparks shot out its back, spraying like a bucket of wash water. Silence gasped at the horrid, icy pain. Her knife slipped from fingers she could no longer feel. She lurched forward, falling to her knees as the second shade fell backward, then began spinning about in a mad spiral. The first one flopped on the ground like a dying fish, trying to rise, but its top half fell over.

The cold of her arm was so *bitter*. She stared at the wounded arm, watching the flesh of her hand wither upon itself, pulling in toward the bone.

She heard weeping.

You stand there, Silence. Grandmother's voice. Memories of the first time she'd killed a shade. *You do as I say. No tears! Forescouts don't cry. Forescouts DON'T CRY.*

She had learned to hate her that day. Ten years old, with her little knife, shivering and weeping in the night as her grandmother had enclosed her and a drifting shade in a ring of silver dust.

Grandmother had run around the perimeter, enraging it with motion. While Silence was trapped in there. With death.

The only way to learn is to do, Silence. And you'll learn, one way or another!

"Mother!" William Ann said.

Silence blinked, coming out of the memory as her daughter dumped silver dust on the exposed arm. The withering stopped as William Ann, choking against her thick tears, dumped the entire pouch of emergency silver over the hand. The metal reversed the withering, and the skin turned pink again, the blackness melting away in sparks of white.

Too much, Silence thought. William Ann had used all of the silver dust in her haste, far more than one wound needed. It was difficult to summon any anger, for feeling flooded back into her hand and the icy cold retreated.

"Mother?" William Ann asked. "I left you, as you said. But he was so heavy, I didn't get far. I came back for you. I'm sorry. I came back for you!"

"Thank you," Silence said, breathing in. "You did well." She reached up and took her daughter by the shoulder, then used the once-withered hand to search in the grass for Grandmother's knife. When she brought it up, the blade was blackened in several places but still good.

Back on the road, the city men had made a circle and were holding off the shades with silver-tipped spears. The horses had all fled or been consumed. Silence fished on the ground, coming up with a small handful of silver dust. The rest had been expended in the healing. Too much.

No use worrying about that now, she thought, stuffing the handful of dust in her pocket. "Come," she said, hauling herself to her feet. "I'm sorry I never taught you to fight them."

"Yes you did," William Ann said, wiping her tears. "You've told me all about it."

Told. Never shown. *Shadows, Grandmother. I know I disappoint you, but I won't do it to her. I can't. But I am a good mother. I will protect them.*

The two left the mushrooms, taking up their grisly prize again and tromping through the Forests. They passed more darkened shades floating toward the fight. All of those sparks would draw them. The city men were dead. Too much attention, too much struggle. They'd have a thousand shades upon them before the hour was out.

Silence and William Ann moved slowly. Though the cold had mostly retreated from Silence's hand, there was a lingering . . . something. A deep shiver. A limb touched by the shades wouldn't feel right for months.

That was far better than what could have happened. Without William Ann's quick thinking, Silence could have become a cripple. Once the withering settled in—that took a little time, though it varied—it was irreversible.

Something rustled in the woods. Silence froze, causing William Ann to stop and glance about.

"Mother?" William Ann whispered.

Silence frowned. The night was so black, and they'd been forced to leave their lights. *Something's out there,* she thought, trying to pierce the darkness. *What are you?* God Beyond, protect them if the fighting had drawn one of the Deepest Ones.

The sound did not repeat. Reluctantly, Silence continued on. They walked for a good hour, and in the darkness Silence hadn't realized they'd neared the roadway again until they stepped onto it.

Silence heaved out a breath, setting down their burden and rolling her tired arms in their joints. Some light from the Starbelt filtered down upon them, illuminating something like a large jawbone to their left. The Old Bridge. They were almost home. The shades here weren't even agitated; they moved with their lazy, almost butterfly, gaits.

Her arms felt so sore. That body felt as if it were getting heavier every moment. Men often didn't realize how heavy a corpse was. Silence sat down. They'd rest for a time before continuing on. "William Ann, do you have any water left in your canteen?"

William Ann whimpered.

Silence started, then scrambled to her feet. Her daughter stood beside the bridge, and something dark stood behind her. A green glow suddenly illuminated the night as the figure took out a small vial of glowpaste. By that sickly light, Silence could see that the figure was Red.

He held a dagger to William Ann's neck. The city man had not fared well in the fighting. One eye was now a milky white, half his face blackened, his lips pulled back from his teeth. A shade had gotten him across the face. He was lucky to be alive.

"I figured you'd come back this way," he said, the words slurred by his shriveled lips. Spittle dripped from his chin. "Silver. Give me your silver."

His knife . . . it was common steel.

"*Now!*" he roared, pulling the knife closer to William Ann's neck. If he so much as nicked her, the shades would be upon them in heartbeats.

"I only have the knife," William Ann lied, taking it out and tossing it to the ground before him. "It's too late for your face, Red. That withering has set in."

"I don't care," he hissed. "Now the body. Step away from it, woman. Away!"

Silence stepped to the side. Could she get to him before he killed William Ann? He'd have to grab that knife. If she sprang just right . . .

"You killed my men," Red growled. "They're dead, all of them. God, if I hadn't rolled into the hollow . . . I had to *listen* to it. Listen to them being slaughtered!"

"You were the only smart one," she said. "You couldn't have saved them, Red."

"Bitch! You killed them."

"They killed themselves," she whispered. "You come to my Forests, take what is mine? It was your men or my children, Red."

"Well, if you want your child to live through this, you'll stay very still. Girl, pick up that knife."

Whimpering, William Ann knelt. Red mimicked her, staying just behind her, watching Silence, holding the knife steady. William Ann picked up the knife in trembling hands.

Red pulled the silver knife from William Ann, then held it in one hand, the common knife at her neck in the other. "Now the girl is going to carry the corpse, and you're going to wait right there. I don't want you coming near."

"Of course," Silence said, already planning. She couldn't afford to strike right now. He was too careful. She would follow through the Forests, along the road, and wait for a moment of weakness. Then she'd strike.

Red spat to the side.

Then a padded crossbow bolt shot from the night and took him in the shoulder, jolting him. His blade slid across William Ann's neck and a dribble of blood ran down it. The girl's eyes widened in horror, though it was little more than a nick. The danger to her throat wasn't important.

The blood was.

Red tumbled back, gasping, hand to his shoulder. A few drops of blood glistened on his knife. The shades in the Forests around them went black. Glowing green eyes burst alight, then deepened to crimson.

Red eyes in the night. Blood in the air.

"Oh, hell!" Red screamed. "Oh, *hell*." Red eyes swarmed around him.

There was no hesitation here, no confusion. They went straight for the one who had drawn blood.

Silence reached for William Ann as the shades descended. Red grabbed the girl around and shoved her through a shade, trying to stop it. He spun and dashed the other direction.

William Ann passed through the shade, her face withering, skin pulling in at the chin and around the eyes. She stumbled through the shade and into Silence's arms.

Silence felt an immediate, overwhelming panic.

"No! Child, no. No. *No* . . ."

William Ann worked her mouth, making a choking sound, her lips pulling back toward her teeth, her eyes open wide as her skin pulled back and her eyelids shriveled.

Silver. I need silver. I can save her. Silence snapped her head up, clutching William Ann. Red ran down the roadway, slashing the silver dagger all about, spraying light and sparks. Shades surrounded him. Hundreds, like ravens flocking to a roost.

Not that way. The shades would finish with him soon and would look for flesh—any flesh. William Ann still had blood on her neck. They'd come for her next. Even without that, the girl was withering fast.

The dagger wouldn't be enough to save William Ann. Silence needed dust, silver dust, to force down her daughter's throat. Silence fumbled in her pocket, coming out with the small bit of silver dust there.

Too little. She *knew* that would be too little. Her grandmother's training calmed her mind, and everything became immediately clear.

The waystop was close. She had more silver there.

"M . . . Mother . . ."

Silence heaved William Ann into her arms. Too light, the flesh drying. Then she turned and ran with everything she had across the bridge.

Her arms stung, weakened from having hauled the corpse so far. The corpse . . . she couldn't lose it!

No. She couldn't think on that. The shades would have it, as warm enough flesh, soon after Red was gone. There would be no bounty. She had to focus on William Ann.

Silence's tears felt cold on her face as she ran, wind blowing her. Her daughter trembled and shook in her arms, spasming as she died. She'd become a shade if she died like this.

"I won't lose you!" Silence said into the night. "Please. I won't lose you. . . ."

Behind her, Red screamed a long, wailing screech of agony that cut off at the end as the shades feasted. Near her, other shades stopped, eyes deepening to red.

Blood in the air. Eyes of crimson.

"I hate you," Silence whispered into the air as she ran. Each step was agony. She *was* growing old. "I hate you! What you did to me. What you did to us."

She didn't know if she was speaking to Grandmother or the God Beyond. So often, they were the same in her mind. Had she ever realized that before?

Branches lashed at her as she pushed forward. Was that light ahead? The waystop?

Hundreds upon hundreds of red eyes opened in front of her. She stumbled to the ground, spent, William Ann like a heavy bundle of branches in her arms. The girl trembled, her eyes rolled back in her head.

Silence held out the small bit of silver dust she'd recovered earlier. She longed to pour it on William Ann, save her a little pain, but she knew with clarity that was a waste. She looked down, crying, then took the pinch and made a small circle around the two of them. What else could she do?

William Ann shook with a seizure as she rasped, drawing in breaths and clawing at Silence's arms. The shades came by the dozens, huddling around the two of them, smelling the blood. The flesh.

Silence pulled her daughter close. She should have gone for the knife after all; it wouldn't heal William Ann, but she could have at least fought with it.

Without that, without anything, she failed. Grandmother had been right all along.

"Hush now, my dear one . . ." Silence whispered, squeezing her eyes shut. "Be not afraid."

Shades came at her frail barrier, throwing up sparks, making Silence open her eyes. They backed away, then others came, beating against the silver, their red eyes illuminating writhing black forms.

"Night comes upon us," Silence whispered, choking at the words, "but sunlight will break."

William Ann arched her back, then fell still.

"Sleep now . . . my . . . my dear one. . . . Let your tears fade. Darkness surrounds us, but someday . . . we'll wake. . . ."

So tired. *I shouldn't have let her come.*

If she hadn't, Chesterton would have gotten away from her, and she'd have probably died to the shades then. William Ann and Sebruki would have become slaves to Theopolis, or worse.

No choices. No way out.

"Why did you send us here?" she screamed, looking up past hundreds of glowing red eyes. "What is the point?"

There was no answer. There was never an answer.

Yes, that *was* light ahead; she could see it through the low tree branches in front of her. She was only a few yards from the waystop. She would die, like Grandmother had, mere paces from her home.

She blinked, cradling William Ann as the tiny silver barrier failed.

That . . . that branch just in front of her. It had such a very odd shape. Long, thin, no leaves. Not like a branch at all. Instead, like . . .

Like a crossbow bolt.

It had lodged into the tree after being fired from the waystop earlier in the day. She remembered facing down that bolt earlier, staring at its reflective end.

Silver.

Silence Montane crashed through the back door of the waystop, hauling a desiccated body behind her. She stumbled into the kitchen, barely able to walk, and dropped the silver-tipped bolt from a withered hand.

Her skin continued to pull tight, her body shriveling. She had not been able to avoid withering, not when fighting so many Shades. The crossbow bolt had merely cleared a path, allowing her to push forward in a last, frantic charge.

She could barely see. Tears streamed from her clouded eyes. Even with the tears, her eyes felt as dry as if she had been standing in the wind for an hour while holding them wide open. Her lids refused to blink, and she couldn't move her lips.

She had . . . powder. Didn't she?

Thought. Mind. What?

She moved without thought. Jar on the windowsill. In case of broken circle. She unscrewed the lid with fingers like sticks. Seeing them horrified a distant part of her mind.

Dying. I'm dying.

She dunked the jar of silver powder in the water cistern and pulled it out, then stumbled to William Ann. She felt to her knees beside the girl, spilling much of the water. The rest she dumped on her daughter's face with a shaking arm.

Please. Please.

Darkness.

"We were sent here to be strong," Grandmother said, standing on the cliff edge overlooking the waters. Her whited hair curled in the wind, writhing, like the wisps of a shade.

She turned back to Silence, and her weathered face was covered in droplets of water from the crashing surf below. "The God Beyond sent us. It's part of the plan."

"It's so easy for you to say that, isn't it?" Silence spat. "You can fit anything into that nebulous *plan*. Even the destruction of the world itself."

"I won't hear blasphemy from you, child." A voice like boots stepping in gravel. She walked toward Silence. "You can rail against the God Beyond, but it will change nothing. William was a fool and an idiot. You are better off. We are *Forescouts*. We *survive*. We will be the ones to defeat the Evil, someday." She passed Silence by.

Silence had never seen a smile from Grandmother, not since her husband's death. Smiling was wasted energy. And love . . . love was for the people back in Homeland. The people who'd died to the Evil.

"I'm with child," Silence said.

Grandmother stopped. "William?"

"Who else?"

Grandmother continued on.

"No condemnations?" Silence asked, turning, folding her arms.

"It's done," Grandmother said. "We are Forescouts. If this is how we must continue, so be it. I'm more worried about the waystop, and meeting our payments to those damn forts."

I have an idea for that, Silence thought, considering the lists of bounties she'd begun collecting. *Something even you wouldn't dare. Something dangerous. Something unthinkable.*

Grandmother reached the woods and looked at Silence, scowled, then pulled on her hat and stepped into the trees.

"I will not have you interfering with my child," Silence called after her. "I will raise my own as I will!"

Grandmother vanished into the shadows.

Please. Please.

"*I will!*"

I won't lose you. I won't. . . .

Silence gasped, coming awake and clawing at the floorboards, staring upward.

Alive. She was alive!

Dob the stableman knelt beside her, holding the jar of powdered silver. She coughed, lifting fingers—plump, the flesh restored—to her neck. It was hale though ragged from the flakes of silver that had been forced down her throat. Her skin was dusted with black bits of ruined silver.

"William Ann!" she said, turning.

The child lay on the floor beside the door. William Ann's left side, where she'd first touched the shade, was blackened. Her face wasn't too bad, but her hand was a withered skeleton. They'd have to cut that off. Her leg looked bad, too. Silence couldn't tell how bad without tending the wounds.

"Oh, child . . ." Silence knelt beside her.

But the girl breathed in and out. That was enough, all things considered.

"I tried," Dob said. "But you'd already done what could be done."

"Thank you," Silence said. She turned to the aged man, with his high forehead and dull eyes.

"Did you get him?" Dob asked.

"Who?"

"The bounty."

"I . . . yes, I did. But I had to leave him."

"You'll find another," Dob said in his monotone, climbing to his feet. "The Fox always does."

"How long have you known?"

"I'm an idiot, mam," he said. "Not a fool." He bowed his head to her, then walked away, slump-backed as always.

Silence climbed to her feet, then groaned, picking up William Ann. She lifted her daughter to the rooms above and saw to her.

The leg wasn't as bad as Silence had feared. A few of the toes would be lost, but the foot itself was hale enough. The entire left side of William Ann's body was blackened, as if burned. That would fade, with time, to grey.

Everyone who saw her would know exactly what had happened. Many men would never touch her, fearing her taint. This might just doom her to a life alone.

I know a little about such a life, Silence thought, dipping a cloth into the water bin and washing William Ann's face. The youth would sleep through the day. She had come very close to death, to becoming a shade herself. The body did not recover quickly from that.

Of course, Silence had been close to that, too. She, however, had been there before. Another of Grandmother's preparations. Oh, how she hated that woman. Silence owed who she was to how that training toughened her. Could she be thankful for Grandmother and hateful, both at once?

Silence finished washing William Ann, then dressed her in a soft nightgown and left her in her bunk. Sebruki still slept off the draught William Ann had given her.

So she went downstairs to the kitchen to think difficult thoughts. She'd lost the bounty. The shades would have had at that body; the skin would be dust, the skull blackened and ruined. She had no way to prove that she'd taken Chesterton.

She settled against the kitchen table and laced her hands before her. She wanted to have at the whiskey instead, to dull the horror of the night.

She thought for hours. Could she pay Theopolis off some way? Borrow from someone else? Who? Maybe find another bounty. But so few people came through the waystop these days. Theopolis had already given her warning with his writ. He wouldn't wait more than a day or two for payment before claiming the waystop as his own.

Had she really gone through so much, still to lose?

Sunlight fell on her face and a breeze from the broken window tickled her cheek, waking her from her slumber at the table. Silence blinked, stretching, limbs complaining. Then she sighed, moving to the kitchen counter. She'd left out all of the materials from the preparations last night, her clay bowls thick with glowpaste that still shone faintly. The silver-tipped crossbow bolt still lay by the back door. She'd need to clean up and get breakfast ready for her few guests. Then, think of *some* way to . . .

The back door opened and someone stepped in.

. . . to deal with Theopolis. She exhaled softly, looking at him in his clean clothing and condescending smile. He tracked mud onto her floor as he entered. "Silence Montane. Nice morning, hmmm?"

Shadows, she thought. *I don't have the mental strength to deal with him right now.*

He moved to close the window shutters.

"What are you doing?" she demanded.

"Hmmm? Haven't you warned me before that you loathe that people might see us together? That they might get a hint that you are turning in bounties to me? I'm just trying to protect you. Has something happened? You look awful, hmmm?"

"I know what you did."

"You do? But, see, I do many things. About what do you speak?"

Oh, how she'd like to cut that grin from his lips and cut out his throat, stomp out that annoying Lastport accent. She couldn't. He was just so blasted *good* at acting. She had guesses, probably good ones. But no proof.

Grandmother would have killed him right then. Was she so desperate to prove him wrong that she'd lose everything?

"You were in the Forests," Silence said. "When Red surprised me at the bridge, I assumed that the thing I'd heard—rustling in the darkness—had been him. It wasn't. He implied he'd been waiting for us at the bridge. That thing in the darkness, it was you. *You* shot him with the crossbow to jostle him, make him draw blood. Why, Theopolis?"

"Blood?" Theopolis said. "In the night? And you *survived*? You're quite fortunate, I should say. Remarkable. What else happened?"

She said nothing.

"I have come for payment of debt," Theopolis said. "You have no bounty to turn in, then, hmmm? Perhaps we will need my document after all. So kind of me to bring another copy. This really will be wonderful for us both. Do you not agree?"

"Your feet are glowing."

Theopolis hesitated, then looked down. There the mud he'd tracked in shone very faintly blue in the light of the glowpaste remnants.

"You followed me," she said. "You *were* there last night."

He looked up at her with a slow, unconcerned expression. "And?" He took a step forward.

Silence backed away, her heel hitting the wall behind her. She reached around, taking out the key and unlocking the door behind her. Theopolis grabbed her arm, yanking her away as she pulled open the door.

"Going for one of your hidden weapons?" he asked with a sneer. "The crossbow you keep hidden on the pantry shelf? Yes, I know of that. I'm disappointed, Silence. Can't we be civil?"

"I will never sign your document, Theopolis," she said, then spat at his feet. "I would sooner die, I would sooner be put out of house and home. You can take the waystop by force, but I will *not* serve you. You can be damned, for all I care, you bastard. You—"

He slapped her across the face. A quick but unemotional gesture. "Oh, do shut up."

She stumbled back.

"Such dramatics, Silence. I can't be the only one to wish you lived up to your name, hmmm?"

She licked her lip, feeling the pain of his slap. She lifted her hand to her face. A single drop of blood colored her fingertip when she pulled it away.

"You expect me to be frightened?" Theopolis asked. "I know we are safe in here."

"City fool," she whispered, then flipped the drop of blood at him. It hit him on the cheek. "Always follow the Simple Rules. Even when you think you don't have to. And I wasn't opening the pantry, as you thought."

Theopolis frowned, then glanced over at the door she had opened. The door into the small old shrine. Her grandmother's shrine to the God Beyond.

The bottom of the door was rimmed in silver.

Red eyes opened in the air behind Theopolis, a jet-black form coalescing in the shadowed room. Theopolis hesitated, then turned.

He didn't get to scream as the shade took his head in its hands and drew his life away. It was a newer shade, its form still strong despite the writhing blackness of its clothing. A tall woman, hard of features, with curling hair. Theopolis opened his mouth, then his face withered away, eyes sinking into his head.

"You should have run, Theopolis," Silence said.

His head began to crumble. His body collapsed to the floor.

"Hide from the green eyes, run from the red," Silence said, taking out her silver dagger. "Your rules, Grandmother."

The shade turned to her. Silence shivered, looking into those dead, glassy eyes of a matriarch she loathed and loved.

"I hate you," Silence said. "Thank you for making me hate you." She retrieved the silver-tipped crossbow bolt and held it before her, but the shade did not strike. Silence edged around, forcing the shade back. It floated away from her, back into the shrine lined with silver at the bottom of its three walls, where Silence had trapped it years ago.

Her heart pounding, Silence closed the door, completing the barrier, and locked it again. No matter what happened, that shade left Silence alone. Almost, she thought it remembered. And almost, Silence felt guilty for trapping that soul inside the small closet for all these years.

Silence found Theopolis's hidden cave after six hours of hunting.

It was about where she'd expected it to be, in the hills not far from the Old Bridge. It included a silver barrier. She could harvest that. Good money there.

Inside the small cavern, she found Chesterton's corpse, which Theopolis had dragged to the cave while the Shades killed Red and then hunted Silence. *I'm so glad, for once, you were a greedy man, Theopolis.*

She would have to find someone else to start turning in bounties for her. That would be difficult, particularly on short notice. She dragged the corpse out and threw it over the back of Theopolis's horse. A short hike took her back to the road, where she paused, then walked up and located Red's fallen corpse, withered down to just bones and clothing.

She fished out her grandmother's dagger, scored and blackened from the fight. It fit back into the sheath at her side. She trudged, exhausted, back to the waystop and hid Chesterton's corpse in the cold cellar out back of the stable, beside where she'd put Theopolis's remains. She hiked back into the kitchen. Beside the shrine's door where her grandmother's dagger had once hung, she had placed the silver crossbow bolt that Sebruki had unknowingly sent her.

What would the fort authorities say when she explained Theopolis's death to them? Perhaps she could claim to have found him like that. . . .

She paused, then smiled.

———

"Looks like you're lucky, friend," Daggon said, sipping at his beer. "The White Fox won't be looking for you anytime soon."

The spindly man, who still insisted his name was Earnest, hunkered down a little farther in his seat.

"How is it you're still here?" Daggon asked. "I traveled all the way to Lastport. I hardly expected to find you here on my path back."

"I hired on at a homestead nearby," said the slender-necked man. "Good work, mind you. Solid work."

"And you pay each night to stay here?"

"I like it. It feels peaceful. The Homesteads don't have good silver protection. They just . . . let the shades move about. Even inside." The man shuddered.

Daggon shrugged, lifting his drink as Silence Montane limped by. Yes, she was a healthy-looking woman. He really *should* court her, one of these days. She scowled at his smile and dumped his plate in front of him.

"I think I'm wearing her down," Daggon said, mostly to himself, as she left.

"You will have to work hard," Earnest said. "Seven men have proposed to her during the last month."

"What!"

"The reward!" the spindly man said. "The one for bringing in Chesterton and his men. Lucky woman, Silence Montane, finding the White Fox's lair like that."

Daggon dug into his meal. He didn't much like how things had turned out. Theopolis, that dandy, had been the White Fox all along? Poor Silence. How had it been, stumbling upon his cave and finding him inside, all withered away?

"They say that this Theopolis spent his last strength killing Chesterton," Earnest said, "then dragging him into the hole. Theopolis withered before he could get to his silver powder. Very like the White Fox, always determined to get the bounty, no matter what. We won't soon see a hunter like him again."

"I suppose not," Daggon said, though he'd much rather that the man had kept his skin. Now who would Daggon tell his tales about? He didn't fancy paying for his own beer.

Nearby, a greasy-looking fellow rose from his meal and shuffled out of the front door, looking half-drunk already, though it was only noon.

Some people. Daggon shook his head. "To the White Fox," he said, raising his drink.

Earnest clinked his mug to Daggon's. "The White Fox, meanest bastard the Forests have ever known."

"May his soul know peace," Daggon said, "and may the God Beyond be thanked that he never decided we were worth his time."

"Amen," Earnest said.

"Of course," Daggon said, "there *is* still Bloody Kent. Now, *he's* a right nasty fellow. You'd better hope he doesn't get your number, friend. And don't you give me that innocent look. These are the Forests. Everybody here has done something, now and then, that you don't want others to know about. . . ."

DANGEROUS WOMEN

PARTS I, II, AND III

IN PAPERBACK - OUT NOW

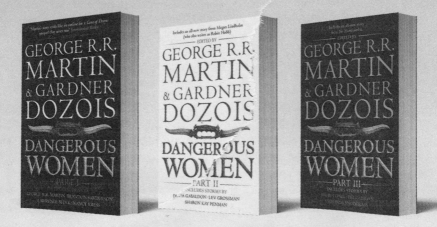